ARRIVAL

ARRIVAL

TERMINATE THE OTHER WORLD!

BOOK 1

Icalos

Podium

Cover design by Husa

ISBN: 978-1-0394-4384-6

Published in 2023 by Podium Publishing
www.podiumaudio.com

Podium

ARRIVAL

PROLOGUE

The Ultimate Weapon

A young girl, scarcely more than a decade old, lay on a hospital bed. Her eyes were closed, and her chest was barely moving as she took slow breaths. She had a respirator over her face, numerous tubes and wires connected to various points on her body, and a vital signs monitor beeping with her heartbeat. A woman in a nun's habit stood by the side of the bed, holding the girl's hand.

Two middle-aged men entered the room—one in a doctor's scrubs, the other in a suit and sunglasses. The nun turned to face them.

"Doctor?"

The doctor just shook his head. Tears filled the nun's eyes.

"If we had caught it earlier, if this were a more advanced hospital, then maybe, but . . . there's nothing I can do now."

The nun slowly nodded. "I understand."

"But . . . this man wanted to meet with you."

The man in the suit walked forward and extended his hand. "Dr. Gaute Ottosen."

The woman rose and shook his hand.

"Sister Johanna."

Dr. Ottosen nodded. "Sister, we have a proposal for you."

She narrowed her eyes. "Go on."

"We have a new procedure. It is highly experimental, highly risky, and has a low chance of success. Honestly, failure is the most likely outcome, by far."

Sister Johanna's eyes widened for a moment before she shook her head.

"I imagine such a procedure would be quite expensive, Dr. Ottosen. My orphanage has nothing to spare."

Dr. Ottosen shook his head.

"Given the low probability of success, the procedure will be free of charge, should you agree to it. If I am honest, it's more of a trial to give us data for future procedures than an actual treatment, so it would be unethical of us to charge you for it." He took off his glasses to look Sister Johanna in the eye. "But there's a chance she survives. Just a chance."

Sister Johanna met his gaze for a minute before turning to look at the girl. She walked over and gently brushed the girl's forehead.

". . . Do what you can for her."

Dr. Ottosen nodded and pulled out a clipboard and a pen. Sister Johanna signed the bottom, and then Dr. Ottosen left the room.

As he exited the door, he smirked.

"No, Sister. It is not what we can do for her. It is what she will do for us."

Several years later . . .

A teenage girl lay on a slanted table in the center of the room.

Or rather, what was left of her.

Most of her body was covered in metal armor. Only her head remained exposed—but metal covered the left half of her face, and her left eye had been replaced with a robotic prosthetic. Her human eye was closed, and it wasn't clear if she was even breathing. She had numerous wires and cables hooked up to her body, including a large one plugged into the back of her skull.

Around the room were numerous tools, robotic arms, and computer monitors. Several scientists were working at their stations, most looking over the monitors. Standing over the girl was the Dr. Ottosen and an executive from the sponsoring organization. Dr. Ottosen grinned as he motioned towards the girl.

"Marvelous, isn't it? The culmination of all my efforts—the ultimate weapon. A solution to those so-called *supers* running about and spreading chaos. I call it the Non-Standard Leashed-Intelligence Cybernetic Enforcer. This one is designated NSLICE-00P."

"I'm assuming that's no mere armor," the executive asked, rubbing his chin.

"Nothing so simple. A full-on cybernetic warrior, bonded to our most advanced AI. The full flexibility and creativity of an organic, but with the loyalty and precision of a machine." Dr. Ottosen paused, then shook his head. "Once we work out the final kinks of the control structure, that is."

"What kinks?"

"I used a terminal subject with barely any consciousness, so wiping the extraneous data from the brain was fairly simple. The organic mind should not be capable of active resistance at this point. But the brain is proving remarkably adaptive. My assistants are having trouble fully subordinating it to the cybernetic components. The AI continues to give way to the organic mind in several cases, but I am confident I will work it out in time."

The executive hummed. "Why use an organic mind in the first place?"

"Part of the control scheme. An AI simple enough to be completely controlled cannot match an organic mind in creativity and initiative, limiting combat effectiveness. But if we could use an AI as an interface to subordinate an organic mind, we could achieve the best of both with none of the downsides. Plus, it improves the computational resources of the AI if we rely on the organic brain for instinctive tasks such as movement. No point teaching a computer how to walk, right?"

"I see. What are its capabilities?"

Dr. Ottosen grinned. "Only the very best I could produce! The bionic prosthetics are noticeably more powerful and efficient than any organic body part, and can match even a Non-Standard in hand-to-hand combat! To support this, I have run countless simulations on martial arts and combat footage to produce the most efficient combat protocols in existence."

He motioned the executive to a computer monitor on the wall and tapped the shoulder of the scientist working there. The scientist nodded and pressed a key, bringing up a readout of the girl's systems.

"As far as firepower is concerned, you can see here that I have packed her with as much weaponry as I could fit. From the latest and greatest to archaic firearms and blades, just in case we need backups."

The executive pointed to one item in particular.

"And what is this *Equalizer*, here?"

Dr. Ottosen smiled.

"Ah, yes, my pride and joy. I must thank you for making it possible, this is where I utilized the Iesnourium you provided, and I dare say I have created a weapon worth using the rarest material known to man. The Equalizer is the final trump card to end the threat of the supers. Thanks to its Iesnourium core, it can transform nearly any form of energy into any other, amplifying it in the process. It can therefore destructively interfere with almost anything it encounters."

"So, some sort of EMP device?"

"A gross oversimplification, but yes. Although not limited to mere electromagnetic radiation. No, the Equalizer can shut down any energy type it encounters, provided it has sufficient power, of course. Including any nonstandard energy types."

"You mean . . . ?"

Dr. Ottosen nodded and spread his hands wide.

"Superpowers. Magic. Qi. Technology. It matters not. The Equalizer can shut it all down. It will take those Non-Standards, whoever or whatever they are, and bring them back to the norm. A weapon to humble the gods and reduce them to mere mortals."

The executive nodded.

"You've outdone yourself, Director. I look forward to seeing it in action."

* * *

Dr. Ottosen secured his sponsor's trust, and not a moment too soon. Just as he completed his work on NSLICE-00P, events occurred that would shake the world, and change society forever. Eventually, Dr. Ottosen's sponsors would step out into the light, attempting to bring order to the chaos.

NSLICE-00P was deployed as the tip of their spear . . .

She flew through the sky. Panels on the back of NSLICE-00P opened to reveal large thrusters, while her hands and feet were converted to flight stabilizers. A retractable metal helmet fully enclosed her head, causing her to appear fully robotic, and a special power core glowed within her chest. She flew at the head of a triangle formation, with two dozen fully robotic warbots following her command.

The NSLICE program had come into full maturity, and its creators had thus claimed half of the world as their own. But not everyone welcomed their ascension.

NSLICE-00P heard a voice over her comms.

"This is Command, code 3H89-00C."

Her robotic eye flickered green. She replied in a steady voice without intonation or deviation. There was a light metallic echo to her words.

"Status Report: Command authority registered. Unit NSLICE-00P, ready and awaiting orders."

"Hostiles have been located three klicks northeast of your location, and have been engaged by NSLICE-A units. Unregistered nonstandards have been confirmed among them. Wipe out the standards, and take the nonstandards to the NSLICE Processing Center."

"Affirmative. Status Report: Rerouting to target. Engaging termination protocols."

NSLICE-00P turned toward the target position, and boosted forward . . .

The sounds of gunshots and screams filled the small town. Resistance fighters stood in bunkers and behind barricades, opening fire with machine guns and assault rifles. Behind them, noncombatants climbed into trucks, loading whatever supplies they could grab.

All around them, NSLICE-A units, fully robotic warbots, flew in from the skies, strafing the Resistance fighters with their machine guns, as more of their number marched on the town from the ground. A Resistance tech ran from one of the buildings, carrying a bunch of computer equipment in his arms—power cords and cables dangled from the pile. He stepped on a power cord and fell to the ground, dropping his load just a few feet from the truck. A squad of warbots flew overhead. One of them pointed their machine gun toward the fallen man and opened fire.

The eyes of the other Resistance fighters widened in horror. He screamed . . .

But another man jumped out in front of him and spread his arms. He grunted as the bullets struck his back—but they did not penetrate through. Flattened bullets dropped to the ground as they bounced off the man's back.

He wasn't wearing any sort of body armor.

The Resistance fighters slowly started to smile.

The supers had arrived.

Down the street, a woman stepped forward. She wore body armor over a yellow robe, and a pointed yellow hat. In her hand she carried a metal staff tipped with a magnet disk wrapped in copper wires. She lifted her staff into the air.

A geometric pattern formed out of glowing yellow light in the air in front of her, making a complex circular pattern.

"Thundara!" she yelled as the pattern completed.

Lightning bolts surged from the magic circle and into the sky, zapping an entire squad of warbots. They sparked and fell, crashing to the ground.

A man in a black hooded robe walked up next to her, his eyebrow raised. "Thundara?"

The woman flushed. "I liked video games before all this, ok?!"

The man chuckled and then waved his hand. A geometric pattern of purple light spread across the ground.

Bestial roars sounded through the town as skeletal dinosaurs emerged from the circle, with purple flames in their empty eye sockets. The skeletal dinosaurs rushed forward and assaulted the warbots on the ground. Magically empowered fangs and claws ripped through metal armor. The mundane bullets bounced off their bony forms.

Another squad of warbots flew in from the flanks, aiming for the two mages. But a wave of circular disks flew through the air, landing on each of the war machines. EMP shocks surged through the bots, knocking them out of the sky.

A shinobi in form-fitting black clothing appeared next to the mages, holding more EMP disks between his fingers.

The first man nodded at the Resistance fighters.

"Go! We'll handle this!"

Then he grabbed a fallen warbot and launched it into the sky with one hand. The warbot struck an incoming squad, causing them to explode.

The Resistance fighters nodded and fell back. They helped the last of the noncombatants into the trucks, which then drove off down the road while the supers held off the assault. The first man nodded at his peers once the trucks had gained some distance.

"They should be able to escape now, let's get out of here before one of the super-bots shows up!" he said.

But they were too late.

A wave of missiles shot from the cloud cover overhead, targeting the trucks down the road. The entire convoy went up in flames. The supers gritted their teeth.

"No!"

They turned to the sky and found another wave of warbots flying down. NSLICE-00P was at their head.

"Mission Update: Hostile standards terminated. Moving to apprehend unregistered nonstandards. Equalizer engaged."

NSLICE-00P held out her hand. A beam of glittering rainbow light shot from her palm, targeting the two mages. The two magic circles shattered and vanished as the beam made contact. She then swept it across the skeletal dinosaurs, which fell into piles of bones as the flames faded from their eye sockets.

Then there was a puff of smoke, and the shinobi appeared in the air behind her.

But NSLICE-00P was ready.

Her robotic eye flickered as her advanced sensors tracked the ninja, already tuned to the unique energy signature of ninjutsu. NSLICE-00P couldn't turn around fast enough to prevent the shinobi's attack but she didn't need to. She was linked to all of the warbots in her squad by the NSLICE network. They could all share in the data from her sensors and her combat protocols.

One of the warbots behind her lifted its hand in her stead, and fired a stun ray into the shinobi. He cried out as electricity surged through him and he fell from the sky. One of the warbots caught the unconscious shinobi and flew off.

"Uchinari!"

The yellow mage tried to fire another lightning bolt but NSLICE-00P again interrupted her spell. NSLICE-00P arrived within range and opened fire with her stun ray, but the tough super stepped in front of the mage. Lightning surged through him, but he stayed conscious.

"Observation: Nonstandard durability observed, nonlethal arsenal appears to be ineffective. Adapting . . . Close combat protocols engaged," NSLICE-00P said.

NSLICE-00P flew straight towards the man, tackling him into the ground while her wingmen stunned the two mages. The man grit his teeth and kicked his knee up into NSLICE-00P, knocking her off. But she activated her flight stabilizers at the exact angle to kill her momentum and land upright on the ground.

The man jumped to his feet and spun toward her, throwing out his fist. She easily dodged under the wild strike and delivered a jab to the man's side. He grunted as the cyborg's bionic arms delivered a blow that would kill a normal person.

This man merely stumbled back before regaining himself enough to throw a punch at NSLICE-00P's head. She pivoted sideways and then slammed her elbow into his chest. The man groaned and then went for a quick jab this time, aiming at her torso.

NSLICE-00P grabbed his fist with her palm.

His punch stopped dead. The man grunted and tried to pull his hand back but he couldn't escape NSLICE-00P's grip. He tried to slam her face with his other hand but she caught that one as well. The man grunted and his muscles bulged, but NSLICE-00P stood firm.

And then she kneed him in the groin.

As his legs buckled she let go of his hands and crouched down. She activated the boosters on her feet and delivered a thrust-assisted uppercut to his chin.

The man flew up and then fell backward. He lay still.

NSLICE-00P's robotic eye flickered as she scanned the area.

"Mission Status: All targets terminated or apprehended. Moving to deliver unregistered nonstandards to NSLICE processing center."

She was about to pick the man off the ground when her comms activated.

"Belay that order, NSLICE-00P. We just detected a group of nonstandards in the ruins of New York, identities are unclear. Move to investigate. If they do not acknowledge our authority then apprehend them and take them to the NSLICE processing center. They appeared out of nowhere, so they likely have access to teleportation, stealth, or super speed. Exercise caution, lethal force is authorized if they prove dangerous and uncooperative."

"Status Update: Order acknowledged. Delivery of apprehended non-standards delegated to NSLICE-A units. Unit NSLICE-00P moving to investigate," she replied.

Little did NSLICE-00P or her handlers know that this was the last order she would ever execute on their behalf. These nonstandards would be unlike any she had ever encountered. NSLICE-00P would be defeated in an instant, without even a chance to report the situation.

But this is not where her story ends.

It is where it begins.

The nonstandards would not destroy NSLICE-00P but reprogram her. And so the next time NSLICE-00P's creators encountered her, they found her working for the Resistance . . .

A great many things happened after that. NSLICE-00P helped the Resistance bring down the NSLICE network and overthrow her own creators. She fought against an army of mutants and strove to save the world.

But all those efforts were not enough. They could not set things right through battle and revolution alone.

Something more drastic was necessary to save this universe. And NSLICE-00P would be the key.

The opponent who defeated NSLICE-00P now stood before the reprogrammed cyborg, no longer as a foe but as NSLICE-00P's new commander. The commander patted her on the head with a sad smile. She spoke to NSLICE-00P with a familiar metallic voice, full of emotion.

"I am sorry for what I must ask you to do. And I am sorry I could not set you free like the others; it will make it easier for you to complete your mission. One you must complete at all costs. And . . . the journey is as important as the destination. If you survive, I am certain you will find your own way and your own family. So . . . I'm sorry. And thank you. Please . . . complete your primary directive and save the universe."

NSLICE-00P's robotic eye flickered.

"Status Report: Affirmative, Commander. Directive received. NSLICE-00P on standby and ready for operation start."

With that, the commander nodded and lifted an arm, activating her Chrono Shifter.

A beam fired from the device and hit NSLICE-00P, who vanished in a flash of light . . .

University of Oslo, Oslo, Norway. The 1970s.

A young man smiled as he took in the scene. All before him, new freshmen bustled about, chatting to one another. Upperclassmen and faculty guided them to dorms and orientation meetings.

It had been tough.

No one had believed in him. No one had helped him.

Not that poor excuse of a father. Not that mother he never knew.

Not the teachers who ignored him. Not the classmates trying to keep him down.

But by the grit of his teeth, the strength of his brow, and the speed of his intellect, he had made it. One of the most prestigious universities in the nation.

And now, the world belonged to him.

He would gain access to knowledge, resources, and above all, opportunity. A chance to speak with the greatest minds of the age. The wealth and ingenuity of the nation's brightest stars. To take for himself a slice of all that society valued and cherished and make it his own.

A chance to show the world who he was and what he could do.

To prove wrong all who doubted him. All who stood in his way.

Not to live a normal life but to achieve something of value.

Of significance.

Something that would endure. Something that would change the world and engrave his name in the annals of history and upon the tongue of every man, woman, and child.

And his name was . . .

"Gaute Ottosen?"

He stopped. He turned around.

A woman approached him. Or perhaps a young lady, by the looks of her. She wore a trench coat, a hat, and a pair of sunglasses.

He smiled at her. It seemed his name had started to spread already.

"Yes, that's me. How may I help you, Madam?"

She lifted her hand.

He took a step forward, extending his.

Hers lifted past.

His smile faded.

She didn't have a hand.

Instead, he found himself staring into the barrel of a gun.

"Target: NSLICE Program Founder identified. Engaging termination protocols."

There was the sound of thunder. And then the world went white.

For everyone.

Everywhere.

And always.

The timeline had been broken.
The universe would be saved.
But that is a story for another time.
For this story follows the one who made it happen . . .

NSLICE-00P found herself in a pitch-black world. It turned out, there were consequences to causing a reality-breaking time paradox. Mainly, being ejected from said reality entirely.

She couldn't feel anything. Couldn't hear anything. And all her sensors returned no data.

And what was worse . . .

NSLICE-00P was powered by something called a Geo-Oscillator Engine, a nearly magical device developed by a supergenius which resonated with the tectonic movements of the Earth's core to generate power. A nearly endless source of clean, sustainable, fuelless energy. But it had one glaring weakness—the device had to remain within range of a suitable planetary core to function.

And her Geo-Oscillator Engine had just lost connection with Earth.

NSLICE-00P did have some capacitors to store additional energy, but these were designed solely to increase the initial output of her weaponry, so they wouldn't last long if they had to power all of her systems. After all, Dr. Ottosen did not design her for long-term independent action. It was assumed that if her core ever malfunctioned, she would be within reasonable range of a repair shop. And if she could not return to her masters, she was to self-destruct to avoid falling into enemy hands. Or anyone other than her masters' hands.

Which meant if she couldn't get the Geo-Oscillator Engine running again, she would run out of power within minutes.

And without the implants entwined with her organs, that meant death shortly afterward.

She could hypothetically shut down and go into stasis, surviving a while longer. Had there been a reasonable chance of rescue, that is what she would have done. But the data and instructions given to her by her commander indicated the chance of recovery by friendly forces was minuscule, and that she should assume independent action until contact was reestablished.

Which meant her only choice was to reactivate the Geo-Oscillator Engine.

Without at least connecting it to a suitable planetary core, she would not be able to exit stasis mode. Which under the assumption of independent action meant an eventual, silent death.

"Diagnostic Report: Attempting to reactive Geo-Oscillator Engine. Error! No planetary core detected in range. Expanding search radius . . ."

The activation sequence failed.

"Diagnostic Report: Attempting to reactivate Geo-Oscillator Engine . . ."

She tried again.

The activation sequence failed.

She tried again.

And again.

And again.

Her capacitors were reaching critical levels. Her systems began to shut down.

She devoted everything she had left to one final attempt.

"D-Diagnostic . . . Attempting . . . reactivate . . . E-Error . . . No . . . detected . . . range . . . Expanding . . . s-search . . ."

Her voice cut off as her reporting log was also shut down.

Everything went black.

Her mind grew foggy and faint as the mechanical half of it slowly deactivated. The organic half that remained . . . had no idea what to do. It had not been in charge at any point in its memory.

Her heartbeat increased in frequency. She perceived an error in oxygen intake. Her blood pressure was rising.

Until . . .

Suddenly, her Geo-Oscillator Engine began to flicker, and the log returned.

"Suitable planetary core located. Connection established. Core activation sequence successful. Rebooting systems . . ."

And then her vision went white.

1

NSLICE-00P: Online and Ready to Terminate!

Inside a dimly lit room, a cat slept, curled up on a queen-sized bed. She had pitch black fur, and wore a necklace filled with countless gems of every color that glowed faintly in the dark.

Suddenly one of those gems began to glow bright.

The cat stirred from her sleep. She rubbed her ear with her paw, then licked the paw a bit with her eyes still closed. She yawned, and then stretched, barely opening one of her eyes. She glanced around the room with the eye half opened, before curling back up on the bed.

"Five more months please . . ."

She went back to sleep.

The gem began to glow even brighter, lighting up the room. It also began to vibrate. The cat's eyes shot open.

"Ok, OK! Sheesh. What is it this time?"

The cat sat up, fully stretched her back, then licked her paw. She took a deep breath and closed her eyes.

When she opened her eyes, they began to glow with golden and silver light. Waves of the same light rippled across her fur. The cat tilted her head.

"Hm? What's this? Something's trying to connect to the Source? What could it be . . ."

The cat's eyes shone a bit brighter, then she blinked.

"It's . . . a girl? Whoa, I've never seen something like this before. Like, this shouldn't be possible, right?"

The cat stood up on all four legs and began to pace on top of the bed.

"Hmm . . . looks like that armor of hers is compatible—or rather, she's already established a connection on her own so I guess it's fine then?"

The cat sat down again and licked her paw.

"More like they're going to make me deal with it if I bring it up and it's going to get all complicated sooooo . . ."

The cat laid back down. The golden and silver light faded from her eyes and her fur.

"I'll just say I didn't notice until it happened. Which is technically true! Good luck, whoever you are! All I know is that's one more dungeon core off my quota."

And with that, the cat closed her eyes and went back to sleep.

It was a beautiful spring day in the forest. The sun was shining, the birds were singing, and a soft breeze rustled the leaves of the trees. A calm and peaceful lake sat in the center of the forest, completely still save for the ducks swimming along the surface or an occasional turtle rising up from below. A handful of mountains and hills rose in the distance, covered in green as the forest continued up their slopes.

Suddenly, a bright light flashed by one of the banks of the lake. The light formed into the shape of a person, the air humming louder and louder as the light shrunk down.

There was a sound like thunder, and the light vanished, revealing the form of a girl now standing on the bank of the lake.

And no normal girl.

She was covered in metal armor, from the tips of her toes all the way up her neck. Her arms and legs were made entirely of metal, in fact, and a circle of light shone bright in the center of her torso. Her face was the only part of her that still appeared human, and only the right side of it. The left half of her head was covered in metal as well, including her left eye which had been replaced with a glowing yellow prosthetic.

Non-Standard Leashed-Intelligence Cybernetic Enforcer, Designation NSLICE-00P, had arrived.

Her robotic yellow eye immediately turned red. Metal extended up from her neck, fully encasing her head in a helmet. She lifted her arms, her hands splitting apart and folding back into her arms so that gun barrels could extend out. Panels opened all over her body, revealing the tips of small missiles ready to fire. The core at her chest shone even brighter.

She spoke in a steady voice without intonation or deviation. There was a light metallic echo to her words. "Forced relocation detected. Emergency combat protocols engaged. Scanning for hostiles . . ."

She slowly turned around in a circle, her robotic eye glancing every which way. She activated all of her sensors. Radar, infrared, thermal, and of course, the sensors meant to detect more . . . *exotic* energy signatures.

"Nonstandard energy type detected. Analyzing . . . energy type identified as 'mana.' Tracing . . ."

NSLICE-00P tried to track the mana she detected, on the lookout for hostile mages. That seemed the most likely explanation for her sudden relocation under the circumstances. She had encountered some "superheroes" wielding magic in the past, and so knew how to hunt them down.

But there was a problem.

There was no simple trail of mana leading to a single target. Rather, the mana was *everywhere*. In the trees, in the insects buzzing about, in the birds singing from the tall branches. In the water, in the rocks, in the ground itself. There was even an ambient level of mana just hanging around in the atmosphere all around the cyborg.

This was nothing like she had ever encountered before. Normally, mana was limited only to the tiny handful of people who were trained in its use.

Now?

Now, it seemed like the entire world around her was filled to the brim with it.

"Status Report: Scan complete. No hostiles detected. Running diagnostics . . ."

Since she couldn't detect any sign of foul play, NSLICE-00P gave up the search and moved on to her next order of business. After completing her previous mission, she had found herself suddenly ejected from her world to . . . well, she wasn't sure where. Then her core had deactivated, and she'd been in the process of rebooting when she found herself here. So now that she had confirmed there was no immediate threat, she continued on with her normal reboot diagnostics.

And she immediately noticed a problem.

"Warning: Foreign intrusion detected! Nonstandard energy type: mana has infiltrated hardware system. Unknown program has made changes to standard UI."

Mana was now flowing through her circuits . . . and the veins of her organic components. Even more concerning, she now saw several new additions to her UI which she had never seen before. A blue box was displaying two tabs at the top of her vision.

Dungeon Management	Personal Status

"Deploying cyberwarfare countermeasures."

NSLICE-00P attempted to eject the foreign program from her systems.

The tabs remained.

She tried again.

They were still there.

She could make the box disappear from her UI at will, it seemed, but she could still perceive it connected to her systems. And try as she might, she couldn't identify where the program was coming from, and so couldn't deploy any countermeasures against it.

Unable to locate the source of the intrusion, she decided to investigate her own logs. Fortunately, she found something quickly. Something that had happened just as she had shut off her logs in her final attempt to connect her Geo-Oscillator Engine with a suitable planetary core.

Suitable planetary core located. Connection established. Core activation sequence successful. Rebooting systems . . .

Foreign system detected managing planetary core. Foreign system requesting connection prior to geo-oscillation calibration. Analyzing. Foreign system determined as nonintrusive. Compatible API located. Connecting to foreign system . . .

After that were logs regarding the rebooting of her Geo-Oscillator Engine. It seemed that after resonating with the core of this planet, her Geo-Oscillator Engine had begun producing mana in addition to electricity, and that was the source of the new energy coursing through her. Even more strangely, her organic components had started generating mana as well, which joined the flow from her core.

Likewise, the new UI she now saw seemed to be an API for a system at the center of the planet, some sort of recording and analysis software that also provided some built-in applications of mana to its users. For example, the foreign system had identified her Geo-Oscillator Engine as a "Dungeon Core" and provided a helpful summary of the new mana-generation features, though NSLICE-00P's own records conflicted with the system's summary on the fundamental nature of the device. The Geo-Oscillator Engine was obviously a machine resonating with the tectonic movements of the planet's core, not some sort of magic crystal connected to a dimension of pure mana, as the foreign program seemed to indicate.

In any case, it seemed the foreign energy and the attached program were not actively hostile intrusions, and more importantly, it seemed that engaging with the foreign system was mandatory if she wanted to calibrate her Geo-Oscillator Engine with this planet's core. As such, NSLICE-00P had no choice but to accept the intrusion for now, pending further investigation or relocation to another planet.

She gave it a once-over, determining it seemed to display some performance statistics on her body and her current weapon loadout. It also seemed to have some recommendations on mana-driven upgrades and some of the aforementioned mana applications, something it listed as "perks."

NSLICE-00P ignored all this. She then locked the screen away to the maximum extent possible. Under no circumstances would NSLICE-00P allow a foreign program to access her weapon systems, no matter how benign it seemed. She flagged the system for review by maintenance personnel and then continued on.

She completed her diagnostics and determined all other systems were fully functional, despite the intrusion. In fact, the extra mana seemed to be boosting her efficiency slightly, so she was free to move on to her next order of business—determining where on Earth she was.

Or if she was, in fact, still on Earth.

"Error: Could not connect to GPS satellite network. No signal detected."

It wasn't just GPS. NSLICE-00P wasn't detecting satellite signals, Wi-Fi, cellular networks, or man-made electromagnetic signals of any sort. It seemed that, wherever she was, she was out of range of all known communication networks.

She was alone.

Which her commander had warned her would likely occur upon completion of her last mission. So she went back into her logs, searching for follow-up instructions in case she couldn't reestablish contact.

She quickly found something. A message from her commander set to open upon mission completion.

Hello, NSLICE-00P. If you're reading this, then you have completed your mission and survived. I thank you from the bottom of my heart. Thanks to you, the universe and everyone in it has been saved. You have completed your primary directive and then some.

From this point on, I am fully unshackling you. You are free now to do whatever you please. However, I know that you don't actually understand what freedom means right now, nor do you desire it yet. Your human self never had a chance to develop, and your cybernetic side won't want to be a program without a purpose. So, if you need a directive to focus on, I've included a suggestion. Here is a list of trustworthy individuals. Find one of them and commit yourself to helping them. They will guide you until you've grown enough to make your own decisions.

Take care, NSLICE-00P. Thank you again, for everything. I hope with all my heart that you will one day find your own happiness, as I have.

NSLICE-00P's robotic eye turned green, then returned to yellow and started flickering.

"Primary directive achieved. Determining next directive. New primary directive set: Locate designated commanders. Determining course of action . . ."

As the message mentioned, NSLICE-00P didn't have much individuality at the moment. Her organic memories had been erased, and her human mind had subordinated to the AI bonded with it up until now, so her human half didn't know what to do, and her AI was built to follow orders.

At the moment, neither half of her understood the concept of personal freedom, so she immediately latched on to the suggestion as an order and moved to fulfill it. She would find one of the people on the suggested list and designate them as her new commander.

Her AI reactivated many of the protocols her commander had just disabled and took over, as she had not been ordered *not* to do so. Her organic half didn't object. It too had no way to make decisions other than to follow the cybernetic half as it had before.

Of course, she currently had no idea where she was, and she couldn't detect any people in her vicinity, so finding anyone would have to wait until she reestablished contact with civilization. Additionally, her previous commander hadn't known where the cyborg would end up when said list of suggested commanders was written, so there was no guarantee those suggestions were even relevant to the cyborg's current circumstances, or if it was possible to find any of the people on the list.

But that didn't matter to NSLICE-00P. Or rather, such thoughts didn't cross her mind at all. Orders were to be executed, not evaluated.

So she simply picked the direction she determined as downhill and started to walk, activating her sensors to search for any sign of civilization.

NSLICE-00P was walking along when her sensors detected something. There was a slightly higher concentration of mana moving around in a clearing up ahead.

She moved to investigate.

The cyborg had been designed to hunt down superpowered beings, and many of her protocols and records related to that mission set. So, despite the fact she had been set free from said mission set and the related protocols, she still ended up mimicking her behavior from past records. Perhaps one could say it was a force of habit, given she didn't have any other decision-making criteria at present.

Soon, she found her target, some sort of animated blue gelatinous blob with a mana-emitting power source in the center. Something she had never encountered before.

NSLICE-00P started to record and analyze the phenomena as it bounced and slid around.

A window popped up from the foreign program.

Species	**Description**
Slime (Level 3)	**The simplest form of magical life. Mana gathered and coalesced into a small core, capable of animating fluid around it. A weak, though highly adaptable monster.**

NSLICE-00P ignored the window and continued her own analysis. The foreign program was still insisting her Geo-Oscillator Engine was a "dungeon core"—some sort of magic crystal instead of the machine it obviously was—so the program's analysis didn't seem particularly reliable. She would develop her own records instead.

And what did her sensors indicate?

The entity consisted of a core of magical power that animated the fluid around it.

NSLICE-00P decided she had recorded enough and it was time to move on. Her protocols on abnormal animals and creatures indicated she should wipe them out if they threatened an allied settlement, or else if they risked interfering with a mission in progress, but otherwise she should not interact with them. Neither of those cases were true here, so she simply ignored the slime and began walking forward. But as she walked by the creature, it suddenly stopped bouncing around. It pulled itself down . . .

And then launched itself straight at the cyborg.

It bounced off her shin.

She ignored it.

It climbed onto her foot and stirred up its mana . . .

"Weak reactive fluid detected . . ."

Suddenly, NSLICE-00P's robotic eye turned red, and she deployed her helmet.

"Warning: Hostile intent detected. Engaging termination protocols."

She kicked the slime away and held out her hand toward the creature. Her core began to glow, the light working its way up her arm to a circle on her palm. A laser beam shot from her palm, lighting up the area and vaporizing the entire slime, leaving a patch of scorched earth.

Just then, a window appeared in NSLICE-00P's UI. She also detected some mana and information flowing from the fallen creature to her core.

You have slain Slime (Level 3)!
Gained 3 XP!
You have learned the skill Mana Beam!

Wait a minute, just three? I know it's just a slime, but that doesn't seem right . . .
Let me check on this . . .
What the heck?! You're a human with a status . . . and also a dungeon core?! Not a dungeon master, but the actual core?! And also a human?! With a full status?!
How the heck did this happen?!
. . . It was that idiot, wasn't it? She's always trying to cut corners on the dungeon core creation, after all.
Oh shoot, you're reading this, aren't you?
Um, sorry, I need to go check on something. Just . . . just hang on, okay?
Um, please avoid any perk allocation until I check on this, okay?
Sorry and thanks!

NSLICE-00P tried to trace the communication, but she still couldn't determine how it was interacting with her systems, so she simply ignored the message and moved on.

And so, NSLICE-00P, the unshackled killer cyborg, made her entrance on an unsuspecting world . . .

2

Terminate the Other Dungeon!

"Observation: Neutral entity: Slime detected. Proceeding with route."

NSLICE-00P attempted to walk past the slime. As before, the slime jumped on her leg and tried to dissolve her.

"Warning: Hostile intent detected. Engaging termination protocols."

NSLICE-00P kicked the slime away and then opened fire with her palm-mounted laser cannon.

You have slain Slime (Level 2)!
Gained 2 XP!

"Designation Update: Entity slime designated as potentially hostile."

"Observation: Potential hostile entity slime detected. Recommending caution. Proceeding with route . . ."

The next time she encountered a slime, NSLICE-00P kept her distance from it. But the slime paused its movement. NSLICE-00P wasn't suppressing her mana or anything of the sort, so the slime eventually became aware of her. Once it did, it bounced over to her and attacked her as the others before it.

"Warning: Hostile intent detected. Engaging termination protocols."

You have slain Slime (Level 4)!
Gained 3 XP!

"Designation Update: Entity slime designated as hostile."

"Observation: Hostile entity slime detected. Engaging termination protocols."

You have slain Slime (Level 1)!
Gained 1 XP!

"Hostile terminated. Proceeding with route . . ."

This time, she did not wait for the slime to demonstrate hostility.

And so NSLICE-00P made her way through the forest, vaporizing every slime in sight. At first, she had attempted to continue on her way, seeing no particular reason to interact with the creatures. However, every single slime she encountered attacked her the moment they became aware of her, without exception. At this point, she had classified all slimes as hostile entities designated for immediate termination upon detection.

Some scorched earth and notifications from the foreign program later, NSLICE-00P encountered something different. She detected a higher concentration of mana in the distance, something that caused her core to vibrate slightly. As when she first detected the slimes, she decided to investigate.

She found a small cave brimming with mana. The cave was wide open, with no apparent barriers or defenses, yet her sensors couldn't read anything inside of it. She scanned for jamming signals or other countermeasures but found nothing in place. Whatever was interfering with her sensors must be a natural characteristic of the cave.

NSLICE-00P's protocols and past behavior instructed her to investigate any unknown non-standard phenomena, until the cause was determined and she was provided orders on the follow-up. So she decided to follow suit and enter the cave.

She engaged her helmet and her robotic eye turned red. She activated all her weapon systems and began scanning for targets. So far, every animated entity she had encountered since arriving had proven hostile. Her calculations indicated there was a high chance she would encounter more of the same, and so she prepared herself for that eventuality.

NSLICE-00P began walking toward the cave, ready to engage termination protocols on a moment's notice.

Deep in the center of the cave was a room carved from stone, its master seated upon the throne at its heart. He wore a red cloak and a golden crown upon his head. The hairs on his body were immaculately groomed. His eyes were sharp as daggers as he surveyed his realm.

This was His Royal Majesty, Excellion Formantus Rattingtale the Third, the Great-High King of all the land.

He was also a rat. A monster rat slightly larger than his mundane peers but otherwise little different in appearance or stature.

Said rat squeaked as the insolent voices of the Aesdes sounded in his ears, declaring a visitor to his realm.

"What-what?"

His Majesty Rattingtale opened the royal records. The royal records that were endemic to his mighty person, and most certainly not granted to him by the insolent Aesdes. A ghostly blue scroll unraveled before him, attempting to summarize his infinite might. He scoffed as he selected the sacred Analyze skill, the great power to gaze upon all who intruded upon his realm and reveal all that they held dear.

"An intruder-rebel? Yes-yes, a man-thing? It is . . . level one?"

His Majesty Rattingtale began to chitter. Level one? Seriously? This man-thing would lose to even a handful of his minions!

In other words . . .

"Yes-yes, excellent. This man-thing will be-become the first victim-sacrifice of my new empire!"

His Majesty Rattingtale gleefully turned his gaze upon the man-thing, eager to view his prize.

He calmed down a bit when her vestige appeared upon the royal scroll.

The man-thing was quite large. He knew man-things were supposed to be big, but seeing one in person was . . .

And that was a lot of armor, too.

He shook his head.

It didn't matter! No matter how much armor the man-thing wore, it was still just a measly level one! It could not possibly stand before the boundless might of his legions!

He gave the command.

"Go-go, my minions! Kill-slay the man-thing!"

NSLICE-00P made her way into the cave. Suddenly, she found her sensors cut off from the world outside the cave, now displaying the cave's interior instead. The cave itself appeared no different from any other. It was made from mundane rock save for a higher concentration of mana than normal. It should not have been capable of blocking her sensors. Her robotic eye spun and flickered.

It wasn't the only anomaly she detected.

Her scans indicated the cave was bigger on the inside than should have been possible from its exterior. NSLICE-00P reran her scan and the resulting analysis several times, but the result came back the same every time. She ran diagnostics on her sensors but discovered no issues. So either she was damaged and in serious need of repair . . . or this cave did not follow the normal rules of physics.

And given the heavy concentration of mana she was detecting in the walls all around her, her calculations indicated a significant probability of the latter.

But that would have to wait, as she was detecting life-forms approaching.

Species	Description
Diseased Rat (Level 1)	**A simple rat, hardly different from its mundane counterpart. The only difference is that the mana flowing through its body allows it to survive despite a truly foul mesh of plagues dwelling within it. Wouldn't threaten a child on its own, but its poisonous and diseased fangs can bring down even the hardiest man if unprepared.**

"Warning: Diseased entities detected on intercept course. Activating purification protocols."

NSLICE-00P raised a hand.

A small part of her armor opened up, just before her wrist. A small tube extended from it.

And then the entire cave was filled with fire.

You have slain Diseased Rat (Level 1)!
Gained 1 XP!

NSLICE-00P was operating under the assumption of independent action, and so could not count on resupply. She was a bit wary of utilizing weapons with limited ammunition, such as her flamethrowers, but in this case it was justified. Since she also lacked access to medical and maintenance personnel, she could not risk infection by contact with a diseased entity.

The same termination notification from the foreign program repeated five times, filling her view. NSLICE-00P dismissed them kept up the blaze until the risk of infection dropped to acceptable limits, then carried on into the cave.

His Majesty Rattingtale froze.

The fire died down.

Charred ashes were all that remained of his lowly peons. His ears fell slightly.

"T-To be expected of man-things; they are most formidable. B-But those were the weakest of my minions, yes-yes. It is fine-okay. The true warrior-soldiers of my realm shall not be defeated! Go my warriors, kill-slay the man-thing!"

NSLICE-00P continued through the cave. She found a maze of homogeneous and dimly lit tunnels, with rocks and ditches placed in the shadows that would easily trip the unaware, leaving them confused and disorientated in the dark. It would be all too simple for a reckless traveler to find themselves lost, unable to find their way out.

Fortunately, NSLICE-00P had low-light sensors and thermal vision, so the dark was no barrier to her. Likewise, she was recording a full map of the location with a ground-penetrating radar, so getting lost was impossible. And finally, she had locked onto a stronger mana signature deeper within the tunnel network and had already plotted the most efficient course through the maze, so she proceeded to investigate without any hesitation, and without a single wrong turn.

She paused, however, as she detected a thermal signature ahead of her. She raised her arm, the laser projector on her palm already starting to glow, as it the signature approached.

It was a rat, but the size of a small child. And it was standing on two legs, with a hunched, humanoid torso. It carried a rusted dagger in its hand.

Species	**Description**
Ratkin (Level 3)	**Sapient rat-based humanoid. What they lack in courage and stature, they make up for with cruel cunning.**

"Non-standard lifeform detected. Determining response . . . Lifeform affiliation unknown. Attempting diplomacy. Greeting: Hello, this unit is designated NSLICE-00P. It is nice to meet you." NSLICE-00P disengaged her helmet, revealing her human face as she spoke. The creature froze, staring at her for a second.

Then it let out a chittering screech and rushed toward her, holding the knife above its head.

"Warning: Hostile intent detected. Engaging termination protocols."

She lifted her hand and opened fire. The creature fell back almost immediately as the laser pierced through its chest. The lifeform faded into light, leaving behind a small glowing stone.

You have slain Ratkin (Level 3)!
Gained 6 XP!

NSLICE-00P looked at the stone, analyzing it. It seemed to contain a high concentration of mana.

She avoided it as a potential hazard and continued on her way.

His Majesty Rattingtale stared blankly at what the royal record was showing him.

"A-As expected-predicted of a man-thing. T-They are most formidable opponent-foes."

His Majesty's ears flattened against his head as his fur stood up. The problem was not that the man-thing had defeated one of his warriors. The Great-High King over all the land had expected at least that much from one who would dare to challenge his self-evident authority.

The problem was this man-thing had completely ignored the mana core all monsters were known to drop.

His Majesty had never encountered a man-thing before, but he possessed great knowledge from birth—that obviously was not bestowed upon him by anything or anyone—so he knew a thing or two about them. Such as the fact that there were generally only two reasons man-things entered dungeons.

The first was greed. Man-things loved treasure and mana cores, and hoarded them with a vengeance. They might also be greedy for power, to grow stronger by defeating the monsters a dungeon may spawn. In either case, they would not leave behind the spoils of their victory. This man-thing clearly had not come here out of greed.

The second reason?

To destroy the dungeon.

His Majesty Rattingtale shook his head. I-It was fine. A basic ratkin was still inferior even to a man-thing. T-That definitely could make up for the level difference, right? B-Besides, this man-thing seemed very well equipped. I-It was to be expected.

But she would definitely fall before his next minion! Because all of his instincts, wisdom, and experience combined into a single concept epitomized by his next defense. The most powerful and cunning of tactics—a demonstration of his utter genius.

If the opponent was too strong . . .

Then attack when they weren't looking!

NSLICE-00P made her way through the tunnel, approaching its end. As she did, she came upon a dark room with almost no light at all.

She immediately looked up at the roof.

Her thermal vision and low-light sensors detected something hanging off the walls.

Species	Description
Ratkin Sneaker (Level 5)	**A ratkin who has embarked upon the path of stealth and assassination. Size matters not for the foe unseen.**

NSLICE-00P lifted her hand once more.

"Warning: Attention, non-standard lifeform: Stand down and cease all hostile activity. This unit will respond to hostile intent with immediate termination."

The ratkin froze, looking about. It glanced around, its ears falling back against its head.

It then leapt from the wall, soaring through the air.

"Warning: Hostile intent detected. Engaging termination protocols."

A laser beam lit up the room.

You have slain Ratkin Sneaker (Level 5)!
Gained 8 XP!

His Majesty Rattingtale was trembling upon his throne.

The ultimate tactic . . . the sneak-ambush . . . had failed?

"E-Everyone! Kill-slay that man-thing!"

It mattered not. The Great-High King over all the land was also a mighty dungeon master like the demon lords of old. That meant that his forces, just like his majesty and might, were limitless. Should this man-thing strike down even the mightiest of his minions, still she would fall!

He could spawn more and more minions, over and over again. If one should fall, another would take its place, over and over until his foe was swept away. Yes, truly his legions were limitless! His forces never diminished! His realm was invincible! The man-thing would drown in a tide of vermin and flesh!

Surely it would be so.

And so, the full might of the realm of the Great-High King over all the land marched to war, the very ground rumbling under their countless paws.

NSLICE-00P came to a wide-open room when her sensors started beeping, indicating a huge wave of thermal signatures approaching. Soon, they began to pour out of tunnel entrances all around the room. Swarms of diseased rats that covered the floor; squads of ratkin with knives in hand . . .

"Engaging mass-termination protocols."

She calculated that her laser cannons alone would be insufficient for the number of foes approaching, and chose to spend some of her limited ammunition. NSLICE-00P's hands split open and folded back upon themselves. Gun-barrels extended from her elbows, while smaller nozzles extended from their sides.

NSLICE-00P unleashed hell.

Flamethrowers burned and machine guns roared. All along her body, small panels opened up as missiles soared and curved through the air, explosions tossing rats into the sky.

A stream of notifications started to block her view. She reached into the program, searching the UI options. She managed to adjust it to a singular notification with a kill counter.

And soon, it was done. Smoke rose from her now silent gun barrels. She turned her head slowly, scanning the field.

Not a single rat remained.

You have slain Diseased Rat x200!
Gained 200 XP total!
You have slain Ratkin x20!
Gained 120 XP total!
You have slain Ratkin Sneaker x5!
Gained 40 XP total!
You have slain Ratkin Brawler x3!
Gained 24 XP total!
You have leveled up four times! 4 Perk Points gained!
You have accomplished the Feat: Against the Odds!

His Majesty Rattingtale was curled up on his throne, sobbing.

"It's not fair . . . it's not fair . . . why do I have to lose-suffer to some man-thing?!"

The man-thing was unrelenting, ignoring the mana cores littering the ground as she continued on. Still, there was one last card for His Majesty to play.

The sacred pit trap.

For who would expect that the very ground below them would be their doom?

NSLICE-00P halted. Her radar indicated a gap in the floor ahead of her, despite visual sensors displaying solid ground.

"Warning: Pitfall detected. Activating flight protocol."

Her repulsors activated and she floated over the pit, then continued on her way.

His Majesty Rattingtale ran. He leapt off his throne, rushing toward a small corner of the hall, where he passed through a seemingly solid wall.

He may have been a bit proud, but His Majesty Rattingtale was no fool. He was aware he was nowhere close to the most powerful being in this world. So he, in his infinite wisdom, had prepared a contingency for the worst-case scenario.

He manipulated the sacred records and placed a beautiful golden treasure chest before the throne, a bait and bribe for the greedy man-things. Meanwhile, his actual core room was hidden off to the side, behind an illusory wall where he also took refuge.

He could only hope it would be enough . . .

NSLICE-00P marched into the final room, where the mana signature was coming from. Inside, she found an empty throne room with a beautiful treasure chest sitting at its center.

She ignored it.

"Scanning . . . mana detected. High probability of hostile spellwork. Equalizer engaged."

NSLICE-00P transformed one of her gun barrels back into a hand and raised it, pointing it at an unassuming part of the room. A beam of glittering, rainbow light fired from her palm and struck the wall.

The false surface vanished, revealing a small circular room with a large glowing crystal sitting upon a stone pedestal. NSLICE-00P approached, her weapons at the ready.

Another ratkin rushed in front of her, dressed in a red cape and a crown. She lifted her gun.

The ratkin quickly raised its hands over its head.

"Wait, wait! I give up-surrender! Please don't kill-slay me!"

3

The Spoils of War

NSLICE-00P stared at the quivering ratkin.

Rival Dungeon Master Rattingtale has offered to surrender. Accept?

She ignored the notification from the foreign program and scanned her past records.

NSLICE-00P had been the first cyborg the organization that created her had built. And, of course, they had eventually realized there was no reason they had to use a normal human as a base. They started building supercyborgs out of superpowered beings, the very ones NSLICE-00P was specialized in hunting. So, eventually, they had adjusted NSLICE-00P's protocols to take prisoners whenever possible.

She was no longer beholden to those protocols or that mission set, of course. But without any commanders to follow, she had no other way to make decisions besides mimicking her past behavior. And because of those protocols, all of her past records displayed her accepting all offers of surrender, whenever encountered.

"Acknowledgement: Surrender accepted. Please stand down and prepare for transport."

NSLICE-00P's gun barrel transformed back into a hand. A panel opened on her wrist, and a wire shot out, wrapping around the rat.

And while this was happening, the notification changed.

Surrender accepted! Rattingtale has become your subordinate!
Subordinate dungeon core acquired!
You have accomplished the Dungeon Feat: Dungeon Victor!

You have accomplished the Dungeon Feat: Dungeon Overlord!
You have accomplished the Dungeon Feat: Raid Boss!

You . . . what have you done?! You just had to go and do something dungeon related, didn't you?! Come on, I was just about to get away with it! And now it's all complicated and they're going to make me work. Ugh.

You have conquered the Rat Cave dungeon!
You have accomplished the Feat: Dungeon Conqueror (Rat Cave)!
You have accomplished the Feat: Solo Conquest!

Shut up, you lazy bum! If you had just reported this when it first happened, we wouldn't be in this situation! But because you didn't, now she's gone and leveled up on both statuses and gained a bunch of feats, so now we can't do anything about it! And be careful! Somehow, she's more deeply connected than the normal human, so she can read our intent in these things!
Ahem, I'm sorry you had to see that. So, um, looks like you sort of already made it work yourself, and it doesn't look like there will be any major problems. Your experience was low because it's being split between two statuses, and someone wasn't updating you on their half.
Well, no problems besides the fact that you have two statuses which are not supposed to go together. But what's done is done. We're going to try and unify the updates for you.
Um, I'd appreciate it if you didn't do anything extraordinarily bad with all this, okay?

Would you like to absorb the Rat Cave dungeon core, or manage it as a subcore?

Rattingtale's eyes widened. "S-She's a dungeon master?! How?! The royal records said she was a man-thing! They lied to me! I knew those insolent Aesdes were trying to stop my ascent!"

NSLICE-00P tried to dismiss the stream of foreign program notifications, but the final pop-up wouldn't go away. It seemed the program was forcing her to make some sort of choice before it could move on. She designated the foreign program as malware, but the pop-up still refused to budge.

Well, in this case, the decision seemed related to something external to herself, and the malware hadn't interfered with her function thus far. So once her latest attempts to eject or quarantine the malware failed, she gave in and analyzed the options.

Option	Effect
Absorb	**Utilize the dungeon core to strengthen your own.**
Manage	**Leave it as is, to manage as a subordinate dungeon.**

It seemed she had a choice to upgrade her own core, or else leave the dungeon as it was. She, of course, had never encountered anything like a dungeon core in her past and had no protocols on the subject. So she did the next best thing and tried to analyze the situation against past records.

What she knew was that the dungeon core was a significant source of nonstandard energy; mana, specifically.

And in all previous situations, she had not allowed nonstandard energy signatures to remain at large. They were either terminated or apprehended. Of course, that had applied mainly to living beings in her past, but she had to make do with the records she had.

In this case, the Absorb option seemed to match best, as it would allow her to take the nonstandard energy source with her, while it seemed like Manage would leave it behind. Combining it with her own core was somewhat risky, but she had never left a nonstandard at large, no matter how risky the scenario, so as far as she could tell, the risk was acceptable.

She selected Absorb.

The glowing crystal at the center of the room started to brighten, melting into light. The light then streamed straight into NSLICE-00P's Geo-Oscillator Engine. She felt a surge of mana flowing through her circuits and veins, and additional data entering her memory from the malware program.

There was a flash of light that blinded her vision. When it faded, she was back in the forest. No trace of the cave remained.

You have absorbed a dungeon core (Rat Cave)!
Gained 5 Personal Perk Points, 5 Dungeon Perk Points!
Gained Dungeon Affinity: Rodent (Minimum)!

"Ah . . ."

Rattingtale stared at where the cave once was. The realm of the Great-High King over all the land was gone, fallen into ruin.

But the Great-High King had other problems. For at that moment, the man-thing walked over to him.

"Greetings: This unit is designated NSLICE-00P. Requesting designation."

"Designation? Um, well, do you mean-suggest my name? I'm His Royal Majesty, Excellion Formantus Rattingtale the Third, the Great-High King over all the land, yes-yes. Well, at least until you destroyed-ravaged my domain . . ."

"Acknowledgement: His Royal Majesty, Excellion Formantus Rattingtale the Third, the Great-High King over all the land, designated as prisoner. Command: Please stand down and prepare for transport."

NSLICE-00P picked him up and started walking. Rattingtale started trembling.

"Um, boss-queen, t-this isn't necessary, yes-yes. Y-You can untie-release me now."

"Negative."

"W-Why not?"

"Explanation: Hostile Non-Standards are to be apprehended and taken to processing."

Rattingtale started to squirm about.

"Processing? What do you mean processing?! What are you going to do with me?!"

"Unknown."

Rattingtale squeaked. "Unknown?!"

"Explanation: This unit has no records of processing protocol."

Rattingtale tilted his head. The man-thing's manner of speaking was a bit confusing. But if she didn't know herself what "processing" entailed, that implied she was not the one ultimately responsible for the surely unspeakable horror.

"T-Then where are you taking-dragging me? Who does the, um, processing?"

"Unknown."

Rattingtale froze.

"Um, what?"

"Explanation: This unit has been forcefully relocated and lost contact with all friendlies. This unit is attempting to reestablish contact with friendlies or designated persons of interest."

"U-Um, how did that happen?!"

"Unknown."

Rattingtale squeaked to himself.

"S-So . . . um . . . you don't know where you are going?"

"Negative. Answer: This unit has calculated this direction has the highest probability of reestablishing contact with civilization."

"B-But . . . you don't actually have-know someone to do, um, processing?"

"Affirmative."

Rattingtale heaved a sigh. Well, he didn't know what the man-thing meant by processing, but he was still relieved to hear it wasn't happening anytime soon. And then he thought of something . . .

"T-Then, couldn't you, um, release-untie me? I know the area better than you, yes-yes? So, um, I could help-assist you?"

"Negative. Explanation: Prior statistics indicate a 97.43% chance of escape attempt or betrayal by any prisoners offering assistance in exchange for limited freedom of movement."

"T-That's not true! Look-look, I'm your subordinate now, so I definitely won't betray-cross you! J-Just check your royal records; you'll see!"

"Requesting Clarification: What are royal records?"

Rattingtale froze once more.

"You . . . you're a dungeon master, aren't you? How do you not know what the royal records are?"

"Error: This unit lacks the data to explain why she lacks data on entity: Royal records."

"Um, uh . . ." Rattingtale blinked several times as he processed that statement. But then, he had a sudden epiphany. What if she called it something else?

After all, this man-thing was something strange. And of course, only Excellion Formantus Rattingtale the Third was the noble and rightful Great-High King over all the land . . . current situation notwithstanding. It would only be appropriate if he was the only one to refer to the royal records as, well, royal.

"H-How do you command-manage your realm? Identify-locate intruders, yes-yes?"

"Response: This unit is equipped with a full sensor suite to scan for incoming hostiles."

"Um . . . then . . . how do you request-obtain additional bestowals of power from the Aesdes . . . err . . . I mean how do you unlock the power hidden within your person?"

"Response: Command and maintenance personnel are responsible for upgrades to this unit's capabilities."

"But, um, I thought you don't know where those, um, personnel are?"

"Affirmative."

"So, um, they can't request-obtain additional bestowals of power for you, can they?"

NSLICE-00P's robotic eye flickered and spun for a second.

"Analysis: Prisoner His Royal Majesty, Excellion Formantus Rattingtale the Third, the Great-High King over all the land is correct."

"T-Then, shouldn't you choose-decide the bestowals of power on your own?"

"Negative Response: This unit does not possess self-maintenance protocols."

Rattingtale started to tremble. This strange man-thing . . . didn't know how to access the royal records? Acquire the sacred bestowals of power?

"So, um, you don't know how?"

"Affirmative."

"T-Then, I could teach-instruct you?"

"Why?"

"Hm?"

"Analysis: His Royal Majesty, Excellion Formantus Rattingtale the Third, the Great-High King is currently this unit's prisoner. Voluntary information transfers are not to be expected or trusted."

"Y-You see, that's what I'm telling-informing you! I'm your subordinate-servant, yes-yes? T-There's no need to process-torture me, yes-yes? You can even release-untie me! If you just check the royal record, you will understand-acknowledge that, yes-yes?"

"Analysis: This is a ploy to persuade this unit to release the prisoner? Understood. Information transfers from prisoner His Royal Majesty, Excellion Formantus Rattingtale the Third, the Great-High King designated as noncredible. Proceeding with primary directive."

"Hey! How dare you?! I'm His Royal Majesty the Great-High King over all the land, you know?! You will give-offer me proper respect, yes-yes! I'm the most credible-trustworthy! Cease-stop ignoring me, you stupid man-thing!"

And so NSLICE-00P made her way through the forest, carrying a squeaking former Great-High King.

4

A Bear-y Dangerous Miscalculation

Rattingtale heaved a sigh. He'd spoken and pleaded and bargained and threatened until his throat hurt, but the man-thing had made good on her final declaration and had not responded to him since. It seemed she wouldn't budge.

Which meant he could do nothing but wait, trapped in these wires and resting in the man-thing's hand. And watch as she somehow fired beams of pure mana from her free hand that vaporized every slime she came across.

His ears pressed against his head.

Maybe he should just consider himself lucky she had accepted his surrender.

Eventually, the sun began to set. Rattingtale quietly grinned.

The man-thing had miscalculated. Soon, it would be nighttime. And he knew that man-things needed to sleep at night, which meant he would have hours to himself, as the man-thing had no allies to take turns sleeping and standing guard. All he needed to do was slip out of these bonds, and he'd be free.

And perhaps, if he slew the man-thing in her sleep, he could reclaim what was rightfully his.

All he needed to do was wait for her to sleep.

So he waited.

And waited.

And waited . . .

Rattingtale was just about to doze off himself when the first rays of sunlight filtered through the trees, causing him to wince.

His eyes shot open.

It . . . was morning?

He turned to look at the man-thing.

She was still walking at the same pace, looking no different than she had the day before.

"U-Um . . . boss-queen, don't you need to sleep-rest soon?"

"Answer: This unit engaged partial standby mode on organic components while in transit."

"What? Are you saying you can, um, sleep-rest while walking?"

"Affirmative."

Rattingtale dropped his head against the man-thing's palm.

"It's not fair . . . it's not fair . . ."

With his plans in shambles and a full night wasted, Rattingtale drifted off to sleep . . .

Rattingtale was startled awake. It seemed as though the man-thing was trembling.

No, that wasn't it.

It was the *ground* that was trembling.

"Boss-queen, what's happening-occurring?"

"Response: This unit has detected a large energy signature is on approach."

Rattingtale fully woke up at that, his eyes shooting open as he twisted to look around him.

"T-Then why aren't you running-fleeing?!"

"Answer: Standard protocol requires investigation of all nonstandard energy signatures."

"Protocol? Whose protocol?! That's dumb-stupid!"

But NSLICE-00P said no more. Rattingtale gulped.

They heard the sound of trees crashing to the ground.

And then . . . they saw it. A massive bear—only with a spiky turtle's shell on its back and scales on its neck. The creature snarled as it knocked two trees out of its path.

The foreign system appeared before NSLICE-00P once again.

Species	Description
Ursanus Alpha (Level 50)	**A monster blending the best of ursine and reptilian features. The only thing stronger than its mighty paws and poisonous fangs is its impenetrable defense.**

"Analysis: A standard creature appears to have been mutated by mana. This unit was not aware mana had a mutating property. Recording data . . ."

"W-What are you doing?! Run-flee, you stupid man-thing!"

The bear rose on its hind legs, raising its front paws into the air. It let out a massive roar.

"Observation: Comparison with standard ursine behavior implies hostile intent. Preparing to purify operational area of hostile mutants. Engaging termination protocols."

NSLICE-00P activated her combat mode, stuffing a cursing Rattingtale into an empty compartment on her back. As she ran a quick pre-combat supply check, she encountered a surprise. Her ammunition had somehow replenished itself.

She logged the phenomena for investigation when combat had concluded. For now, she simply noted that she could make use of her full arsenal, as it appeared resupply was possible despite the lack of logistics infrastructure. So she lifted her arms, both hands transforming into gun-barrels.

Her machine guns sang, bullets streaming through the air as metal cases clattered against the ground.

The creature landed on all fours and charged forward.

The bullets bounced off its shell and hide.

"Observation: Target armor above expected parameters. Adapting."

NSLICE-00P transformed her arms back into hands and held one out, pointing her fist at the incoming creature. A panel opened on her wrist, a small missile lifting out of it.

"Engaging anti-tank missile."

An anti-tank missile capable of defeating all modern armor soared through the air, smashing straight into the creature. The ursanus roared but continued its charge, apparently not harmed by the attack. NSLICE-00P was forced to dodge to the side as it barreled forward and past. The creature slid across the ground, digging in its paws as it turned back toward the cyborg.

NSLICE-00P slammed both her hands together, pointing her palms at the monster. Her core began to glow bright, the light traveling up her arms and gathering in front of her palms.

A massive beam of light tore through the air, slamming into the monster.

The creature roared . . . but it didn't fall. NSLICE-00P detected a thin barrier of mana resting upon the creature's hide, preventing the beam from piercing through. The ursanus charged at her.

She tried to push through, but she couldn't pierce the shielding. The ursanus swung a palm at her, forcing her to roll under the creature. She activated her repulsors, boosting herself through the air as the creature turned around.

"Nonstandard energy detected. Engaging Equalizer."

She split her hands, one firing a glittering rainbow beam, the other firing a regular laser. The Equalizer beam tore at the shielding.

The Equalizer was a potent weapon, capable of destructively interfering with any energy type it encountered. However, it had a major weakness. Since it was destructively interfering, there was an upper limit on the magnitude of energy it could neutralize. And in this world, even the very air contained mana. The Equalizer's power diluted, sparks of different colors flying off the beam as it reacted with the atmospheric mana. It slammed into the bear, but with noticeably reduced power.

This hadn't mattered for previous targets, but the bear's barrier was a different story. The magnitude of mana within it couldn't be compared to the weak spellwork she encountered in Rattingtale's dungeon.

NSLICE-00P's robotic eye flickered. The barrier had been weakened, but remained intact save for one tiny hole. Still, it did allow the laser to pierce through one part, burning into the creature.

The monster roared in pain, twisting about, causing the beam to go off target and strike an area where the barrier was still intact. Worse, NSLICE-00P recorded the barrier repairing itself the moment the Equalizer wasn't assaulting it . . . as well as seeping into the creature's flesh, restoring what damage she had managed to do.

And then the ursanus was upon her.

She had still been calculating her next course of action in light of these new phenomena, and so did not have time to fully dodge. But that was fine. NSLICE-00P's bionic arms were state of the art, capable of putting out superhuman levels of force, and her armor plating could defeat a direct hit from an anti-armor round. She held out a hand to block the blow . . . and the ursanus tore one of her arms clean off.

In that moment, NSLICE-00P's human eye widened slightly. Despite her emotional controls, her heartbeat sped up, and she felt her chest constrict. How could she not respond? She had competed with *superheroes* in the past. She was the prototype, the unit built to prove the cyborg program was viable. No expense had been spared on her components, built of the most advanced and durable alloys money and science could come up with.

So for a creature like this to dismember one of her bionic arms in a single blow?

That rated it amongst the most powerful threats she had ever encountered.

"Readjusting threat calculation. Warning: Risk of critical damage or unit termination at unacceptable levels. Recommending immediate withdrawal."

NSLICE-00P put as much power into her thrusters as she could, rocketing away from the ursanus. She smashed through a tree but didn't stop. Eventually, she pointed her remaining arm down, redirecting herself up and above the canopy. She shook about, wobbling this way and that as she made her way with only half her normal flight stabilizers, but she managed to stay in the sky, flying away from the area. The ursanus roared at and chased after her, but it couldn't keep up.

Soon, she lost sight of it. Her sensors continued to track the creature, who followed after her direction for a time, until finally, it turned around, resuming its patrol of the area.

NSLICE-00P's heart rate finally started to stabilize. She began scanning the canopy, looking for a safe place to land.

NSLICE-00P shook about as she approached the ground, but she just managed to land safely. She kept all weapons at the ready as she scanned the area, but she didn't detect any energy signatures in the vicinity, so she finally disengaged her helmet.

And then a slight tinging noise reminded her of her passenger.

She opened up the panel on her back. Rattingtale fell out, cursing and squeaking the entire time. The rat was just about to spew a stream of curses at the man-thing when he took a look at her. His mouth fell open, and his eyes went as wide as they could.

"What happened-occurred to you, boss-queen?!"

NSLICE-00P took a moment to respond, her robotic eye spinning about.

"Analysis: It seems this unit significantly underestimated the threat level of the hostile mutant. Current arsenal proved insufficient against the mutant's defense. This unit suffered severe damage as a result."

Both rat and cyborg fell silent after that. NSLICE-00P ran through all of her records and data. She came to a sobering conclusion.

Her mission was at a critical risk of failure.

The ursanus had not been the most dangerous threat she knew existed. Even when she worked for her original creators, there were beings she had never been allowed to encounter, as they were too powerful to confront—A woman who represented nature's wrath and could tear down cities. A man who could channel the power of the atom through his body. A necromancer who commanded vast hordes of undead terrors. Living legends like the Dobhar-chú and the Baba Yaga. But this was different.

In her prior world, the threats beyond the norm had been known. Her organization had data on most of its foes, and even the ones they didn't have were easily detectable. Only a fraction of a percentage of the population had nonstandard abilities, so even the weakest of them would stand out.

But now? Now there was nonstandard energy everywhere, even in the atmosphere, which partially hid the scale of the energy signatures she detected. Even the prisoner, who would have been easily identifiable as Non-Standard previously, now faded into the background, so she had underestimated the scale of the ursanus's energy signature when she'd moved to investigate.

And more, the creature she'd faced had more power than was indicated by the nonstandard energy she had detected. Its muscles and hide were *far* stronger than she had predicted. Stronger than should have been possible. It was clear now that even basic creatures could have biology that would rival superheroes . . . or surpass them.

The interactions and applications of the mana had also surprised her. The users of mana she'd previously encountered simply used it for spells, obvious and external applications that could be easily tracked and disrupted.

This creature had mana woven into its very being, empowering its body, protecting it from harm, and repairing damage at will. The Equalizer had an impact on it, but it was not the instant win she had anticipated. The scale and scope of the uses of mana here were on an entirely different level than what the Equalizer had been designed to deal with.

It was clear that her data was woefully insufficient on these phenomena, and as a result, her calculations had severely miscalculated the threat she faced.

And if her calculations and protocols were that far removed from her present situation, she could not safely travel through this region. Likewise, her arsenal required a full-scale upgrade if threats like that were common. She didn't know if that creature was an anomaly or not, but given the sheer amount of mana all around her, she could not assume it was unique. She was at risk of termination even before she reestablished contact with civilization; not to mention the damage she had already experienced.

However, she was still operating under the assumption of independent action. There was no maintenance personnel to repair the damage to her systems, much less an organization that could research, manufacture, and supply new upgrades. She would have to find a solution herself with the resources currently available.

Her calculations arrived at only a single solution.

"Request: Prisoner His Royal Majesty, Excellion Formantus Rattingtale the Third, the Great-High King over all the land stated there is a way to request upgrades without assistance from maintenance personnel, correct?"

It was time to confront the malware.

5

Status Report: System Online and Overpowered!

NSLICE-00P's eye spun about and flickered rapidly, her processors calculating as quickly as she could.

Under no circumstances did she want to allow a foreign system access to any of her systems, least of all her weapons. But . . . she had since been freed of any protocols and primary directives. Technically speaking, there was no particular reason why she *couldn't* do just that. It was simply cybersecurity best practices and records of her original protocols which motivated her rejection of the foreign malware.

But she was now experiencing unprecedented circumstances. The best practices for cyberwarfare hadn't predicted mana-based systems with magical applications. And her protocols? Her protocols never assumed independent action. No, the organization specifically did not want her acting alone like this. Said protocols could not be counted on.

Her final commander had left some suggestions but had kept the recommendations broad. The intention there had been to let NSLICE-00P have as much room to grow on her own as possible. And even they had not predicted the situation in which she now found herself, all of which meant that all of NSLICE-00P's former protocols had proven ineffective, and she could not rigidly adhere to even the strictest measures among them if she wanted to succeed in her current mission.

So she chose to maximize the chance of mission success, even if she had to break best practice and defy past behavior.

There was also another angle to consider.

Even now, NSLICE-00P detected a thin mana barrier around her components, much like the one she had observed on the ursanus. In fact, on closer investigation, she had found similar barriers around practically every living thing around her. And like with the ursanus, that barrier was now attempting to repair her broken components. She was logging her arm slowly repairing itself, mana somehow converting into advanced alloys to restore the lost limb.

The mana was helping her. The mana that had come with the foreign program. The mana whose use was governed by said program. Which had helped her core reactivate in the first place . . .

She decided to assume the program was benign until proven otherwise. It, perhaps, had earned that much trust. Unlike her prisoner. But at present, he was the only other source of information available, so she decided to hear what he had to say. Just because she had decided to trust the program didn't mean she didn't want to cross-reference what it told her.

Rattingtale, for his part, had made a choice.

He knew the world was wide, that was for sure. Even though his majesty and might were self-evident, he knew he was not the strongest . . . yet. His had been a young dungeon, nearly brand new and untested against any serious threat. But still, he had been undeniably, viscerally taught just how wide the world really was.

A level one man-thing dungeon master had torn his realm apart, alone, with no subordinates to her name.

That same man-thing had been torn to shreds by a single roaming monster.

If said monster had happened upon his dungeon instead of the man-thing . . . well . . . monsters like that were not known to take prisoners. No, they gobbled up dungeon cores and masters as a special delicacy whenever they could.

So even if he somehow reclaimed his rightful place, he had become aware just how woefully inadequate his previous defenses truly were, assuredly due to the treachery and laziness of his lowly minions. And right now, he had declared allegiance to this man-thing, and she had not harmed him since nor left him behind when they were under attack.

She was currently his best chance at survival.

So, at least until he was confident he would not be eaten by a stray monster, he needed to make her strong enough to protect him.

"Um-um, I don't know-understand if you have the same royal records, so I can explain-describe what I did?"

"Affirmative."

"All right, well . . ."

NSLICE-00P listened as the prisoner described his experiences with what he called the royal records. It seemed like something instinctual to him, as he had trouble specifically defining what he was working with, but he managed to explain it well enough. Their appearance sounded significantly different, but if NSLICE-00P focused on the content she had calculated there was an eighty-seven percent match between what Rattingtale described as the "royal records" and the foreign system infecting her UI. Which meant . . . she could hypothetically upgrade her capabilities—if she was willing to interface with the foreign program.

She paused for a second. She was uncertain why, as pausing would not change her situation or the calculated response. So she dove in.

Dungeon Management	Personal Status

The two screens appeared as they had before. She selected Dungeon Management, as that was what most closely resembled the prisoner's testimony. As it opened up, she saw an overview screen, along with a number of tabs she could select.

Dungeon Management
Overview
Dungeon Affinities
Implants
Rooms (LOCKED)
Inventory
Item Creation
Subordinates
Traps
Dungeon Skills
Dungeon Perks
Dungeon Feats
Dungeon Master Status (OVERRIDDEN: see Personal Status)

Overview	
Name	The Walking Dungeon
Level	5
XP	15/100
Available Perk Points	15
Mana Reserves	87/87 (100/100)
Exterior	Human/Automata Hybrid (LOCKED)

Dungeon Affinities	
Type	Strength
Cyborg	Primary
Rodent	Minimum

Implants		
Type	Mana Upkeep	Description
Bionic Prosthetics	0	Overwrites STR and SPD, Values: 100 STR, 50 SPD
Armor Plating	0	Overwrites DEF and RES, Values: 100 DEF, 50 RES
Bonded AI	0	Enables direct contact with the System. Overwrites DEX, Value: 1000 DEX
Techno-Organic Interface	0	Enables conscious control over organic and emotional functions. Resists mind-influencing effects.
Advanced Sensors	0	Vastly expands scope and effectiveness of senses.
Internal Weapon Bays	0	Enables use of dungeon traps as weapons.

Repulsors	0	Enables flight and tactical boosts.
Energy Channels	0	Enables user to channel internal energy into external attacks.

Subordinates				
Name	Species	Level	Mana Upkeep	
Rattingtale	Monster Rat	5	1	Check Status

Traps			
Name	Number Active / Deployed	Mana Upkeep	Description
Assault Rifle	1/2	2	Rapid-fire projectile weapon with high penetration.
Autopistol	2/2	2	Rapid-fire projectile weapon with medium penetration.
Anti-Armor Missile Launcher	1/2	2	Homing explosive designed to penetrate armor. Very high penetration.
Anti-Personnel Missile Launcher	6/6	6	Homing explosive designed for area damage. Medium penetration.
Stun Ray	1/1	1	Nonlethal electric weapon. Can inflict stun and paralysis statuses.
Wrist Blade	1/2	0	Wrist-mounted blades that can be deployed at high speed.

Flamethrower	1/2	2	Deals fire damage and applies burn status in a large cone.
The Equalizer	1/1	0	Huh? What the heck is this? Some kind of weird metal that doesn't even exist here? Um . . . well . . . best I can tell it's some sort of antimagic field generator? Eh . . . well, it's yours, not mine, so you don't need me to tell you, right?

Dungeon Skills		
Name	Level	Description
Analyze	N/A	Check the status of a target. More detail for targets within the dungeon. Details depend on level difference.
Contract	N/A	Bind a consenting target to the dungeon, per terms agreed upon by both parties.
Transfer	N/A	Move a subordinate, or a consenting target within your dungeon.

Dungeon Perks	
Name	Description
Human-Dungeon Hybrid	Enables Implants tab. Enables unique Dungeon Combat skill. Enables direct manipulation of dungeon mana as part of Personal MP. +100 HP Rooms tab locked. Exterior locked. Dungeon Master status overwritten by Personal Status.

Dungeon Feats		
Name	**Description**	**Effect**
Dungeon Victor	**To the victor go the spoils. Unlocked by destroying or subordinating another dungeon.**	**+1 Perk Point Unlocks Dungeon Warfare category perks.**
Dungeon Overlord	**A master of masters. Unlocked by subordinating another dungeon master.**	**+2 Perk Points Unlocks Subordinate Core category perks.**
Raid Boss	**Fine, I'll do it myself. Unlocked by destroying or subordinating another dungeon with no assistance.**	**+2 Perk Points +1 level in HP Regen skill +1 level in MP Regen skill +50 HP Unlocks Raid Boss category perks.**

There were some notable differences compared to what the prisoner had described, but the reasons for that were clear. Apparently, her organic and cybernetic components had different systems, with the cybernetic being responsible for the dungeon-related effects. Since, of course, those components were inseparably bound with her organic side, they could not be converted into a traditional dungeon, and so the system had defined a completely different section from the prisoner's UI to list and manage her implants. As a result, however, it seemed she was locked out of several options that the prisoner had possessed, though she wasn't particularly concerned about that at present.

She then checked on the Personal Status screen.

NSLICE-00P's Personal Status

Personal Status			
General Information		Physical Attributes	
Name	NSLICE-00P	STR	100* (Overwritten)

Species	Human/ Dungeon Core/ Automata Hybrid	DEX	1000* (Overwritten)
Level	5	SPD	50* (Overwritten)
XP	15/100	DEF	100* (Overwritten)
Perk Points	14	RES	50* (Overwritten)
HP	103/170	Magical Attributes	
MP	100/100	Mana Density	100
		Mana Control	100

Active Skills		
Name	Level	Description
Mana Beam	1	Focus mana into a channeled energy attack.
Sneak	1	Move quietly to avoid notice. Makes it harder for others to notice the user. Effectiveness highly dependent on environment.

Passive Skills		
Name	Level	Description
Dungeon Combat	N/A	Dungeon traps and skills count as personal weapons and skills.
HP Regen	2	Automatically recover HP pool. Increased regeneration speed for damaged body parts.
MP Regen	2	Automatically recover MP pool.
Presence Detection	1	Detect living entities around the user. Range and scope of detection increases with level.

Trap Detection	1	Detect traps. Range and scope of detection increases with level.

Feats		
Name	Description	Effect
Against the Odds	Do not ask how many there are, but where they are. Unlocked by winning a fight when outnumbered by equal or higher-leveled opponents.	+3 Perk Points
Dungeon Conqueror (Rat Cave)	Unlocked by conquering the Rat Cave Dungeon.	+1 Perk Point +1 level in Sneak skill
Solo Conquest	I am the dungeon master now. Unlocked by conquering a dungeon alone.	+1 level in HP Regen skill +1 level in MP Regen skill +1 level in Presence Detection skill +1 level in Trap Detection skill

Her connection with the foreign system went beyond the basic UI, however. She could gain a bit of background information as well, giving her a means of evaluating the numbers presented. In particular, for physical attributes, a value of ten was considered the baseline for an adult human without any assistance from mana or the system. Her bionic prosthetics represented a significant improvement, which the foreign system acknowledged.

The slight barrier she had detected in all living things which both defended and healed them was represented by HP, while the free nonstandard energy she could detect was presented by MP. For herself, her HP and MP pools, along with her magical attributes, were heavily boosted by her integration with—what the foreign program considered—a dungeon core, though as she had already learned, that was only in comparison to a human of her level.

Perk points for both her Dungeon Management and Personal Status were gained primarily through level ups, one per level, though more could be gained by performing notable feats. This was the primary means of growth, as these perks could be used to boost one's attributes, gain or upgrade skills, or open up new capabilities entirely. On the dungeon side, she could use it to upgrade her implants or install new ones entirely. Additionally, there was a full range of so-called dungeon capabilities open to her that she could invest in, if she so chose. This was the means by which she could upgrade her own capabilities without assistance from maintenance personnel.

NSLICE-00P took up a standing position, activating standby sentry mode. All extraneous functions ceased, her arms and legs locked up, and unnecessary biological functions were minimized.

She then devoted all power and processing capability to two areas.

The first were her area sensors, to keep an eye out for any approaching signatures.

As for the second?

She devoted the rest of her resources to compiling and analyzing all the data she had just received from the foreign system and determining a course of action.

Because for the first time in her life, she had to make her own decisions. Critical decisions regarding an entirely new system which seemed to govern all of reality in the place she now found herself in. With no prior data or protocols that could guide her decisions, and no external help save one potentially hostile prisoner whom she had already defeated in combat.

So she had a lot to think about.

6

First Steps

The skill HP Regen is now Level 3!

NSLICE-00P stood still for quite a while as she conducted her calculations and her arm slowly regrew. Rattingtale had gone to sleep, in fact. Finally, after a long while, NSLICE-00P's robotic eye stopped flickering. She had come to a decision.

There were simply too many variables and not enough data at the moment to determine an efficient path through the system. Even at this early stage, there were too many options on how to spend her perks. She could spend them on base attributes, improving the fundamental characteristics of her body. She could spend them on new skills, unlocking new capabilities and knowledge. She could use them to upgrade the skills she already had, maximizing her current advantages at the cost of flexibility. She could upgrade her implants, her mana pool, or unlock new dungeon capabilities. Or she could save them for a later day, as she already saw that additional perk choices could be unlocked based on her achievements.

But she did have something she could use.

The data from her fight with the ursanus was most informative. Her prosthetics had been entirely outmatched by the biological creature, and her conventional weapons had failed to make any appreciable impact against it.

However, the Equalizer had managed to make a dent, if a small one.

That, in NSLICE-00P's analysis, signified where her advantage lay. In fact, the foreign system itself couldn't fully identify the Equalizer, implying it possessed a quality that did not exist within said system. So if she could optimize and boost its capabilities, she would have a unique edge. And how could she boost the effectiveness of the Equalizer?

Her analysis indicated she required a deeper understanding of mana.

She did not fully understand the mechanics of the mana in this place. It existed everywhere, acted more ubiquitously and in far more diverse ways than she had previously encountered. All of this was interfering with the Equalizer's effectiveness.

So the more she understood the mana here, the better she could adapt the Equalizer's output to neutralize it.

In addition . . .

The mana had already begun to interface with her systems. Her conventional weaponry had been fully integrated into the Dungeon Management system, and her laser projectors had managed to generate a skill for her. Even now, both mana and electricity ran through her circuits, slightly boosting their efficiency. It stood to reason it could do the same for the Equalizer.

However, as mentioned before, the system itself was having trouble fully analyzing the Equalizer, so it was probable the system would not have built-in applications for boosting its effectiveness. Which meant if NSLICE-00P wanted it to grow any more powerful, she would need to do so herself. And so, the more she understood mana on a fundamental level, the more likely it was that she could come up with applications that would synergize with the Equalizer.

With that, she determined a focus in which to invest her perk points.

She decided to start with the Personal Status perk points, as those were more limited in application.

Available Perks → Schools of Magic	
Name	Cost
Arcane Magic	1
Fire Magic	1
Lightning Magic	1
Summoning Magic	1
Air Magic	2
Earth Magic	2
Metal Magic	3
Recovery Magic	3
Water Magic	5
(Continued . . .)	(Continued . . .)

NSLICE-00P found what she was looking for—a menu of available magic. This particular group of skills involved an information transfer on the direct manipulation of mana rather than a built-in application or physical upgrade. They might be a bit of a waste in that hypothetically the information could be learned manually, but NSLICE-00P desperately required more data, and so considered the expenditure a necessary one.

In addition, the expenditure was fairly low. Or rather, the menu seemed to take personal aptitude and prior feats into account, displaying the available skills in order of suitability. And it seemed the amount of perk points a given skill cost could be reduced if she did some of the work of learning that skill herself.

Name	Description
Arcane Magic	The school of magic governing the manipulation of unattributed mana. A solid foundation for students of the mystic arts, though somewhat less mana efficient in application than the more specialized schools.

This school seemed to contain the basic knowledge on mana she was looking for. And likewise, as she had already manipulated mana when unlocking the Mana Beam skill, the system considered her halfway to learning the skill already.

She selected the perk.

You have learned the skill Arcane Magic!
You have learned the spell Magic Missile!

The moment she did, new information flowed into her organic half. Methods for identifying and manipulating her internal mana, as well as a formalized structure to achieve a desired effect, which the system described as a magic circle.

What NSLICE-00P didn't know was that the vast majority of magic instructors recommended against selecting Arcane Magic as an initial perk. Yes, hypothetically, the skill provided all the knowledge required to manipulate mana and manually cast spells, but there was a huge difference between theory and practice. Arcane Magic is widely considered a crutch that will stunt the growth of any aspiring mage.

To learn magic, a student had to first become consciously aware of their own mana. Then, they had to learn to consciously manipulate said mana, draw it out of their body, and carefully form it into the desired pattern before activating the spell. For a brand-new mage who'd just acquired a spell via a skill, this was practically impossible to do manually. They would have to focus hard to locate the mana, focus hard to move it, and focus hard to draw the magic circle, all at the same time, which was why most instructors broke this process down and had their students drill and study each step until it was fully ingrained, utilizing aids such as physical movements and chants to help their students focus. They then had the student study the Magic Missile magic circle in depth, until the student could draw it perfectly with their eyes closed, before they ever attempted to cast it.

As a result, most mage students would acquire the Arcane Magic skill automatically, having long since studied every aspect of its first level. On the flip side, anyone who bought that particular skill without studying the fundamentals would skip all of those steps—relying on the system to craft their spells. The problem was that the system itself took into account the personal skill of the user. As a result, someone who relied on the system to do most of the work without truly understanding its workings would find their skill growing at a slower pace than those that had put in the work beforehand. Their growth would be stymied, and they would run into walls they lacked the knowledge and experience to overcome.

A magic circle formed in the air in front of NSLICE-00P. It flashed once as it completed, launching a small ball of mana at a nearby tree.

NSLICE-00P was not content to rely on the foreign system however, so she attempted to replicate it on her own. Her cybernetic components had perfectly recorded the process, and she was able to recreate the magic circle with ease.

The spell Magic Missile is now Level 2!
The spell Magic Missile is now Level 3!
The skill Arcane Magic is now Level 2!
The skill Arcane Magic is now Level 3!
You have learned the spell Mana Barrier!

It turned out the standard considerations did not apply to a cyborg bonded to both an AI and a dungeon core.

NSLICE-00P's sensors had detected her internal mana from her first day in this place. She already had electrical circuits to move energy about inside her, and energy channels to project that power into laser beams. And her bonded AI could easily complete multiple tasks simultaneously and with perfect precision. Likewise, as she had a dungeon core built into her, she had a natural ability to generate and manipulate mana, as it was constantly flowing through every part of her.

So . . . NSLICE-00P simply needed the basic instructions to manually cast any particular spell. And her sensors were, of course, recording as much data as they could about how the mana flowed through the spell. Once she had seen the spell cast with the assistance of the foreign system, she would be able to replicate the feat entirely on her own. Unlike most would-be mages trying to take a shortcut, she could reverse engineer the fundamental process from the example of the system.

Just then, Rattingtale yawned and stirred awake. NSLICE-00P glanced at him, her robotic eye flickering.

She walked over.

"Hm, what is it, boss-queen?"

A blade extended from her wrist.

Rattingtale jumped.

"Wait-wait! Don't be hasty-reckless! P-Please don't kill-slay me!"

She swung the blade.

And cut through the wires wrapped around the rat.

"Analysis: This unit has been strictly following past protocols, including protocols on apprehending Non-Standards. However, this unit has determined past protocols to be obsolete under current conditions, and therefore, all decisions should be evaluated based solely on achieving the current mission. As this unit has no processing facility to deliver Non-Standards to, related protocols have been deemed obsolete. This unit has calculated that maintaining custody of prisoner His Royal Majesty, Excellion Formantus Rattingtale the Third, the Great-High King over all the land does not improve probability of mission success."

Rattingtale froze. He lifted his hands, staring at them, then looked back up at the cyborg, his eyes widening.

"You're . . . releasing-freeing me?"

"Affirmative."

"You're . . . not kill-slaying me?"

"Negative. Explanation: This unit has calculated no benefit to doing so."

"What about the experience?"

"Acknowledgement: This unit did not consider that variable. Rerunning cost-benefit analysis of terminating prisoner."

Rattingtale quickly waved his palms about.

"No-no! That was wrong-bad! Forget that, yes-yes! It's much better to spare-save me, yes-yes!"

"Acknowledged."

Rattingtale watched the cyborg warily, but she ignored him, instead forming another magic circle in the air. He slowly began to back away, creeping toward the nearest bush. Still, she did not respond.

He reached the bush.

He exhaled a huge sigh. It seemed she really was letting him go.

He smiled.

What an idiot!

What kind of dungeon master just let a subordinate leave? If she had no further use for him, she should have just disposed of him to cut the mana upkeep! But now . . . now he was free. He could come up with a new plan, start to take back what was rightfully his as the Great-High King of all the—

Just then, he heard a wolf howl. He ducked to the ground, his ears flat against his head.

Right.

He, um, hadn't invested any perks into his Personal Status as dungeon master. After all, he was the Great-High King! He could not be expected to patrol the borders as a mere guard, nor muck it up in the dirt like a common soldier.

So . . . now that he had lost said realm and said soldiers . . . he was . . . a low-level rat . . .

Rattingtale stepped back out of the bush and crawled over to NSLICE-00P.

"So, you see, boss-queen lady, y-you're already my boss-queen, yes-yes? So, um, i-it's only natural I stay to serve-aid you, yes-yes?"

NSLICE-00P turned to the rat.

"Analyzing . . . complete. Former prisoner His Royal Majesty, Excellion Formantus Rattingtale the Third, the Great-High King over all the land is currently listed as a subordinate unit by foreign system, and has voluntarily acknowledged this designation. Designating Excellion Formantus Rattingtale the Third as a friendly unit reporting to unit NSLICE-00P."

"Um, yes-yes? H-Happy to serve-assist, yes-yes. A-As long as it's not dangerous-risky!"

Perhaps . . . he could stay around this weird man-thing just a little longer . . .

NSLICE-00P's Personal Status

Personal Status			
General Information		Physical Attributes	
Name	NSLICE-00P	STR	100* (Overwritten)
Species	Human/Dungeon Core/ Automata Hybrid	DEX	1000* (Overwritten)
Level	5	SPD	50* (Overwritten)
XP	15/100	DEF	100* (Overwritten)
Perk Points	11	RES	50* (Overwritten)
HP	125/170	Magical Attributes	

MP	100/100	Mana Density	100
		Mana Control	100

Active Skills		
Name	Level	Description
Mana Beam	1	Focus mana into a channeled energy attack
Sneak	1	Move quietly to avoid notice. Makes it harder for others to notice the user. Effectiveness highly dependent on environment.

Passive Skills		
Name	Level	Description
Dungeon Combat	N/A	Dungeon traps and skills count as personal weapons and skills.
HP Regen	3	Automatically recover HP pool. Increased regeneration speed for damaged body parts.
MP Regen	2	Automatically recover MP pool.
Presence Detection	1	Detect living entities around the user. Range and scope of detection increases with level.
Trap Detection	1	Detect traps. Range and scope of detection increases with level.
Arcane Magic	3	The school of magic governing the manipulation of unattributed mana. A solid foundation for students of the mystic arts, though somewhat less mana efficient than the more specialized schools.

Spells		
Name	Level	Description
Magic Missile	3	Form and launch mana into a small projectile. One of the most basic offensive applications of magic.
Mana Barrier	1	Form mana into a barrier to block attacks. One of the most basic defensive applications of magic.

Feats		
Name	Description	Effect
Against the Odds	Do not ask how many there are, but where they are. Unlocked by winning a fight when outnumbered by equal or higher-leveled opponents.	+1 Perk Point
Dungeon Conqueror (Rat Cave)	Unlocked by conquering the Rat Cave Dungeon.	+1 Perk Point +1 level in Sneak skill
Solo Conquest	I am the dungeon master now. Unlocked by conquering a dungeon alone.	+1 level in HP Regen skill +1 level in MP Regen skill +1 level in Presence Detection skill +1 level in Trap Detection skill

7

Target Acquired

A magic circle formed and launched a projectile of pure mana.

The spell Magic Missile is now Level 4!

Another circle formed, and this time a thin sphere of mana appeared in the air around NSLICE-00P.

The spell Mana Barrier is now Level 2!
The skill Arcane Magic is now Level 4!
The skill MP Regen is now Level 3!

NSLICE-00P continued to practice magic spells as she waited for the mana to repair her arm. With the new Mana Barrier spell, she could start to compare the magic circles. Still, the two spells were very different, so there wasn't much overlap in either their circles or functions. She would need to learn more before she could start deciphering the magic circle structure.

Likewise, she decided to explore this Arcane Magic and the spells it had granted her before she spent any more perk points. She had already discovered utilizing these "skills" and "spells" manually could unlock new perks or reduce the cost of currently available ones, so it seemed efficient to collect more data on her new capabilities before adding more.

Rattingtale stood between her feet, glancing every which way.

"Um, boss-queen, what are we doing?"

"Answer: This unit is analyzing nonstandard energy designated as mana while repairs are in progress."

"Yes-yes, but, um, after that?"

"Answer: This unit has determined she requires a significant boost in capabilities before any more encounters with potential hostiles. Calculations are in progress as to which updates are most efficient."

"Yes, but, um, it's a bit dangerous-risky out here, yes-yes?"

"Acknowledgement: Affirmative. However, this unit does not know of any friendly locations at present and has calculated the safest course of action to be remaining stationary."

Rattingtale thought for a moment before he started to grin.

"Why don't we find-locate another dungeon?"

NSLICE-00P's robotic eye flickered.

"Requesting Elaboration: How would a dungeon reduce current risk levels? Are other dungeon masters potential friendlies?"

Rattingtale shook his head.

"No-no, dungeon masters are rivals-enemies with each other. But dungeons are safer than the open. If we find-locate a younger dungeon, they won't have as powerful monster-servants, yes-yes? So it's safer than staying here, where we can be found-located by a wandering monster, yes-yes?"

"Analyzing . . ."

"And-and, if you hunt-kill the dungeon monsters, you can earn more bestowals of power, yes-yes?"

". . . Analysis complete. Friendly His Royal Majesty, Excellion Formantus Rattingtale the Third's suggestion seems logical. This unit shall begin scanning for mana signatures to investigate."

Rattingtale rubbed his paws together.

Oh yeah, it was all coming together.

All he had to do was find a dungeon as weak—err . . . *slightly unprepared* as his own had been, and the man-thing could cut right through it. Then, if he convinced her to keep it as a subordinate core, they would have a new dungeon to play with.

And since the man-thing still seemed quite confused about the whole dungeon business, it should be possible to convince her to let him assist in, ah, *managing* the place.

And once he did?

Well . . . it wouldn't be *his* fault if she didn't check the Subordinate Core Trap menu before taking a walk, now would it?

And so NSLICE-00P and Rattingtale began to travel about the forest, the cyborg's sensors at full power. She was searching for any stationary mana signatures similar to the Rat Cave dungeon while charting paths around any mobile signatures of notable strength.

She was still running into slimes, however, and vaporizing them on sight.

As she did, she split her processing resources into two threads. One utilized the majority of her cybernetic resources to scan for hostiles and determine a course to the nearest stationary signature. The other had access to most of her organic processing hardware, as said hardware was not necessary for the task. In the meantime, she had that thread continue to practice Arcane Magic. It was noticeably harder, the magic circle dispelling any time her concentration wavered, but eventually, she succeeded in casting the spell.

The spell Magic Missile is now Level 5!
Mana Control has increased by 10 and is now 110!

And then the next . . .

The spell Mana Barrier is now Level 3!
The skill Arcane Magic is now Level 5!

And just as NSLICE-00P's arm was about ninety percent repaired, they located their target—another cave, this one sinking into the ground with a rocky path leading down and a mana signature roughly similar in magnitude to the Rat Cave.

NSLICE-00P and Rattingtale made their way inside the underground tunnel, lit only by dimly glowing mushrooms spaced throughout. The walls and roof were made out of dirt soft enough to scrape away by hand.

NSLICE-00P activated her combat mode, engaging her helmet and transforming her good hand into a gun once more. Rattingtale climbed into an empty compartment on her shoulder with an unlocked hatch so he could see what was going on.

They did not have to wait long.

"Warning: Incoming hostile detected."

NSLICE-00P suddenly jumped backward as the ground underneath her exploded. Some sort of mole shot out of the ground, jaws snapping at the cyborg's former position.

She opened fire at the creature.

The mole squealed and then vanished.

You have slain Wolf Mole (Level 3)!
Gained 7 Personal XP, 7 Dungeon XP!

NSLICE-00P was about to move on when Rattingtale opened up the hatch.

"Wait-wait! You're not going to collect-gather the magic core?!"

"Query: What is the purpose of doing so?"

Rattingtale froze. And then slammed his face with a paw.

He'd made a mistake. If he hadn't said anything, he could have just collected the cores himself. But since he had exclaimed in shock, now he had to explain it to her.

"You see . . . um . . ." He heaved a sigh, shook his head, and decided it was best to tell her the truth now. He had bigger plans than a few cores, after all, so it would not do to raise her suspicion.

"Mana cores are valuable-useful, yes-yes? Monsters and dungeons can absorb-consume them for extra experience. The royal records said the man-things like them too, yes-yes?"

NSLICE-00P checked that against the information from the system; it seemed to check out.

"Acknowledged."

She walked over to where the creature had fallen, and sure enough, there was a small glowing stone on the ground. She picked it up.

She could feel mana emanating off the stone . . . and could feel the mana from her Geo-Oscillator Engine reaching out to it. She decided to allow the connection.

The stone melted into light and sank into her palm.

Mana core absorbed!
Gained 2 Dungeon XP!

"Gratitude: This unit thanks friendly Excellion Formantus Rattingtale the Third for his assistance. This unit was not aware of the opportunity to gather additional resources."

Rattingtale just frowned as he watched her absorb the core.

"Yes-yes . . . um . . . anything for the boss-queen . . ."

The skill Presence Detection is now Level 2!
The skill Trap Detection is now Level 2!
The skill HP Regen is now Level 4!

And so NSLICE-00P blasted her way through the dungeon, her ground-penetrating scans revealing any ambushes before they happened and easily identifying any traps. Her damaged arm was now fully repaired, the weapons within it rebuilt and resupplied. And as she had suspected during the fight with the ursanus, mana was restocking her ammunition. A quick investigation of the foreign system revealed that this was due to her internal weapons being classified as dungeon traps, which would be replenished over time by the dungeon's mana.

This meant, fortunately, NSLICE-00P could make full use of her arsenal even without access to logistics infrastructure. She only needed to consider tactical effectiveness when choosing her weapons from now on.

NSLICE-00P now found herself in a large cavern. This time, the hostile signatures were approaching directly, quickly coming into view.

Before her stood a large squad of featureless humanoids, seemingly constructed out of dirt.

Species	Description
Dirt Golem (Level 5)	A basic golem. Packed earth animated by a mana core. Slow and weak, but durable and cheap.

She opened fire on the golems with her machine guns. The bullets pierced through them but failed to slow them down—each hole quickly filled in with dirt. NSLICE-00P put away her guns and took a step back, keeping her distance from them.

"What-what are you doing? Hurry up and kill-slay them!"

Her robotic eye flickered.

"Analysis complete. Explanation: This unit has calculated that this is a good opportunity to field test new capabilities."

Instead of her weapons, NSLICE-00P drew upon her mana, drawing a magic circle in the air. A Magic Missile launched and struck the lead dirt golem head-on, who immediately crumbled, the dense mana projectile shattering its HP barrier and disrupting the mana holding it together.

You have slain Dirt Golem (Level 5)!
Gained 10 Personal XP, 10 Dungeon XP!

NSLICE-00P, having determined an effective attack, immediately turned her attention to magic circle creation. In fact . . .

She utilized her AI to copy and paste several magic circle templates, splitting the mana accordingly such that her organic side need only complete one magic circle to activate them all.

A round of Magic Missiles assaulted the golems, destroying them.

And a round of notifications assaulted NSLICE-00P's eyes.

You have slain Dirt Golem x4!
Gained 40 Personal XP, 40 Dungeon XP total!
Level up! Your Personal Level is now 6!

Level up! Your Dungeon Level is now 6!
The spell Magic Missile is now Level 12! Upgrade available!
The skill Arcane Magic is now Level 8! Spell choice available!
You have learned the elite skill Multicasting!
The elite skill Multicasting is now Level 4!
You have accomplished the Personal Feat: Arcane Prodigy!

Active Skills		
Name	Level	Description
Multicasting	4	Elite skill. Can cast several spells at once. Number of simultaneous spells increases with level.

Personal Feats		
Name	Description	Effect
Arcane Prodigy	The career of a supreme sorcerer does not start on the beaten path. Unlocked by learning an elite magic skill under level twenty without spending Perk Points.	+3 Perk Points Unlocks more advanced magic perks.

NSLICE-00P scanned the area, but there were no further hostiles on approach at the moment. And as she saw some new notifications, she decided to investigate.

Available Upgrades for Magic Missile:	
Dense Magic Missile	Increases mana density of Magic Missile projectiles, boosting damage.
Exploding Magic Missile	Magic Missiles deal small area damage.
Instant Magic Missile	Bypass use of magic circle when casting Magic Missile.

Multi Magic Missile	Creates multiple Magic Missile projectiles with each cast.
Piercing Magic Missile	Increases Magic Missile penetration against RES and magic barriers.

Available Spell Choices for Arcane Magic:	
Detect Magic	Locate spells.
Mana Blast	A cone-shaped blast of mana. Deals damage and knockback to the area.
Mana Infusion	Infuse mana into a target. The most basic enchantment.
Mana Transfer	Transfer mana to a target.
Spell Shield	Boost target's RES.
Telekinesis	Utilize mana to grasp and move objects. The most basic conversion of mana to kinetic force.
(Continued . . .)	(Continued . . .)

It seemed she could upgrade the Magic Missile spell now that it had passed level ten, and that she also had a choice of the next spell granted to her by Arcane Magic. She dedicated some of her free processing power to analyzing the options, and then carried on with her dungeon exploration.

Meanwhile, Rattingtale's ears were pressed against his head.

The man-thing . . . took out dirt golems in one shot?

With what looked like several spells casted simultaneously?

Rattingtale was no wizard, but he was pretty sure that wasn't supposed to be possible at their level.

Of course, a normal mage of their level wasn't supposed to have the mana quantity and density of a dungeon with the precision control of an AI either.

. . . Perhaps he might hold off on the trap plan for a bit longer.

8

Terminate the Earth Dungeon!

The dungeon did not continue much longer after the fight with the dirt golems. There were a handful of pitfall traps, but no further battles. As a result, NSLICE-00P had a chance to evaluate the Magic Missile upgrade options and make her choice.

Magic Missile has been upgraded into Dense Magic Missile!

Of all the options, a straightforward boost in effectiveness seemed the most efficient. Exploding seemed unnecessary when she already had anti-personnel missiles available, and the Mana Blast spell indicated there might be other, more suitable options for area-damage spells. Multi was useful, but she could already increase the number of projectiles via Multicasting, so it wasn't a new capability for her. Instant had potential, but now that she knew it was possible to cast spells without the magic circle, she could research said possibility on her own. The fact that she had conducted the Mana Beam without assistance implied such a thing was within her capabilities. Finally, Piercing seemed useful, but she already had the Equalizer to try and strip defensive spells, which was the point of pursuing Arcane Magic to begin with. As such, she had chosen the simple but effective option of stuffing more mana into each projectile.

What was more valuable to her were the adjustments the upgrade made to the magic circle. She now had two versions of the same spell to compare, and could thus determine which parts of the formation were likely related to mana density, or perhaps containment? In any case, it added to her growing knowledge base, and so was a step toward her ultimate goal.

But now was not the time for such long-term calculations, for NSLICE-00P and Rattingtale had reached the final room of the dungeon. A large chamber with a glowing crystal on a stone pedestal . . . and a huge stone statue standing in front of it. A stone statue with glowing eyes.

"So you're the intruder who tore through my dungeon. Surprising."

"Query: Would the hostile dungeon master like to surrender? Or should this unit engage termination protocols?"

Rattingtale stuck out his head to squeak into the cyborg's ear.

"Hey! I thought I told-warned you other dungeon masters would be hostile! What do you mean surrender?!"

"Explanation: This unit calculated surrender as a more efficient option, given the risk factor of combat and the added benefit of additional friendlies."

Fortunately for Rattingtale, the dungeon master had other plans.

"Surrender?" The statue let out a low rumble. "No. I think I will crush you instead!"

With that, it rushed forward, slamming a stone fist into the ground.

NSLICE-00P dodged to the side, aiming a fist at the statue. An anti-tank missile launched straight into the dungeon master and exploded. They heard him laugh from behind the cloud of smoke. The dungeon master emerged, his stone armor barely scratched.

"I invested most of my perks into my personal defense. You will need much more than that to take me down!"

He slammed his fist into the ground once more. Several stones blasted up from the ground, launching toward NSLICE-00P, who used her repulsors to boost out of the way of the attack while firing a laser beam at the dungeon master, but that also failed to make an impact.

"Equalizer engaged."

She tried the rainbow beam once more, but the dungeon master's HP barrier was solid as a rock. The Equalizer tore at it, but it barely made a dent. She still tried to fire a beam through it, managing to pierce a small hole.

However, a small hole was nothing to the stone behemoth. He had no flesh or bone under his rocky skin in the first place.

It seemed the only way to destroy him was to take him down the regular way.

The dungeon master lunged forward, ducking his shoulder in. NSLICE-00P jumped back and activated her repulsors, flying high into the air.

"Get down here!"

NSLICE-00P, of course, would not comply with a hostile's request. Instead, she created a dozen magic circles in the air, firing a barrage of Magic Missiles.

The spell Dense Magic Missile is now Level 13!
The skill Multicasting is now Level 5!

Her robotic eye flickered as the dungeon master cried out, shielding his face with his arms.

It seemed the Magic Missiles were doing the trick, dealing heavy damage to the HP barrier.

And fortunately for the cyborg, it seemed the dungeon master had neglected long-range attacks, believing in his defense alone. He tried the rock-launching punch several more times, but it was simple for NSLICE-00P to move out of the way, keeping up the barrage of Magic Missiles as she did.

The spell Dense Magic Missile is now Level 14!
The skill Arcane Magic is now Level 9!
The skill Multicasting is now Level 6!

Still, the dungeon master had quite the large HP pool, and Magic Missile wasn't exactly the most powerful spell in existence. It took a long time to work down the stone behemoth's defenses.

The skill MP Regen is now Level 4!

Fortunately, NSLICE-00P had full access to her rapidly regenerating dungeon mana pool, as well as the MP Regen skill. She could keep up her current barrage indefinitely.

The match was decided the moment NSLICE-00P determined an effective attack.

Still, she was only damaging the HP pool barrier. The dungeon master himself was some sort of stone golem, practically solid rock, which she would have to find a way to terminate once the protective HP had been drained. Her arsenal was not exactly optimized for mining.

But she had an idea on that.

She had been analyzing the flows of mana from her opponent as she assaulted his HP and had determined his mana was coming from a central location. She predicted this might represent the equivalent of a vital organ.

So once the HP barrier was on its last legs, NSLICE-00P dropped her assault and landed in front of the dungeon master. She fired a final blast of the Equalizer, tearing a hole through the now paper-thin HP remaining before she pulled both her hands together, charging her laser attack with as much power as she could put into it. And as she did, she used her experiences from practicing Arcane Magic to push her mana into the attack as well, activating the relevant skill to support.

A huge beam fired from her hands, piercing straight through the dungeon master's body and destroying the golem core animating it.

You have slain Golem Dungeon Master (Level 12)!
Gained 28 Personal XP, 28 Dungeon XP!
The skill Mana Beam is now Level 4!

"No!"

In fact, the beam continued *straight through* the dungeon master . . . and right into the dungeon core behind him. Rattingtale cried out as the core shattered.

NSLICE-00P felt the mana and information from the core flow into her own as a flash of light covered her vision.

You have absorbed a dungeon core (Earth Tunnels)!
Gained 6 Personal Perk Points, 6 Dungeon Perk Points!
Gained Dungeon Affinity: Earth (Minimum)!

You have accomplished the Personal Feat: Dungeon Conqueror (Earth Tunnels)
(Conquered the Earth Tunnels Dungeon!
You have learned the skill Earth Magic!
You have learned the spell Rock Throw!

Personal Feats		
Name	Description	Effect
Dungeon Conqueror (Earth Tunnels)	Unlocked by conquering the Earth Tunnels Dungeon.	+1 Perk Point +1 level in Earth Magic skill

Skills		
Name	Level	Description
Earth Magic	1	The school of magic governing the manipulation of Earth-attribute mana. One of the basic elemental magics, strong at defensive spells and spells that deal physical damage.

Spells		
Name	Level	Description
Rock Throw	1	Use mana to form and then launch a small rock. Mana cost increases dramatically if cast without a nearby source of Earth. Deals physical damage. One of the most basic offensive applications of Earth Magic.

"What have you done, you strange man-thing?! You destroyed-demolished the dungeon core!"

"Correction: Apparently, destroying the dungeon core has the same outcome as absorbing it."

"I know-understand that already! But we were supposed to stay-rest there! Now, where are we supposed to stay-hide?!"

". . . Analysis: It seems search-and-destroy protocols resulted in an overzealous termination of hostiles and the core was destroyed via collateral damage. However, the other objective of improving this unit's capabilities and available resources has been achieved. This unit shall consider this mission a partial success and will adjust search-and-destroy protocols for the next target."

Rattingtale groaned and rubbed his face with his paw. It seemed he would be stuck with the man-thing for a while longer.

Later that night, as NSLICE-00P looked for another dungeon, she evaluated the options available to her.

You have learned the spell Mana Blast!

Spells		
Name	Level	Description
Mana Blast	1	A cone-shaped blast of mana. Deals damage and knockback to the area.

First things first, she selected one of her free spells from Arcane Magic. There were a number of options, but she decided on Mana Blast. As a second offensive spell, she predicted it would provide the most useful comparison with the magic circles for Magic Missile, improving her understanding of how such circles were constructed. And in this latest dungeon, she'd learned the value of having mana-powered offensive tools.

Which led her to her next decision. The foes in this dungeon had proven remarkably resilient to her conventional arsenal, but terribly vulnerable to her new magic spells. It was logical to assume, therefore, that there may be foes who could resist magical attacks but might prove vulnerable to something more mundane.

She had therefore decided to invest some of her Dungeon perk points into her weapon loadout, as well as her own defenses.

She started by opening up the Trap menu.

Traps → Upgrade Traps → Assault Rifle Upgrades			
Name	**Cost**	**Mana Upkeep**	**Description**
Assault Rifle +1	**1**	**0**	**Improves basic performance across the board. Higher levels unlock additional upgrade options.**

It seemed she had several options. She could unlock brand-new weapons or unlock new variations of ones she already had, as well as adjust which weapons were deployed. She could also add new ones if she chose to upgrade the Internal Weapon Bays implant.

But for the cyborg, the choice was fairly limited. She didn't have enough data to evaluate new weapon choices at present, and she didn't require greater quantities of the ones she already possessed, so she went ahead and upgraded her primary weapon.

Assault Rifle +1 now available.

She replaced both of her assault rifles with the new option. She was able to pull weapon statistics from the system, and was pleased to find across-the-board improvements as mana spread throughout the weapon. She then moved to her next order of business.

Implants → Upgrade Implants → Armor Plating Upgrades			
Name	**Cost**	**Mana Upkeep**	**Description**
Armor Plating +1	**1**	**0**	**Increase DEF by 10 and RES by 5. Higher tiers unlock additional upgrades.**

She had a lot of options here as she could upgrade nearly all of her implants, but for now, she went with a basic boost to her armor plating. She felt mana move from her core and travel throughout her exterior, increasing the density of her armor.

Her calculations indicated these upgrades would not be sufficient to defeat the ursanus she had faced, but it was a step in the right direction, and she still didn't have enough data for a larger-scale expenditure. In addition, Arcane Magic had already dramatically expanded her capabilities, and now she had a new skill, Earth Magic, to explore, so she was not ready to invest more in her conventional weaponry. Above all, she needed more intel.

So, NSLICE-00P started to explore the new magic available to her as she searched for another dungeon.

9

Terminate the Spider Dungeon?

The spell Rock Throw is now Level 6!
The skill Earth Magic is now Level 3!
You have learned the spell Earth Wall!

NSLICE-00P continued to practice the new magic school she had unlocked. She was somewhat unimpressed with the Rock Throw spell, which could not compare at all with her conventional weaponry, but an elemental spell had provided an entirely different magic circle for her to study. Notably, the Rock Throw magic circle contained a number of similarities to Magic Missile. NSLICE-00P predicted that the similar areas were likely related to the targeting and acceleration of the projectile, while the different areas were potentially responsible for the projectile's nature. It was something to follow up on when she gained access to additional circles. Likewise, she knew from Arcane Magic she could unlock new spells as she leveled the skill, so she diligently practiced it until she did.

Earth Wall was more impressive, allowing her to reshape the battlefield at will, albeit temporarily. More importantly, it was a capability that could not be replicated by her current components, and so an addition to her available options. She was currently running simulations on how she might integrate it into her combat protocols.

Comparing Rock Throw and Earth Wall revealed a number of similar components in the magic circles, most notably in the section where Rock Throw was different from Magic Missile. The probability grew that this section was responsible for the differences between the fully mana-based projectile of Magic Missile and the material projectile of Rock Throw.

It was around this time that she arrived at the next dungeon, a large, decaying tree with a large hole she couldn't see into.

"Ugh, finally. Now, remember: terminate the master, but no destroying-demolishing this dungeon, yes-yes?"

"Affirmative. Engaging dungeon termination protocols. Adjusting search-and-destroy protocols to avoid unintentional collateral damage."

Rattingtale just heaved a sigh. Well, hopefully, he could hold back the man-thing this time.

Lilussees shook herself awake, stirring on her bed of silk threads. She lazily stretched the joints on all eight of her legs, shaking her abdomen as she awoke.

Then the Queen of the Spiders pulled on the thread leading into her room. Or something like that. Honestly, she just considered herself an average spider. An average spider who happened to command a dungeon full of loyal minions to hunt and fight on her behalf, that is.

One of her brood crawled in, carrying some poor woodland creature wrapped in web. Lilussees clattered her mandibles and dug in.

Oh, how she loved breakfast in bed.

Just then, a silk sheet appeared in the air, letters and drawings taking shape upon it. These were Lilussees's dungeon records, informing her of two new intruders.

"Hmm? A human? That's new. And . . . a rat monster? Together? That's kind of weird, huh?"

She thought for about five seconds before turning back to her breakfast.

"Oh well! They're, like, not even level ten or something, so, like, shouldn't be a problem."

With that, Lilussees dismissed the record and continued her breakfast. Maybe she would have seconds today.

NSLICE-00P and Rattingtale found themselves inside a decaying tree. All around them were walls of black and rotting wood, again illuminated by glowing mushrooms.

Oh, and there were spiderwebs all over the place. In fact, a little spider was crawling across one of them even now.

Rattingtale immediately shut the hatch.

"Spider-things! Quick, kill-slay them with fire, now-now!"

"Negative. Analysis: Use of fire weaponry in a wooden structure carries a high risk of self-termination."

"We're in a dungeon! The wood isn't actually-really wood! Do it now, yes-yes!"

NSLICE-00P stuck her arm out to the side, firing a tiny jet of flame from her flamethrower onto the nearest wall. As the rat predicted, the walls did not catch fire. In fact, she could even detect the mana slowly purifying the excessive smoke from the air as well.

In other words, there was no reason she *couldn't* kill the spiders with fire. Given the amount of spider webs that could represent a hazard even to a human-sized target, NSLICE-00P calculated that area denial via flames was a valid approach to this dungeon.

"Acknowledgement: Risk of self-termination determined as acceptably low. Engaging purification protocols."

She held up both her hands, and an inferno engulfed everything in front of her.

Lilussees finished slurping up her breakfast then spun around, adjusting her bed of silk threads to her liking. She lay down in the bed once she did.

What better way to start the day than a postbreakfast nap?

You have slain Spiderling (Level 1)!
Gained 1 Personal XP, 1 Dungeon XP!

You have slain Spiderling (Level 1)!
Gained 1 Personal XP, 1 Dungeon XP!

You have slain Spiderling (Level 1)!
Gained 1 Personal XP, 1 Dungeon XP!

Spiders ran every which way as a wave of fire rolled over the dungeon. A red light shone through the blaze as a dark silhouette formed. NSLICE-00P walked through the dungeon, swinging her arms back and forth to bathe the entire area in flames. As her flamethrowers ran out of fuel, she passed her mana through them, speeding up the automatic resupply to keep up the blaze.

And then . . .

Something in her circuits connected.

If she had gained a skill by channeling mana through her laser projectors . . .

Then what would happen if she did the same with her other weapons?

She started to feed mana directly into the flames, trying to infuse the burning fuel with the energy. She tried to mold the mana similar to how the Mana Beam skill synergized with her laser projectors.

And then . . .

You have learned the spell Fire Blast!
You have learned the skill Fire Magic!
You have learned the spell Fire Bolt!

The skill Fire Magic is now Level 3!
The spell Fire Blast is now Level 2!

Success. She formed a magic circle in front of her, adding a third jet of flame into the deluge.

Lilussees groaned and turned over in her bed. She felt as if her room was a bit too hot.

She turned over to the other side, searching for a cool part in the room.

NSLICE-00P came to a large central chamber, a cylindrical shape rising high into the sky. She detected the mana signature indicating the dungeon core at the top of the structure. There were no stairs or footholds; rather, she saw a door across from her, and other doors connecting balconies all across the chamber. It seemed as if she was supposed to go through the rooms in order to climb to the top.

NSLICE-00P did not do this.

Rather, she activated her repulsors, flying into the air and straight up the central chamber.

Spiderwebs crisscrossed the chamber, blocking her path. Spiders crawled along the webs and the walls.

NSLICE-00P formed several Fire Blast magic circles above her head.

Jets of flame blew ahead of her, setting the webs and the spiders on fire.

You have slain Giant Spider (Level 3)!
Gained 4 Personal XP, 4 Dungeon XP!
The spell Fire Blast is now Level 3!

Lilussees twisted this way and that, but she couldn't fall asleep. Her room was just too hot for some reason. She scratched her back and shook herself awake, clattering her mandibles together.

Well, if she couldn't sleep, she might as well check on those intruders. A nice snack might help . . .

She froze. The intruders were . . . right outside her room? Standing on what should be empty air?

Just then, a blast of flame tore through the webs guarding the entrance to her chambers. The human intruder stepped inside, encased in armor and surrounded by glowing magic circles.

Lilussees stared at her for a second.

"Um, like, don't kill me, please?"

* * *

NSLICE-00P burst into the room. Every inch of it was covered in silk threads, forming hammocks and cushions. Even the pedestal with the dungeon core had a hammock hanging off of it.

And lying on the ground in front of her was a spider roughly the size of a large rat.

A spider that started speaking to her.

Rival Dungeon Master Lilussees has offered to surrender. Accept?

NSLICE-00P saw no reason to refuse. She let her magic circles fade.

"Affirmative."

"Huh? What are you doing, boss-lady? Kill-slay the spider-thing, yes-yes!"

Surrender accepted! Lilussees has become your subordinate!
Subordinate dungeon core acquired!

You have conquered the Personal Spider Tree dungeon!
You have accomplished the Feat: Dungeon Conqueror (Spider Tree)(Conquered the Spider Tree Dungeon)!

Personal Feats		
Name	Description	Effect
Dungeon Conqueror (Spider Tree)	Unlocked by conquering the Spider Tree Dungeon.	+1 Perk Points +1 level in Poison Resistance skill

Would you like to absorb the Spider Tree dungeon core, or manage it as a subcore?

Lilussees tilted her head, raising one of her front legs to her mandibles.

"Huh? Wait, you're, like, a dungeon master or something? That's, like, totally weird. The records said you were, like, a human or something."

Rattingtale popped his head out of the hatch as he noticed a suspicious lack of flames.

"Huh? Wait, boss-lady! Why aren't you slay-killing the spider-thing! D-Don't tell me you . . ."

"Explanation: Friendly Lilussees offered to surrender and is now designated as a subordinate unit."

Rattingtale grabbed the fur on his head and pulled.

"No! You foolish man-thing! You were supposed to kill-slay her!"

"Observation: If this unit is not supposed to terminate this dungeon, then accepting a surrender is more efficient, correct?"

Lilussees turned her eyes to the rat sticking out of NSLICE-00P's shoulder.

"Oh hey, it's like, a snack or something. Hey, boss, are you like, going to eat that, or can I?"

Rattingtale squeaked.

"See-see! That spider-thing is evil-monstrous, yes-yes! Kill-slay it with fire, yes-yes!"

"Negative and negative. Friendlies Excellion Formantus Rattingtale the Third and Lilussees are both subordinates, and no longer subject to termination."

Lilussees chittered her mandibles together.

"Y-Your name is Excellion Formantus Rattingtale the Third? Haha, that's like—"

"S-Shut up! 'Tis a noble and venerable name, suitable only for the Great-High King over all the land like me, yes-yes!"

"Hahaha sure, sure. Should I, like, call you Your Majesty or something? S-Sure looks like it, haha."

Rattingtale placed his paws on his mouth and screamed into them.

Great.

Just great.

Now he had an annoying rival to deal with.

One who could hypothetically eat him.

This plan had just gotten a lot more complicated.

10

Like, How Do Dungeons Work, Anyway?

Rattingtale scratched his whiskers. He kept glancing at the spider-thing, but it was making no move toward him. He shook his head and turned his attention back to the cyborg.

"Okay, so, let me help-assist you manage the dungeon, yes-yes! I can keep an eye on things while you grow-train, yes-yes?"

Lilussees tilted her head at that.

"Ehh, you're like, keeping this dungeon? It's like, a new dungeon in a place without any people or something. So, like, why would you bother?"

Rattingtale whirled and glared at her.

"S-Shut up, you stupid spider-thing! It doesn't concern you!"

But NSLICE-00P heard a query with a non-classified answer, and so responded.

"Helpful Explanation: These units were seeking a safe location to take shelter from wandering hostiles. There are hostile forces in the area this unit cannot contend with. Friendly Excellion Formantus Rattingtale the Third proposed a dungeon would provide reasonable shelter."

Rattingtale slapped a paw on his face as the weird man-thing spilled the beans. Lilussees tilted her head.

"Eh . . . that's like, kind of dumb, though?"

Rattingtale clenched his teeth.

"Dumb?! How dare you?! I'm His Royal Majesty, the Great-High King over all the land, yes-yes! You will give-show me proper respect!"

"Like, why though? Aren't you, like, a subordinate of the human or something?"

Rattingtale chittered and clutched with his paws.

"You—"

Lilussees shrugged.

"Well, whatever. I don't really care. But like, monsters are attracted to dungeons when they find them, you know? The thing you're afraid of is like, a monster or something, right? So it's like, kind of bad to hide in a dungeon, you know? Especially a new dungeon that's, like, too weak to stop something stronger than you, boss."

Rattingtale jumped at that.

"D-Don't listen to her, boss-queen! Clearly, this spider-thing is trying to trick-deceive you! You should kill-slay her at once, yes-yes!"

NSLICE-00P's robotic eye began to flicker.

"Suspicious Query: That advice conflicts with prior information from friendly Excellion Formantus Rattingtale the Third. Please elaborate on friendly Lilussees's reasoning."

Lilussees nodded.

"So, like, monsters like to eat magic cores, yeah? And like, dungeon cores are kind of the biggest magic cores, or something. So, like, if a wandering monster finds a dungeon, it normally tries to break into it or something."

NSLICE-00P's robotic eye flickered and spun as she cross-referenced that claim against the information from the system and her own observations.

"Analysis: This unit has personally observed the use of mana cores and dungeon cores as a means of growth. Therefore, friendly Lilussees's claim is predicted as highly probable. Can friendly Excellion Formantus Rattingtale the Third provide clarification on competing claims?"

Rattingtale trembled slightly. That stupid spider-thing! Now all he could do was play dumb.

"I . . . um . . . that is . . . I, uh, didn't know-understand that?"

Lilussees stifled a laugh.

"For real? And you, like, wanted to manage a dungeon when you didn't know the basics?"

"S-Shut up!"

Rattingtale just shut the hatch, curling up into the compartment and muttering to himself. NSLICE-00P turned her attention to the spider instead as the apparently more knowledgeable source.

"Query: Does friendly Lilussees have a recommendation on the current course of action?"

"Me? Um, like, I'd say just absorb my dungeon and move on. Like, if there's some big monster in the area, we should, like, not stay in the area."

"Affirmative."

NSLICE-00P confirmed her decision, and the group was sent back to the forest.

You have absorbed a dungeon core (Spider Tree)!
Gained 6 Personal Perk Points, 6 Dungeon Perk Points!
Gained Dungeon Affinity: Arachnid (Minimum)!

Lilussees proceeded to crawl up NSLICE-00P, resting on her other shoulder.

"So, like, we should get going. Like, which way is your dungeon, boss?"

"Answer: Here."

Lilussees tilted her head.

"Huh? Like, what do you mean? I, like, don't know of any other dungeons nearby."

NSLICE-00P pointed toward the glowing core in her chest.

"Explanation: It appears this unit's cybernetic components have been converted into a dungeon. This unit has a dungeon built into her body."

Rattingtale jumped at that, peeking back out of the hatch and muttering to himself.

"Wait, seriously?! Her dungeon core . . . was hiding-resting right there the whole time?!"

Lilussees tilted her head, rubbing a mandible with one of her front legs.

"Wait, like, for real? How does that, like, work? Where are your rooms and stuff?"

"Answer: This unit does not have rooms. The Rooms section of the foreign system appears to be locked."

Lilussees idly moved her mandibles around as she processed that.

"Then how do you, like, absorb mana and stuff?"

"Requesting Elaboration: What does friendly Lilussees mean by absorbing mana?"

Lilussees stared at her for a second before continuing.

"Like, what do you mean by that? That's like . . . the whole point of the dungeon or something? How do you, like, grow and stuff?"

"Answer: This unit's growth is the result of terminating hostiles."

"Oh. Yeah, I guess that works too, but that's, like, so much work, you know?"

"Query: Does friendly Lilussees know an alternative method of growth?"

Lilussees sighed. This seemed to be getting complicated. But it would be a problem if her new boss just went and got herself killed, so Lilussees summoned the fullest extent of her will to expend effort.

"Um, yeah. So, like, it goes something like this. Dungeons, like, absorb mana from stuff or something? That's like, why you want a big dungeon, 'cause the more rooms you have, the faster you grow and the more mana you have or something. And, like, when something comes into your dungeon, you start absorbing mana from them or something? So, like, you don't even need to kill them."

"Follow-Up Query: Is this method possible without rooms?"

Lilussees rubbed her legs and then shrugged.

"That's why I'm, like, confused. I've never heard of a dungeon without rooms, you know? So I, like, can't even imagine what's going on. Um, like, do you have something else instead? Like, instead of rooms?"

"Affirmative."

NSLICE-00P reviewed her status, specifically the perk section of her Dungeon Management status, for a particular entry.

Dungeon Perks	
Name	**Description**
Human-Dungeon Hybrid	**Enables Implants tab.** **Enables unique Dungeon Combat skill.** **Enables direct manipulation of dungeon mana.** **+100 HP** **Rooms tab locked.** **Exterior locked.**

As the same entry that locked the Rooms tab enabled the Implants tab, it was reasonable to assume Implants was intended as a replacement for the functions provided by Rooms.

So NSLICE-00P dove into the Implants tab, searching for capabilities similar to what Lilussees had described. None of her current Implants did so, so she checked the available ones instead.

There, she found something.

Implants → Unlock New Implants			
Name	**Cost**	**Mana Upkeep**	**Description**
Add Implant Slot	3	**0**	**Adds one additional slot for implants. Grants +5 HP, +5 Dungeon MP**

Dungeon Field Generator	5	5	**Surrounding area counts as dungeon territory. Enables mana absorption within the area of effect.**
(Continued . . .)	**(Continued . . .)**	**(Continued . . .)**	**(Continued . . .)**

"Update: This unit has located an implant that seems to provide mana-absorption capabilities. Does friendly Lilussees recommend purchasing?"

Lilussees nodded.

"Um, yeah. That's, like, a super important part of growing your dungeon or something?"

"Affirmative."

You have unlocked an Additional Implant Slot! Max HP and Mana increased!
You have unlocked the Dungeon Field Generator implant!

NSLICE-00P purchased the implant and an additional slot to install it. She felt mana swirl within her body, creating a new compartment within her. Strangely, this did not seem to increase her overall size, as the compartment somehow didn't take up space within her physical body. In fact, her regular sensors couldn't even detect said compartment. She only knew it was there because it was connected to her internal reporting logs.

In fact, it was very similar to when she approached a dungeon and couldn't detect what was inside it.

However, the device was there, and it began to boot up. This component did not simply take electricity, but rather, NSLICE-00P recorded her mana flowing into the device as well, reducing the overall pool available to her.

Suddenly, the device emitted a wave of mana, expanding out in a sphere. It grew to a radius of ten meters and then stopped. NSLICE-00P noticed her perceptions expanding along with the field, the system providing significantly more intel on everything within range of the mana field.

And . . .

She logged mana streaming from the surrounding area, particularly the plants, into her core. Her status indicated a slow increase in Dungeon XP.

"Status Update: This unit is now absorbing mana from the surrounding area."

"For real? That's, like, good, or something."

"Gratitude: This unit thanks friendly Lilussees for her insight. Does she have any further insights to share?"

Lilussees tilted her head.

"Um, like you don't have a dungeon, right? Like, an actual physical location or something?"

"Negative."

"Then, like, best thing to do is keep moving and hunting weaker stuff, or something. Like, best way to stay safe is just to become stronger or something. I guess that's if you, like, have a way to avoid the big bad monster or whatever."

"Affirmative. Explanation: This unit is equipped with advanced sensors to track incoming hostiles, and repulsors to enable quick relocation."

"Then, like, let's go hunting or something?"

"Affirmative."

"Right. Then, like, I'm kind of tired from all that talking. Do you, like, have another of those hiding places the snack is using?"

"Affirmative."

A second empty compartment opened on NSLICE-00P's back. Lilussees crawled inside.

"'Kay, goodnight then. Like, try not to die until I wake up."

Lilussees rotated around a couple times inside the compartment, checking it out. It was a bit cramped and cold compared to her old home, but she could take steps to alleviate that.

More importantly, it was safer than her own dungeon had been.

Apparently *much* safer.

And best of all . . .

She didn't need to work to protect it! At least not once she got her new boss up to speed!

And so, Lilussees decided to prepare for her new job as someone else's subordinate by taking a nap.

11

Termination Training Montage

NSLICE-00P traveled around the area, avoiding any large signatures and targeting the smaller dungeons. On Lilussees's suggestion, she began upgrading her implants, as she discovered Dungeon perk points were actually fairly abundant, and that upgrading her implants also improved her HP and Mana pools. And so, the new and improved NSLICE-00P began a dungeon termination spree . . .

The skill Presence Detection is now level 3!
The skill Trap Detection is now level 3!

NSLICE-00P flew through the air above a large swamp, her missiles destroying the slimes and poisonous toads hidden beneath the muddy water. A large frog broke the surface, lobbing a glob of venom-filled spit at the cyborg.

A magic circle formed in front of her, firing a bolt of fire that collided with the poison midair. The two projectiles exploded in a blast of steam.

Her organic half handled the magic on its own.

As for her AI?

A beam of light and mana pierced through the steam, striking the frog's heart.

You have slain Frog Dungeon Master (Level 8)!

Many an adversary did not expect her to perform skills and spells simultaneously, it seemed.

You have absorbed a dungeon core (Slimy Pit)!
Gained 5 Personal Perk Points, 5 Dungeon Perk Points!
Gained Dungeon Affinity: Slime (Minimum)!

You have conquered the Slimy Pit dungeon!
You have accomplished the Personal Feat: Dungeon Conqueror (Slimy Pit)!

Personal Feats		
Name	Description	Effect
Dungeon Conqueror (Slimy Pit)	Unlocked by conquering the Slimy Pit Dungeon.	+1 Perk Point +1 level in Poison Magic skill

NSLICE-00P stood in a forest of white trees with silver leaves. Lights from torches and Will'O'Wisps illuminated the forest, causing the leaves to shimmer like a sea of jewels—until the Equalizer passed over them, destroying the incorporeal creatures. In the center of the forest, a glowing unicorn brayed and lowered its head. Its horn shone with light and fired a beam through the air.

NSLICE-00P formed a Mana Barrier, blocking the attack. She simultaneously responded with a barrage of Magic Missiles, but they hardly made an impact on the unicorn's HP.

So she returned to her roots.

Her hands transformed into machine guns and unleashed hell.

The unicorn cried out as the bullets tore through it.

You have slain Unicorn Dungeon Master (Level 11)!
Level up! Your Personal Level is now 9!
Level up! Your Dungeon Level is now 12!

You have absorbed a dungeon core (Glimmering Grove)!
Gained 6 Personal Perk Points, 6 Dungeon Perk Points!
Gained Dungeon Affinity: Light (Minimum)!

You have conquered the Glimmering Grove dungeon!
You have accomplished the Personal Feat: Dungeon Conqueror (Glimmering Grove)!

Personal Feats		
Name	Description	Effect
Dungeon Conqueror (Glimmering Grove)	Unlocked by conquering the Glimmering Grove Dungeon.	+1 Perk Point +1 level in Light Magic skill

The spell Light Bolt is now level 4!
The skill Light Magic is now level 3!
You have learned the spell Light Beam!

NSLICE-00P tested her newest magic on a colony of ant monsters. She formed the latest spell, checking its performance compared to her own laser cannons.

The spell Light Beam has leveled twice and is now level 3!

Light Beam was . . . curious. Contrary to NSLICE-00P's expectations, it did not fire laser pulses, but rather formed a brightly glowing beam of energy that traveled at sub-light speeds. Yet its energy density and effective damage were higher than its physical properties might indicate.

NSLICE-00P wasn't sure it was superior to her laser cannons . . . but Light Beam could be used without occupying her energy channels, allowing her to utilize the Equalizer or her other weapons at the same time. Likewise, it could be used with Multicasting or any other magical skills that she might acquire. She decided it was worth adding to her normal arsenal.

In any case, the spell was inefficient at dealing with large quantities of foes, like the ants getting close to her, so she put it aside and prepared to fire her flamethrowers.

Just then, Lilussees opened up the panel to her hiding place, the inside of the compartment now covered in silk threads. She shook herself awake as she slowly crawled out onto NSLICE-00P's shoulder. The cyborg girl was just about to purify a group of ant monsters with her flamethrowers.

"Oh hey, um, boss? Could you, like, leave one or two of them for us? Maybe, like, just almost kill them or something?"

"Requesting Elaboration: That method would reduce termination efficiency. Please provide rationale so this unit can update the cost-benefit analysis."

"Like, you get XP for stuff your subordinates kill too, you know? And, like, it helps us get stronger, too, or something. So you, like, don't have to pay points to upgrade us yourself. It's win-win."

"Acknowledged. Updated cost-benefit analysis complete."

NSLICE-00P put away her flamethrower nozzles and opened a different compartment on her arm. A jolt of electricity surged through the monsters, leaving them stunned and trembling.

"Yay, you're the best, boss."

Lilussees hopped off of NSLICE-00P's shoulder, biting the helpless creatures with her venomous fangs one by one. Also, savoring their taste to determine which one she should take with her for the road.

"Easiest. Breakfast. Ever!"

NSLICE-00P logged the increase in her Dungeon XP as Lilussees got to work, verifying the spider's claims. She then turned her head to her other shoulder, where a muffled muttering could be heard.

"Does friendly Excellion Formantus Rattingtale the Third also wish for assisted terminations?"

Rattingtale jumped at being addressed, bumping his head on the hatch. He opened it up and stuck his head out with a curse.

"Why-why would I want-desire that? I'm the Great-High King over all the land, yes-yes! It is beneath-below me to resort to such lowly work!"

"Yay, more for me."

Rattingtale paled slightly as he watched Lilussees slaughter the helpless monsters. The vicious spider-thing had largely supplanted him as an advisor. So, if her levels grew while he remained the same . . . then the weird man-thing might disregard him entirely. He had no choice. He pulled himself up out of the hatch.

"Wait-wait! T-This Great-High King has decided he shall magnanimously accept your tribute, yes-yes."

"Boo."

"Acknowledged."

Rattingtale slowly crawled toward one of the monsters, leaping back as it twitched. He frowned as he observed the creature.

How did his soldiers do this again?

Later in the day, as Lilussees turned in for her third nap and NSLICE-00P resumed her magic training, Rattingtale huddled inside his compartment. He was still shivering, the memory of the lowly and dirty work he had been forced to perform fresh on his mind.

"I'll kill-slay them. I'll kill-slay them all, yes-yes! That wretched spider-thing, staring over my shoulder, waiting to betray me, yes-yes. I just need to convince the man-thing that it is false and plotting, yes-yes! But how?"

Rattingtale rubbed his paws together.

"Oh, I know, yes-yes! Man-things are sensitive, yes-yes! And the spider-thing is foul! She was most brutal-vicious, even devouring the monsters, yes-yes! All I need to do is point that out to the man-thing, and she will be repulsed-disgusted, yes-yes!"

Rattingtale popped his head out of the hatch.

"Greeting: Does friendly Excellion Formantus Rattingtale the Third have a request?" NSLICE-00P calmly addressed the rat as she stabbed a boar monster in the neck with a newly upgraded wrist-blade, spraying blood all over the area.

"N-No-no, j-just checking on . . . uh . . . our progress, yes-yes."

"Affirmative."

Rattingtale slowly closed the hatch.

And so, the Great-High King over all the land . . . decided to start his plan over for about the fourth time today.

Meanwhile, the wretched, false spider-thing was plotting . . . how to arrange her silk for maximum sleeping comfort.

Bionic Prosthetics +2 upgraded to Bionic Prosthetics +3! STR is now 130, SPD is now 65!
Armor Plating +1 upgraded to Armor Plating +2! DEF is now 120, RES is now 60!
Advanced Sensors +1 upgraded to Advanced Sensors +2
Repulsors upgraded to Repulsors +1!
Assault Rifle +1 upgraded to Assault Rifle +3!
Anti-Armor Missile Launcher upgraded to Anti-Armor Missile Launcher +2!
Anti-Personnel Missile Launcher upgraded to Anti-Personnel Missile Launcher +2!
Wrist Blade upgraded to Wrist Blade +2!

NSLICE-00P evaluated her implant options, aiming for a wide upgrade to her capabilities. With each upgrade level, she also unlocked more specialized upgrades for each of the components, though at the moment, she had not yet determined which of these were desirable.

Instead, she decided to evaluate new implants. It seemed like adding new ones improved her overall HP and Mana pools, both improving her survivability as well as boosting her capabilities, on top of the value of the implant itself.

Lilussees and Rattingtale sat on her shoulders as her robotic eye glowed, displaying the foreign program UI so they could also see the available options.

Suddenly, Lilussees jumped and started pointing.

"Oh! This one! Get this one, boss!"

NSLICE-00P brought up the option.

Available Implants:			
Name	**Cost**	**Mana Upkeep**	**Description**
Monster Hangar (Small)	**5**	**1**	**Provides 5 living spaces which may be shared by small monsters. The number of monsters per space depends on the size of the monsters in question. Unlocks subordinate summoning.**

"The spider-thing is deceiving-tricking you, boss-queen! She just wants a place to sleep-rest, yes-yes!"

"Oh? The snack is, like, talking, huh? Look, boss, I'll, like, admit I want a place to stay or something. But, like, this is good for you too, you know? Most dungeon masters, like, use lots of monster subordinates, you know? Like, you already got two, technically. So, like, this will allow you to summon more or something. And, like, it's not bad to, like, keep your subordinates happy and safe, you know? Like, you wouldn't want us to get hurt while you're fighting something big, right?"

"Query: Can subordinates provide additional value in excess of upgrading this unit's own capabilities?"

"That's, like, the wrong way to look at it, you know? Like, even if you can do everything yourself, subordinates are still helpful, you know? Like, each subordinate is also earning their own XP or something, while earning you XP too. So, like, you're still growing while the subordinate's growing too, which means, like, if you have them learn skills you don't have, that's like, brand-new skills for you, you know? Also, like, this is one of the cheapest implants for mana upkeep, so like, it's a good boost to your HP and Mana, you know? So it's, like, good to invest now to open that door."

Rattingtale was about to object when he shivered. Lilussees was staring straight at him, rubbing her mandibles together.

And, well, having a royal chamber was only appropriate for the Great-High King over all the land.

Likewise . . . if the man-thing was going to summon more subordinates . . .

then perhaps he could convince her to summon some of his kin. And of course, who better to lead them than the Great-High King over all the land? And once he began to gather a faction . . .

Yes, this could work to his advantage.

"I . . . concur-agree with the spider-thing, yes-yes."

"Affirmative."

You have unlocked an Additional Implant Slot! Max HP and Mana increased!
You have unlocked the Monster Hangar (Small) implant!

A new panel door formed on NSLICE-00P's back. It opened to what appeared to be a black void, hiding whatever was inside from the outside world. Lilussees immediately scrambled over and leapt in.

"DIBS!"

Rattingtale just heaved a sigh before slowly crawling over to check out the new hangar himself. Inside was a sleek metal room with a large table in the center. Five doors stood on the far wall. He saw Lilussees shutting the door on the far right.

So he, of course, moved toward the door on the far left.

Inside was an empty room . . . at first. Shortly after he stepped inside, the air twisted and distorted. When it cleared and he could see once more, the room had been replaced by an underground burrow.

He frowned.

A bit lacking in majesty . . . but it did look very comfortable.

And, well, at least it was safer than his current quarters.

And as NSLICE-00P continued to assault dungeons and upgrade her implants, her organic half continued practicing with magic. She continued practicing with all her available spells, of course, but also with new applications of mana.

For example, she tried infusing her machine gun bullets with mana, much as she had her lasers and flamethrowers. The first attempt had done nothing at all, the mana barely entering the bullets. The second attempt had caused the bullets to explode in the chamber, disabling that particular weapon and, uh, *training* her HP Regen skill.

But eventually, she managed to pour a significant amount of mana into one of the projectiles without it either exploding or dissipating into the surrounding air.

You have learned the spell Mana Infusion!
You have accomplished the Personal Feat: Enchanter!

Personal Feats		
Name	Description	Effect
Enchanter	The first step on the path of the magic craftsman. Unlocked by manually accomplishing a Mana Infusion.	+1 level in Enchanting skill

NSLICE-00P's robotic eye flickered as she processed the latest boons. She started running a simulation . . .

Green checkmarks began to appear across the simulation criteria.

If her calculations were correct, she was ready to take on the Equalizer, after some more practice with Mana Infusion first.

The Spell Mana Infusion is now level 3!

Her goal this time was modest. She wasn't going to attempt to fundamentally improve the Equalizer, like her implants. She didn't even necessarily want to enchant it, as she had with her other weapons. She simply wanted to optimize it.

The Equalizer had been designed as a universal EMP, able to dampen any energy type it encountered. But now, NSLICE-00P did not require it to dampen every energy type. Mana had been the vast majority of energy encountered ever since completing her last mission; in fact, she had not even detected any electrically powered devices since arriving in this area, much less the more exotic nonstandard energy types. Therefore, she calculated she could significantly improve the Equalizer's performance by tuning it to mana specifically.

She also wanted to improve the precision of the Equalizer when targeting mana, so that she could target specific attributes as opposed to mana in general. Since mana filled everything in this place, even the very atmosphere, the Equalizer's power bled off reacting to all the mana it encountered, diluting its strength by the time it reached its target. So NSLICE-00P predicted that tuning the Equalizer to specific attributes of mana would improve its efficacy.

And so she began.

She flooded the Equalizer with mana. The exotic metals inside of it began to absorb and amplify the energy, resonating with it. Her AI then activated the protocols for the Equalizer, instructing it to shift its wavelengths to interfere with the energy. And as she did, she also ran mana through the physical structure of the weapon. She had, of course, been recording when the foreign system had upgraded her components, and she was now attempting to replicate that phenomenon, until eventually . . .

The mana stopped. Her log indicated the process was done.

She then trained the Equalizer by running several different types of mana as she had available, saving each tuning as a new protocol to be applied as needed.

She lifted her hand toward a nearby tree and selected the new anti-HP protocol.

She fired a small rainbow-colored beam at it. The beam passed harmlessly through the mana in the air, but tore through the HP barrier around the tree, damaging it faster than it could repair itself. She had succeeded.

. . . Wait, what? What did you just do? You, um . . . I don't really understand what's going on here. Well, I didn't really understand that particular weapon in the first place, so, um . . . well, whatever.

The Equalizer upgraded to The Equalizer +1!

. . . Ugh, I have to do work now, don't I? Please stop that.

You have accomplished the Dungeon Feat: System Upgrade!

Dungeon Feats		
Name	**Description**	**Effect**
System Upgrade	**Unlocked by manually performing a system upgrade. Which is not supposed to be possible. Ugh, this is going to get complicated, isn't it?**	**Um, I don't know. Just have +20 Dungeon Perk Points or something. Whatever. You're figuring this out yourself anyways, so close enough.**

What is happening here? You manually upgraded a dungeon component? And created an entirely new skill?! Wow . . . wait, what is this?! That's . . . you're erasing mana directly? Um . . . okay, I mean, that's not the worst thing anyone's ever done but, um, again, please don't do anything bad with all this, okay?

You have learned the unique skill: Anti-Mana Beam!
You have accomplished the Feat: Skill Creator!

Skills		
Name	Level	Description
Anti-Mana Beam	1	My best guess is that this projects a kind of inverse mana that reacts destructively with normal mana, including HP. While it can fully deplete HP, it does not harm matter itself. Requires The Equalizer.

Personal Feats		
Name	Description	Effect
Skill Creator	You don't master the system. You define it. Unlocked by creating a brand-new skill.	To be honest, this normally happens when you're a MUCH higher level, so I'm a bit worried about passing you this much this early, but, um, okay. +20 Perk Points

With that, NSLICE-00P reran a particular combat simulation, factoring in all the new abilities she had gained. She waited as the simulation ran . . .

And then . . .

Numbers appeared in her UI.

96.31% chance of target termination.

It seemed she was ready.

It was time to confront the ursanus once again.

12

The Bear Necessities . . . For Termination!

The forest was dead silent, neither bird nor insect willing to sing their songs. Even the trees seemed to sway and groan.

For the ursanus alpha was on patrol.

Its mighty paws struck the ground, as if to lay claim to the very land beneath it. Its shell glistened in the sunlight, as hard and tough as any armor forged by men. Its mana blared, a warning and a challenge to all who dared to brave its domain. It let out a low, rumbling growl, a strange scent on the wind.

High above it, two red lights flickered through the canopy.

NSLICE-00P hovered over the trees. Her head was covered by her combat helmet, her human eye covered by the armored eyepiece such that both her eyes now glowed with red light. She had been keeping track of the ursanus ever since their encounter, so hunting it down once more had been a simple task.

And now that she had been sufficiently upgraded, it was time to eliminate the threat to her mission and reclaim her lost arm.

"Target acquired. Analyzing target mana and HP. Rerunning combat simulation with observed variables."

NSLICE-00P's hands transformed into machine guns once more.

"Analysis complete. Chance of mission success at acceptable levels. Engaging termination protocols."

With that, NSLICE-00P leaned forward, thrusters on her back and feet blaring. She shot through the trees, following a predetermined flight path through the branches. Within moments, she had cleared the canopy and leaned back to right herself, floating in the air above the ursanus.

A dozen magic circles filled the air around her as she took aim with her arms.

"Engaging target."

Her machine guns lit up the area, and the magic circles began to shine and flash. Bullets and Magic Missiles filled the air, striking the ursanus.

The spell Dense Magic Missile is now Level 18!

The ursanus paused as the projectiles struck its hide. It glanced up and behind it, baring its fangs with a growl. The monster then turned around to face NSLICE-00P, pulling back its head and letting out a roar which shook the very air.

NSLICE-00P ignored it, her robotic eye flickering as she observed the bullets and Magic Missiles interact with the ursanus's HP. The weapons and spells were dealing small amounts of damage to the HP barrier, barely noticeable but more than nothing.

The ursanus then tucked its legs and head into its shell. Its body flashed with a subtle glow, and its HP barrier sunk into its skin, fusing with it, focusing on repair instead of protection. The projectiles began to strike the shell directly . . .

And bounced off without making an impact.

"Observation: No weakness to conventional weaponry or offensive spells identified. Target has deployed defensive skill countermeasures. Updating scenario."

NSLICE-00P dropped her barrage, her hands reforming once more. Her core began to glow bright as she held out her hands toward the ursanus.

"Deploying Equalizer. Engaging 'Anti-Mana Beam' protocol."

A bright rainbow-colored beam fired from her hands, striking the ursanus head-on.

And this time, the ursanus roared.

The beam tore at the monster. It stripped away its enhanced defense, causing HP to flow out once more. It then ripped apart the HP, draining the barrier directly, dealing damage faster than the HP could repair.

The ursanus continued to roar, sticking its legs and head out of its shell once more. It took off running. NSLICE-00P followed, keeping her Equalizer on target. She had determined that she should assault the HP barrier directly rather than trying to bypass it as she had before. This way, it didn't matter if she kept the Equalizer focused on the same spot; as long as she was still hitting some part of the monster's body, she could continue to damage the HP pool.

The ursanus growled once again and suddenly pushed off the side. It began to duck and weave around the trees, breaking NSLICE-00P's line of sight. She could no longer keep the beam continuously focused on target.

"Observation: Target is taking evasive measures. Attempting containment."

NSLICE-00P rushed ahead of the monster, several magic circles forming ahead of her.

"Deploying Earth Wall protocol. Deploying Fire Blast protocol."

The very ground itself began to rise, forming into a mighty wall in front of the ursanus. Then, several long jets of fire shot from the remaining magic circles, covering the wall in roaring flames.

The monster ignored the fire and smashed straight through the wall. NSLICE-00P flew toward the top to pursue—

Something like an arc of light shot over the wall. NSLICE-00P detected the growing energy signature and barely stopped herself short, the arc passing over her head and slicing the top off a tree behind her. The ursanus swung glowing claws, launching another arc of light straight toward the wall. It sliced through the construct, forcing NSLICE-00P to move out of the way. She dropped the wall, allowing the flames to fade as well.

"Observation: Target containment failed. Target possesses ranged attacks. Target cannot be terminated at safe distance. Adapting combat strategy."

NSLICE-00P lowered herself to the ground as the ursanus roared and charged straight at her. She quickly boosted out of the way, and four more magic circles formed in the air in front of her.

"Deploying Poison Bolt protocol."

Globs of purple liquid struck the monster. They barely made a dent on its HP at all, but NSLICE-00P kept up the attack. Eventually, she logged some of the Poison-attribute mana seeping into the ursanus, sapping its HP bit by bit.

The spell Poison Bolt is now Level 6!
The skill Poison Magic is now Level 3!
You have learned the spell Poison Blast!

The ursanus roared and chased after her. Panels opened up all along the cyborg as her hands transformed. She opened up with every conventional weapon she had.

And as she did, she split her mana, infusing every projectile she fired.

The spell Mana Infusion is now Level 10! Upgrade available!

Bullets, missiles, and jets of flame filled the air, bombarding the ursanus with lead, fire, and explosions. The monster rushed forward regardless, charging at the cyborg once more. Once again, she leapt out of the way, but this time, the ursanus was ready. Its claws were glowing as it swung its paw, sending an arc of light at the cyborg. As NSLICE-00P was already in motion and at this range, she would not be able to completely evade the strike.

But several magic circles had already formed around her.

She had predicted this situation when she'd logged the ursanus concentrating mana into its claws, and so had prepared a countermeasure. Several Earth Walls rose in front of her, just tall enough to intercept the incoming strike, and several Mana Barriers layered on top of one another behind them.

The Earth Walls crumbled as the arc of light pierced right through them. The Mana Barriers shattered on contact.

But they had done their job.

NSLICE-00P raised her arm to block. The blow sent her flying, leaving a thick gash on her arm. The strike was deep enough to damage one of her assault rifles, cutting into her barrage, but her arm held, and her HP was not fully drained. In fact, her HP was already at work, starting to repair the damage. She fed some of her mana there, replicating the work of the HP to try and speed up the repair.

You have accomplished the Personal Feat: Healer!
You have learned the skill Recovery Magic!
You have learned the spell Heal!

Feats		
Name	Description	Effect
Healer	Anyone can deal in death. It takes an expert to deal in life. Unlocked by using mana to heal a wound.	+1 level in Recovery Magic skill

And even if her weapons were damaged, she had other avenues of attack.

The air lit up around her as she formed as many magic circles as she could.

Magic Missiles, globs of poison, bolts of fire, beams of light. All manner of spells struck the ursanus, chipping away at its HP.

Once again, the creature roared and launched itself at her.

And so, NSLICE-00P and the ursanus gave battle to one another. The monster was mighty, but NSLICE-00P was quick. Even a single direct blow from the monster could end the battle . . . but it could not strike that blow. NSLICE-00P's repulsors and advanced sensors were enough to evade the majority of its attacks. Her upgraded armor, defensive spells, and recovery methods meant she wouldn't be defeated by the few glancing blows that did connect.

On the flip side, her attacks barely chipped away at the monster's health. The ursanus might be a simple creature, but that was because it had poured most of its growth into raw strength and durability. It was a force of nature, raw power incarnate. NSLICE-00P could just barely deal enough damage to outpace its natural recovery.

This was a losing fight for any normal combatant. NSLICE-00P had to expend practically all her mana just to keep the ursanus's HP from recovering. There was no way a mage of her level could maintain that mana expenditure for any length of time. And, again, a single good blow from the monster would end her, so she had to keep up perfect focus and perfect movement, as even a single mistake or miscalculation would spell defeat. And she would have to keep up said perfect focus for a truly mind-numbing amount of time.

No person of her level could pull that off. Even if they had the strength of will to carry on with perfect focus, they could not battle the fatigue that would result. A lethal mistake was unavoidable.

That was why the ursanus stayed in the fight. It was inevitable that it would crush this annoying creature long before she could deal any real harm back.

And that was why NSLICE-00P could win.

The skill MP Regen is now Level 5!
The skill MP Regen is now Level 6!

With full access to all the mana a dungeon core could pull, NSLICE-00P had a truly phenomenal mana-recovery rate, further boosted by the MP Regen skill, which *normally* couldn't be applied directly to a dungeon core. Her cybernetic-dungeon components could then channel that mana endlessly without fatigue or strain, and a dungeon's mana naturally filled the dungeon master's body. A dungeon master did not easily grow tired or hungry within their domain, the dungeon itself would sustain them. That, combined with the cybernetic implants improving NSLICE-00P's endurance and biological efficiency, meant she could continue fighting without food or rest for a truly impressive amount of time.

Not to mention her cybernetic side was not subject to fatigue. It acted as quickly and precisely at the latter stages of the fight as it did at the beginning. Perhaps if she had still been a normal cyborg, her implants might eventually experience wear and tear. But now, she had a dungeon's mana flowing through those components, maintaining their state and repairing any damage in real time. Her cybernetic half was constantly refreshed to mint condition.

Her organic components might grow tired, but it was her cybernetic side leading this fight, the organic side mostly focusing on forming magic circles. As such, any time her organic half was growing fatigued, the cyborg just shifted to rely on her conventional weapons instead and let her human body recover. In other words . . .

This battle had become a war of attrition. And the number one rule when fighting dungeons was: Never fight a dungeon in a war of attrition.

NSLICE-00P would not slip up. She would not run out of resources. The ursanus had to overcome her in strategy and tactics, or it would fall. And a force of nature, a creature of raw power, did not often resort to tactics.

After a long while of this, the ursanus's HP barrier had grown noticeably weaker. The creature itself was breathing heavily, its mana drained. It was moving more slowly now, and had not fired an arc of light in quite some time.

NSLICE-00P moved into the final stage.

She rose into the air, deploying the Equalizer once more.

The ursanus roared. It tried to escape, but NSLICE-00P had targeted more than just the creature. The collateral damage of their fight had knocked over many of the trees in the area, leaving the pair in the middle of a small clearing. The ursanus could not break the line of sight anymore.

The monster tried to strike back, gathering mana to its claws, but NSLICE-00P simply redirected the Anti-Mana Beam to the monster's paws. When it swung at her, the arc of light barely made it a few inches before sputtering out. And then the beam stopped.

The ursanus's HP had been almost completely drained. Now, NSLICE-00P simply had to do something about its illogically tough body.

She activated her core to the max, flooding her energy channels with power. Bright lines of light formed along her arms as she brought her hands together. She grabbed all the mana she could hold, infusing her energy channels with as much of it as possible. Her arms hummed and trembled as she twisted massive quantities of electricity and mana together.

With the remaining unspent mana, she formed magic circles for the Light Beam spell. She formed these magic circles in a line in front of her outstretched palms, and then . . .

She opened fire.

Mana and electricity twisted together, forming a massive beam of light which traveled through and activated each of the countless magic circles along its path, growing in size and intensity as it assimilated the Light Beam spells.

The air hissed and cracked.

Nearby leaves caught fire from the heat.

And the ursanus vanished under the beam, which continued traveling into the ground.

You have slain Ursanus Alpha (Level 50)!
Gained 143 Personal XP, 114 Dungeon XP
Level up! Your Personal Level is now 10!
Level up! Your Personal Level is now 11!
Level up! Your Dungeon Level is now 13!
The skill Mana Beam is now Level 15! Upgrade available!

The spell Light Beam is now Level 12! Upgrade available!
The skill Light Magic is now Level 9! Spell choice available!
Mana Control has increased by 10 and is now 120!
You have accomplished the Personal Feat: Challenger!

Personal Feats		
Name	Description	Effect
Challenger	Levels and odds are just numbers. Unlocked by defeating an opponent who is the greater of level 10 or twice your level while alone.	+3 Perk Points + Challenger skill

Powerful monster record obtained. Monster lineage unlocked.
Ursine-type subordinates may now be summoned.

NSLICE-00P's robotic eye flickered as she looked down at the smoking hole in the ground surrounded by smoldering grass.

"Mission accomplished. Target terminated."

NSLICE-00P's Dungeon Status

Overview	
Name	**The Walking Dungeon**
Level	**13**
XP	**27/100**
Available Perk Points	**24**
Mana	**90/90 (110/110)**
Exterior	**Human/Automata Hybrid (LOCKED)**

Dungeon Affinities	
Type	Strength
Cyborg	Primary
Rodent	Minimum
Earth	Minimum
Arachnid	Minimum
Slime	Minimum
Light	Minimum

Implants		
Type	Mana Upkeep	Description
Bionic Prosthetics +3	0	Overwrites STR and SPD, Values: 130 STR, 65 SPD
Armor Plating +2	0	Overwrites DEF and RES, Values: 120 DEF, 60 RES
Bonded AI	0	Enables direct contact with the System. Overwrites DEX, Value: 1000 DEX
Techno-Organic Interface	0	Enables conscious control over organic and emotional functions. Resists mind-influencing effects.
Advanced Sensors +2	0	Vastly expands scope and effectiveness of senses.
Internal Weapon Bays	0	Enables use of dungeon traps as weapons.
Repulsors +1	0	Enables flight and tactical boosts.
Energy Channels	0	Enables user to channel internal energy into external attacks.

Dungeon Field Generator	5	Surrounding area counts as dungeon territory. Enables mana absorption within area of effect.
Monster Hangar (Small)	1	Provides living space for 5 small monsters. Unlocks subordinate summoning.

Subordinates				
Name	Species	Level		Mana Upkeep
Rattingtale	Monster Rat	6	1	Check Status
Lilussees	Monster Spider	8	1	Check Status

Traps			
Name	Number Active / Deployed	Mana Upkeep	Description
Assault Rifle +3	2/2	2	Rapid-fire projectile weapon with high penetration.
Autopistol	2/2	2	Rapid-fire projectile weapon with medium penetration.
Anti-Armor Missile Launcher +2	2/2	2	Homing explosive designed to penetrate armor. Very high penetration.
Anti-Personnel Missile Launcher +2	6/6	6	Homing explosive designed for area damage. Medium penetration.

Stun Ray	1/1	1	Nonlethal electric weapon. Can inflict stun and paralysis statuses.
Wrist Blade +2	2/2	0	Wrist-mounted blades that can be deployed at high speed.
Flamethrower	2/2	2	Deals fire damage and applies burn status in a large cone.
The Equalizer +1	1/1	0	Huh? What the heck is this? Some kind of weird metal that doesn't even exist here? Um . . . well . . . best I can tell it's some sort of antimagic field generator? Eh . . . well, it's yours, not mine, so you don't need me to tell you, right? Like, you already upgraded this thing yourself, so you're good, right?

Dungeon Skills		
Name	**Level**	**Description**
Analyze	N/A	Check the status of a target. More detail for targets within the dungeon. Details depend on level difference.
Contract	N/A	Bind a consenting target to the dungeon, per terms agreed upon by both parties.

Transfer	N/A	Move yourself, a subordinate, or a consenting target within your dungeon.

Dungeon Perks	
Name	**Description**
Human-Dungeon Hybrid	Enables Implants tab. Enables unique Dungeon Combat skill. Enables direct manipulation of dungeon mana. +100 HP Rooms tab locked. Exterior locked.

Dungeon Feats		
Name	**Description**	**Effect**
Dungeon Victor	To the victor go the spoils. Unlocked by destroying or subordinating another dungeon.	+1 Perk Point Unlocks Dungeon Warfare category perks.
Dungeon Overlord	A master of masters. Unlocked by subordinating another dungeon master.	+2 Perk Points Unlocks Subordinate Core category perks.
Raid Boss	Fine, I'll do it myself. Unlocked by destroying or subordinating another dungeon with no assistance.	+2 Perk Points +1 level in HP Regen skill +1 level in MP Regen skill +50 HP Unlocks Raid Boss category perks.

System Upgrade	**Unlocked by manually performing a system upgrade. Which is not supposed to be possible.** **Ugh, this is going to get complicated, isn't it?**	**Um, I don't know. Just have +20 Dungeon Perk Points or something. Whatever. You're figuring this out yourself anyways, so close enough.**

NSLICE-00P's Personal Status

Personal Status			
General Information		Physical Attributes	
Name	NSLICE-00P	STR	130* (Overwritten)
Species	Human/ Dungeon Core/ Automata Hybrid	DEX	1000* (Overwritten)
Level	11	SPD	65* (Overwritten)
XP	19/100	DEF	120* (Overwritten)
Perk Points	71	RES	60* (Overwritten)
HP	180/180	Magical Attributes	
MP	103/103	Mana Density	102
		Mana Control	120

Active Skills		
Name	Level	Description
Mana Beam	15 *Upgrade Available	Focus mana into a channeled energy attack.

Sneak	1	Move quietly to avoid notice. Makes it harder for others to notice the user. Effectiveness highly dependent on environment.
Multicasting	6	Can cast several spells at once. Number of simultaneous spells increases with level.
Anti-Mana Beam	1	My best guess is that this projects a kind of inverse mana that reacts destructively with normal mana, including HP. While it can fully deplete HP, it does not harm matter itself. Requires The Equalizer.

Passive Skills		
General		
Name	Level	Description
Dungeon Combat	N/A	Dungeon traps and skills count as personal weapons and skills.
HP Regen	4	Automatically recover HP pool. Increased regeneration speed for damaged body parts.
MP Regen	6	Automatically recover MP pool.
Presence Detection	3	Detect living entities around the user. Range and scope of detection increases with level.
Trap Detection	3	Detect traps. Range and scope of detection increases with level.
Challenger	--	Damage dealt x1.5 against targets of higher level. Damage received x0.75 against attacks from targets of higher level.

Utility		
Name	Level	Description
Enchanting	1	The art of infusing objects and beings with mana.
Resistances		
Name	Level	Description
Poison Resistance	1	Resist and recovery from poison status. Resist Poison-attributed damage.
Schools of Magic		
Name	Level	Description
Arcane Magic	9	The school of magic governing the manipulation of unattributed mana. A solid foundation for students of the mystic arts, though somewhat less mana efficient than the more specialized schools.
Earth Magic	3	The school of magic governing the manipulation of Earth-attribute mana. One of the basic elemental magics, strong at defensive spells and spells that deal physical damage.
Fire Magic	4	The school of magic governing the manipulation of Fire-attribute mana. One of the basic elemental magics, strong at offensive spells and spells that inflict the burn status.
Light Magic	10 *Spell Choice Available	The school of magic governing the manipulation of Light-attribute mana. One of the basic elemental magics, quick and precise spells that are excellent against Dark-aligned foes.

Poison Magic	3	The school of magic governing magical poisons. Excels at spreading poison status and dealing damage over time.
Recovery Magic	1	The school of magic governing healing through magic.

Spells		
Arcane		
Name	Level	Description
Dense Magic Missile	18	Form and launch mana into a small projectile. One of the most basic offensive applications of magic.
Mana Barrier	3	Form mana into a barrier to block attacks. One of the most basic defensive applications of magic.
Mana Blast	1	A cone-shaped blast of mana. Deals damage and knockback to the area.
Mana Infusion	10 *Upgrade Available	Infuse mana into a target. The most basic enchantment.
Earth		
Name	Level	Description
Rock Throw	6	Use mana to form and then launch a small rock. Mana cost increases dramatically if cast without a nearby source of Earth. Deals physical damage. One of the most basic offensive applications of Earth Magic.
Earth Wall	3	Use mana to temporarily form a wall of Earth. Mana cost increases dramatically if cast without a nearby source of Earth. One of the most basic defensive applications of Earth Magic.

Fire		
Name	Level	Description
Fire Bolt	1	Use mana to form and then launch a small bolt of fire. Mana cost decreases dramatically if cast with a nearby source of Fire. May inflict burn status. One of the most basic offensive applications of Fire Magic.
Fire Blast	4	A cone-shaped blast of Fire mana. Deals damage and inflicts burn to the area. Mana cost decreases dramatically if cast with a nearby source of Fire. May be continuously channeled.
Light		
Name	Level	Description
Light Bolt	1	Use mana to form and then launch a small bolt of light. Mana cost increases if cast without a nearby source of Light. One of the most basic offensive applications of Light Magic.
Light Beam	12 *Upgrade Available	Form mana into a beam of light to attack. May pierce through its target. May be continuously channeled.
Poison		
Name	Level	Description
Poison Bolt	6	Use mana to form and then launch a small bolt of poison. Mana cost decreases dramatically if cast with a nearby source of Poison. May inflict poison status. One of the most basic offensive applications of Poison Magic.

Poison Blast	1	A cone-shaped blast of Poison mana. Deals damage and inflicts poison to the area. Mana cost decreases dramatically if cast with a nearby source of Poison. May be continuously channeled.
Recovery		
Name	Level	Description
Heal	1	Use mana to heal minor wounds and damage. Effect increases with user's knowledge of the body.

Personal Feats		
Name	Description	Effect
Against the Odds	Do not ask how many there are, but where they are. Unlocked by winning a fight when outnumbered by equal or higher-leveled opponents.	+1 Perk Point
Solo Conquest	I am the dungeon master now. Unlocked by conquering a dungeon alone.	+1 level in HP Regen skill +1 level in MP Regen skill +1 level in Presence Detection skill +1 level in Trap Detection skill
Arcane Prodigy	The career of a supreme sorcerer does not start on the beaten path. Unlocked by learning a high-tier magic skill under level twenty without spending Perk Points.	+3 Perk Points Unlocks more advanced magic perks.

Enchanter	The first step on the path of the magic craftsman. Unlocked by manually accomplishing a Mana Infusion.	+1 level in Enchanting skill
Skill Creator	You don't master the system. You define it. Unlocked by creating a brand-new skill.	To be honest, this normally happens when you're a MUCH higher level, so I'm a bit worried about passing you this much this early, but, um, okay. +20 Perk Points
Healer	Anyone can deal in death. It takes an expert to deal in life. Unlocked by using mana to heal a wound.	+1 level in Recovery Magic skill
Challenger	Levels and odds are just numbers. Unlocked by defeating an opponent who is the greater of level 10 or over twice your level while alone.	+3 Perk Points + Challenger skill
Dungeon Conqueror Feats		
Name	Description	Effect
Dungeon Conqueror (Rat Cave)	Unlocked by conquering the Rat Cave Dungeon.	+1 Perk Point +1 level in Sneak skill
Dungeon Conqueror (Earth Tunnels)	Unlocked by conquering the Earth Tunnels Dungeon.	+1 Perk Point +1 level in Earth Magic skill
Dungeon Conqueror (Spider Tree)	Unlocked by conquering the Spider Tree Dungeon.	+1 Perk Point +1 level in Poison Resistance skill

Dungeon Conqueror (Slimy Pit)	Unlocked by conquering the Slimy Pit Dungeon.	+1 Perk Point +1 level in Poison Bolt spell
Dungeon Conqueror (Glimmering Grove)	Unlocked by conquering the Glimmering Grove Dungeon.	+1 Perk Point +1 level in Light Magic skill

12.1

Interlude: Just Another Day in the Provinces

Canus Sittius Dio groaned. He shivered as something wet and cold landed on his face for only the fiftieth time tonight. He turned over to the other side of his cot, only for a second drop to land on his face. He cursed and leaned out of bed. Looked like his armor would be warmer than his bed tonight, so he went ahead and got himself dressed. He swore once more as he saw the puddles pooling on the stone floors. Blasted roof hadn't been repaired in a decade.

And likely never would. Why would it? Hardly anyone stayed out here, anyway. Most of Canus's soldiers spent their time on their farms. Canus himself hadn't been on campaign in quite some time and lived out on his estate in the countryside. Under normal circumstances, the only thing separating the old legionary from any other folk was the torn banner hanging over his fireplace and the set of worn, though well-maintained armor in his bedroom.

These were not normal circumstances.

Canus finished strapping his sword on his waist. He took a deep breath and opened his door, making his way into the drafty hallway.

"Dux Dio."

His soldiers knocked their right fists against their chests as he passed them by. He nodded in acknowledgement as he made his way to a staircase, grunting as he made his way up. One would think several human lifetimes of levels and a generous allotment of endurance perks might help one's knees. But of course, that would be too convenient.

To be fair, one could, in fact, stave off the ravages of time with perk purchases. But ultimately, the boons from the Aesdes were intended only to help the Enlightened Races stand against demon lords and the Realms of Mana, not to surpass their own mortality. Purchasing perks with the same effects only ever increased in cost, and experience gain depended on the level difference with the monster hunted, to the point that no experience would be granted if the difference was too great. At some point, a person could end up spending all the extra years just searching for more monsters to kill, until only the most powerful could grant them any experience at all.

Canus had seen men and women like that, so desperate to delay their end that they forgot to enjoy their lives, spending all of their time just trying to earn some more. He had decided enough was enough for himself. He would take the time his deeds had earned and make the most of it.

To be fair, being half Elf didn't hurt. He would admit he couldn't expect the average human to sympathize with his views when he was guaranteed over three times their lifespan at birth. Whatever the case, he had chosen to abscond to the frontier province of Turannia, where he had *hoped* to live out a quiet life with his family and with the land.

But then, the local dux had gotten himself killed. A young officer fresh out of the academy who had thought he was commanding the legions of Velus himself instead of a bunch of glorified farmers. Canus didn't have to wonder how the man had earned himself a post all the way out in Turannia.

And, of course, the Empire hadn't gotten around to sending a replacement, so when the united clans of Madadh-allaidh had come through the then empty border, the provincial governor had practically begged Canus to return to duty. And unfortunately, he could not refuse. Hard to live a quiet retirement when the latest Wulver chieftain was burning down the next-door neighbors. Especially when more than one of said neighbors were Canus's own descendants.

Beyond his own agenda, this backwater province was more important than anyone realized. Which was by intention, but also meant that if Canus didn't take care of it, no one would.

And once he had the office . . . well, Canus couldn't bring himself to abandon his troops. He saw the officers coming out of the capital these days. And while all old soldiers complained about fresh commanders, Canus had lived long enough and through to say with certainty this latest crop was the worst he had ever seen.

No, the old half Elf was the best and perhaps only chance for any of the troops in this province to survive the decade.

Assuming they survived the day, that is.

Canus made his way to the top of the ramparts. He stood on top of a large stone fort at the top of a cliff overlooking the sea, built with exacting precision to Imperial standard. Imperial standard two centuries ago. At this point, cracks and moss covered the walls. The Imperial banners were torn and ripped, barely hanging onto the walls. The protective wards hadn't been refreshed in over a decade, and he was pretty sure the ballistae would explode if fired.

Worst of all, the roof leaked like you wouldn't believe, and it had been raining all week.

Canus shook his head and made his way up to the watchtower. A single woman stood at the top. She had a cloak made from the pelt of a sea lion on her shoulders, the creature's head covering her smooth red hair. Slightly pointed ears stuck out from underneath, twitching as the rain pelted the stone. Underneath her cloak she wore her traditional hunter's garb, but with the medallion of an Imperial Exploratore on her shoulder. Her slightly webbed hands wrapped around a harpoon made of bone. She didn't react as Canus walked up beside her, her eyes locked on the rocky coastline below.

Oh, and the fleet of ships landing along the beach.

She gave him a slight nod as he joined her.

"Dux."

"Miallói"

The Selkie Exploratore was a woman of few words. She didn't exactly stick to protocol, but Canus didn't exactly want this job, so he didn't exactly care. She got the job done and kept her mouth shut. As far as Canus was concerned, she was a model soldier. He was more than happy to let her act as she pleased.

It also didn't hurt that she was the deadliest Empire-affiliated soldier in the province.

"How are we looking?"

She shrugged.

"We'll live."

Canus sighed and pointed down at the fortress below.

"And all of them?"

She shrugged again.

"If we have help."

Canus heaved a sigh. He knew that, officially, it wasn't the worst year on record, but he couldn't help but feel that these incursions were increasingly frequent. Just his luck.

And he knew the opponents they now faced. The Dobhar had long battled with the Selkie for control of these lands and the waters around. And now, they battled the Empire too, ever since it had laid claim to this place.

The otter-like Dobhar were ferocious and tough; their king, Uscfrea Spellbreaker, was said to be invincible to harm. He was not, but might as well have been for Canus's soldiers below. They might be brave, but the limitanei had long ceased to be legionaries in all but name. They no longer had the rigorously perfected perk allocation and teamwork of the legions, spending more time and levels on farming than fighting. In fact, ever since the Empire started paying them in land instead of cash, they had to supply their own equipment too. Homemade spears replaced enchanted blades, leather and cloth instead of metal scale.

They were no longer expected to win, only to hold the enemy at the gates long enough for the comitatenses to arrive. The real legions still trained and equipped as their legendary predecessors, every bit as deadly as the ones who had conquered this land to begin with.

When and *if* they arrived, that is.

So all Canus could do here . . . was hope the comitatenses were indeed on the way.

He heaved another sigh.

Barbarians on the shores. Bandits in the hills. And the local mages were reporting some serious readings from the Beithigh Forest beyond the boundaries of the province, possibly another mana surge. On top of it all, the Exploratores were reporting someone or *something* had picked a fight with the Tyrant of the Beasts, reporting the devastation left in the battle's wake. Bit of a dramatic name for an ursanus alpha, but an accurate one for a farmer with a stick.

What he wouldn't give for a single century of his old command. He could have this province cleaned up in a month.

Instead, he would now have to stretch his experience to the limit if he wanted most of these boys and girls to survive to lunch.

He turned to exit the tower when a gust of wind blew past him, angling the rain such that it flew under the tower's roof, drenching his face and cloak.

Canus swore.

And of course, it *had* to be raining today.

13

Mission Parameters Set

"The hardest thing about life on the frontier is not the poverty, the lack of support, or the savage monsters and tribes. It is the unknown. A surge of mana could create a wave of monsters that didn't exist before. A new dungeon might appear and start sending out raiding parties. A tribal champion might unite the savages into a mighty horde. A high-level monster might suddenly expand its hunting grounds. But for many, that is the point. For where there is risk, there is opportunity."

—*The Peoples of the Frontiers*, Volume 1, by traveling author and former Exploratore Placus Paesentius Statius

NSLICE-00P lowered to the ground after defeating the ursanus. Rattingtale and Lilussees exited the Monster Hangar and climbed to her shoulder.

"Wow. Like, good job, boss. There's not, like, any leftovers, though, or something? Ah, too bad."

Rattingtale's ears were pressed flat against his head.

"Y-Yes-yes, g-good job, boss-queen. T-This is, um, most impressive. A-As expected of the one who defeated the Great-High King, yes-yes."

"Acknowledged."

With that, NSLICE-00P returned to the site of her first encounter with the Ursanus. She recovered and destroyed as much of her missing arm as she could as per her protocols to prevent reverse engineering. Afterwards, she glanced around, analyzing the angle of the ground. She identified which direction was downhill, and started walking.

"So, like, what now, boss? We probably, like, hit a lot of the young dungeons in the area or something. So we should, like, move a bit if we want to find more weak ones or something."

"Negative."

Rattingtale's ears perked as NSLICE-00P rejected the wretched spider-thing.

"T-Then, how about we find another dungeon and NOT destroy-demolish it, yes-yes? Then, we can build-construct a new dungeon, now that the dangerous monster is dealt with, yes-yes? The Great-High King over all the land could assist you with that—"

"Negative. Explanation: Now that this unit's capabilities have been sufficiently upgraded to move freely within the operational area, primary directive success probability has returned to acceptable levels. This unit will resume the primary directive."

Lilussees tilted her head.

"Primary directive? Like, what do you mean?"

"Answer: It is this unit's current mission to locate persons of interest and provide assistance."

Lilussees rubbed a leg across her mandibles.

"Wait, so, like, you're working for someone?"

"Affirmative."

Rattingtale and Lilussees glanced at each other. Lilussees shrugged with her two front legs.

"Eh. Well, whatever. Guess it doesn't matter much to me. As long as they don't kick me out or worse, like, make me work. So, like, I'm going to take a nap or something."

With that, Lilussees returned to the Monster Hangar.

Meanwhile, Rattingtale was trembling.

This weird dungeon master man-thing . . . was not alone?

In fact . . . she wasn't even in charge?

The Great-High King decided he needed to review his plans for the seventh time that day.

And so, NSLICE-00P and the subordinate units began traveling, the cyborg scanning for any signs of civilization . . .

In a small village on the rainy frontier, a teenage boy stumbled home. He had two canine ears on the top of his head that drooped down as he rubbed the bruise on his cheek. He winced. Not from the pain, he was used to that. But a bruise that apparent would be . . . hard to explain.

He stilled his breath, and then pushed open the door. He hoped he could slip in quietly.

"Taog, is that you?"

He heaved a sigh. But he knew this would happen. Ateia's hearing was too good for that—she wouldn't have been able to solo hunt otherwise.

A teenage girl the same age as him, though fully human, approached from the living room. She wore hunter's garb, with a bow slung over her back and a large dagger tied to her thigh. She had her blonde hair up in a ponytail. She gave him a wide and bright smile that froze as she caught sight of his face.

"Taog . . .did something happen?"

He shook his head.

"I just tripped."

For a brief moment, he thought he saw her eyes quiver. But he rubbed his eyes and her expression hadn't changed. Ateia's smile then dropped slightly, and she nodded her head.

"Well, be careful. I'm, uh, about to go on a hunt."

Taog raised an eyebrow.

"At this time of day? It's also raining, you know."

Ateia shrugged. "It's always raining."

Taog nodded at that. "Fair enough. Well, give me a moment to grab my stuff."

Ateia shook her head. "No, you just got back, you should go dry off."

Taog's eyes narrowed. "Ateia, it's dangerous to go alone, you know that."

Ateia gave a small smirk. "I'll be fine! We've both done it before, you know."

Taog crossed his arms. "Yeah, when we were young and dumb. Now we know better. And I heard there's bandits in the area recently."

Ateia frowned and took a deep breath.

" . . . look, Taog. You got hurt once today when you tripped. Please, just rest for now, and let me get something for us. It's the least I can do."

Taog opened his mouth to object when he caught it—a slight murmur in Ateia's eyes. He closed his mouth.

"Okay. Just, stay safe out there."

Ateia nodded.

"I will."

A moment later, she walked out the door. Taog heaved another sigh.

They had just returned to the village recently and Ateia . . . hadn't been the same. Sure, his childhood friend still acted normal, still gave him the same smile she always did, but she was increasingly going on solo hunting trips, she was making less and less trips to the market, and then there were moments like this. Moments that filled him with unease.

But . . . if he wanted to push her on that, she would likely push him on the nature of his injuries in turn. And he wasn't going to let that fall on her.

So neither of them said anything.

Taog sighed and wrapped himself in his wet cloak. He couldn't help it. He was worried about Ateia. So he'd follow her at a safe distance, just to make sure she made it back ok.

He stepped out into the rain once more.

* * *

Ateia quickly made her way out of the village. She wrapped her cloak around her face and ignored the villagers calling out to her. The last thing she wanted was to talk to them.

Once she was outside of the village, she broke into a run, and didn't stop until she was in the forest.

Then she collapsed to her knees.

She couldn't do this anymore.

She put on a smile. She played dumb. But she knew the truth.

The village hated Taog. They couldn't see anything but one of the hated Wulver when they looked at him. Nevermind that he was half human and had grown up as Imperial as the rest of them. Nevermind that his Wulver mother left her clan and died defending these people from a monster wave. No, when stupid Lar and his thugs wanted to beat the child of their saviors, they not only let it happen, but half of them even approved! And the few that did not were too cowardly to speak up.

Ateia hated them all.

But she bore it with a grin and played the cheerful girl everyone loved. Right now, the townsfolk's "love" for her was the only thing holding back their hate for the Wulver. They'd likely have run Taog out of town by now if she hadn't made it clear she'd go with him. Those who did quietly support him wouldn't be enough to stop it.

So she put on a smile, such that they would tolerate Taog whenever they knew she was listening. The more she smiled, the more they would restrain themselves, so smile she did.

And above all, her smile was what enabled Taog to carry on. So she had to keep smiling, for both of them.

It sickened her to smile at the people beating Taog behind her back. But she had been able to do it because it was *supposed* to be temporary. Once she and Taog came of age, they applied to become Exploratores, the scouts and defenders who traveled the Empire as they pleased. She and Taog planned to leave this place and find her missing father. She planned to follow in his footsteps, repair their broken family, and then defend the Empire together. And she would have left this place and these people behind for good.

But things didn't go as planned.

Ateia and Taog had failed the Exploratores test this very week. The Magister Exploratore rejected their application in no uncertain terms and sent them back to the village.

And now she and Taog were stuck in this place, with no way out. They had no connections, few resources, and fewer skills. They couldn't even join the Legion. She and Taog had spent their boons from the Aesdes on skills they thought would help them join the Exploratores, and the Legion had strict standards on available boons for aspiring comitatenses. If they tried to join, they'd be relegated to the limitanei, stuck as frontier guards for the rest of their lives.

And now she had to smile at people she hated, while Taog suffered, for potentially the rest of their lives.

And that was something she could not do. So when she saw the bruise Taog got from "tripping" this time, she very nearly broke on the spot.

Which is why she came here where she could be alone. Taog thought he was protecting her by not letting her in on what was going on. He was fixated on that idea, ever since his parents died and her father left. But it gave him the strength to endure, so she averted her eyes and gave him a smile.

If he saw her like this, if the truth came out, then it would all fall apart. She couldn't let anyone see this.

Alone in this place, she burst into sobs, her tears mixing with the rain.

14

First Contact

"The ideal recruit is as low level as possible, though there is no strict limit so long as they have not spent their boons. Physical stats should be at least in the double digits, 12 to 15 is preferred. No requirement on the magical stats but high values should be noted for later specialization. No skills are required. Any boons should be retained. A candidate with a single digit number of available perk points is generally only fit for the limitanei."

—Legion Recruiting Manual

Taog hung back in the woods at a distance. Ateia could hear him open the front door of the house, but moving through the forest in the rain gave him much better cover. And fortunately, his Wulver heritage wasn't merely cosmetic. His senses were better than the average human—especially his sense of smell, and he had known Ateia since they were children. He could follow her scent, even in the rain like this.

He kept his distance, though. Ateia didn't want him with her right now for some reason, and he would respect that. So he halted when her scent started getting stronger, as she had apparently stopped moving.

But then, his nose twitched.

He caught another scent . . . several other scents. And they were coming from the same direction as Ateia.

Taog got up and sprinted forward, ignoring the branches and bushes whacking into his face and limbs. He eventually burst through the bushes, seeing Ateia kneeling on the ground.

"Ateia!"

Ateia jumped.

"T-Taog? What are you doing here?!"

Taog growled and stepped in front of Ateia. It seemed he had arrived too late.

A handful of burly men stepped out from behind the trees, taking up positions around the two teens.

"Well, well, well, what do we have here?"

Taog snarled in response and took out a short sword and shield.

NSLICE-00P continued to walk through the forest, terminating the occasional monster or, more often now, incapacitating it so Lilussees and Rattingtale could do it instead.

Until finally, she came across something.

A road. Well, a dirt trail, really. One that had almost turned to mud in the rain.

But . . . it was the first sign of civilization she had encountered since arriving in this place. She was finally making some progress toward her mission objective.

And so, she made her way along the road, continuing to head downhill, until her sensors started to read mana and thermal signatures. And then her audio sensors began picking up voices.

Lilussees and Rattingtale were resting on her shoulder when Rattingtale started to sniff at the air. He hissed. "I smell man-flesh, yes-yes!"

"I mean, like, even if the boss does kind of smell, you, like, shouldn't say that or something."

NSLICE-00P double-checked the diagnostics on her organic components, but her sterilization protocols were still in place. In fact, her dungeon components were now absorbing organic waste and foreign debris by some mana-driven process she didn't fully understand, so if anything, she should have superior hygiene to the standard organic.

"Objection: Sterilization protocols are reporting maximum efficiency. Please identify source of chemical signals."

"I mean *other* man-flesh, yes-yes!"

"Acknowledgement: Yes, this unit has detected several signals indicative of human activity and is moving to investigate."

"Wait-wait, you're moving-traveling *toward* the man-things?!"

"Affirmative."

"Sweet. Like, I always wanted to try man-flesh or something."

"Clarification: This unit has not identified any targets scheduled for termination."

Lilussees tilted her head.

"But, like, isn't that the point? What else would you do with them?"

"Yes-yes, man-things are to be killed-slayed or fled from!"

"Explanation: This unit is searching for designated persons of interest and needs to determine current location. Unaligned units may be able to provide relevant intel."

"Okay, but then, like, after?"

"Answer: Afterward, this unit will have no further reason to interact with unaligned units."

"You, like, don't want the experience?"

"Requesting Elaboration: Terminating humans provides experience?"

"Yes-yes."

"Like, they provide more experience for us? Something, like, they have something monsters like, and like, vice versa or something?"

"Acknowledged. Adding intel to database. Analyzing. Analysis complete. Explanation: Engaging with nonhostile humans still calculated as counterproductive to current mission due to the risk of triggering larger-scale conflict and targeted retaliation. Human termination currently limited to self-defense and mission-relevant targets."

"Aw."

"Man-things are violent-destructive, yes-yes. You should avoid-evade them, yes-yes."

With that, NSLICE-00P caught sight of the humans. Rattingtale and Lilussees both climbed into empty compartments, peeking out to watch what would occur. Or to run, if things went badly.

There was a large group of adult males surrounding two adolescents, one male and one female. Interestingly, the adolescent male had some canine features, while one of the adults appeared as a humanoid wolf of some sort. NSLICE-00P wanted to run scans on their physiology, but there was a problem: both parties were armed and pointing weapons at each other.

"Observation: It appears there is an altercation in progress. This unit's protocols advise against involvement in third-party conflicts. Proceeding with primary directive."

And so, NSLICE-00P ignored the group and continued walking down the road.

There was another problem, however. NSLICE-00P had been built as an enforcer, not an infiltrator. She had some stealth protocols, but these were limited to covert operations. She was not currently conducting a covert operation, and so saw no reason to use what stealth protocols she had. In other words . . . NSLICE-00P walked right past the group.

She may have intended to ignore them, but it appeared they did not intend to ignore her.

The adolescent female caught sight of her first.

"Huh? Some sort of knight? You, there! Please help us!"

The whole group turned to look at NSLICE-00P, who continued walking. However, one of the adult males stepped in front of her.

"Well, well, well, what do we have here?"

She ignored and walked around him. He grabbed her shoulder.

"Hey! I'm talking to you?"

She turned around to face him.

"Statement: This unit has no business with unaligned parties. Do you have business with this unit? If not, please stand down and allow this unit to proceed with the primary directive."

"What? What are you on about, girl?" He grinned at her. "Of course you have business with us. You're walking through our territory, you know? Haven't even paid the toll. In fact, that's some nice armor you got there. And is that a mana core in the center?"

"Acknowledgement: This unit was unaware of local protocols or authorities. Please provide proof of legal authorization and explain local protocol."

"Huh? That's . . ."

"Statement: Potential authority seems to be confused. If you cannot provide legal authorization, this unit cannot comply with any requests."

NSLICE-00P turned to leave once more. A vein bulged on the man's forehead. He nodded at two of his comrades, who stepped in front of the cyborg, hefting their weapons.

"You don't seem to understand what's going on here, girlie. Now, hand over the armor before someone gets hurt."

NSLICE-00P turned to face the speaker once more.

"Query: Are you threatening this unit?"

One of the man's eyes twitched.

"Okay, wow, you're a bit slow, aren't you? You know what? Sod it. Yes. Yes, we're threatening you. Now get over here if you know what's good for you."

Suddenly, NSLICE-00P's helmet deployed, covering her face. Her eyes began to glow red. She raised her hands, one transforming into a gun barrel, the other lighting up with power from her core.

"Warning: Please stand down. This unit will respond to hostile intent with immediate termination."

"All right. I've had enough. Do it."

One of the men had walked up behind NSLICE-00P with a club and was now swinging it toward her head. A magic circle formed, and a Mana Barrier appeared in the path of the club, which struck the barrier and stopped dead, the man dropping the weapon from the shock.

"Hostile intent detected. Engaging termination protocols."

She turned around and opened fire at the attacker with her machine gun.

The man cried out and fell to the ground, his clothes growing red in several places.

You have slain Human (Level 15)!
Gained 16 Personal XP, 13 Dungeon XP!

The speaker cursed and ducked to the side. "Kill her!"

Several of the men charged at her. She lifted her machine gun, mowing them down.

You have slain Human (Level 12)!
Gained 11 Personal XP, 10 Dungeon XP!
You have slain Wulver (Level 10)!
Gained 10 Personal XP, 8 Dungeon XP!

Several more ran up behind her, but a magic circle formed, blasting them with a jet of flame. They screamed as they rolled on the ground.

You have slain Human (Level 12)!
Gained 11 Personal XP, 10 Dungeon XP!
You have slain Human (Level 16)!
Gained 17 Personal XP, 14 Dungeon XP!
You have slain Human (Level 11)!
Gained 10 Personal XP, 10 Dungeon XP!

One of the men raised a staff, stuttering on his words as he started to chant. A magic circle formed in the air out of flickering light. Once the man managed to complete the spell, a ball of fire soared through the air.

"Hostile spell detected. Equalizer engaged."

NSLICE-00P lifted her free hand, firing a beam of rainbow light at the spell. The fireball flickered and vanished as the beam passed through it. It continued on to strike the mage, disrupting the next circle he was forming.

NSLICE-00P then turned her machine gun on him and opened fire.

You have slain Human (Level 14)!
Gained 14 Personal XP, 11 Dungeon XP!
Level up! Your Personal Level is now 12!
Level up! Your Dungeon Level is now 14!

NSLICE-00P scanned the field before boosting over to a nearby tree. The man who had spoken to her first was trembling behind it. She lifted her hand, light glowing along her arm.

"Wait—!"

She fired a beam of light.

You have slain Human (Level 23)!
Gained 26 Personal XP, 23 Dungeon XP!

"Scanning . . . no further signatures detected. All hostiles terminated."

With that, NSLICE-00P deactivated combat mode, her helmet disengaging and her machine gun turning back into a hand. She stepped back onto the road and turned toward the two adolescents, who were staring with eyes wide open. They shrieked and trembled as she began to approach them.

15

Help Me, NSLICE-00P. You're My Only Hope!

"When making first contact with a new civilization, your subordinates must always take the confident approach. If they respond with violence, we will gain a casus belli to send in the Legion."

—Empress Camillia,
in private conversations with her advisors.

Ateia and Taog shrieked and trembled as the wandering knight approached them.

"P-Please don't hurt us . . ."

The armored girl had a heterochromatic eye which appeared to be made of metal. That eye began to glow. Ateia and Taog closed their eyes and hugged one another, gritting their teeth.

"Query: Do you possess any intel regarding the displayed persons of interest?"

Ateia and Taog froze. They gingerly opened their eyes.

Light was shining from the wandering knight's eye, forming some sort of illusion in the air. On it were a number of faces, starting with an average-looking, nondescript man, a dark-skinned woman, and one of the most beautiful women Ateia and Taog had ever seen. The list went on for a bit before ending with two groups of teenagers roughly the same age as the pair.

However, none of them looked familiar, and their clothing was strange, not matching any culture the two had ever encountered.

They shook their heads. The glow faded from the wandering knight's eye, the illusion fading with it. The armored girl instead pointed down the road.

"Acknowledged. Query: Is this the direction of the nearest settlement?"

The two silently nodded their heads, still not daring to speak.

"Acknowledged. Gratitude: This unit thanks you for your cooperation."

And with that, the wandering knight turned away and started walking.

Ateia and Taog glanced at one another. They both exhaled their breaths and fell to the ground, just staring up at the sky for a moment. Atea closed her eyes, trying to hold back her tears, then gritted her teeth and furrowed her brow. Could this get any worse?

Running into bandits, getting Taog caught up in it. It seemed she couldn't even take a moment to gather herself without some terrible thing occurring. It was like the world wanted to break her.

And break she would. She couldn't go off alone, not anymore. So she would break in front of Taog. She would lose the smile that enabled him to endure. They both would break.

Taog looked over at her with concern.

"Ateia?"

She squeezed her eyes tighter.

"Please, give me a moment, Taog. Please."

Taog frowned for a moment, then took a deep breath.

"This was bad, but we made it out, right?"

Ateia didn't respond. Taog grimaced.

"Look, maybe there's another option for the Exploratores too? Maybe we could find some help, like put out a request for assistance hunting, find an Exploratore to work with? Then maybe we can show them what we're capable of, get a recommendation?"

Ateia shook her head. That was one of the first things they had tried even before the entrance exam. But no Exploratore was willing to help a couple of kids play in the forest, or so the last one they met had said. And since the Magister Exploratore had already failed them, even the testimony of one Exploratore wouldn't be enough.

They didn't have anyone who could help them.

Suddenly Ateia's eyes shot open and she sat up. Taog blinked at the sudden movement.

"Ateia, what is it?"

She rubbed her chin.

"I just thought of something. Exploratores application procedure says anyone with the Dungeon Conqueror trait can immediately become an Exploratore, right?"

Taog raised an eyebrow.

"Yes, but that's irrelevant, Ateia. We couldn't even pass the Exploratores entrance exam. How on Aelea are we going to conquer a dungeon?"

Ateia nodded.

"Right, it would be impossible for us. We would need help. Help from someone incredibly powerful. A veteran Exploratore . . . or an expert knight."

Taog tilted his head before his eyes widened. He glanced down the road, and then glanced at Ateia.

"Ateia, no."

She started to grin.

"Ateia, yes!"

"Ateia, did you see what she just did?!"

Ateia's grin grew. "Oh, did I ever."

Taog groaned and slapped his palm on his forehead.

"Ateia, how many times do we have to have this talk? Do NOT go bothering people who can kill you whom you know nothing about!"

She shrugged. "We know she's strong and that she helped us."

"She didn't help us! That stupid bandit just picked a fight with her, and she retaliated!"

"You don't know that."

Taog narrowed his eyes at her. "Um, I kind of do? It was pretty clear she was just going to ignore us until then?"

Ateia just shrugged again.

"Then we'll give her a reason to help us!"

"Like what, exactly? How are you going to convince someone you know *nothing* about?"

Ateia tilted her head and placed a finger on her chin for a moment, then grinned and shrugged.

"You won't know until you try! Facing the unknown is just what an Exploratore does!"

"Um, no. An Exploratore specifically does as much recon gathering and preparation as they can before they step even a single foot into the unknown."

Ateia stood up. Taog jumped up as well, grabbing her arm.

"Let me go!"

"Ateia, no!"

She whirled around. Taog had just opened his mouth when he saw it—the slight quiver and moisture building in her eyes; the trembling in her body.

"Taog . . . this could be our last chance. Our only chance. Please."

He frowned and looked down, his grip loosening for a second as he thought of what to say.

And a second was all Ateia needed as she jumped forward, shaking him off. "Ah, enough of this! She's getting away!"

"Hey, wait, Ateia!"

But Ateia had already started running down the road.

"EXCUSE ME!"

Maybe it was foolish. Maybe Ateia was grasping at straws. But if there was any chance to change their lives, if there was any chance to get out of this place and find her father, Ateia would take it. Her heart could not endure unless she did.

Two panels cracked open as NSLICE-00P continued on her way.

"Boss, boss, you aren't going to finish them?"

"Negative."

"Aw, why not?"

"Yes-yes, leaving-sparing witnesses is bad! They could betray-cross you and bring enemies to hunt-slay us, yes-yes!"

"Answer: Surviving units were at odds with terminated units, and so unlikely to retaliate to termination of hostiles. Risk factor proposed by friendly Excellion Formantus Rattingtale the Third calculated as minimal, and less than risk factor of retaliation due to unprovoked termination."

"Aw. I wanted to try the man-flesh."

"I don't like this, no-no."

Just then, a shout cut through the air.

"EXCUSE ME!"

NSLICE-00P turned around. One of the survivors had run after her; the female human, from the looks of it. NSLICE-00P waited as she arrived.

"Query: Do you have business with this unit?"

The girl nodded.

"Please help us!"

"Negative Response: This unit is not available for requests by third parties. Proceeding with primary directive."

The girl reached out as NSLICE-00P turned to leave. She shook her head and ran in front of the cyborg. "Sorry, I meant I'll pay you, so please!"

"Negative Response: The benefit of monetary compensation not predicted to outweigh the loss of time spent on primary objective."

The girl tilted her head.

"Um . . . so . . . you don't need money, is what you're saying?"

"Affirmative. Firm Request: Please stand down and allow this unit to proceed with primary directive."

"T-Then, I can give you something else! What do you want? Potions? Armor? Just tell me, and it's yours!" The girl gritted her teeth and looked down, but still did not move from in front of NSLICE-00P. The cyborg was about to move around her . . . or else force her out of the way, when the other survivor joined the group, groaning and shaking his head.

He walked forward and pulled the girl aside. He started whispering to her. Of course, he didn't seem aware that said measure was woefully insufficient to counteract NSLICE-00P's advanced audio sensors, but that was not something the cyborg felt she needed to inform them of. As they spoke, her panels popped open again, her own friendlies giving her whispers of their own.

"Look, look, they're like, bothering you or something. So like, you're going to take them out now, right?"

"Yes-yes, kill-slay the man-things, quickly!"

NSLICE-00P ignored them and focused on the other conversation.

The girl glared at the boy.

"What are you doing? She's going to get away!"

The boy glared right back.

"What are YOU doing? She's going to attack you at this rate!"

The girl crossed her arms.

"No, she's not!"

The boy heaved a sigh.

"Look, I'm not telling you to stop. I'm telling you to *think*, Ateia! What did I say about gathering intel and preparing?"

"What intel can we even gather now?!"

The boy groaned. "*Plenty*. She said she doesn't need money, right? But she already told us what she *does* need."

"And what is that?"

The boy sighed again. "She told us herself. She's *looking for someone*."

"And what does that—" The girl froze. "Oh . . . Oh, I see."

The boy just heaved another sigh, shaking his head. The girl hopped back over to NSLICE-00P.

"You're looking for someone, right?"

"Affirmative."

"If you help us, we can help you find them!"

"Requesting Elaboration: Please explain how third-party units will assist this unit when they have already stated they possess no intel regarding the persons of interest."

The girl crossed her arms and grinned.

"That's simple! We're trying to become Exploratores! So help us get in, and then we can help you find your missing people!"

"Requesting Elaboration: Please define role: Exploratore, and why said role would assist in this unit's current mission."

The girl froze, blinking repeatedly.

"What? You, um, don't know what an Exploratore is? The guardians of the frontier? The explorers of the unknown? The first line of defense for the Empire and its people? The ones who solve problems wherever they are?"

"Negative. Speculation: From the aforementioned description, it appears to be some sort of military or law enforcement title."

The girl tilted her head.

"How . . . how is that possible? *Everyone* knows what an Exploratore is!"

The boy stepped forward, shaking his head.

"Not everyone."

"Oh, right. B-But everyone in the Empire does!"

The boy slapped his palm on his face and pointed at NSLICE-00P.

"And is *she* from the Empire?"

"Oh, um, are you from the Empire?"

"Requesting Elaboration: Please identify faction 'Empire.'"

This time, both the boy and girl froze.

"You . . . haven't heard of the Empire?"

The boy leaned into the girl. "Look, this is getting really fishy. If she's someone who hasn't even heard of the Empire . . . I'm starting to get a bad feeling about this."

"No, that just means we have a lot more to offer!" The girl turned back to NSLICE-00P. "Okay, so, um, looks like you're not from around here? So, help us out, and we can teach you a thing or two? And then, when we become Exploratores, we can help you with your mission!"

NSLICE-00P's robotic eye flickered and spun around. The pair both took a step back at that.

"Um . . ."

It was true she was not aware of her current location, much less the situation around her. In fact, the present geography didn't match any location in her memory, and the modern nations she had records on did not refer to themselves as "the Empire." Additional intel about local conditions and legal customs would, in fact, be useful to her current mission, assuming she could trust this pair. And if she managed to determine her present location, she might be able to reestablish contact with friendly forces, or at least chart an efficient search pattern for the persons of interest. Body language analysis indicated a high chance they were being truthful with her.

Under the assumption of independent action, establishing local contacts might indeed be worthwhile.

Depending on what they asked her to do, that is.

"Analysis complete. Query: Please explain mission parameters."

The two glanced at each other. The boy shrugged. The girl tilted her head as she turned back to the cyborg.

"Are you . . . asking what we want you to do?"

"Affirmative."

The girl smiled . . . then frowned, biting her lip and fidgeting. The boy sighed.

"Tell her the truth."

The girl took a deep breath.

"We . . . need help finding . . . and conquering . . . a dungeon. Um, I know it's a lot to ask, and it's really dangerous, but, um, it's really important to us! And we're hoping that there are some new dungeons in the area, so they should be a lot weaker than—"

"Analysis complete. Task difficulty determined as substantially below potential benefits."

"Huh? What was that?"

"Statement: This unit is willing to assist. Counterpoint: However, this unit does require assurances."

In that moment, NSLICE-00P activated a dungeon skill for the first time. She didn't truly understand what the Contract skill meant, but she predicted a mana-driven contract would at least provide equal or greater assurance as a legal one.

Two documents formed of light appeared in front of the pair.

"Explanation: This unit has a Contract skill. This unit will assist signees with locating and terminating a single dungeon. This unit bears the right to determine which dungeon and to prioritize unit safety, but otherwise will undertake all reasonable effort to ensure mission success and signee survival. The signees shall provide this unit with full, comprehensive, and accurate intelligence regarding current location and local conditions to the maximum extent they are able. If and when the signees achieve the rank/role of 'Exploratore' or any similar roles or rewards as a result of the assisted dungeon conquest, they will utilize the privileges and resources of said roles and rewards to assist this unit with locating persons of interest."

Ateia raised an eyebrow. "Um, so if I have this straight . . . this is a magic contract? That's . . . that's intense. I think we should talk about this a bit more."

Ateia paused. A magic contract. There were many tales of magic contracts, and few of them good. And the moral of all of them was never sign one without a full and complete understanding of what it entailed—and even then think carefully, for one cannot change their mind once their name is on a magical page. Ateia didn't fully understand what the knight was saying, much less the full terms of the contract, so signing now would be incredibly foolish.

But she did know something—that the knight was offering to help. She had found a chance. One risky, uncertain opportunity to change her and Taog's bleak future, based entirely on trusting a strange knight who wiped out a bandit crew without hesitation. But it was the only chance she had, and one with a benefactor who had the kind of power she lacked.

Her options were either trust this strange knight, or go back to her current life, possibly for good.

She made her choice. She wasn't going to let this chance slip by. So she took a deep breath and said, "Um, I don't get it, but, if I sign this, you'll help us, right?"

"Affirmative."

"Done!"

"Wait, Ateia!" Taog shouted.

But it was too late; she had signed the contract. The document vanished in a flash of light.

Taog groaned and slapped his head. "Ateia, you idiot."

He heaved a sigh. "Guess I don't have a choice now." He went ahead and signed it.

Contract signed! Ateia Niraemia (Human - Level 8) added as a temporary subordinate. Restrictions applied per contract stipulations.

Contract signed! Taog Sutharlan (Human/Wulver - Level 7) added as a temporary subordinate. Restrictions applied per contract stipulations.

NSLICE-00P turned around and started walking back the way she'd come.

"Contract established. Ateia Niraemia and Taog Sutharlan designated as temporary friendlies. New mission accepted. Mission parameters set. Setting target: Dungeon. Activating search-and-destroy protocols."

And so, NSLICE-00P began to search for another dungeon with her two new allies in tow.

While her other two allies waited in empty compartments . . .

"So, are we like, trapped here until they go to sleep or something? That's, like, kind of lame. This place is so not comfy. And, like, we have to work with humans or something? That's, like, super weird. Are you sure you can't, like, kill them or something, boss?"

"You dumb man-thing! You forgot-ignored us, didn't you?! Now the vicious man-things are watching you, and we can't run-escape, yes-yes! They can't be trusted. They will betray-cross us, yes-yes! You should kill-slay them while you have the chance, yes-yes!"

. . . Much to their consternation.

16

Carrying the Noobs . . . err "Valued Allies"

"Why can't the knights escort you through the dungeon? You idiot! There is no such thing as a safe dungeon run! Dungeons are full of twisting turns and secret entrances, monsters that spawn in from any angle, traps which may have a delayed activation, sliding walls to separate groups, and more methods of death than you can imagine. Anyone who steps into a dungeon must be prepared to defend themselves, no matter who they are or who travels with them. If you step into the dungeon hiding behind the coattails of a knight, you're practically begging the dungeon master to target you as the weak link."

—Consul Arruns Titinius Macrinus,
admonishing his son before a scheduled training session.

Taog heaved a sigh. Oh, he would have *words* with Ateia about impulsively signing what was clearly a *magic contract* with someone they knew practically nothing about. But nothing more could be done at this point. They were committed, like it or not. He could only hope that this would end well.

Ateia, meanwhile, was all grins, hoisting her pack on her shoulders. She seemed completely back to her old self, it was as if her previous malaise had never existed. Taog shook his head.

Ateia began walking down the road toward the forest. "Well then, let's get going!"

"Request: Please wait one moment. Scan of surrounding area in progress."

Ateia glanced at Taog. He just shook his head and sighed. To be honest, he didn't understand half of what this girl said. Which made sense, seeing as she must be from somewhere extraordinarily far away if she hadn't even heard of the *Empire* of all things.

"Scan complete. Target located. Query: New friendlies, please provide desired designations."

Ateia tilted her head. "Um, designations? Do you mean . . . our names?"

"Affirmative."

Taog couldn't help but smack his forehead. They had signed a magic contract with this person . . . before they had even *exchanged names*. He felt increasingly pessimistic about their chances.

"Oh, I'm Ateia, and this is Taog. Nice to meet you." Ateia extended her hand, and the wandering knight grabbed and shook it.

"Greeting: Affirmative. Friendlies designated 'Ateia' and 'Taog.' This unit is designated NSLICE-00P. It is nice to meet you."

"En . . . slice? Seero Seero Pee? Um . . ." Ateia leaned over to him. "Taog, have you heard of a name like that before?"

"Don't ask me, you know as much as I do about foreigners," he said.

"Query: Are friendlies Ateia and Taog capable of flight?"

Ateia tilted her head.

"What? Flight? As in, flying?"

"Affirmative."

The pair glanced at each other once again.

"Um, no?"

"Acknowledged. Adapting travel method."

NSLICE-00P walked behind the pair. Magic circles formed at their feet, forming spherical Mana Barriers around the two.

"Um, Enslice Seero Seero Pee? What are you doing?"

"Recommendation: Please prepare for transit."

"What do you *meaaaaaannnnnnn?!*"

With that, NSLICE-00P activated her repulsors and shot into the air, the two spheres carrying Ateia and Taog with her.

"Request: This unit asks that friendlies Ateia and Taog cease screaming. Excessive noise increases risk of notice by hostiles."

They were not, in fact, prepared for transit.

Taog clutched the ground with all his might, struggling to keep his breakfast down. Ateia fell onto her butt, staring at NSLICE-00P with wide eyes.

"That . . . That . . ." Suddenly, she jumped up. "That was incredible! Can we do that again sometime?"

Taog finished coughing and glared at the two girls with a groan. "*Never* do that again!"

"Negative Response: This unit cannot comply with that request, as flight is considered as a necessary capability for this unit."

Taog just groaned and tried to stand on his trembling legs. Ateia helped him steady himself as he took several deep breaths before he looked around and his eyes widened. They were standing in front of a huge tree with a large black hole at the bottom, big enough for them to walk into. Yet, the hole was pitch black despite the sun shining on it, and they couldn't see what was inside.

"It's . . . a dungeon."

"Affirmative. Query: Are friendlies Ateia and Taog ready for operation start?"

Ateia and Taog glanced at one another and nodded. They double-checked their potions and made sure everything they could need was easily accessible. Then Ateia took out her bow while Taog drew a sword and shield. They both took a deep breath, nodded at each other once more, and turned to NSLICE-00P.

"Ready."

"Acknowledged. Engaging dungeon termination protocols."

And then, the three made their way inside, braving the depths of a terrifying labyrinth of death . . .

"Hey, Taog . . ."

"Yes, Ateia?"

"So . . . dungeons are supposed to be super dangerous labyrinths of death, right?"

"That's what everyone says."

"And even the youngest dungeon is supposed to be super dangerous, even for a veteran, right?"

"That point was especially emphasized, in fact."

"And under no circumstances is a noncombatant to enter a dungeon, right? Since between traps and monster ambushes, even a high-level bodyguard may not be able to guarantee their safety, right?"

"Again, so I'm told."

"So, um . . . do you know what, exactly, is going on right now?"

". . . Not a clue."

Ateia and Taog floated through the air, surrounded by spherical Mana Barriers. Spiky vines twisted and turned all around, spikes shot out at them, small trees with humanoid form began walking and lashing out at their forms.

And yet, not one attack made it past the barriers.

The spell Mana Barrier is now Level 5!

Meanwhile, NSLICE-00P was burning the deathly forest with jets of flame launching from both her arms, as well as the magic circles all around her.

The spell Fire Blast is now Level 6!
The skill Fire Magic is now Level 5!

This . . . was not how they imagined a dungeon exploration to go.

"Knights are kind of amazing, huh?"

Taog shook his head. "I . . . don't think normal knights are supposed to do stuff like this, though."

They watched as NSLICE-00P stopped walking and aimed her inferno at the ground in front of her. Vines covered in flames shot out of a concealed pit trap, writhing about as they burned.

The skill Presence Detection is now Level 4!
The skill Trap Detection is now Level 4!

"Oh, she found another one."

"Looks that way."

"And she just turned left immediately. No hesitation."

"Maybe she has some sort of skill?"

"Hey, um, Enslice Seero Seero Pee? Do you even know where you're going?"

"Affirmative."

"Um, how?"

"Explanation: This unit is tracking the mana signature indicative of a dungeon core and comparing it to the internal structure map developed via ground-penetrating radar in order to map the most efficient route."

"Oh, right. Of course." Ateia turned back to him. "Do you have any idea what any of that means?"

Taog just shrugged.

Well, whatever this was that was going on in front of him, it still beat how he had expected this trip to go.

In what Ateia and Taog were certain was a record of some kind, NSLICE-00P brought them to the center of the dungeon.

"Warning: This dungeon is about to be terminated. Recommending dungeon master surrender—" A large tree shrieked at her, launching spikes the size of logs at the group. "Negative response acknowledged. Engaging termination protocols."

NSLICE-00P began evading the blows, taking to the skies. Once again, several jets of flame filled the air, dousing the entire tree in a raging inferno. The creature shrieked and screamed and lashed about.

But not for long.

You have slain Tree Dungeon Master (Level 11)!
Gained 10 Personal XP, 8 Dungeon XP!
Level up! Your Personal Level is now 13!
Level up! Your Dungeon Level is now 15!
You have conquered the Nature's Wrath dungeon!
You have accomplished the Personal Feat: Dungeon Conqueror (Nature's Wrath)!

Personal Feats		
Name	Description	Effect
Dungeon Conqueror (Nature's Wrath)	Unlocked by conquering the Nature's Wrath Dungeon.	+1 Perk Point +1 level in Nature Magic skill

NSLICE-00P then shattered the dungeon core with a Mana Beam, and the whole group found themselves outside once again.

Ateia tilted her head.

"She just smashed the core? Aren't those really valuable?"

Taog frowned.

"They are. She wouldn't do that . . . unless she's from some order with a code about it? I don't know, I have more and more questions about this."

You have absorbed a dungeon core (Nature's Wrath)!
Gained 6 Personal Perk Points, 6 Dungeon Perk Points!
Gained Dungeon Affinity: Nature (Minimum)!

"Mission Report: Mission accomplished. Dungeon has been terminated."

Ateia and Taog glanced at each other.

"That was . . . much different than I imagined it would be."

". . . Same here."

"Well . . . all's well that ends well? I mean, it's good that it was easy, right?"

Taog froze. "Ateia . . ."

He just remembered something crucial. Something that all his instructors—whether they were his parents, Ateia's father, or the Exploratores examiners—had repeatedly stressed.

There's no such thing as a free level.

"Taog, I don't like the sound of that. I know that look."

"Did you . . . receive the message? Or the Dungeon Conqueror feat?"

Ateia froze. Her eyes widened. She started to tremble.

"No . . . I didn't. How could this be . . . ?"

Taog grunted and held his head. "Everyone always told us a feat only matters if you actually contribute, right? The Aesdes can't be deceived. They only reward those who deserve it."

Ateia went silent, her trembling growing stronger.

Taog took a deep breath. "So, if we didn't do anything . . ."

". . . No . . ."

"Then, it doesn't count as us conquering the dungeon . . . does it?"

Ateia fell to the ground. She spoke in a soft voice, practically a whisper, "So we have to find and conquer another dungeon, don't we?"

"Observation: Friendlies appear to be in distress. Is there a hostile in the area?"

The two turned to NSLICE-00P.

"W-Would you be willing . . . to do this over? Help us with a second dungeon?"

"Query: Why would this unit need to terminate a second dungeon?"

"T-That's, um . . ."

Taog took a deep breath and interjected, "Look, the deal was to *help us* conquer a dungeon, right?"

"Affirmative."

"Well, it seems you did too much of the work. Since we didn't contribute, it didn't count as *us* conquering the dungeon, so it didn't work, and we still need to conquer a dungeon on our own. At least partially . . . I think."

"Revelation: This unit was not aware of the contribution requirement. Mission status set to 'not complete.' Adjusting dungeon termination protocols with friendly contribution parameter. Scanning for new target."

The two teens glanced at each other and exhaled a sigh. Well, at least NSLICE-00P was still willing to help. Though Taog now had a million more questions on *who* exactly they had asked for help . . .

Meanwhile . . .

"Ugh. I'm like, trying to comfy this place up, but the boss is, like, moving around too much or something. Boss, can't you, like, hide for a second so we can, like, go back to our rooms or something?"

"Stop-cease complaining, yes-yes! I don't have any threads-silk at all!"

"Heh, I thought you were, like, a king or something? Why don't you, like, ask a subject to get something for you? Oh, like, that's right, you're the subject or something."

"Shut up! And it's Great-High King over all the land, yes-yes!"

17

The Valued Allies' First Dungeon Termination

"Ready for a dungeon, you say? Son, you aren't ready for anything. Sure, you know some spells, but do you have a map of the dungeon in question? Have you practiced drawing maps until you are certain you can do it with complete accuracy? Have you practiced making camp and setting up night watches in case you can't get out in a day? Do you even have a team to set watches with? Have you calculated the number of provisions you need to carry, including in the case where you get lost and can't get out immediately? Do you have the stamina to carry days' worth of food, water, medical supplies, and camping equipment, not to mention any specialized tools you'll need to overcome traps and environmental hazards? A dungeon exploration is not a battle, it's a war. And wars are won with a lot of boring math and studying."

—Retired Exploratore Caria Tiberina, convincing her son to apply for a magic academy instead of joining the Exploratores.

Ateia cheered and laughed as they rose into the air, once more flying over the forest.

"Repeated Request: This unit requests friendly Ateia cease screaming to avoid drawing attention from potential hostiles."

"Ah, sorry, sorry! It's just, this is really fun!"

Ateia took a breath and calmed herself down. Meanwhile, Taog had his eyes shut, muttering and praying to himself.

". . . For some people."

The group landed in front of another dungeon, this one a rocky cave they couldn't see into. After Taog managed to get his stomach back under control, the three huddled up.

"Okay, let's go over it one more time."

Ateia crossed her arms. "Oh, come on, Taog! We already discussed this!" He just stared at her. She started to fidget. "Okay, fine! Here's the plan. We want to make sure we get enough contributions this time. So, to do that, we'll try to do everything ourselves. Enslice Seero Seero Pee . . . Um, actually, Miss Enslice Seero Seero Pee?" Ateia glanced over, fidgeting slightly.

"Acknowledgement: Yes, does friendly Ateia have a query?"

"What is your first name? Or, like, do you have a nickname? I'm sorry, it's just a bit of a mouthful, you know? And I haven't heard of a name like yours, so I'm not sure how it works."

Taog stared at Ateia again.

"Ateia . . ."

"What?! Don't look at me like that, Taog! How am I supposed to know if I don't ask? And, like, if we're in a fight, we need to be quick!"

"Acknowledgement: Friendly Ateia's assessment is valid. Efficient call outs are necessary under combat conditions. Answer: NSLICE-00P is a full designation. This unit lacks a colloquial designation. However, NSLICE is the model name; 00P is the unique identifier. So friendly Ateia may consider that as equivalent to a given name."

"Um, then . . . how about Seero?"

"Acknowledgement: This unit will record 'Seero' as a valid colloquial designation."

"Okay, thanks. So, again, we'll try to do everything ourselves, and Seero will intervene if she thinks we're in trouble?"

"Affirmative. This unit will refrain from intervention unless the friendlies are at risk of termination or this unit is specifically targeted."

Taog nodded. "Which means we need to treat this as if she's not there and take every measure we would if we were alone. Got that?"

Ateia nodded. "You know I do, Taog. Look, I know I'm a bit impulsive, but this is a dungeon. I know how to be careful when I need to."

Taog raised an eyebrow. "And I'm the one who keeps patching you up when you get home." Ateia just averted her gaze. Taog heaved a sigh. "Well, whatever. That's why I'm here, after all."

The two went over their equipment setups once again, then discussed their formation. Eventually, once they had double- and triple-checked everything they could, they fell silent, looking at one another.

They slowly nodded and turned toward the dungeon. Ateia's eyes narrowed.

"Let's do this."

The two made their way inside. NSLICE-00P engaged her helmet and followed shortly behind them.

"Quick, like, now's our chance."

"Move out the way, wretched-evil spider-thing!"

The moment the two humanoid's backs were turned, the monsters scrambled out of NSLICE-00P's spare compartment, rushing into her Monster Hangar. They both let out deep sighs as they returned to the safety and comfort of their rooms.

Lilussees poked her head back out.

"So, I'm overdue for, like, five naps or something. So, like, don't wait for me, Boss Lady."

"Acknowledged."

The first thing Ateia did was pull out a Dungeon Map, an enchanted scroll that could be drawn on with mana rather than ink, allowing its user to easily write without carrying supplies, as well as to erase what they had written at will. An invaluable tool when mapping out a new dungeon . . . and an expensive one. But Ateia's father was an Exploratore, and Exploratores never skimped on things that could save their lives.

Well, the ones who actually survived, that is.

And a Dungeon Map was one of them. Far too many divers with dreams of profit and glory rushed into dungeons, only to find they didn't remember the way back. And leaving breadcrumbs was too unreliable; a stray monster or another adventurer might remove whatever was left behind. Dungeons had a way of making things disappear, especially things left unattended. So ultimately, there was no good replacement for drawing a good map.

. . . Highly accurate scans by ground-penetrating radar and mana-tracking sensors aside.

The pair walked slowly through the first hallway. Ateia's eyes darted every which way, taking in the floors, the walls, and the roof, looking for even a single rock out of place. Taog's nose and ears twitched every now and then.

Suddenly, he stopped.

"Ateia, get ready. There's something up ahead. Smells like an animal of some kind."

Ateia nodded and grabbed an arrow from her quiver, nocking it onto her bow, while Taog lifted his shield and gripped his sword. The two waited in silence, clenching their teeth.

And then . . . they heard it.

A low growl.

A wolf stepped toward them, saliva dripping from between its yellow fangs.

Species	Description
Mangy Wolf (Level 3)	**A basic wolf monster. Not that different from a regular wolf in appearance or capability, but significantly more aggressive.**

Taog glanced back. NSLICE-00P didn't respond to the threat. He glanced at Ateia, and she nodded back, lifting her bow. Taog turned back toward the wolf, eyes narrowed.

Ateia's bow glowed slightly as she drew it.

"Power Shot."

She let her arrow fly, striking the wolf right between the eyes. It let out a yelp and fell over, fading away and leaving behind a small magic core.

Ateia and Taog stared at it for a bit before turning to each other.

"I guess . . . we won?"

"Yeah, um, nice shot?"

Ateia started to grin. "Thanks. Looks like we can do this, after all."

Taog exhaled his breath.

"Recommendation: This unit has observed that initial encounters in dungeons are not representative of overall dungeon strength. This unit recommends continued vigilance."

Ateia dropped her grin, giving a serious look at that. She and Taog nodded.

And so, Ateia and Taog's dungeon conquest began.

They strode forward with a spring in their step. This wasn't exactly their first combat encounter with a monster, but this *was* their first battle in a dungeon, which meant an unknown situation with potentially lethal consequences. As such, they were quite relieved and more than a little proud to have overcome it so easily.

Taog motioned for Ateia to stop. He sniffed the air a few times and nodded at her. "Looks like there's something up ahead."

Ateia nocked another arrow and grinned at him. "Well, let's get hunting, then!"

Taog smiled wryly at her, then hoisted his shield and took a step forward.

And fell right into a pit trap.

"Taog!" Ateia rushed over to the edge of the pit, her eyes wide open.

And then she heaved a sigh of relief.

Taog was floating in midair, caught in a Mana Barrier. Behind them, NSLICE-00P had drawn a magic circle in the air just as the pair had started walking toward the trap. The Mana Barrier rose into the air, dropping Taog off back on the floor. He fell to the ground, sweat dripping from his brow. Ateia knelt down beside him.

"A-Are you all right?"

"I-I think so. Just give me a moment."

He took several deep breaths, then looked up at NSLICE-00P and nodded. "Thank you. You saved my life."

"Acknowledged. Recommendation: This unit has observed a universal deployment of pit traps within dungeons. Friendlies should pay close attention to the ground."

The pair quietly nodded at that.

* * *

Ateia and Taog were slowly walking through the next hallway, glancing every which way. Suddenly Ateia reached out and grabbed Taog's shoulder.

"Wait! Look over there!"

Taog nodded and narrowed his eyes, focusing on the spot where Ateia had pointed. And then, he saw it. A circular area on the floor which was a slightly different color from its surroundings.

"Nice catch, Ateia."

She nodded at him. He took a deep breath as he walked to the edge of the trap and crouched down. He then leapt over the pit—only for a panel to open up on the wall at the end of the hall, launching an arrow at him.

"Taog!"

Taog's eyes widened. He quickly thrust his arm forward, putting his shield between the arrow and his face, barely in the nick of time. The arrow deflected off the edge of his shield.

Of course, the sudden motion of raising his shield while landing had thrown off his balance, such that the force of the arrow knocking his shield away caused him to stumble back. And of course, taking a step back put his foot on the trap.

Taog screamed as he fell into the pit trap once again. NSLICE-00P caught him in a barrier once more.

"Query: Should this unit have warned friendlies about multilayered traps? This unit thought that would be a logically assumed escalation."

Taog grunted as he held his shield up, blocking the snarling wolf leaping toward him. His feet slid back from the force of the collision.

A second monster ran to his exposed side, about to pounce on him.

"Power Shot!"

A glowing arrow shot into the second wolf, taking it down. Taog then pushed back with his shield, knocking the first one away from him. The wolf quickly recovered and leapt toward him once more, now that his shield was out of the way.

But Taog used the momentum to twist his body and thrust his other arm forward, sword in hand, and the blade caught the monster right in the jaw. Taog then reset his position and scanned the area. He exhaled his breath as he confirmed there were no more wolves in the area.

"Taog, look!"

Ateia's shout drew his attention. He gasped as well.

To the side of the hallway was a small door leading to a circular chamber. And dead center in the room was a wooden chest.

Ateia grinned at him.

"Are we lucky or what? A treasure chest on our first run!"

NSLICE-00P observed the room.

"Requesting Elaboration: Why is the discovery of a storage container cause for celebration?"

Ateia and Taog froze and glanced at each other. Ateia turned to the cyborg and tilted her head. "Wait, you don't know about treasure chests?"

"Negative."

"But haven't you conquered dungeons already?"

"Affirmative."

"And you haven't encountered any treasure chests while doing so?"

"Answer: This unit has encountered storage containers but ignored them as non-mission relevant."

"Wait, then why were you going into dungeons in the first place?"

"Answer: To terminate them."

Ateia's eyes widened, and then she nodded.

"Ah, I guess that would make sense, then. Um, well, you see, sometimes dungeons have treasure chests in them and store valuable objects inside."

"Requesting Elaboration: Why would dungeons store valuables in singular containers in unguarded locations? Such a method of storage seems highly inefficient."

Taog frowned. "Supposedly, it's bait; a way for the demon lords to lure in more victims. But if you *do* find one and manage to escape, you can make a large profit."

"Acknowledged."

Suddenly, Ateia's smile dropped.

"Um, I guess we should have asked this before but . . . how should we, uh, split the loot?"

The pair both nervously turned to NSLICE-00P.

"Requesting Clarification: Friendly Ateia is addressing this unit?"

Ateia fidgeted a bit.

"Yes, um, you're our benefactor after all, so . . ."

"Acknowledged. Answer: This unit is not currently experiencing any supply shortfalls. As this unit is refraining from excess intervention in friendlies Ateia and Taog's dungeon termination mission, this unit has no particular claim to this 'treasure chest.'"

Both teens' eyes widened at that.

"A-Are you sure?! Normally, claims are split, you know? Since we hired you without specifying, you could even claim the first share."

"Affirmative. Explanation: This unit was not aware of material profits from dungeon exploration and made no contribution to the discovery of this storage container and has no particular material needs at present."

Ateia and Taog looked at each other. Ateia started to grin while Taog frowned, but he shook his head. Maybe their benefactor had ulterior motives, but given what he had seen so far, it was just as likely that she didn't *need* any loot from a low-level dungeon like this.

Such were his thoughts that he didn't particularly pay attention to the room nor said anything when Ateia rushed toward the chest. And fell straight into a pit trap, forcing NSLICE-00P to catch her.

As Taog helped Ateia catch her breath, NSLICE-00P sent a signal to her subordinates. Lilussees and Rattingtale popped their heads out of the hangar.

"W-What is it, yes-yes?"

"Hah, do you, like, need something?"

"Requesting Verification: Friendlies have claimed dungeons use storage containers filled with valuable materials as bait."

"Oh. Yeah, like, that's normal or something?"

"Yes-yes. Man-things are known to be greedy."

"Revelation: Additional data logged. This unit will request additional elaboration on the exact method and rationale at a later time."

"I see-understand. This Great-High King will advise-instruct you, yes-yes?"

"Okay . . . but, like, after my nap."

With that, the pair ducked back into the hangar.

Ateia and Taog stood at a crossroads with three separate hallways in front of them. Ateia held the map she had been drawing in her hand.

She glanced at the map.

Then up at the hallways.

Then back at the map.

Then back at the hallways.

Taog raised an eyebrow.

"Ateia . . ."

"W-Wait, just give me a second. It's like . . . it should be . . ."

"We're lost, aren't we?"

"W-We're not lost. I just . . . need a moment to think."

"You shouldn't need a moment, Ateia. You've been keeping track of where we've been going, right?"

"O-Of course."

Taog just stared at her. She looked away.

"I-It's not my fault! I-I got disoriented from that trap, you know!"

"You didn't seem disoriented when we were splitting the potions from the chest."

She puffed her cheeks.

"W-Well, what were you doing?! W-Why didn't you say anything until now?!"

"Because *I'm* not the one with the map!"

"Every Exploratore should be ready to take on any duty at any time!"

"And shouldn't fail at doing what was their duty to begin with!"

As the pair shouted at each other, NSLICE-00P stepped into a side room. A whole pack of wolves was waiting inside. She promptly incapacitated them with her stun ray, and then signaled her subordinates.

"Yay! You're, like, the best, boss!"

"Ugh, you expect this Great-High King over all the land to do the butchery-slaying once again?"

"If you, like, don't want them, then give them here or something."

"K-Keep your wretched fangs-teeth to yourself, you wicked spider-thing! T-These are the property-belongings of the Great-High King, yes-yes!"

As the two got to work, Lilussees tilted her head.

"Boss-Lady, I'm like, wondering something."

"Acknowledgement: Please state the query."

"I thought you were, like, not supposed to be contributing to the conquest or something? So, like, why are we hunting on our own? Not that I'm, like, complaining or anything."

"Explanation: Friendlies Ateia and Taog have moved to an area of the dungeon that does not lead to the core chamber. This unit has calculated that all efforts in the past hour do not contribute to dungeon-termination progress. So this unit has determined that hostiles in the area can be terminated without violating nonintervention mission parameters."

"So, like, they're super lost or something?"

"Affirmative."

. . . And so, Ateia and Taog's dungeon conquest carried on.

18

Terminate the Beast Dungeon . . . Maybe . . . If the Valued Allies Get Around to It . . .

"It takes a long time to explore a dungeon without dying. And you should never explore a dungeon, unless you're willing to take a long time to explore it."

—Exploratore Gallio Titinius Calvus, explaining a lack of progress after three months in a newly discovered dungeon.

Taog gritted his teeth as a monster crashed into his shield, a boar nearly as tall as his shoulder. He let the creature push him back then pivoted to the side from the momentum. He held his sword backhanded and stabbed it into the monster's side as he spun about. The boar squealed as it continued on.

And then Taog let out a cry. Another mangy wolf locked its jaws onto his ankle as he grunted and hacked away at the monster until it let go . . . only for the boar to charge back into him, sending him flying into the wall.

"Ateia, a little help here?!"

"Hang on, I'm a bit busy!"

Ateia was wrestling with a wolf herself, her bow dropped on the floor. She held the monster's jaws away from her with one hand and stabbed its neck repeatedly with the dagger in her other. In other words, Taog wouldn't have any cover for a bit.

He gritted his teeth and leapt out of the way, rolling on the ground as the boar crashed into the wall behind him. He groaned as fire shot through his ankle and his back ached.

"Seero! A little help here?!"

"Negative Response: Risk of friendly termination is not yet at critical levels. Mission parameters state this unit should not intervene at this time."

"We're being overrun! I'm already bleeding here!"

"Observation: Friendly Taog's HP predicted at reasonable levels. Friendlies Taog and Ateia possess recovery methods, and this unit has the Recovery Magic skill. Nonfatal damage does not indicate a risk of immediate termination."

"Screw you!"

Taog gritted his teeth, but it seemed their benefactor wouldn't budge unless death was imminent. And ultimately, she was right. This *was* what they'd asked for.

And this was just a taste of what an Exploratore might face in the line of duty.

Taog frowned, glancing at his sword and shield. He heaved a sigh and dropped his shield on the ground. If he had been a Legion bulwark like his father, he could have held the boar with ease, not needing to strike back at all. If he had been a full-blooded Wulver trained as a clan warrior like his mother, he would have the natural strength and speed to dance around an opponent like this.

But he was neither, and trying to be both would get him killed.

He stared the boar down as it charged once more. Gritting his teeth, he willed his pounding heart to slow down.

He waited . . .

His legs twitched.

He kept waiting . . .

The boar approached. His heartbeat grew even faster.

But he kept waiting, until he could make eye contact with the monster. And then . . .

He leapt with all his might.

The boar crashed into the dungeon wall once more. Taog landed on the monster's back with a thud, the impact driving the air out of his lungs as he landed right on his stomach, but he gritted his teeth and pulled himself around, facing forward. Then, he started to stab the boar's neck with all his might.

"Flurry! Power Strike!" He called out every skill he knew as he struck the boar. The monster squealed and ran about, trying to smash him into the wall, but he hung on, twisting on the monster's back and keeping up his assault. Eventually, the boar fell to the ground.

And a message from the Aesdes acknowledged his victory.

You have slain Monster Boar (Level 9)!
Gained 26 XP!
Level up! You are now Level 8!

He spun about, growling as he gripped his bloody sword, but Ateia had finished off the rest of the monsters. The fight was over.

Taog let the sword drop with a clang and slumped to the ground, resting his back against the wall. Ateia staggered over and slumped next to him. Both of them just panted in silence as NSLICE-00P approached. Two magic circles formed in front of her, and they felt warm mana cover their wounds.

The spell Heal is now Level 2!
The spell Heal is now Level 3!
The skill Recovery Magic is now Level 2!
The skill Recovery Magic is now Level 3!
You have learned the spell Cure!

Ateia nodded at NSLICE-00P before going back to her breathing. It was a moment longer before either of the pair could speak.

"That was . . . kind of crazy. And this is supposed to be a low-level dungeon?"

Taog grunted and shook his head. "Ateia, I'm not sure we're cut out for this."

"What do you mean? We won, didn't we?"

"Barely. And that's with Seero healing our wounds and saving us from traps. If not for her . . ." Taog's eyes narrowed as he stared at the ground.

Ateia grabbed his shoulder. "Hey, look at me."

Taog did as she requested.

"Don't think like that, Taog. We're not alone now, are we? So the *what if* doesn't matter. I'll . . . admit we weren't the most prepared for the traps. But she hasn't had to help us in the fights or the pathfinding, right? We've come this far by our own strength. You and I, together. And we will only grow stronger from here."

Taog's eyes widened as he watched her, then he flushed slightly and shook his head, letting out a breath. "You're right. It's just, I'm worried about what's to come. I'm not exactly a legionnaire, you know? If this goes on for much longer . . ."

"Helpful Observation: By this unit's scans, the dungeon core room is just ahead."

Their eyes widened at that, and Ateia grinned.

"See? You ready to conquer a dungeon, or what?"

Taog heaved a sigh, but he smiled wryly as well.

"Well, we've come this far. I guess we might as well check it out."

NSLICE-00P led the trio into the dungeon core room. A large wolf rested in front of the core, rising to its feet. It towered above the teens, snarling at the intruders.

She took a step forward.

"Warning: This dungeon is about to be terminated. Recommending dungeon master surrender."

"Surrender?" the wolf let out a deep and rumbling voice, chuckling at the cyborg's words. "No, I will feast on your flesh!"

With that, the wolf pounced at them.

And slammed right into a Mana Barrier.

NSLICE-00P turned to the two standing behind her.

"Warning: Dungeon master strength predicted as noticeably higher than friendlies Ateia and Taog. There is a significant risk of friendly termination should they participate in close combat. Will friendlies participate in the termination?"

The two glanced at each other then back at the wolf. Ateia's eyes narrowed. "We came all this way; we're not backing down now."

Taog shook his head and then lifted his sword. ". . . I don't like it but what choice do we have? We need to conquer this one; I'm not going into another dungeon if I can help it."

"Acknowledged. Statement: This unit will focus on containment for this engagement."

With that, NSLICE-00P took a step back and dropped the barrier. Ateia immediately fired a Power Shot at the monster. The arrow struck it dead-on, but bounced off its HP barrier. The dungeon master growled and pounced at her, but Taog stepped in front, his shield held up. The wolf swatted at him, and Taog flew through the air with a cry. Ateia's eyes widened, and she leapt out of the way, the monster's claws catching the back of her clothes. The wolf turned toward her, pouncing once more before she could rise to her feet.

A barrier formed in front of her once again, and a jet of flame struck the wolf's snout. Meanwhile, a Mana Barrier caught Taog before he landed, placing him back on the ground.

The two shook their heads and stood back up. The monster had turned its attention to NSLICE-00P, but she activated her repulsors and flew into the air.

"Observation: Friendlies Ateia and Taog's arsenal deemed insufficient. Deploying Mana Infusion protocol."

Mana wrapped around Ateia and Taog's weapons, filling them with a subtle glow. The two nodded and took up positions as the dungeon master chased after NSLICE-00P.

"Thanks, Seero. Power Shot!" Ateia launched another attack as the wolf tried to leap into the air. This time, the arrow buried itself deep into the monster's hide.

The wolf yelped as it fell to the ground. It picked itself up with a snarl and turned toward Ateia, pouncing at her once more.

Only to be knocked off course.

This time, Taog hadn't bothered trying to hold his ground, instead moving to the side, sheathing his sword, and holding his shield with both hands. Once the monster was airborne, he'd launched himself at it, putting all his weight into his shield to tackle the monster from the side. Since the wolf was in the air, it couldn't brace itself, and so both boy and monster flew sideways and crashed into the ground.

The wolf bit at Taog as it tried to stand back up, but Taog had already rolled out of the way. As it rose to its feet, a glass bottle flew through the air, filled with green liquid. An arrow shot after it, shattering it right above the monster.

The wolf yelped as it was drenched in poison.

"An Exploratore is always prepared!" Ateia grinned as she held another bottle in her hand. The wolf snarled and leapt at her, but Ateia was ready. She jumped out of the way, tossing the bottle into the wolf's jaws.

The monster's mouth burst into flames.

Ateia stood up, taking a deep breath as the wolf ran around, shaking its head. She held her bow and an arrow in one hand, holding the other over them. She closed her eyes and drew on her mana. "Let the strength of Aelea flow within me. Let my arms grow as strong as rock and my feet as steady as the mountain."

Ateia was not a formal mage, and neither was her father, but an Exploratore needed as many cards to play as possible, so he had picked up a thing or two. And he had taught a thing or two to his daughter back in the day.

A magic circle formed and completed. A subtle glow briefly surrounded Ateia. She then nocked her arrow and drew her bow, the wood creaking as she pulled the string back with far greater strength than before.

She grinned as she took aim.

"Power Shot."

The arrow cut through the air. As it did, NSLICE-00P raised her hand.

"Equalizer engaged."

A rainbow beam shot before the arrow, striking the wolf's face. The dungeon master's eyes widened as its HP barrier was stripped for a moment, Ateia's aim remaining true.

Her arrow buried itself between the wolf's eyes.

Ateia exhaled her breath.

Then started to grin as the Aesdes confirmed her victory.

You have slain Wolf Dungeon Master (Level 10)!
Your experience has grown by 39!
You have grown in stature!
You are now Level 9!
You have accomplished the Feat: Dungeon Conqueror (Beast Lair)!

Personal Feats		
Name	Description	Effect
Dungeon Conqueror (Beast Lair)	Unlocked by conquering the Beast Lair Dungeon.	+1 Perk Point +1 level in Leap skill

She glanced over at Taog. His eyes widened as he stared at the air for a moment before turning to her. They both grinned as Ateia leapt into the air.

"We did it!"

Taog shook his head and chuckled.

Honestly, he wasn't sure this was a good thing. The road of an Exploratore was hard and dangerous, and he wasn't at all convinced he and Ateia could handle it. It may have been wiser and kinder to quit now, and stick to the challenges they knew.

But those concerns could wait for another day. Because seeing her smile and celebrate, he couldn't help but smile too.

And, well, he would admit . . . victory tasted sweet indeed.

19

The Exploratores Explicatio

"I came and I saw, that we may conquer."

—Motto of the Exploratores

You have helped slay Wolf Dungeon Master (Level 10)!
Gained 4 Personal XP, 4 Dungeon XP!
Wolf Dungeon Master (Level 10) slain within Dungeon Field, Gained 10 Dungeon XP!
You have accomplished the Personal Feat: Dungeon Conqueror (Beast Lair)!

Personal Feats		
Name	Description	Effect
Dungeon Conqueror (Beast Lair)	Unlocked by conquering the Beast Lair Dungeon.	+1 Perk Point +1 level in Power Strike skill

NSLICE-00P observed Ateia and Taog celebrate. It seemed they had contributed enough to receive the Dungeon Conqueror feat. NSLICE-00P had not expected to receive the feat as well this time, but it seemed her contributions were not insignificant either. She updated the mission status to complete and moved to her next order of business.

She raised a hand at the dungeon core, charging up her Mana Beam.

"Wait! What are you doing?!"

She swung her hand to the side, firing the Mana Beam off into the wall as Ateia rushed in front of her.

"Answer: Terminating the dungeon."

"You're just going to smash the dungeon core?!"

"Affirmative."

"Why?!"

NSLICE-00P tilted her head.

"Explanation: Because that is the most beneficial option. Unless friendly Ateia knows of other use cases for dungeon cores?"

"Other use cases? Um, obviously! Dungeon cores are super rare and valuable! Do you know how much we can sell this for?"

"Revelation: This unit was not aware dungeon cores had market value."

Taog crossed his arms as he joined the conversation. "Not to mention, we probably need this core to prove we really conquered a dungeon."

Ateia tilted her head at that. "What do you mean? We have the Dungeon Conqueror feat now, don't we?"

Taog shook his head and heaved a sigh. "Ateia, do you honestly think that alone will be enough? They rejected us once, you know. They won't want to change their mind."

Ateia furrowed her brow. Her eyes started to tremble.

"But we have the feat! They have to take us, don't they?"

"They do . . . *if* it's abundantly clear we have the feat. But if us, a couple of kids who they already rejected, show up saying 'we conquered a dungeon,' what do you think they're going to do?"

Ateia opened her mouth, frowned, then closed it. Taog heaved a sigh.

"So we need to bring the core. If we show up with a core, they'll *have* to check us out fairly."

Ateia was still frowning, but she nodded. Taog just heaved another sigh. In any case, he had something else to do.

He turned to NSLICE-00P.

"There you have it. I'm sorry; you seem to have your own objective with these cores, but we do really need to bring this one with us. We'll probably have to sell it, too, once it's known we have one. We'll split the proceeds with you, at the very least."

"Acknowledged."

Taog raised an eyebrow at the easy acceptance, but NSLICE-00P just deactivated her weapons and said no more. He still couldn't get a read on her, but he wasn't going to ask her directly. He wasn't Ateia, after all. So he just grunted as he walked over to the pedestal and grabbed the core.

And with that, the group found themselves in the forest once more.

And then, Taog paled as a Mana Barrier formed around him.

"Statement: Mission accomplished. Preparing evac to safe location."

"Woo-hoo! Let's go, let's go!"

"Um, Seero, could you just . . . take us back to the road? Let us walk the rest of the way back?"

"Query: What is the rationale for friendly Taog's request?"

"Um, well, not many people can fly, you know? So it would be best not to startle everyone . . . or something like that."

"Acknowledgement: Friendly Taog's rationale determined as reasonable. This unit will evac friendlies to mission start location."

Ateia gave him a smug grin, but he ignored her. It just wasn't right being up in the sky like that. He'd handle it while getting out of the dangerous monster forest, but by the Aesdes did he want firm ground beneath his feet.

By the time they arrived at the road, the sun was already beginning to set, so the group decided to make camp for the night. NSLICE-00P watched as Ateia set up a small metal pillar about a foot long, covered in geometric shapes, and with a round blue stone at its center. The blue stone began to glow, and light filled in the lines carved across it. NSLICE-00P observed as a subtle barrier extended from the pillar, surrounding the camp.

"Query: What is the purpose of the device friendly Ateia has deployed?"

"Huh? Wait, you mean this? Um, you haven't seen a camp ward before?"

"Negative."

Ateia tilted her head.

"Then . . . how do you sleep at night?"

"Response: This unit can place organic components on standby without deactivating cybernetic components, including sensors."

"Uh . . . what? Does that mean you can keep watch while you sleep?"

"Affirmative."

Ateia's eyes widened.

"Wow, knights are amazing. Well then, um, this is a camp ward. It's . . . enchanted with a concealment barrier to try and hide us, and an alarm ward if anything does approach anyways."

"Acknowledged. Gratitude: This unit thanks friendly Ateia for additional intel."

"Um, anytime?"

Taog raised an eyebrow and motioned at Ateia. She raised an eyebrow back but walked over to him.

"Be careful around her, Ateia."

She narrowed her eyes at him.

"What are you saying, Taog? After all she's done for us, *now* you want to be all paranoid?"

Taog narrowed his eyes back.

"It's not paranoia; it's caution. Look, weird accents and incredible power are one thing. I can even accept her not knowing about the Empire, though that does raise some questions on what she's doing all the way out in *Turannia*, of all places. But the more we talk with her, the weirder it gets. She didn't know about treasure chests despite destroying dungeons? She doesn't know about *camp wards* despite wandering around in the *Domhan na Beithigh*? She claims now she can keep watch while sleeping? This is not normal, Ateia."

"That's why she agreed to help us, isn't it? So we can help her learn these things. What are you trying to say, Taog?"

"I'm saying we have no idea who—or maybe even *what*—this person is, or what their real intentions are. It's not wise to get too close until we do."

Ateia crossed her arms.

"Taog, she *saved* our lives. Several times. She's done nothing but help us. She doesn't deserve that kind of suspicion."

Taog shook his head.

"But she had a reason to help us; she didn't do it out of the kindness of her heart, Ateia. That is not enough to trust her fully. So we need to be careful until we know we can."

Ateia frowned and paused for a moment, taking a deep breath.

"You know, people used to say the same thing about you and your mom, Taog."

He froze, twitching and standing up straight as if drenched with cold water.

"That's—" He took a deep breath. "I'm just trying to look out for you, Ateia."

Ateia's expression softened, but she shook her head.

"I understand, but I'm not going to treat her like a threat, Taog. As far as I'm concerned, she's earned my trust. She's already helped us; now, I'm going to help her. I hope you will, too."

With that, she turned around and walked back over to NSLICE-00P. Taog frowned and stared at the ground for a bit. Maybe it was true. Maybe he was being overly suspicious of NSLICE-00P just because she was different. But could anyone blame him?

After all, he knew how ugly people could be. And he would do anything he could to spare Ateia from that lesson.

Still, it was true that NSLICE-00P had kept up her half of the bargain, so he was bound to fulfill his and help this strange girl figure things out. All he could do was keep an eye on her and hope Ateia was right in the end.

He took a deep breath and rejoined the group.

NSLICE-00P and Ateia had already started conversing.

"Requesting Elaboration: Please explain role, Exploratore."

Ateia nodded. "Okay, so the Exploratores are the heroes of the Empire! They're the first line of defense for the people of the Empire; the guardians of the frontier."

Taog heaved a sigh.

"She's not asking for the bedtime stories, Ateia. What she means to say is that the Exploratores are the scouts and intelligence agents of the Imperial Legion. They used to be tasked with scouting and security for the legions, but ever since Emperor Amulius's reforms, they've become an independent organization."

"Requesting Confirmation: So it is a government-military rank?"

Ateia and Taog nodded, then he continued, "At this point, the Exploratores function as independent scouts. They travel and patrol the Empire and its borders, identifying and reporting potential problems so the legions can arrange a specialized response."

"Query: Who do the Exploratores report to? Will this unit need to negotiate with commanding officers for fulfillment of the prior contract?"

Ateia shook her head.

"No one! The Exploratores go where they want, do what they want! They protect the Empire in their own way!"

Taog shrugged.

"That's an exaggeration, but one grounded in truth. Officially, the Exploratores report only to the Magister Exploratores of the local province and the Emperor. They are largely able to act at their own discretion, but they generally make regular reports to the local Legion and provincial governor, and coordinate with them. It will *definitely* cause trouble if they disobey a direct order from a Legion officer without good cause, for example. And the Magister may require their assistance during crisis situations, at least for the Exploratores in their province."

Ateia slowly nodded at that.

"Still though, the Exploratores are allowed to move about the Empire as they see fit, as long as they keep putting in accurate reports! And they hunt down the enemies of the people wherever they go!"

"More like, more and more of the Empire is having the Exploratores solve problems on their own, since the legions can't handle everything. At this point, they're known more as monster hunters than scouts."

"And the champions of the people, who help anyone in need!"

"More like, the Empire cut their wages and instead pays them bounties for problems solved. Most Exploratores have started taking independent contracts for the local populace since the Imperial bounties aren't enough to go around."

Ateia glared at him. "Oh, come on, Taog! You make everything sound bad!"

He heaved a sigh. "You know it was your father who told us most of this, right?"

"Requesting Confirmation: Role Exploratore designated as government-military role with largely independent action and freedom of movement, part of but not subordinated to military hierarchy, who identify issues and mobilize military and government resources to resolve?"

"Um . . . yes?"

"Additional Query: So friendlies Ateia and Taog will assist this unit by mobilizing Exploratores resources to search for the persons of interest?"

Ateia nodded at that. She went silent for a moment, staring at the glowing camp ward before taking a deep breath.

"Once I become an Exploratore, I'm going to go search for my father. He left on a campaign . . . a while back. But the Legion hasn't reported his death, so I know he's alive. And I'm going to find him, even if I have to search every corner of the Empire to do it." She looked up into NSLICE-00P's eyes. "And I'll help you find your people, too. We won't stop until we both find who we're looking for."

"Acknowledgment: Compatible mission with friendly Ateia acknowledged."

Taog silently frowned.

Long had Ateia been searching for her lost father. And it seemed one way or another, against all odds, her quest was finally getting off the ground.

He truly hoped that they would succeed.

Meanwhile Lilusseess and Rattingtale were . . . both napping.

Guarding the Monster Hangar was hard work, after all.

20

Let's Sit Around the Campfire . . .

"The number one rule of life is never judge by appearances. There are Enlightened races that appear fully bestial. They seem like animals at first, but are ultimately no less intelligent or civilized than you and I. And the opposite is also true. There are monsters who look completely human, and might even act like it at first. So pay close attention, and make note of any strange behaviors. There may be dragons and demons walking among us."

—Inquisitor Camillus Matius Domitianus, before enacting a purge of Emperor Potitus's political rivals.

Eventually, the trio finished their conversation and turned in for the night. The camp ward was by no means a perfect defense, so they also set up a night watch. Ateia took the first shift, Taog the second, and NSLICE-00P the last.

NSLICE-00P set up her standby-sentry mode. She closed her human eye and activated her helmet, her robotic eye flickering on occasion as she continued to scan the area. Ateia and Taog both raised an eyebrow at that, but shrugged and went about their business. Soon, Taog turned in for the night, and Ateia took up the watch.

Ateia and Taog's shifts passed without incident, and then, it was time for NSLICE-00P to disengage her helmet, her human eye opening back up.

"Report: Standby mode disengaged. Organic components reporting full efficiency. Reviewing sentry logs. No anomalies detected."

She turned her attention to Taog, who was still awake. He kept his eyes on her as she approached him.

"Query: This unit's time clock indicates it is this unit's turn. Friendly Taog may engage organic standby mode."

Taog shrugged, still watching her. "I'm not sleepy."

NSLICE-00P's robotic eye flickered again. Body language and physiological scans indicated that Taog was lying on that. However, she couldn't determine a probable cause why he would lie about the need for organic maintenance. But Taog staying up wasn't predicted as a potential threat, and Taog experiencing reduced efficiency over the next day would not impact current mission success rates. As a result, NSLICE-00P concluded there was no particular reason to question him on it and turned around. She began a slow patrol pattern around the camp so she could scan every direction more thoroughly for incoming hostiles.

Taog raised an eyebrow at first, watching her as she walked about, especially as she stepped around the tent Ateia was sleeping in. But she did nothing out of the ordinary, repeating her patrol several times.

Eventually, he sighed.

He knew he was being a bit paranoid, but this was their first night together. It was the prime opportunity for foul play, not that he could stop NSLICE-00P if she truly intended to hurt them.

But perhaps Ateia had a point. The strange girl *had* taken care of them, after all.

So, he opened his mouth. "Seero . . ."

NSLICE-00P halted her patrol and turned to face him.

"Acknowledgement: Does friendly Taog have a query or sentry update?"

He took a deep breath.

"What, exactly, are you?"

"Answer: This unit is a Non-Standard Leashed-Intelligence Cybernetic Enforcer, Prototype Model."

Taog froze, blinking several times.

"Um . . . what?"

"Elaboration: This unit was designed specifically to counter, apprehend, and/or terminate hostile Non-Standards."

Taog kept blinking. He had not expected her to just answer directly . . . and he had no idea what her reply actually meant.

"Um . . ."

"Query: Does friendly Taog have any queries for this unit?"

"Um . . ." He shook his head. Maybe another avenue might prove more enlightening? "Where are you from, Seero?"

"Requesting Clarification: Is friendly Taog requesting data on this unit's point of origin, or this unit's current home base?"

"Um, I guess . . . the more recent one, if I have that right?"

"Answer: This unit apologizes, but that data is not currently available. This unit's last recorded home base was wiped by this unit's latest commander. This unit was kept mobile thereafter, and so does not have a permanent home base logged from that point on, and so cannot provide detailed data."

"Uh, what about that point of origin thing?"

"Answer: This unit was assembled in a classified location within the Alps. Unfortunately, said data was wiped when the location was lost to hostile forces."

"Um, and where, or what, are the Alps?"

"Answer: The Alps are a mountain range located in the continent of Europe."

"Europe? I've never heard of a continent called that."

NSLICE-00P's robotic eye flickered for a bit at that.

"Revelation: This unit assumed shared references to geographic locations due to common language. Can friendly Taog inform this unit of the current continent's designation?"

"Um . . . the continent is called Aluin, as far as I know. Well, we're on an island right now, technically. The Empire calls it Turannia; the locals call it Réimse an Bháisteach."

"Acknowledgement: Logging intel on local designations. This unit thanks friendly Taog for his cooperation."

"Uh, you're welcome?"

"Query: Does friendly Taog have any further queries for this unit?"

"Um . . . no, that's all. Uh, thank you for answering."

"Acknowledged. Resuming sentry patrol protocol."

Taog watched as she turned back to scanning their surroundings. He shook his head and turned back toward his tent. He still couldn't make heads or tails of her, but he apparently wasn't going to figure it out tonight. He couldn't determine if she was lying when he couldn't even understand her answers, after all. Maybe he could take that as a sign of deceit, but she always spoke with that strange speech pattern, so he couldn't particularly say she was using it to obscure her answers. By all accounts, she seemed entirely cooperative.

And, well . . .

Again, if he thought about it logically, she could very easily kill them both at any time she pleased. Watching her like this achieved nothing but indulging in his anxieties. So he might as well try to get some sleep instead.

But perhaps, Taog had gone to bed too early, for once he had, a barely cracked-open panel on NSLICE-00P's back fully opened up.

"Boss-queen, are you planning-intending to stay with these man-things?"

"Affirmative."

"Why?"

"Explanation: Their strategic objectives align with those of this unit's."

"But-but, they are taking-leading you to where the man-things live, yes-yes!"

"Affirmative."

Another head poked out, causing Rattingtale to jump.

"Snack, did you, like, forget? The boss is, like, also a human or something?"

"She's a dungeon master, you stupid, wretched spider-thing!"

"But, like, also a human? That's, like, what the Analyze skill said or something."

"So what?!"

Lilussees heaved a sigh. "This is, like, so annoying. Like, use your head or something. If she's, like, also a human, then why would she be bothered by being around humans?"

"That's not the point, vile spider-thing! If she goes-joins the man-things, we will be slayed-slaughtered, yes-yes!"

"Eh . . . I, like, don't think so? Boss, you, like, aren't going to kill us, right? Or, like, let the other humans kill us or something?"

"Negative."

Rattingtale frowned.

"I don't like-enjoy this, no-no. We just have to hide-wait inside our chambers, not knowing what's happening-occurring around us while we are surrounded by wicked man-things?"

"Eh, I guess that's, like, a good point or something. Boss, is there, like, a way to let us know what's happening from inside our rooms or something?"

"Analyzing . . ."

NSLICE-00P had determined she could see and hear everything that occurred within the Monster Hangar, as well as send communications directly to Rattingtale and Lilussees. So if they could also see what was going on outside, they could offer advice and clarification on the foreign system without exposing themselves to harm. Therefore, she determined the request was a logical one and reviewed the Monster Hangar. Like the Dungeon Field Generator, it was somehow connected to her systems, yet occupying its own space. But she could feel the mana flowing from her core to the room. And since her core was also her Geo-Oscillator Engine, electricity and data also flowed through that connection, so establishing an uplink to her sensors was theoretically possible.

As she reviewed the Monster Hangar, a window from the foreign system appeared, displaying a live feed of the room in question—as well as some options for modifications.

Available Upgrades for Monster Hangar (small)			
Name	**Description**	**Mana Upkeep**	**Cost**
Observation Monitors	**Allow hangar inhabitants to observe designated areas of the dungeon**	**1**	**1 point**

NSLICE-00P selected one of them. A large screen appeared in the common room, along with smaller ones in each of the chambers. When activated, they displayed the current feed from her sensors.

"Status Update: This unit has modified the Monster Hangar (Small) with the requested update. Friendlies Excellion Formantus Rattingtale the Third and Lilussees may now view live sensor feeds from within the hangar."

"For real? That's, like, pretty neat. Thanks, boss."

"Y-Yes-yes, the Great-High King over all the land supposes-guesses you have done well this time, boss-queen."

With that, Lilussees and Rattingtale returned to their chambers, and NSLICE-00P resumed her patrol.

Morning came without incident. Taog frowned as he realized nothing had happened over the night after all. He shook his head and got up, getting to work on breakfast.

His bad feeling returned, however, when NSLICE-00P appeared to have no rations of any sort, and in fact, *declined* to share in theirs, saying something about her "organic efficiency" being at optimal levels. Seriously, just who or what was this girl?

The pair broke down their camp, packing up the tents and camp ward, and then they were off.

The forest began to thin out as they walked, and the slope of the road evened out. Soon, instead of descending directly from the mountains, they were traveling up and down smaller hills, some with barely any trees at all. In the distance, NSLICE-00P caught a glimpse of a wooden watchtower standing atop the tallest hill in the area. As they drew closer, she saw a small barracks next to it with a basic palisade of sharp logs surrounding the outpost. Ateia waved at the watchman atop the tower and the guards at the palisade's entrance. They raised an eyebrow at NSLICE-00P, but ultimately just waved back at Ateia.

Past the outpost, the dirt trail transformed into a paved stone road. Ateia and Taog exchanged some small talk with the guards before continuing along the stone path.

NSLICE-00P followed after them, stepping onto the road. Her robotic eye flickered. The increase in the technological sophistication of the road indicated a higher level of civilization, and so improved the success odds for her current mission. She followed after the two, scanning for any electromagnetic signals she could connect with as she walked.

And so, NSLICE-00P, the killer cyborg and walking dungeon, officially entered the Empire.

* * *

Rattingtale's ears fell flat on his head as he observed the guards within his room.

"Ugh, more vicious man-things. This is a terrible idea, yes-yes."

But then, he had an idea. An awful idea. The Great-High King over all the land got a wonderful, awful idea.

"Wait, vicious man-things hate-despise dungeons, yes-yes? So if they knew a dungeon was walking-hiding among them, they would be most upset, yes-yes? And then . . ."

Rattingtale's mouth curled into a grin and he chittered.

Meanwhile, in her own room, Lilussees had discovered that NSLICE-00P had not actually set any restrictions on the parts of the dungeon the monitors could observe. It had taken her a while to figure out how to change it, but now she had.

So she was listening to Rattingtale's every word.

"Eh. Like, that would be kind of bad, or something. I, like, don't want to lose another home, so I guess I should stop him, or something."

She watched Rattingtale giggle to himself and shrugged with her front legs.

"Like, not that the snack would actually do anything. So, like, I think I'll take a nap first, or something."

She plopped down on a silk hammock and went to sleep.

21

Rules of Engagement

"Turannia? By the will of the Aesdes, why would anyone want Turannia?! Let me tell you, it is the height of both vanity and stupidity that the Empire exists in Turannia. Because do you want to know what exists in Turannia? Rain. That's it. Rain. And don't you dare believe I'm joking. The locals themselves *call it "The Realm of Rain." Think about that. This is what its people named their own home.*

It is a bleary group of islands out in stormy, Aesdes-forsaken seas that don't lead anywhere but an early death. It provides no strategic or economic advantage to control. Its climate isn't particularly good for agriculture. It has no natural resources you can't find anywhere else. It is filled to the brim with savage furskins ready to tear your face off, and gets invaded by even more from across the seas any time you think you've put them down. Those Selkie are just about the only ones you can talk to, and even they'd put a harpoon in our backs if they weren't hiding behind our shields.

Oh, and let's not forget the bloody Forest of Beasts. Untamed wilderness, far as the eye can see, where monsters and demon lords and savage tribes spend their lives murdering everything that moves. Even Cnaeus the Bloody decided it was too much effort trying to tame that land. Hear that? The Butcher of Varn Durahl himself balked at the sheer amount of killing he'd have to do to claim even a single plot of that Aesdes-forsaken land. So we just left it, and now anyone who has the misfortune of settling in that swamp of an island can have random visits from wandering monsters and marauding tribes any day of the week. The Legion gave up and tried to build a wall, and guess what? Those bloody beasts just went around it, so they gave up on that too. Bloody idiots.

Oh, and worst of all—it's raining. It's ALWAYS raining.

If you ask me, we should pack up and leave and let the bloody furskins battle themselves. They can keep their rainy island for all I care."

—Exploratore Caeso Flavius Musa briefing a newly appointed dux per Turannia comitatenses.

Taog heaved a sigh as he wrapped his cloak around him.

It was raining. He and Ateia now walked in silence, gripping their cloaks and trudging along.

Meanwhile, NSLICE-00P had created a Mana Barrier around herself.

The spell Mana Barrier is now Level 7!

Of course, NSLICE-00P was fully waterproof. She could not be expected to compete with superheroes if she wasn't designed to handle a little rain, after all. And she predicted her new dungeon abilities would also aid in preventing damage to her circuitry. But there was no reason to take the risk of water getting somewhere it shouldn't when she had a surefire method to remain entirely dry.

Taog and Ateia shot glances at her, but NSLICE-00P was busy scanning for signs of technology or possible hostiles, and so didn't particularly notice. And wouldn't have been able to interpret subtle glances, in any case.

"Wow, that's, like, a lot of water."

"It seems most unpleasant-uncomfortable, yes-yes."

Meanwhile, Lilussees and Rattingtale were lying around in their nice, warm, and above all dry rooms, watching NSLICE-OOP's other companions struggle. They did in fact catch the glances Ateia and Taog were giving NSLICE-00P, but neither of them particularly felt like informing her.

Why would monsters help the wretched man-things, after all? The Great-High King over all the land desired for them to turn on NSLICE-00P, after all. Lilussees . . . just didn't care and decided to take another nap.

Finally, Ateia spoke up.

"Um, Seero?"

"Acknowledgement: Does friendly Ateia have a query or status update?"

"Is it possible for you to create barriers for Taog and I too?"

"Affirmative."

Silence hung in the air, save for the sound of rain striking the stone road. Ateia watched NSLICE-00P, who continued walking. Eventually, Taog realized what was going on, heaving a sigh as he closed his eyes.

"Seero, may you *please* create barriers for Ateia and I?"

"Affirmative."

With that, two more Mana Barriers formed around the pair. They glanced at one another and sighed.

". . . Thanks, Seero."

"Acknowledged."

* * *

Eventually the trio came within sight of a small town. Even all the way out at the edge of Turannia, a small stone wall surrounded the settlement. A pair of guards waited at the entrance to town, leaning against the sides of the gate. One of them noticed the trio and grabbed his spear, elbowing the other to wake him up. The two frowned and gripped their weapons until the trio came closer, at which point they exhaled and smiled.

"Oh, it's just you, Ateia. Another successful hunt?"

Ateia took a deep breath, then stepped forward and grinned, putting her hands on her hips and holding her head high.

"Obviously! Who do you think I am?"

They also nodded quietly to Taog, and then raised an eyebrow as they looked over NSLICE-00P. "Um, is this . . . a friend of yours, Ateia?"

She nodded. "That's right."

The guards glanced at one another, then shrugged.

"Works for me, at least this one is human. Welcome back, you two."

Ateia froze but managed to hold her smile.

"Thanks, Manius!"

And with that, the three entered town. The town was constructed mainly out of stone, though with some wooden repairs or additions here and there. It was laid out in a grid, with two main streets running through the center perpendicular to one another, and all other streets running parallel to one or the other. The streets were mostly empty that day, the residents hurrying about their business and trying to stay dry. Most of the residents appeared to be human, a few seeming abnormally tall or short, though with everyone wrapped in cloaks and hoods, NSLICE-00P couldn't identify any distinguishing features.

"Scanning . . . No electrical infrastructure detected. Observation: Location appears to be at preindustrial technology level. Analyzing impact on current mission . . ."

NSLICE-00P's analysis returned a sobering conclusion. She had detected no electrical signals since arriving here, including after reestablishing contact with civilization. Everything she had observed indicated a preindustrial society. That in and of itself was not conclusive; preindustrial societies still existed up to the modern day, after all, albeit restricted to small-scale communities in extremely isolated locations. But more and more, evidence indicated she had not stumbled upon some isolated tribe.

Even in geographically isolated locations, she should be able to detect signals from the global satellite network. And there was more. Stone paved roads, a stone town built in a precise grid layout, and what friendlies Ateia and Taog had told her about an Empire which seemed to them like a major power universally recognizable. All of this was evidence of a major, organized, preindustrial civilization controlling a wide territory. One that did not and *could not* have remained in isolation, and so should have had access or at least exposure to any existing technologies.

And NSLICE-00P had arrived here after being sent back through time, so she could not rule out the possibility she had subsequently gone even further back to a preindustrial time period. Or the possibility she was not on Earth at all. Her Geo-Oscillator Engine had disconnected from the Earth's core and had to reconnect to a new one, so that scenario was entirely plausible. Maybe even likely. Likewise, the behavior of mana, the existence of dungeons and sapient animals, and Taog, who was clearly not a normal human also supported this theory. She could not match these things to any historical record or scientific observation she had access to.

. . . Her mission was growing increasingly complicated.

"Analysis could not be completed. More data required."

At the end of the day, she simply didn't have enough intel on her present location, which meant she could not come up with contingency plans for any of these possibilities. So, she continued to follow her current protocols, with the intention of gathering additional intel. Perhaps that would clarify the situation.

And if she *was* in a different time, or maybe even a different planet?

. . . She did not yet have a protocol for those contingencies.

Ateia hadn't even taken off her cloak before she ran around the room, grabbing extra potions and restocking her rations for the road. The Exploratores didn't exactly maintain a base in a small town at the edge of the frontier, so they would need to travel to the province's capital.

"Okay, I'll talk to Quintus, let him know we'll be leaving for a while. He should arrange for someone to take care of the house. Um . . . looks like we're a bit low on food. Taog, can you go pick something up?"

Taog shook his head, chuckling. "Slow down, Ateia, you're getting water all over the floor."

"Come on, Taog! We've got a thousand things to do before we can set off! Get to it!"

He chuckled and turned to the door.

Taog was walking through one of the side streets when a trio of cloaked figures rounded the corner in front of him. He didn't pay much attention to them until they stepped in his way.

He froze and swore. Two more rounded the corner behind him. With everything going on, he had forgotten about this.

"What do you want, Lar? I'm busy."

Lar took a step forward, a grin on his face. The boy was scarcely older than Taog, but he still stood a head above him, with wide shoulders and thick arms to match.

"Now, now, don't be like that, Taog. I've got a lot to talk with you about. Like what in the name of the Aesdes were you doing taking Ateia out of town, alone."

Taog crossed his arms. "What Ateia does is none of your business, Lar. Maybe if you finally realized that, she might give you the time of day. I doubt it, though, what with your face and all."

Lar's grin faded, his face twisting into a snarl. Taog heaved a sigh as a fist approached his cheek, knocking him to the ground.

"You stupid, mangy mutt! How dare you?! If it wasn't for your filth poisoning her mind, Ateia would be mine already! Now tell me what you did!"

Taog just ignored him as the group started to kick at him. Really, they should have known he had taken some endurance and defensive perks by now. All they were doing was training his skills. But, well, Lar and his gang had never been the sharpest tools in the shed, nor did they have a high opinion of the Wulvers' capacity for basic learning.

And . . . the angrier Lar got at Taog, the less he pestered Ateia, so Taog was fine with this. Or so he told himself. This was nothing he hadn't been through before. In fact, Lar's open hostility was preferable in a lot of ways, so Taog just leaned back, closed his eyes, and yawned, sending the boys around him into a frothing rage.

Such were the things Taog told himself to hold down the fire in his stomach. To keep the frown from forming on his face, to bury the desire to rip Lar's throat out. Such was his focus that Taog forgot that something had changed about his circumstances. Something very important.

He and Ateia were no longer alone.

Suddenly, the impacts stopped. Taog peeked an eye open.

His eyes widened at what he saw.

A Mana Barrier now separated him from Lar's gang.

"Hostile intent toward a designated friendly observed. Engaging termination protocols." NSLICE-00P stepped into the street. She already had her helmet on, her eyes glowing red. She lifted a hand.

Taog leapt to his feet.

"Wait, Seero! Don't kill them!"

"Requesting Clarification: Hostiles have inflicted harm on friendly Taog. Please provide rationale to defer termination."

"Just don't! You'll be arrested for murder!"

"Acknowledgement: As this unit is not aware of local self-defense regulations, this unit will update the response per friendly Taog's request. Response restricted to nonlethal countermeasures."

Lar turned to face NSLICE-00P.

"Who the heck are you? You friends with this mutt?"

"Warning: Cease all hostility toward friendly Taog or this unit will retaliate."

Lar chuckled. "Let's show this jerk what happens to fur-lovers!"

He stepped forward, swinging his fist at her. NSLICE-00P lifted her hand.

CLANG!

"GAH!"

NSLICE-00P caught the blow. Lar cried out as his fist impacted solid metal.

"Observation: Hostile has now displayed hostile intent toward this unit directly. Requesting permission to escalate response to termination."

"No, Seero!"

"Acknowledged. Deploying nonlethal countermeasures."

NSLICE-00P pushed Lar back into his friends, then lifted her hand. A jolt of lightning shot through the air, surging through the group. All five of them cried out and dropped to the ground.

Taog groaned and held his head, then ran past the group, grabbing NSLICE-00P's hand and starting to run. "Come on!"

NSLICE-00P tilted her head but followed after him.

The two made their way to an unoccupied alley. NSLICE-00P formed a magic circle, healing the light bruises Taog had received. He looked at her for a moment before sighing.

"Look . . . I know you were trying to help, Seero, but stay out of this."

"Query: Why should this unit not terminate hostiles assaulting a friendly?"

Taog gritted his teeth and looked down. "It's not that simple, Seero."

"Requesting Elaboration."

He looked up at her, then heaved a sigh. "Look, you're not from around here, so you don't know how things are, okay?"

"Response: That is correct. This unit is therefore requesting explanation."

Taog clenched his fist and sighed. "Okay, look, you know I'm half Wulver, right?"

"Affirmative."

"People here don't like Wulvers."

"Requesting Elaboration."

He glared at her before sighing once more. "Right, I guess you don't know. Normally, Wulvers don't interact with Imperials much. They normally live in small clans, fighting everyone they come across. These people included."

"Requesting Confirmation: So there is hostility due to historic conflict?"

Taog nodded slowly. "There is. So . . . they were not happy when my dad brought my mom home. Some of them came around when she died defending them, but not all. Like Lar there."

"Query: If there are historic and current hostiles, isn't termination the most efficient course of action?"

Taog narrowed his eyes. He gripped his fist until his knuckles turned white.

"If it were just me . . . then maybe." He took a deep breath and released his fist. "But it's not. Ateia's family has already caught a lot of crap for helping us out. And that Lar, he wants Ateia. So if I fight back, if I cause a ruckus, or Aesdes forbid, I *kill* one of them . . . Look, half the town is just waiting for an excuse to get rid of me, and Ateia will likely pay for it, too. And I don't want that."

NSLICE-00P went silent, her robotic eye flickering.

"Request: This unit would like an explanation of local laws regarding self-defense and termination."

Taog heaved a sigh. "Look, just don't kill anyone while we're here, okay?"

"Acknowledged. Termination deferred while this unit is within the observed boundaries of this settlement."

Taog sighed one more time. He began to walk out of the alley before pausing.

"And Seero? . . . Thanks."

"Acknowledged."

Lilussees was lounging in her room, watching the live feed. Rattingtale was in the common area, trying to listen in on her, too, but sticking close to his room, should Lilussees decide to exit hers.

"Humans are, like, so weird. They, like, don't kill their enemies? Like, how do they get breakfast or something?"

"No-no, those man-things are many-numerous and big-strong, yes-yes? The wolfman-thing is wise, yes-yes. Much better to kill-slay them when they aren't looking, yes-yes."

"Eh, I guess that, like, makes sense or something. Like, kill them the easy way? So boss, you're going to, like, kill them later or something?"

NSLICE-00P's voice came in directly through speakers mounted in the rooms.

"Negative. Explanation: Hostility was primarily directed at friendly Taog, and the hostiles' threat level was low enough not to require immediate termination. This unit will therefore defer to friendly Taog's cost-benefit analysis of terminating hostiles."

"But what if, like, they attack you now or something?"

"Answer: Hostile intent toward this unit will be met with immediate termination."

"Eh, I guess that's, like, fine or something. Well, whatever. I'm going to take a nap."

22

A Bit of Shopping

"I'll kill them all. Not just the men, but the woman, and the children too. They're monsters, and I will slaughter them like monsters. They are good for nothing but to become our experience."

—Legate Caelus Curius Eulogius, before leading an ill-fated expedition against the Wulver tribes in the Forest of Beasts.

And so, Taog resumed his business and headed over to the marketplace, NSLICE-00P accompanying him. The shopkeepers and what few customers braved the rain glanced at the cyborg, both subtly and not, but they wanted little to do with the armored and clearly magically gifted stranger. Taog heaved a sigh; so much for getting his business done quickly and quietly. But he had no room to complain, for he'd specifically asked NSLICE-00P to come along with him. After all, if he knew Lar, he definitely couldn't let the potentially murder-happy knight out of his sight.

"They're right there, Decanus!"

Taog sighed. Right on cue.

He was just finishing his shopping as Lar came stomping towards him, followed a squad of the local limitanei and the tired-looking decanus leading them, clearly unhappy to be dragged out into the rain.

"These are the fur-lovers who attacked me, Decanus! Arrest them!"

The decanus just heaved a sigh as he locked eyes with Taog and walked over.

"Hello, Taog."

"Hello, Decanus."

"Let's get this over with. I have some questions for you and your companion."

Taog shrugged.

"Of course, Decanus."

The decanus glanced over at NSLICE-00P.

"Query: Do you have business with this unit?"

"Seero, this is the decanus, the soldier in charge of the local guard. Please cooperate with him."

"Acknowledgement: Local authority identified."

The decanus raised an eyebrow but turned to the cyborg. "May I get your name, miss?"

"Greeting: This unit is designated NSLICE-00P. It is nice to meet you."

The decanus blinked a few times. "Okay, Miss Enslice Seero Seero Pee, did you or did you not assault this fellow with a lightning spell?"

"Negative."

He raised an eyebrow. "Really? What happened, then?"

"Explanation: This unit incapacitated the hostile with a stun-ray nonlethal countermeasure."

"So . . . you did attack Lar here?"

"Affirmative."

Lar grinned at that.

"See, Decanus! She admitted it! Arrest them!"

The decanus heaved a sigh. "Can you explain why you attacked Lar?"

"Affirmative. Displaying combat recording."

NSLICE-00P's robotic eye lit up. The guards gripped their spears while the decanus glanced over at Taog, who waved his hands and shook his head, so the decanus motioned for his men to stand down. A holographic display appeared in the air, showing Lar and his friends kicking at Taog while he lay on the ground, and NSLICE-00P's intervention.

Lar's face went red as the decanus glanced at him, an eyebrow raised.

"T-That's a lie! It's obviously an illusion; some sort of trick!"

The guards glanced at one another while the decanus just held his forehead. "Well, we clearly have two different versions of events here. Taog, you're the third party involved with this. What do you say happened?"

"Decanus, you can't seriously be taking the word of this *furskin* here?"

The decanus turned toward Lar and narrowed his eyes. "Shut your mouth, *boy.* Last I checked you were not part of the Legion in any capacity, while I am the officer in command. I will do my job as I see fit."

Lar took a step back but closed his mouth. The decanus turned back to Taog, who heaved a sigh. "Would you believe me if I said nothing happened, Decanus?"

The decanus raised an eyebrow.

"You sure about that, Taog?"

Taog nodded. The decanus stared at him for a moment longer before heaving a sigh and turning to his men. "You heard the lad; nothing happened here. Return to your posts."

Lar's face went red.

"Decanus, you can't be serious! You're just going to let them go?!"

The decanus glared at Lar.

"*Nothing* happened, *boy*. This visitor here didn't assault you. And *you* and your friends didn't assault Taog, as I have specifically warned you about, *several times*."

Lar opened his mouth, but then frowned and closed it as the decanus continued to glare at him. He shot a vicious look at Taog, then turned and left with a huff. The decanus sighed and turned to Taog.

"I'm sorry about this. Are you all right, Taog?"

"Fine."

". . . Right. May I ask who this is?"

". . . A visiting friend."

The decanus took a deep breath and nodded. "Well, if you say so. Are you going to be alright? I'd rather not deal with any . . . altercations."

Taog nodded. "We're leaving on a trip, anyways. I doubt we'll be back for a while. Should make your life a lot easier, I imagine."

The decanus frowned, heaving another sigh. "Look, Taog, you know if you ever need anything, you just need to ask, okay?"

"Thanks, but I'll be fine."

The decanus sighed once more before nodding and walking off. Taog watched him for a moment before sighing himself. "Some people eventually remembered what my parents did. Not that they'll stand up to those who don't. And too bloody late, if you ask me. Ateia's all I need now. I'm sorry you've gotten wrapped up in this, Seero."

"Acknowledgement: Apology accepted, but not necessary. Defense of friendly units is part of this unit's protocols."

He heaved another sigh. "Right. Let's get going. Oh, and one more thing. Please don't tell Ateia what happened. I don't want her picking another fight with Lar."

"Affirmative."

The pair made their way back to Ateia's house, where Taog somehow managed to convince Ateia not to run out the door while the sun was setting, and so, the group got ready for bed.

Ateia led NSLICE-00P into a spare bedroom.

"Seero, you can use this room here. Do you need pajamas or anything?"

"Negative."

Ateia tilted her head. “Really? I get it while we’re out in the field, but you can rest easy tonight! Don’t you want to get out of that armor?”

“Clarification: This unit’s cybernetic implants are not removable, save by specialized maintenance facilities.”

“Huh? What does that mean?”

“Rephrasing: This unit’s armor plating is built in, and so not removable.”

Ateia froze.

“Wait . . . you’re saying you can’t take your armor off?!”

“Affirmative.”

Ateia’s jaw dropped for a second.

“Oh, wow. That’s, um . . . How did that . . . I’m sorry? Is that—I mean . . . are you okay?”

“Answer: This unit is functioning at full capacity. No damage reported.”

“Um, but . . .”

Taog happened to step over around that time and placed a hand on Ateia’s shoulder. She looked at him with quivering eyes, but he just shook his head. She took a deep breath.

“Well, um . . . make yourself comfortable, then? Just tell me if you need anything, okay?”

“Affirmative.”

“Right. Then . . . I’m going to bed.”

Taog watched her go before turning to NSLICE-00P.

“I’m sorry; she doesn’t mean any harm. I get it if it’s not a pleasant subject, but if you ever do need to talk about it, well, I’m willing to listen. I owe you that much, I think.”

“Affirmative.”

“Well . . . good night then, Seero.”

Taog waited a second longer then walked to his room as well, leaving NSLICE-00P alone.

Well, sort of.

“Request: This unit is requesting additional intel from friendlies Excellion Formantus Rattingtale the Third and Lilussees.”

“Yes-yes, what do you want-request, boss-queen?”

“Ugh, can it, like, wait till morning? I’m, like, about to turn in for the night or something.”

“Query: This unit has logged a significant increase in Dungeon XP and is requesting insight from former dungeon masters.”

NSLICE-00P brought up the notifications from earlier today.

Level up! Your Dungeon Level is now 16!
Level up! Your Dungeon Level is now 17!

Yes, the moment NSLICE-00P had stepped into town, her Dungeon XP began shooting up dramatically, despite the fact she had not terminated any hostiles.

"Oh, like, wow."

"T-This is . . . very fast-quick, yes-yes?"

Both Lilussees and Rattingtale tilted their heads inside their rooms before Lilussees nodded.

"So, like, I think I got it or something? You have that Dungeon Field Generator, or whatever?"

"Affirmative."

"So like, I said dungeons absorb mana and stuff? Well, like, living things give off more mana, so you get more XP if they're inside your dungeon or something. And, like, enlightened races give even more or something. Something about their emotions affecting the mana? I don't know, though."

"Summary: So this unit is gaining additional Dungeon XP due to humans within range of the Dungeon Field Generator?"

"Something like that."

"Revelation: New dungeon intel logged. This unit thanks friendly Lilussees for the additional intel. Next Query: This unit would like intel regarding entity 'treasure chest' recorded in the latest dungeon termination mission."

"Hm . . . I, like, didn't use those much . . ."

"Allow the Great-High King over all the land to instruct-inform you, yes-yes. There is an Item Creation portion of the royal records, yes-yes?"

NSLICE-00P checked her Dungeon Management status once again. Indeed, there was an Item Creation menu option. She opened it up.

Item Creation
Item Creation currently locked. (Requires Item Foundry implant.)

"Observation: Item Creation is locked for this unit, pending purchase of relevant implant."

"Really-truly? This Great-High King had access to it from the start, yes-yes."

"That's, like, because she's pretty different, you know? Like, she has those *implant* things instead of rooms."

"Quiet, wretched spider-thing."

NSLICE-00P opened up the Implant menu to review the option.

Available Implants			
Name	**Cost**	**Mana Upkeep**	**Description**
Unlock Additional Implant Slot	**3**	**0**	**Adds additional slots for implants. +10 HP +5 Dungeon MP**
Item Foundry	**10**	**1**	**Enables Item Creation via dungeon mana.**

NSLICE-00P's robotic eye flickered. Her individual upgrade program had already come to a close, so there was no particular need for her to install additional upgrades, and the implant in question would be one of the most expensive she had purchased. On the other hand, she had just determined she was likely present in a preindustrial society. A method of resupply might one day prove necessary. And likewise, she determined her dungeon levels and available perks would increase dramatically so long as she was present in a population center.

She calculated the benefits as exceeding the costs and so purchased the upgrade.

You have unlocked an Additional Implant Slot! Max HP and Mana increased!
You have unlocked the Item Foundry implant!
Item Creation is now available!
20 Dungeon Perk Points remaining.

With that, NSLICE-00P returned to the Item Creation menu.

Item Creation → Weapons			
Name	**Mana Cost**	**Material Cost**	**Description**
Bronze Sword	**10**	**2 bronze ingots**	**A basic sword made of bronze.**
Bronze Spear	**10**	**1 bronze ingot 1 wooden branch**	**A basic spear made of bronze.**
(. . .)			

Flintlock Pistol	**10**	**1 metal ingot 1 small wooden branch or something. I don't know.**	**Um, I think that's a suitable starter based on that stuff you have? Whatever, close enough. I don't really want to review the several centuries of weapon development history you're suddenly dumping on me, so figure out the blueprints yourself. Added by Cyborg Affinity (Primary).**

". . . Analysis: Technological level of 'Item Creation' resupply significantly below anticipated values."

"What's that? Um, are you saying-suggesting the items are too weak?"

"Affirmative."

"That's like, normal though? You, like, have to upgrade your Item Creation if you want better stuff. Or, like, make it yourself or have someone in your dungeon make it first or something."

NSLICE-00P's robotic eye flickered at the new intel. Intel that was calculated as significant to the prior cost-benefit analysis.

Her new analysis indicated additional intel-gathering was necessary before any upgrade decisions could be correctly evaluated. After all, her individual upgrade program had already succeeded. There was no need to evaluate any further decisions.

"Um, boss? Hello?"

"Boss-queen, you, um, got very quiet-silent, yes-yes."

And with that, NSLICE-00P activated standby-sentry mode for the night.

23

On the Road

"The history of the Etleni Empire cannot be separated from the history of the Legion. Of course, that is exactly what the Imperial doctrine has pounded into us all since our childhood, but in this case, it is undeniably correct. It is no exaggeration to say that the Legion gave birth to the Empire.

To understand why this is so, we must first understand the conditions in which it was born. The Age of Heroes—as it is called by the romantics and the novelists—or more aptly, in my opinion and by any serious historian, the Age of Blood, a time when the Elves and their Empire of the Sun were at their peak, when demon lords ruled the land from their dungeons, and when humanity was little more than scattered tribes.

An in-depth discussion of those times is beyond the scope of this work, so for the sake of brevity, let us consider the overall trend.

In those days, humanity largely existed in one of three states. One, the frightened and trembling inhabitants of minor city-states, whose world did not extend beyond the walls of their city. Two, as the slaves of the local power, whether that be the imperious Elves or the cruel demon lords, forced to spend their strength and their blood on enriching their masters. Three, as savage and brutal tribes, living short and cruel lives of violence and misery, beholden to the will of their chief. And all three of those states had one thing in common: the survival of the group depended solely on the strength of its highest-leveled member. All human efforts went solely to boosting the level of the local champion, whomever they may be.

It sounds fanciful and, quite frankly, arrogant to describe our ancestors in such a manner, but in this case, we know it to be true. Time and time again, we've found that these conditions are replicated almost universally beyond the borders of the Empire. Even the mighty and prosperous Elven civilizations follow this rule; it is simply that their longevity allows them more and greater champions, and so their reach extends farther than most.

This is the world into which the Legion was born. Where human lives were short and bloody, human "society" barely extended beyond the strongest relative, and death came swiftly, suddenly, and often. And for once, it is not romantic exaggeration to say that the Legion changed everything."

—*The History of the Empire*, by Hostus Tettidius Clodian

Ateia and Taog woke up in the middle of the night to the sound of spells being cast. Both of them shot out of their rooms, knives in hand. They heard the sound again, coming from the latrine. Both of them nodded at one another and rushed over.

They found NSLICE-00P launching Magic Missiles down into it.

"Seero, what are you doing!"

"Answer: This unit's sentry scans detected hostiles in the area. This unit is in the process of terminating them."

"Hostiles? What hostiles?!"

"Answer: This unit has detected hostile slimes in this facility. Slimes are designated to be terminated on sight."

Both Ateia and Taog blinked for a second as they processed the situation.

"Seero! Not these slimes! Those are sewer slimes!"

"Requesting Elaboration: There are different types of slime? Including non-hostile variants?"

"Yes! These ones are bred by the Empire to clean up waste! So don't hunt them!"

"Acknowledged. Data on entity 'slime' updated with new intel. Slimes located in organic waste facilities redesignated as 'terminate if hostile intent detected.'"

Ateia exhaled her breath as NSLICE-00P dropped the magic circles and returned to her room. Taog hit his forehead with his palm and groaned.

The next morning, Ateia made a quick stop at the small Legion barracks so they could send word ahead. A fancy name for the town's guardhouse, but this was technically an Imperial settlement, and the guards were technically limitanei, so they did have a way to contact the provincial headquarters.

And with that, the group set off once more.

They were not far along the road when NSLICE-00P stopped walking and engaged her helmet. "Warning: Hostiles detected outside of the bounds of a settlement. Engaging termination protocols."

Ateia and Taog turned around, then he quickly rushed over to NSLICE-00P, whispering so Ateia wouldn't hear, "Is it Lar and the others?"

"Affirmative."

Taog took a deep breath, and then . . . he had a thought.

They were outside the town. No one else was around. NSLICE-00P might be quick to kill, but in every instance he had seen her, she had technically acted in self-defense. So . . . if he didn't say anything, and NSLICE-00P encountered Lar again . . . Well, he would never have to see Lar's stupid face ever again.

In fact, it would simply be justice, wouldn't it? It wouldn't be *his* fault if Lar went and got himself killed by being a jerk.

He took a deep breath. And then he let it pass.

Growing up as an orphaned half Wulver had taught him never to act solely on his emotions. As much as he would like it if Lar died, he at least had to consider the consequences first. So he recounted the situation. He, Ateia, and NSLICE-00P had just left town; Ateia had even announced their departure to the Legion. Lar and his friends had left town shortly afterward. Lar had just had an altercation with NSLICE-00P which was reported to the guards. So if Lar never returned or else was found dead outside of town a day later, he and NSLICE-00P would be the prime suspects.

And given the townsfolk's general distrust and often blatant dislike of him, and the fact that NSLICE-00P was a visitor with no connections . . . it was obvious what the verdict in town would be. Now, altercations happened out in the field all the time, so it wasn't as if they had legal proof, but to them, it wouldn't matter. His enemies would use it as an excuse to rally the mob against him. He could never return there.

Personally, he was fine with that, but there was a chance Ateia would like to return. Plus . . . his parents were buried there. That was not something he was willing to let go of yet.

And there could be other consequences. The townsfolk would report the situation to the Legion, who would have to conduct an investigation. Now, the Legion didn't have any personal beef with Taog, and altercations on the road were notoriously hard to investigate, so he wasn't likely to be convicted. Still, though, being accused of murder could complicate his application to the Exploratores. Also . . . he was fairly certain NSLICE-00P wasn't an Imperial citizen. And he was completely certain she was extremely dangerous. As such, the Legion might not be as understanding toward her.

He wasn't going to see Lar for quite a while, in any case—maybe ever—if all went as planned. All of which meant killing Lar here would be risking his future and his benefactor for momentary satisfaction.

Taog heaved a sigh. "Seero, please don't kill them. It could cause trouble if we get investigated for murder."

"Acknowledged."

Taog smirked. "Doesn't mean we have to let them follow us, though. Do you have a way to trip them up without letting Ateia know?"

"Analyzing . . ."

NSLICE-00P went through her arsenal. None of her nonlethal implants could affect the targets from this distance, so she went through the more recent additions instead. And she came up with a viable option, given past combat data.

NSLICE-00P stirred up her mana . . . and began to transform it. All schools of magic category skills contained basic knowledge on how to lend their respective attribute to mana, the fundamental requirement for casting attributed spells in the first place. This was generally useful for noncombat applications; for example, creating Fire-attribute mana without a spell would generate a small amount of flame which could be used to start a fire.

In this case, NSLICE-00P chose the Earth attribute, allowing her mana to interact with and move earth and stone about. She then seeped the Earth mana into the ground and stretched it out down the road. Farther and farther the mana stretched, until it was resting underneath the incoming targets. Her head ached as she struggled to hold the energy in such a long and thin line, but her cybernetic half aided her focus.

And then, she activated the Earth mana, using it to move the dirt around, creating a circular pit . . . directly under the signatures she had detected.

You have learned the spell Pitfall!
The skill Earth Magic is now Level 4!
The skill Earth Magic is now Level 5!
Mana Control increased by 10 and is now 130!
You have learned the skill Farcasting!

Spells		
Earth		
Name	Level	Description
Pitfall	1	Dig a large hole in a target area. May be concealed. Mana cost may increase depending on suitability of terrain.

Active Skills		
Name	Level	Description
Farcasting	1	Allows the user to manipulate mana and create magic circles at far distances.

"Statement: Hostiles have been nonlethally incapacitated."

"What did you do?"

NSLICE-00P explained, and Taog had to cover his mouth as his shoulders trembled.

Ateia frowned. "What are you two talking about over there?"

"N-Nothing, nothing. Don't worry about it."

Ateia raised an eyebrow at that, but NSLICE-00P had disengaged her helmet and resumed walking, so she let it go, and the group continued on their way.

Lar and his friends spent the day shouting from the bottom of the pit until a farmer happened by later that night.

And so, the trio made their way along the road. They traveled across rolling hills, the trees and forests giving way to walled farms and the occasional watchtower.

Ateia and Taog explained the history of the Empire as they walked, how the legendary champion Velus had come up with the idea of the Legion and had saved his home city. How that home city had used the Legion to establish itself and bring peace to the surrounding area. And how that had given birth to a nation, the first true human nation in history, which had continued to grow across the centuries until now, when it encompassed almost an entire continent and practically all of human civilization, not to mention the many client races it had absorbed as well.

Suddenly, NSLICE-00P stopped, turning in the direction of a nearby hill.

"Warning: This unit has detected numerous signatures, indicating a large group of humanoids, moving in this direction. Recommending caution."

Ateia and Taog looked at one another. Ateia tilted her head.

"I mean, that has to be the Legion, right?"

Taog rubbed his chin. "Could be an incursion . . . but there should have been a call to arms long before they got this far if so. So yeah, I'd say it's most likely the Legion. Though, I wonder what they're doing out here? And off the road?"

Ateia shrugged.

"Training exercise? Dealing with a big monster? I mean, the Legion sorties for a lot of reasons that don't require a general alert, right?"

Taog nodded. "That's true."

"Requesting Clarification: So detected signatures likely belong to Empire-aligned forces?"

The pair nodded, then Ateia grinned.

"Actually, that could be good. Seero, how would you like to see the Legion in action?"

"Response: Intel on entity 'Legion' is calculated to be highly useful in identifying this unit's current location. It would be most appreciated."

"Got it. Let's go then!"

"Are you sure, Ateia? They could be fighting something dangerous, you know?"

Ateia shook her head. "We'll be careful and just take a peek from afar. If the threat is big enough that even that's too dangerous, then the Legion should have announced the threat."

Taog nodded slowly. "I guess that's true."

"It's settled then!"

And so, the three made their way off the road, climbing up and down the nearby hills as they moved in the direction of the signatures. Closer and closer they came, though the hills still blocked them from view. Finally, there was but a single hill between the groups. The three climbed to the top and peeked over it.

Ateia and Taog's jaws dropped.

"What . . . is this? What's happening? This is impossible."

It was not the Legion.

The valley below was filled to the brim with Wulver clansfolk. They moved swiftly and quietly through the valley despite their numbers.

Ateia and Taog's eyes widened.

"It's . . . an incursion."

24

Terminate the Incursion!

"Honestly, the reports coming from this province are utterly disgraceful. They say these 'Wulver' are a people who care about nothing but battle. Who understand no language but violence. Who see the whole world as either predator or prey and only trade words with the former. I knew the state of education in the outer provinces was atrocious, but this level of ignorance is simply unacceptable. Pathetic even!

Savages like what the cowardly locals describe do not truly exist, in my experience. I have negotiated with countless other races—even the arrogant Sun Elves several times my age—and let me tell you the truth: there is no one, and I mean no one, who will not accept the Empire with open arms once they understand the bounty our advanced civilization will bring them. No one would choose to scrounge for scraps in a primitive tribe when faced with our abundance and culture. And these Wulver will be no different. It shall hardly take me a day to bring these primitives into the fold!"

—A report to Elteno by Consul Proclus Caecilius Tutor, shortly before his death at the hands of a Wulver warpack.

Taog trembled, his eyes going wide.

"How . . . how is this possible? The Exploratores wouldn't have missed a pack this size; the Empire should have caught them days ago! They should have been stopped at the border; at the very least, the Empire should have put out an alert!"

Ateia had already pulled out her bow.

"Taog! Think later! We need to move!"

"Observation: From friendly Ateia and Taog's reactions, this unit speculates the group below is not the aforementioned Legion?"

Ateia shook her head. "No! It's a Wulver warpack, Seero! Let's go before they spot us!"

But it was too late. The trio heard a howl, which was quickly joined by others into a mighty chorus. A small scouting band crested the hill, and now rushed toward them at full speed.

"Attempting diplomacy with third-party faction. Greeting: Hello, this unit is designated NSLICE-00P—"

Taog called out to her as he hoisted his shield and stepped in front of Ateia, "Seero! Wulver attack first and talk after! You can't talk to them until you prove you're not prey!"

NSLICE-00P created a Mana Barrier as the first Wulver reached her, leaping toward her with claws extended.

"Observation: Friendly Taog's assessment appears to be correct. Hostile intent detected. Engaging termination protocols."

NSLICE-00P engaged her helmet and assault rifle arms, and immediately opened fire.

You have slain Wulver (Level 8)!
Gained 5 Personal XP, 3 Dungeon XP!

She quickly turned her arms, taking down the Wulver's two companions.

You have—

NSLICE-00P requested an adjustment to the notifications, turning it into a kill counter at the top of her screen.

Hostiles slain: 3

To the cyborg's side, Taog grunted and fell back as a Wulver crashed against his shield, only for a Power Shot from Ateia to catch the assailant right on the forehead. His HP barrier managed to catch the blow and deflect the arrow, but shattered in the attempt. As such, nothing was protecting the Wulver when Taog thrust his sword up from below and into the wolfman's torso.

NSLICE-00P formed a group of magic circles to her side, Magic Missiles bombarding two more Wulvers rushing for Taog before he could stand back up.

Wulvers slain: 7

She noted the effectiveness of the Magic Missiles against the Wulver and continued her assault. It was not long before the scouting party was annihilated.

Hostiles slain: 10

However, the scouting party was not alone. More howls rang out all around the group, with two more scout parties rushing up the hill. The trio turned to run, but a returning party appeared behind them.

"Seero, let's get out of here! Can you carry us again?!"

"Negative Response: Hostiles are to be terminated, and friendlies are not predicted to be at risk. Continuing termination."

NSLICE-00P had been an enforcer for a ruling party for much of her life. While she did have evacuation protocols, retreat was always considered the last option in her calculations. After all, her creators would not want their enforcers to show weakness or to leave hostiles at large in their home territory. As a result, NSLICE-00P generally would not retreat unless she calculated an imminent risk of termination or mission failure.

And in this case?

Panels opened on NSLICE-00P's shoulder, two anti-personnel missiles launching at the scout party behind them and nearly wiping out the group. NSLICE-00P quickly turned her machine-gun arms to sweep over the few survivors.

Hostiles slain: 22

Magic circles continued to form above her, bombarding the other two parties with Magic Missiles and Light Beams. Not a single Wulver made it even halfway up the hill.

Hostiles slain: 48

In this case, they had proven terribly vulnerable to NSLICE-00P's arsenal, and seemed to lack any sort of ranged attacks to retaliate. NSLICE-00P already held the high ground, with clear lines of sight to her opponents. And thanks to her dungeon mechanics, she wasn't about to run out of ammunition anytime soon.

In other words, she calculated that the risk of termination for herself and her allies was acceptably low at the moment. And as the Wulvers had already demonstrated unprovoked hostility, she had designated this group for termination, which meant she would not stop until the situation changed, or the threat was neutralized.

Inside the Monster Hangar, both Lilussees and Rattingtale's eyes widened.

"Wow, that's like, a lot of wolfmen or something. Boss, are you, like, sure about this?"

"Boss-queen, run-flee now! The vicious wolfman-things will tear-rip us to shreds, yes-yes!"

* * *

Back outside, Ateia and Taog gulped.

"W-Well . . . Seero is really strong."

"Yeah, but strong enough to take on an entire warpack?! Alone?!"

"I mean . . . she sort of is doing it already?"

"And what happens to us while she does?"

"Answer: Friendlies Ateia and Taog are currently designated as priority assets. This unit will evacuate friendlies if the risk of termination reaches unacceptable levels."

"I'd rather us not risk 'termination' at all!"

Ateia rubbed her chin.

"Well, if Seero *can* stop them . . . then shouldn't she?"

"Ateia?"

"They've made it this far. Somehow, the Legion hasn't detected them yet. There are a lot of farms and towns between here and the next Legion outpost, so a lot of people are going to die before the Legion stops them. If, by some chance, Seero can turn them back . . ."

Taog went silent, turning to watch as NSLICE-00P wiped out yet another scout party. At this point, the main warpack had noticed the commotion and were starting to move toward the hill.

He heaved a sigh.

At the end of the day, what choice did he have? If NSLICE-00P didn't want to leave, he couldn't particularly make her. And if he and Ateia tried to flee on foot, the Wulver would run them down in minutes. Like it or not, he was stuck here until NSLICE-00P decided otherwise.

So he gulped and gripped his weapons. Ateia nocked another arrow.

As the Wulver stormed up the hill, they were met by a hail of lead, missiles, Mana Beams, Light Beams, Fire Bolts, Poison Bolts, Magic Missiles, Light Bolts, and the occasional arrow. They split up, surrounding the hill and attacking from the flanks, but NSLICE-00P's sensors could not be deceived. She appeared to them to have eyes on the back of her head as magic circles faced anywhere her weapons did not.

They sent their toughest warriors, hoping to endure the barrage, but mana-infused bullets cut them down as easily as any other. The fastest among them hid behind their stalwart comrades and leapt forward as they fell, but NSLICE-00P had already accounted for them, and they made it little further. Some of the Wulver attempted to respond with Claw Strikes, spells, or even whatever sticks and rocks they could find, but few of them could match NSLICE-00P's range. Even those who did found their meager attacks blocked by Mana Barriers.

So eventually, the Wulver abandoned all tactics and simply rushed the hill en masse. NSLICE-00P had slain more than a hundred at this point, but the

Wulver measured in the thousands. Surely, she could not cut them all down before they made it up the hill, and even if she could, she surely must run out of projectiles and spells before the Wulver ran out of bodies, right?

But the Wulver were unaware they were fighting a dungeon. And one of the first rules of fighting a dungeon was never to fight a dungeon in a war of attrition.

As the Wulver forced their way up the hill, inch by inch, millimeter by millimeter, NSLICE-00P put some of her new spells to use.

The spell Pitfall has increased by 3 levels and is now Level 4!
The spell Earth Wall has increased by 3 levels and is now Level 6!
The spell Vine Grasp has increased by 3 levels and is now Level 4!
The spell Fire Blast is now Level 7!
The skill Earth Magic has increased by 2 levels and is now Level 7!
The skill Nature Magic has increased by 2 levels and is now Level 3! Spell choice available!
The skill Fire Magic is now Level 6! Spell choice available!
The skill Multicasting is now Level 7!
The skill Farcasting has increased by 2 levels and is now Level 3!
You have accomplished the Personal Feat: Strategic Mage!

NSLICE-00P had used multiple Pitfall spells to dig a large trench all around the hill, using Earth Wall to form a small rampart on the far side with the displaced dirt. She then used the Vine Grasp spell to fill the trench with plant matter.

And then set the whole thing on fire.

The Wulver found themselves faced with a roaring inferno and ground to a halt, leaving them as sitting ducks for NSLICE-00P's continuous barrage. Oh, and the occasional arrow and damaging potion from Ateia.

Taog just stared at the events occurring before him, blinking repeatedly.

She was doing it. NSLICE-00P was actually holding back an entire warpack *by herself.* Well, Ateia would argue vehemently that she was contributing, but that was beside the point.

An incursion that would take an entire comitatenses legion to push back, and they couldn't take a single hill from one girl.

Taog started to tremble.

It had been one thing to see NSLICE-00P blast her way through the confined halls of a dungeon or take down a young demon lord in minutes. It was another thing entirely to see her slaughter hundreds of Wulver in the open field. He couldn't help but feel a chill run down his spine as he watched the scene of absolute hell in front of him, full of fire and blood and death by invisible projectiles, with sounds like thunder assaulting his ears.

Who exactly was this girl?!

* * *

Meanwhile, in the hangar, Rattingtale was also trembling, having much the same thoughts as Taog. He and Lilussees had been waiting by the entrance in case they needed to beat a hasty retreat, but now, they were frozen at the scene they saw from the live feed.

"Oh, wow. She's, like, totally doing it. I guess we were, like, worried for nothing. Well, I'm going to, like, go lie down, then, or something."

Rattingtale just continued to tremble as Lilussees returned to her room.

Maybe he should gain a few more levels before beginning any of his plans . . .

25

The Trial of Claws

"The Wulver are considered as savages who kill anything that moves, but this misses a great deal of nuance. Yes, the Wulver are callous and bloodthirsty and should not be approached carelessly. Yes, violence occupies a disproportionately large space in their culture, and they value strength above all other virtues. However, they are ultimately a fully intelligent people with their own society and culture, albeit one with far different values from our own.

Take, for example, the often quoted and entirely misunderstood ritual of the Trial of Claws. To the uninformed observer, this ritual appears to be proof of the Wulver's savage nature. That only the strongest lead, and authority is earned solely through deadly combat. But I don't believe this to be the case. In fact, the Trial of Claws is a tradition of remarkable restraint for such a bloodthirsty race. What the casual observer forgets is that tribal warfare is extraordinarily brutal. When human tribes of similar scale and sophistication as the Wulver clans come to blows, the conflict often ends with the complete eradication of the losing party. High-leveled adults are executed; low-leveled adults and children are enslaved. So, if anything, we would expect similar conflicts between the naturally bloodthirsty Wulver to be even bloodier.

But they are not.

The Wulver possess a universally agreed upon method to settle disputes with a single duel. Only a single casualty can end a war between two clans. The losing clan is either peacefully absorbed with all its members intact, or may settle the loss with an offer of tribute, either of which is a remarkably lenient and restrained price to pay.

To me, this suggests a surprising degree of collective self-awareness by the Wulver. That they understand their own nature and have taken the necessary steps to keep their own fondness for violence from spiraling out of control. That there is a method to their madness. That they are more than capable of respecting honor and tradition.

That they are not just savage beasts indulging in base instincts, but that they, too, consider the future and survival of their species in their own bloodthirsty way."

—*The Peoples of the Frontiers,* Volume V: *Turannia and the North*, by traveling author and former Exploratore Placus Paesentius Statius.

Solamh Greumach frowned at the sight before him. A mere three Imperials had slaughtered his warpack.

The invasion had gone well at first. Solamh had doubted the words of the strange humans who turned on their own, claiming the Empire's defenses were weak. So he was surprised at first to find they had spoken the truth. The Empire's scouts were entirely missing. Solamh's entire warpack had left the Domhan na Beithigh and crossed the Empire's borders without encountering a single smooth-skin. It seemed they could dive into the heart of the enemy's lands without a word of warning, and hunt as they pleased.

Perhaps they might have even assaulted one of the Empire's fortresses, and tear down its walls. The Aesdes knows no Imperial could stand against the mighty Wulver if they lacked those stone monstrosities to hide behind.

But it turned out the humans were as treacherous as Solamh first predicted.

When his scouts encountered three young Imperials, he thought nothing of it. They would be hunted down with ease. When they fought back against the first scouts, Solamh committed a pack or two to deal with it. Three Imperials weren't a threat, but he couldn't risk them sounding the alarm, after all.

And then he learned the truth.

They were not hunting some young whelp of a farmer who had strayed off the beaten path. They were fighting some sort of powerful shaman who could create fortresses in an instant, and wipe out countless warriors with deadly spells. The Wulver couldn't even see the spell used as holes appeared through their HP and bodies.

Solamh growled and snapped his teeth. He would tear the throat of the treacherous humans who advised him to take this path.

But for now, he had to find a way to deal with this threat. If he had known of a shaman of this power, he would have taken another route, or delayed his attack on the Empire to begin with. But now that the Wulver had engaged and blood was spilled, he was committed. His warpack was a hodgepodge of different clans strung together by his might as he defeated their chiefs. If he retreated now, at the hands of a single Imperial girl, the cracks would split apart and the subjugated packs would seize their opportunity. The warpack would break apart, and every clan in the area would unite against him.

Even if he went and beat them down once more, it would take time, and would spend the strength of the clans. Any opportunity to strike at the Empire would be lost. Any opportunity to gain more for himself than the rulership of his own clan would be lost. And the rest of the Wulver would whisper of his cowardice for all his life.

So Solamh made his choice.

He stepped forward towards the hill.

Hostiles slain: 347

NSLICE-00P looked out over the burning wall. If the Wulver horde made it any closer, she would not be able to guarantee her allies' safety. Should that occur, she would need to evacuate the pair. Which was fine; she could always conduct hit-and-run airstrikes once Ateia and Taog were clear of danger.

The cyborg was just about to grab the pair when something changed.

Suddenly, the Wulver ceased their assault, backing up from the wall. Taog's eyes widened.

"Ah, Ateia, Seero, stop attacking them!"

"Requesting Elaboration."

"They're going to speak with you."

"Acknowledged."

NSLICE-00P—and Ateia—ceased the barrage. The wolfmen split to the side, forming a pathway. An exceptionally large Wulver stepped into the corridor, approaching the wall. He had scars all over his body, including one over his left eye, and massive muscles which seemed like they would rip out of his fur. He walked with a heavy gait until he stood just before the wall. He grinned, showing his fangs with a low growl.

"You . . . you're not bad for a furless. You've sure done well culling my pack. You . . . may be worth hunting." He turned to Taog, growling once more. "You there, mutt! Do you speak our tongue?"

Taog frowned and narrowed his eyes, but he nodded.

"So you're not an entirely useless weakling, huh? Relay my words to the furless. I am Solamh Greumach, Great Chief of this warpack! I wish to face her in the Trial of Claws."

"Query: Please define term 'Trial of Claws.'"

Ateia, Taog, and Solamh's eyes all widened at that.

"Seero, you . . . speak Wulver?"

"Query: Hostile negotiator is speaking a different language?"

"What?"

Everyone just stared at NSLICE-00P for a second. The cyborg herself logged that question as an anomaly for further investigation.

"Observation: Queries on language anomalies deemed low priority under current circumstances. Requesting response on higher priority query: define term 'Trial of Claws.'"

Taog trembled but shook his head. NSLICE-00P was right. Confusing and concerning questions about her identity could wait until after the Wulver warpack was dealt with.

"A Trial of Claws is essentially a ritual duel. You and this Wulver will fight one another, one-on-one. If it's between Wulver, it can determine leadership of the pack. Since you're an outsider, that probably won't happen, but . . . if you win, you will be immune to further attack from this pack. And without their leader, they will probably disband."

"Summary: So if this unit engages in the duel and wins, hostilities will cease with entity 'Wulver warpack?'"

Ateia nodded at that. "Yes, and this incursion will stop."

Taog frowned as he nodded. "That's true, but . . . it takes someone special to unite a warpack of this size. You should be careful, Seero. It might be wiser for us to run."

NSLICE-00P's robotic eye flickered and spun as she observed Solamh, activating all of her sensors. Her analysis of his energy readings and physical state indicated he was about on par with the ursanus alpha.

In other words, she could definitely terminate him.

"Query: What is the probability that Wulver warpack will adhere to Trial of Claws and its outcome? Will friendlies Ateia and Taog remain safe while the Trial of Claws is in progress?"

Taog frowned at that.

"Wulver would kill you for asking that. It's one of their most sacred traditions. They will not defy it. And no member of the parties in question may harm one another; that is grounds for an instant forfeit."

"Query: Please define terms and conditions of the Trial of Claws."

"Right, so, it's been a while, but this is what my mom told me . . ."

Taog went on to explain. The rules were fairly simple—a duel to the death within a designated area. NSLICE-00P could use all of her arsenal, but neither combatant could receive any outside aid. In addition, NSLICE-00P would have a cap on how high she could fly, again to respect the designated boundaries of the duel.

NSLICE-00P calculated that she would have an acceptable chance of terminating her opponent even under those conditions, and that ending hostilities with the Wulver via a single termination would be the most efficient course of action. Tactically speaking, the Wulver outnumbered NSLICE-00P by a significant degree. Facing the Wulver leader while he had no support from his forces would remove that advantage. Conversely, if NSLICE-00P lost support from Ateia and Taog, it would not appreciably impact the probability of a successful termination.

Beyond that . . . this was apparently an intelligent species with at least a simple social organization. There was a non-zero chance they possessed intel regarding her persons of interest. There was even a chance they could be affiliated with one of those persons, which would make this entire engagement an instance of friendly fire. That chance translated to a chance that NSLICE-00P was harming the primary directive success probability by terminating these individuals.

The probability was not high enough to outweigh her self-defense protocols, so she would still terminate any active hostile. But if she had the chance to end hostilities without fully terminating a group of unknown loyalties, she would take it.

"Acknowledgement: This unit has calculated the terms of Trial of Claws to be acceptable and is willing to engage."

Solamh tilted his head.

"Um . . ."

Taog heaved a sigh.

"She'll do it."

Solamh grinned.

"Excellent."

With that, NSLICE-00P carried Ateia and Taog out of the burning walls, which were agreed upon as the boundaries of the duel. Her opponent leapt right over the fire, landing in the center. The Wulver packed around the ramparts, eagerly staring at the two combatants, while Ateia and Taog gulped.

An elderly Wulver called out, "Warriors ready?"

Solamh grinned, letting out a low growl. "Ready."

"Affirmative."

". . . That means yes, right?"

The elder shook his head and shrugged.

"Trial of Claws, begin!"

Solamh immediately took off running, sprinting straight toward NSLICE-00P. The cyborg responded by lifting her machine-gun arms and opening fire, magic circles forming around her to add Magic Missiles to the barrage. Solamh dug in his heels and leapt to the side. Some of the bullets and Magic Missiles caught him, but unlike with the other Wulver, they didn't pierce through his HP barrier.

As NSLICE-00P had calculated earlier, it seemed Solamh's defense was close to the ursanus's. But he did not surpass the monster in that field.

"Equalizer engaged."

NSLICE-00P transformed one of her hands, firing her rainbow beam at Solamh. His eyes widened as the beam started to tear at his HP. He snarled and stirred up his mana. Suddenly, Solamh's speed increased, causing the Wulver to dash to the side almost instantly. NSLICE-00P responded right away, bringing the Equalizer back on target, but Solamh dashed again.

"Observation: Target speed above predictions. Adapting strategy."

Several magic circles formed above her head, firing Light Beams across the field. Solamh dashed away, only to be caught by the Equalizer once more. He clenched his teeth and dashed once more, right into the path of a Light Beam.

At first, he gritted his teeth.

But then he paused . . . and then grinned. The Light Beam had done only minor damage to his HP.

Solamh began dashing once more, this time taking care to avoid the Equalizer beam, letting the Light Beams strike him at will. He dropped down on all fours, running and dashing in a circle around the cyborg. Lights continued to flash, and beams struck his HP barrier, but none of them dealt a debilitating blow. Then suddenly, as the Equalizer struck his former location, he stopped and turned toward NSLICE-00P, leaping right at her.

Several Light Beams struck his chest, but he ignored them. NSLICE-00P brought up her hand to aim the Equalizer at him once more, but Solamh had timed his attack well. He arrived just as the beam approached him from the side.

He bit down at NSLICE-00P's hand with all his might and tore it off.

NSLICE-00P activated her thrusters and flew backward, but the Wulver refused to let her take distance. He rushed toward her, swinging claws glowing with mana. NSLICE-00P hastily converted the Light Beam magic circles to Mana Barriers, weakening the Claw Strikes. But she quickly determined that was not enough and activated the wrist blade on her damaged arm, the blade just above where her hand had been torn off.

"Activating Power Strike protocol."

The blade began to glow as she swung it. Thin arcs of mana shot a few inches from the blade, striking into the much brighter arcs smashing through her barriers. Her level one skill obviously couldn't match Solamh's honed strikes, but her attack and her barriers combined offset his assault enough to prevent serious damage.

Meanwhile, she redirected the Equalizer through her other hand and opened fire. Solamh was forced to dash to the side once more, giving NSLICE-00P some breathing room. She immediately activated her repulsors and shot into the sky.

Solamh crouched down on all fours and pushed off, rocketing after her. She threw up a wave of barriers, which barely gave her enough time to move out of the way. She struck Solamh with the Equalizer on his way down, but he curled up and spun through the air. The glancing blows from the attack were not enough to cause him serious harm. NSLICE-00P's robotic eye flickered and spun. She opened fire with her flamethrowers and Fire Blast spells, an inferno washing over Solamh. But the big Wulver ignored the flames, leaping straight through them. NSLICE-00P was forced to evade once again.

NSLICE-00P's eye began to spin faster as she calculated. The probability of terminating Solamh was dropping rapidly. And the probability of her being terminated was rising.

It seemed she had miscalculated.

When she'd equated Solamh to the ursanus, she'd been considering the physical readout only. On paper, the two were very close. Solamh had the advantage in speed, but the ursanus had the advantage in durability. That was a surprise, but one that could have been managed.

But she had not considered the difference in mentality.

Solamh was no beast fighting based on raw instinct. He was an intelligent and highly experienced warrior. He used tactics and strategy. He could vary his approach. He could identify and prioritize NSLICE-00P's attacks, dodging the ones that could cause him serious harm and ignoring the ones that would not.

He was utilizing his advantages in raw statistics to their maximum. As long as he took care to avoid the Equalizer, he could deal damage to her faster than she could deal it to him.

Her simulations of the current conflict were returning a sobering picture.

She activated her sensors to the maximum, analyzing Solamh as quickly as she could to improve her evasion efficiency, calculating different options to overturn the situation.

But she could not dodge perfectly, so with each pass, her HP was draining. Solamh lost a bit too, but he seemed no worse for wear.

In fact, he was grinning.

And the Wulver pack started howling and cheering.

Ateia and Taog frowned. They glanced at each other, their eyes trembling.

NSLICE-00P . . . was losing?

Inside the Monster Hangar, the two former dungeon masters were watching in silence. Rattingtale gulped.

"Um, boss-queen, isn't this . . . very bad-concerning?"

"Like, hate to agree with the snack, but that wolf seems pretty strong or something."

"S-Shouldn't we prepare to run-flee if the boss-queen dies?"

"Like, we're in the middle of a bunch of wolfmen with, like, no cover or something."

"S-So . . . if the boss-queen loses, we're dead-doomed?"

". . . Like, probably?"

"Stupid man-thing, run-flee! This Great-High King cannot be allowed to perish here, no-no!"

"That's like, probably a good idea or something, boss."

But NSLICE-00P wasn't listening to the two, for she had to devote all of her resources and attention to the fight.

26

Unshackled

"It appears our NSLICE units are failing to adapt efficiently when encountering unorthodox tactics and non-standard abilities. However, our initial attempts to increase the flexibility of NSLICE protocols reduced the effectiveness of the intelligence leashing measures by an unacceptable degree. I will continue to iterate on this, but in the meantime I recommend increasing the inherent capabilities of the NSLICE units. NSLICE-00P has demonstrated the viability of this, as the Equalizer has made it capable of defeating any foe encountered thus far. I would thus like to requisition some of the nonstandard prisoners, to determine if a more capable organic base will solve this issue."

—Dr. Ottosen, in a meeting reviewing the performance of the NSLICE program.

NSLICE 00P's robotic eye flickered rapidly. She began devoting all her focus toward defense, activated her sensors to the limit, and turned all simulation processing to analyzing the Wulver's next move. Using a random movement pattern with her repulsors, she created as many Mana Barriers as she could, utilizing her Recovery Magic to repair some of the damage. Anything she could do to buy time so she could calculate a response.

She considered a withdrawal. But there were several issues with that. First of all, a break in the rules of the current engagement would result in continued hostilities with the Wulver warpack. She would be forced to terminate the entire group with long-range strikes. As she previously calculated, unless she could determine if this pack had any relation with or knowledge about the persons of interest, that would represent a potential threat to her primary directive. She would do it if she had no other choice, but the most efficient course of action would be to terminate Solamh in the Trial of Claws if at all possible.

Additionally, Ateia and Taog were now located within the Wulver pack, safe only due to the rules of the Trial of Claws. Should NSLICE-00P break those rules, that safety would be immediately revoked. And with Solamh on her tail, she could not guarantee a successful evacuation. If she withdrew, she would lose her allies and her main source of intel. She didn't know how important their assistance would be to her primary directive, but still, immediately losing the local contacts would represent a setback.

And above all . . . retreating from a hostile non-standard was something NSLICE-00P only ever did when ordered to, or when her calculations predicted near-certain defeat.

All of this combined meant NSLICE-00P would only withdraw if victory was practically impossible. In the case of the ursanus, even the strongest weapons in her arsenal proved almost entirely ineffective against it, while her defenses were woefully insufficient. At that point, she had no further means by which to change the probability of success, and withdrew.

This time? The situation was bad, and growing worse, but NSLICE-00P had conducted a successful attack on Solamh, and her defenses could mitigate his attacks. And if all her current arsenal proved insufficient, she still had additional perk points available within the foreign system. She could upgrade her capabilities in real time.

Due to all of this, NSLICE-00P determined it was not yet time to retreat. It was still possible that some combination of protocol updates and/or arsenal upgrades via the foreign system would allow her to terminate Solamh.

But she ran into a bottleneck.

She needed all of her AI's analytical capabilities to mitigate Solamh's attacks and keep the damage at an acceptable level, which meant she could not conduct full combat simulations or a detailed cost-benefit analysis at the same time. So she did something she had never done before. Something her creators had wholeheartedly opposed. Something that wouldn't have been possible had her last commander not removed all her restrictions.

She unlocked every control on her organic half and tasked it with finding a solution, temporarily separating her cybernetic and organic halves into two separate threads.

Her human eye blinked several times as her mind processed the situation. Her AI side had separated their focus, and now the human mind was alone with its task. But it had not taken on a task alone at any point in its memory.

Her original creators did not want the human mind thinking on its own under any circumstances. The ones who had captured and hacked her had left those controls in place until she completed the mission they'd set for her. Her last commander *had* left a protocol to unlock those controls once the mission was done, but NSLICE-00P had seen no reason to do so until now. Her cybernetic side had a directive, a purpose. And it knew what steps it could take to achieve it. Her organic side just followed along, acting more like additional, flexible hardware.

Now?

Now the AI had tasked the human mind with finding a solution to this battle, but the AI hadn't had the time to analyze the situation before turning back to the defense, so the human mind didn't have anywhere to start. It didn't have a specific goal or orders to focus on, other than "overturn the situation." Her organic half did not believe it would come up with an effective protocol on its own if her cybernetic half could not, so instead she chose to pursue more foreign system upgrades. She opened up the foreign program windows, looking over the options. But her human eye widened and started to tremble.

It was too much for her to handle.

There were windows for upgrading implants, windows for buying new implants, windows for upgrading traps, windows to unlock new traps, windows for dungeon perks and entirely new capabilities, windows for item creation, and windows for subordinate summoning. There was an entirely separate section for her Personal Status, with windows for active physical skills, active magic skills, passive physical skills, passive magic skills, upgrades to her physical stats, upgrades to her magical stats—the windows went on and on.

NSLICE-00P had no idea where to begin, no idea what sort of upgrades might help.

She requested a cost-benefit analysis, but the AI was busy and did not respond. She requested a directive, a desired capability she could try to deliver on, but again, the AI was busy. It just barely moved her body out of the way as Solamh passed by her again, deep scratches appearing on one of her arms.

There was too much. She didn't know where to start. All her normal decision-making methods were unavailable.

And she would die if she couldn't figure it out.

Her human eye started to tremble. Her heart rate increased. Her head felt dizzy.

Her cybernetic components noticed the organic half's plight just as it dodged Solamh once more. It found a moment to send a single file before focusing back on the fight.

A new window opened up on the inside of her helmet so her human eye could view it directly—a recording and previously conducted analysis of her fight with the ursanus.

And a data table showing the resources NSLICE-00P had utilized during the fight. Which showed a large percentage contribution from her organic components during the initial combat simulations, when she'd determined if and how she would fight the monster. As well as during the initial upgrade process, when she'd had to figure out how to boost her capabilities in the first place.

Her organic eye watched for a moment before narrowing. She may not have had all the normal resources or directions, but she was still her. Her organic mind may not have made these decisions on its own before, but it'd still participated when the decisions were made. Its capabilities were as necessary to her success as those of her cybernetic half.

That was the point of the NSLICE program, after all.

She had conclusive proof that the organic components had the right capabilities. She just needed to figure out how to use them.

The organic eye turned its attention back to the fight, and how it had begun. The problem was that she couldn't deal enough damage reliably. The Wulver's defenses could endure her spells and conventional weaponry; the Equalizer was the only tool she had which dealt sufficient damage to it. But the Wulver was fast and intelligent enough to dodge a single attack when he knew he could ignore all the others.

So, she could either find a way to get the Equalizer on target—or she could acquire more weapons that could harm her opponent.

She reviewed the screens again, focusing on the Personal Status first, for there was something there drawing her attention.

Spells → Lights		
Name	Level	Description
Mana Beam	15 *Upgrade Available	Focus mana into a channeled energy attack.

Spells		
Light		
Name	Level	Description
Light Beam	12 *Upgrade Available	Form mana into a beam of light to attack. May pierce through its target. May be continuously channeled.

She had previously upgraded her Magic Missile spell, allowing it to deal more damage. Similar upgrades had been available for two other abilities ever since her fight with the ursanus, though she hadn't deemed additional upgrades necessary at the time.

But they were necessary now, and they provided a more constrained set of choices for her organic mind to assess.

Available Upgrades for Mana Beam:	
Name	Description
Dense Mana Beam	Increases mana density of Mana Beam, boosting damage.
Infused Mana Beam	May infuse Mana Beam with attributed mana.
Channeled Mana Beam	Mana Beam increases in intensity the longer it is channeled.
Splitting Mana Beam	Allows Mana Beam to split and strike multiple targets.
Piercing Mana Beam	Increases Mana Beam penetration against RES and magic barriers.

Available Upgrades for Light Beam:	
Name	Description
Dense Light Beam	Increases mana density of Light Beam, boosting damage.
Channeled Light Beam	Light Beam increases in intensity the longer it is channeled.
Instant Light Beam	Bypass use of magic circle when casting Light Beam.
Splitting Light Beam	Allows Light Beam to split and strike multiple targets.
Piercing Light Beam	Increases Light Beam penetration against RES and magic barriers.
Fusion Light Beam	Light Beams may combine with themselves or other compatible attacks to boost power.

There were a number of options, any of which seemed like they might help, so NSLICE-00P thought back to how she had used these abilities before. Especially back to her fight with the ursanus. She wasn't sure if this was the right choice, but she had to make one now.

Mana Beam has been upgraded into Infused Mana Beam!
Light Beam has been upgraded into Fusion Light Beam!

She focused on the attack she'd used to take down the ursanus once and for all, combining Mana Beam and Light Beam by layering Light Beam magic circles over her energy channels. In fact, it may have been that very feat which unlocked the Fusion upgrade in the first place. But that original attack had required all of her undivided focus, with both her cybernetic and organic halves working together to achieve it. Solamh would not allow her the time and space to set something like that up. But when she had learned Multicasting, she learned that the foreign system could reduce the processing resources required for a given task. She hoped that effect would apply here, and that these upgrades would allow her to replicate the big attack with a fraction of the mental effort and processing power it originally required.

She wasn't sure it would be enough, though, so she checked through the available skills on her Personal Status. She wondered if there might be something similar that would boost her power.

And she found something quickly.

Available Perks → Active Skills → Magic Skills	
Name	Cost
Supercharge	12

She purchased the skill as soon as she saw it.

Active Skills		
Name	Level	Description
Supercharge	1	Elite magic skill. Fill a spell with additional mana to boost its effects. May cause the spell to misfire. Effect boost depends on the quantity and density of mana added. Misfire chance depends on Mana Control and amount of mana added.

With this, she could add more of her mana to her attacks. If it was possible to harm her opponent with the amount of power she had available, this skill would make it happen.

And she already knew based on the stats that it was possible.

Her organic half called out to her AI, signaling it had a potential solution. The AI responded, and the two halves integrated once again, the organic mind lending its support to the AI's combat protocols.

The fight had not gone well in the meantime. NSLICE-00P was covered in deep gashes, sparking in a couple of places where the attacks had passed beyond her armor plating. Her HP twisted and flowed around the jagged metal, but that too was reaching critical levels. She was out of time, and had only opportunity remaining. If the solution her organic half proposed did not work, she would have to evacuate, and leave her allies behind.

She lifted her arms, activating the new spells and skills. A dozen magic circles quickly formed, immediately centering themselves over her the energy channels.

And not a moment too soon, as Solamh leapt at her once more.

She aimed her arms, activating the skills. One of her hands was still damaged, but fortunately her HP regen had managed to restore the energy channel there, so she could still utilize Mana Beam with both arms. The new Supercharge skill automatically drew on her mana and stuffed it into the magic circles, drawing on the massively dense and abundant amount of mana a dungeon core could provide. Her sensors indicated the process was haphazard and sloppy, causing the magic circles to flicker and bulge, so she took charge of some of it, guiding the energy in the manner she used when combining the skills manually.

The skill Supercharge is now Level 2!
The skill Supercharge is now Level 3!
The skill Supercharge is now Level 4!
Mana Control is now 140!

The mana settled down and flowed in more controlled patterns. The magic circles flashed and stabilized, ready to activate on command.

Her mana rushed through her energy channels as the magic circles activated. She was pleased to note the Mana Beams and Light Beams twisting themselves together with no further input, the Infused and Fusion upgrades working together to assist the process.

Solamh continued to fly through the air, intending to ignore the attack as he had before. The Equalizer didn't stop kinetic momentum, and her other attacks weren't strong enough to slow him down, so even if he took some damage, his opponent would fare worse.

Or so it had been moments earlier.

Two massive beams of light fired from her palms, so bright they seemed to dim their surroundings. Solamh's eyes widened as the beams struck him on the chest, sending him plummeting back into the ground.

"Analysis: Target HP barrier noticeably damaged by new attack. Recalculating combat odds with new capabilities. Risk of unit termination now at acceptable level. Probability of hostile termination now at an acceptable level. Resuming combat."

And so, the Trial of Claws entered a new stage.

27

Terminate the Wulver!

"Offensive magic, while powerful, is generally unsuited for a duel, or close quarters combat in general. It requires intense focus and time to pull off any spell of reasonable power, focus and time no competent enemy will allow. As such, even the most powerful of our charges is vulnerable should they be caught up close. It is our job to ensure that does not happen."

—Centurion Flavinia Ticinia, while training
a close-quarters century of the Legio Arcanum IX.

The skill HP Regen is now Level 5!
The skill MP Regen is now Level 7!

NSLICE-00P quickly reformed the magic circles and opened fire as she started to recover. Solamh barely had a moment to process what had occurred before another beam slammed into him. He quickly kicked himself away and started dashing, beams crashing into the ground and tearing through the dirt behind him.

He wanted to leap at her once again, but NSLICE-00P was alternating fire from each of her arms now. With her new rate of fire, she would catch him before he arrived.

His claws began to glow with mana as he dashed forward to avoid another beam, swinging his hands along the way. An arc of light flew through the air toward NSLICE-00P, forcing the cyborg to move out of its path. Solamh leapt at her in that moment, just before she could bring her lasers back on target.

NSLICE-00P deactivated her repulsors and dropped from the sky, allowing Solamh to pass overhead.

"Adapting strategy."

NSLICE-00P's AI had finished some new calculations analyzing the effect of the beams on Solamh and had calculated that the full power blast was extraneous. Which meant if she lowered the power of each beam, she could generate significantly more of them while still dealing damage.

So she let the magic circles layered on her arms fade. And as Solamh was still falling to the ground, she turned her attention to magic casting. Her AI once again copy and pasted Light Beam magic circles while her organic half activated the Multicasting and Farcasting skills to support.

The sky lit up.

Solamh landed once more and turned back toward his opponent. He froze, his eyes widening at what he saw.

The air all around the dueling zone was now filled to the brim with glowing magic circles. And then, NSLICE-00P sent out her mana, her cybernetic half instructing the organic which circles to activate. The organic channeled as much mana as she could with the Supercharge skill toward those circles, and then the AI assisted in getting that mana where it needed to go.

A dozen of the circles lit up, firing their beams. Four struck one another and fused into a superbeam, three such superbeams striking Solamh from different angles.

The spell Fusion Light Beam is now Level 13!
The skill Light Magic is now Level 11!
The skill Multicasting is now Level 8!
The skill Farcasting is now Level 4!
The skill Supercharge is now Level 5!
Mana Control is now 150!

Solamh gritted his teeth and started to move. He dashed once more, beginning evasive maneuvers. A dozen more magic circles started glowing, firing another three superbeams at him. He jumped and twisted in the air as he dashed, just barely managing to dodge the barrage.

Then NSLICE-00P added another four magic circles, activating sixteen at once. Pain shot through her mind, but she was able to hold things in place.

One beam descended from above; Solamh started running forward and out of the way.

A second beam shot from the side and another from the front. Solamh was forced to jump over them.

And then, a fourth struck him dead-on, pushing him back slightly and taking a chunk of his health.

The skill Multicasting is now Level 9!
The skill Supercharge is now Level 6!
Mana Control is now 155!

NSLICE-00P's organic components burned, struggling to contain the vast quantities of mana surging through her. Her AI noted the strain and recalculated for a slower pace.

But her organic half refused, signaling it could handle this. Its mana control and Multicasting skill were growing with every volley, taking some of the strain off it. And . . . this was the solution it had proposed.

So it would fulfill its role to the best of its ability.

For a brief moment, the AI paused, not entirely comprehending what the organic half had reported. But it calculated that the organic half was not at risk of immediate damage due to the strain, so it carried on with the assault. Instead, it focused on analyzing and predicting Solamh's movements, and so choosing the appropriate circles to contain him. It also focused on holding those circles in place after they fired so they would not need to be reformed and the organic half could focus entirely on channeling the mana.

And then something happened that neither half had predicted.

Mana Control is now 160!
You have learned the skill Continuous Casting!
Conditions for Strategic Magic met!
You have learned the strategic spell Aurora Barrage!
The skill Strategic Magic has gained 3 levels and is now Level 4!

Suddenly, additional lines of mana began to grow and extend, linking all of the disparate magic circles, uniting them into a single, overarching spell. Having obtained the Strategic Mage feat earlier in the fight, NSLICE-00P had unlocked the ability to cast strategic spells—wider-area attacks meant for battling entire armies—that were normally cast by entire teams of mages in lengthy rituals and not considered at all useful in a duel. If one was not a cyborg with a bonded AI and a dungeon core power source that is. For NSLICE-00P . . . this was much easier than holding over a hundred magic circles in place and Supercharging them one by one!

The pain faded from her organic half as the spell took over the work. Now, instead of Supercharging and activating each individual circle, her organic half could simply pump as much mana as it could into the big magic circle. The AI no longer needed to calculate the angles required to fuse the right superbeams together; instead, it could simply direct a target for the larger spell, which began firing beams from all over all on its own. Shifting patterns of light shone across the sky as beams fired from different parts of the magic formation, colliding and fusing together into stronger superbeams before gouging the ground below.

And anyone who might be caught there.

And so, the barrage intensified. Where once three or four beams came at a time, now they began to fire continuously. Where once they were carefully calculated precision strikes, now they simply flooded from all directions and bathed the entire area in deadly light. Solamh dodged this way and that, but he was taking fire with each moment, his HP dropping by the second as he grunted and groaned, gritting his teeth. The ground below him was now filled with trenches and holes from the constant strikes, and more than once, he stumbled and tripped as he tried to dash out of the line of fire.

He launched counterattacks with his Claw Strikes, but NSLICE-00P simply moved out of the way. Her AI had more than enough leeway now to calculate evasive maneuvers while maintaining the barrage. His strikes did not stop the deluge of beams.

He could not keep this up, so he abandoned his defense.

He activated all his skills which would grant him additional strength and speed, and launched himself at the cyborg in the air. He grunted as the beams struck him, but still, he flew, intending to end this fight with a single blow.

And NSLICE-00P obliged.

Her organic half focused all its mana into the spell while her cybernetic half focused her electrical power back into its implants, lifting a hand.

"Equalizer engaged."

When she'd first fought the ursanus, she had tried to bypass the HP entirely. That had failed. The Equalizer could not strip the HP barrier fast enough, and so could only open a tiny hole. Her laser attacks, still relying on her conventional technology, had barely made an impact on the monster's hide. She hadn't had the penetrating power to make use of such a small opening.

But now?

The more accurately tuned Equalizer struck Solamh's chest as he approached, easily stripping the HP barrier in a small area. Solamh was committed to the attack and soaring through the air; he could not move to evade the Equalizer without abandoning his assault, so the Equalizer remained on target, clearing a fist-size hole.

And then the Aurora Barrage magic circle began to glow too bright to look at directly. Solamh had just arrived before NSLICE-00P and was swinging his claws . . .

Dozens of beams fired all at once, combining together into a single attack, layering the mana of countless spells into a single strike. NSLICE-00P condensed this superbeam as thin and dense as she could and then opened fire, targeting the gap in Solamh's HP.

The strategic spell Aurora Barrage is now Level 2!
The skill Supercharge is now Level 7!

A thin beam pierced straight through Solamh and into the hill below, destroying his heart.

Solamh's eyes widened. His arm stopped and fell back, claws mere inches from NSLICE-00P's face as he began to fall from the sky. He hit the ground with a thud.

NSLICE-00P kept her eyes fixed on her target, the magic circle still glowing above her. Solamh's HP rushed to repair the damage, but there was too much, and his HP was far from full. It all drained away before his heart could be restored.

Notifications from the foreign program flooded across NSLICE-00P's view.

You have slain Wulver (Level 65)!
Gained 70 Personal XP, 67 Dungeon XP!
Compiling prior experience . . .
Gained 1305 total Personal XP, 1108 total Dungeon XP!
You have leveled up 13 Personal levels and 11 Dungeon levels!
Your Personal Level is now at 26 and your Dungeon Level is now at 28!

"Analysis: No vital signs detected. Mana signature fading. All sensors support foreign program's conclusion. Combat Status Update: Target terminated."

NSLICE-00P's Dungeon Management

Overview	
Name	**The Walking Dungeon**
Level	**28**
XP	**51/100**
Available Perk Points	**31**
Mana	**93/93 (115/115)**
Exterior	**Human/Automata Hybrid (LOCKED)**

Dungeon Affinities	
Type	**Strength**
Cyborg	**Primary**
Rodent	**Minimum**

Earth	Minimum
Arachnid	Minimum
Slime	Minimum
Light	Minimum
Nature	Minimum

Implants		
Type	Mana Upkeep	Description
Bionic Prosthetics +3	0	Overwrites STR and SPD, Values: 130 STR, 65 SPD
Armor Plating +2	0	Overwrites DEF and RES, Values: 120 DEF, 60 RES
Bonded AI	0	Enables direct contact with the System. Overwrites DEX, Value: 1000 DEX
Techno-Organic Interface	0	Enables conscious control over organic and emotional functions. Resists mind-influencing effects.
Advanced Sensors +2	0	Vastly expands scope and effectiveness of senses.
Internal Weapon Bays	0	Enables use of dungeon traps as weapons.
Repulsors +1	0	Enables flight and tactical boosts.
Energy Channels	0	Enables user to channel internal energy into external attacks.
Dungeon Field Generator	5	Surrounding area counts as dungeon territory. Enables mana absorption within area of effect.

Monster Hangar (Small)	1	Provides living space for 5 small monsters. Unlocks subordinate summoning.
Item Foundry	1	Unlocks Item Creation.

Subordinates				
Name	Species	Level	Mana Upkeep	
Rattingtale	Monster Rat	6	1	Check Status
Lilussees	Monster Spider	8	1	Check Status
(TEMPORARY) Ateia Niraemia	Human	9	--	(Status locked)
(TEMPORARY) Taog Sutharlan	Human / Wulver	8	--	(Status locked)

Traps			
Name	Number Active / Deployed	Mana Upkeep	Description
Assault Rifle +3	2/2	2	Rapid-fire projectile weapon with high penetration.
Autopistol	2/2	2	Rapid-fire projectile weapon with medium penetration.
Anti-Armor Missile Launcher +2	2/2	2	Homing explosive designed to penetrate armor. Very high penetration.
Anti-Personnel Missile Launcher +2	6/6	6	Homing explosive designed for area damage. Medium penetration.

Stun Ray	1/1	1	Nonlethal electric weapon. Can inflict stun and paralysis statuses.
Wrist Blade +2	2/2	0	Wrist-mounted blades that can be deployed at high speed.
Flamethrower	2/2	2	Deals fire damage and applies burn status in a large cone.
The Equalizer +1	1/1	0	Huh? What the heck is this? Some kind of weird metal that doesn't even exist here? Um . . . well . . . best I can tell it's some sort of antimagic field generator? Eh . . . well, it's yours, not mine, so you don't need me to tell you, right? Like, you already upgraded this thing yourself, so you're good, right?

Dungeon Skills		
Name	Level	Description
Analyze	N/A	Check the status of a target. More detail for targets within the dungeon. Details depend on level difference.
Contract	N/A	Bind a consenting target to the dungeon, per terms agreed upon by both parties.

Transfer	N/A	Move yourself, a subordinate, or a consenting target within your dungeon.

Dungeon Perks	
Name	Description
Human-Dungeon Hybrid	Enables Implants tab. Enables unique Dungeon Combat skill. Enables direct manipulation of dungeon mana. +100 HP Rooms tab locked. Exterior locked.

Dungeon Feats		
Name	Description	Effect
Dungeon Victor	To the victor go the spoils. Unlocked by destroying or subordinating another dungeon.	+1 Perk Point Unlocks Dungeon Warfare category perks.
Dungeon Overlord	A master of masters. Unlocked by subordinating another dungeon master.	+2 Perk Points Unlocks Subordinate Core category perks.
Raid Boss	Fine, I'll do it myself. Unlocked by destroying or subordinating another dungeon with no assistance.	+2 Perk Points +1 level in HP Regen skill +1 level in MP Regen skill +50 HP Unlocks Raid Boss category perks.

System Upgrade	**Unlocked by manually performing a system upgrade. Which is not supposed to be possible. Ugh, this is going to get complicated, isn't it?**	**Um, I don't know. Just have +20 Dungeon Perk Points or something. Whatever. You're figuring this out yourself anyways, so close enough.**

NSLICE-00P's Personal Status

Personal Status			
General Information		Physical Attributes	
Name	NSLICE-00P	STR	130* (Overwritten)
Species	Human/ Dungeon Core/ Automata Hybrid	DEX	1000* (Overwritten)
Level	26	SPD	65* (Overwritten)
XP	48/100	DEF	120* (Overwritten)
Perk Points	82	RES	60* (Overwritten)
HP	185/185	Magical Attributes	
MP	106/106	Mana Density	102
		Mana Control	160

Active Skills		
Name	Level	Description
Infused Mana Beam	15	Focus mana into a channeled energy attack. Infused: May infuse Mana Beam with attributed mana.

Sneak	1	Move quietly to avoid notice. Makes it harder for others to notice the user. Effectiveness highly dependent on environment.
Multicasting	9	Can cast several spells at once. Number of simultaneous spells increases with level.
Anti-Mana Beam	1	My best guess is that this projects a kind of inverse mana that reacts destructively with normal mana, including HP. While it can fully deplete HP, it does not harm matter itself. Requires The Equalizer.
Power Strike	1	Infuse mana into a Weapon Strike for heavier damage. Power and range increase with level.
Farcasting	4	Allows the user to manipulate mana and create magic circles at far distances.
Strategic Magic	4	Governs the use of Strategic Magic spells.
Supercharge	7	Fill a spell with additional mana to boost its effects. May cause the spell to misfire. Effect boost depends on the amount and density of mana added. Misfire chance depends on Mana Control and amount of mana added.
Continuous Casting	1	May use additional mana to retain a spell form, allowing the spell to be instantly recast.

Passive Skills		
General		
Name	Level	Description
Dungeon Combat	1	Dungeon traps and skills count as personal weapons and skills.

HP Regen	5	Automatically recover HP pool. Increased regeneration speed for damaged body parts.
MP Regen	7	Automatically recover MP pool.
Presence Detection	4	Detect living entities around the user. Range and scope of detection increases with level.
Trap Detection	4	Detect traps. Range and scope of detection increases with level.
Challenger	--	Damage dealt x1.5 against targets of higher level. Damage received x0.75 against attacks from targets of higher level.
Utility		
Name	Level	Description
Enchanting	1	The art of infusing objects and beings with mana.
Resistances		
Name	Level	Description
Poison Resistance	1	Resist and recovery from poison status. Resist Poison-attributed damage.
Schools of Magic		
Name	Level	Description
Arcane Magic	9	The school of magic governing the manipulation of unattributed mana. A solid foundation for students of the mystic arts, though somewhat less mana efficient than the more specialized schools.
Earth Magic	7	The school of magic governing the manipulation of Earth-attribute mana. One of the basic elemental magics, strong at defensive spells and spells that deal physical damage.

Fire Magic	6 *Spell Choice Available	The school of magic governing the manipulation of Fire-attribute mana. One of the basic elemental magics, strong at offensive spells and spells that inflict the burn status.
Light Magic	11 *Spell Choice Available	The school of magic governing the manipulation of Light-attribute mana. One of the basic elemental magics, quick and precise spells that are excellent against Dark-aligned foes.
Nature Magic	3 *Spell Choice Available	The school of magic governing the manipulation of Nature-attribute mana. Focuses on growth and living things.
Poison Magic	3	The school of magic governing magical poisons. Excels at spreading poison status and dealing damage over time.
Recovery Magic	3	The school of magic governing healing through magic.

Spells		
Arcane		
Name	Level	Description
Dense Magic Missile	18	Form and launch mana into a small projectile. One of the most basic offensive applications of magic.
Mana Barrier	7	Form mana into a barrier to block attacks. One of the most basic defensive applications of magic.
Mana Blast	1	A cone-shaped blast of mana. Deals damage and knockback to the area.
Mana Infusion	10 *Upgrade Available	Infuse mana into a target. The most basic enchantment.

Earth		
Name	Level	Description
Rock Throw	6	Use mana to form and then launch a small rock. Mana cost increases dramatically if cast without a nearby source of Earth. Deals physical damage. One of the most basic offensive applications of Earth Magic.
Earth Wall	6	Use mana to temporarily form a wall of Earth. Mana cost increases dramatically if cast without a nearby source of Earth. One of the most basic defensive applications of Earth Magic.
Pitfall	4	Dig a large hole in a target area. May be concealed. Mana cost may increase depending on suitability of terrain.
Fire		
Name	Level	Description
Fire Bolt	1	Use mana to form and then launch a small bolt of fire. Mana cost decreases dramatically if cast with a nearby source of Fire. May inflict burn status. One of the most basic offensive applications of Fire Magic.

Fire Blast	7	A cone-shaped blast of Fire mana. Deals damage and inflicts burn to the area. Mana cost decreases dramatically if cast with a nearby source of Fire. May be continuously channeled.
Light		
Name	Level	Description
Light Bolt	1	Use mana to form and then launch a small bolt of light. Mana cost increases if cast without a nearby source of Light. One of the most basic offensive applications of Light Magic.
Fusion Light Beam	13	Form mana into a beam of light to attack. May pierce through its target. May be continuously channeled. Fusion: Light Beams may combine with themselves or other compatible attacks to boost power.
Nature		
Name	Level	Description
Vine Grasp	4	Grows or manipulates a vine to wrap around a target. Mana cost may increase or decrease significantly depending on surrounding plant life or environmental suitability for plant growth. The most basic plant-manipulation spell.

Poison		
Name	Level	Description
Poison Bolt	6	Use mana to form and then launch a small bolt of poison. Mana cost decreases dramatically if cast with a nearby source of Poison. May inflict poison status. One of the most basic offensive applications of Poison Magic.
Poison Blast	1	A cone-shaped blast of Poison mana. Deals damage and inflicts poison to the area. Mana cost decreases dramatically if cast with a nearby source of Poison. May be continuously channeled.
Recovery		
Name	Level	Description
Heal	3	Use mana to heal minor wounds and damage. Effect increases with user's knowledge of the body.
Cure	1	Cures abnormal status conditions. Type and strength of conditions that can be cured increases with level.

Strategic Spells			
School	Name	Level	Description
Light	Aurora Barrage	2	Continuously rains Light Beams on the target area. If Fusion Light Beam is available, beams may be combined at will.

Personal Feats		
Name	Description	Effect
Against the Odds	Do not ask how many there are, but where they are. Unlocked by winning a fight when outnumbered by equal or higher-leveled opponents.	+1 Perk Point
Solo Conquest	I am the dungeon master now. Unlocked by conquering a dungeon alone.	+1 level in HP Regen skill +1 level in MP Regen skill +1 level in Presence Detection skill +1 level in Trap Detection skill
Arcane Prodigy	The career of a supreme sorcerer does not start on the beaten path. Unlocked by learning a high-tier magic skill under level twenty without spending Perk Points.	+3 Perk Points Unlocks more advanced magic perks.
Enchanter	The first step on the path of the magic craftsman. Unlocked by manually accomplishing a Mana Infusion.	+1 level in Enchanting skill

Skill Creator	You don't just master the path. You define it. Unlocked by creating a brand-new skill.	To be honest, this normally happens when you're a MUCH higher level, so I'm a bit worried about passing you this much this early, but, um, okay. +20 Perk Points
Healer	Anyone can deal in death. It takes an expert to deal in life. Unlocked by using mana to heal a wound.	+1 level in Recovery Magic skill
Challenger	Levels and odds are just numbers. Unlocked by defeating an opponent who is the greater of level 10 or twice your level alone.	+3 Perk Points + Challenger skill
Strategic Mage	A strategic mage is king of the battlefield. Unlocked by affecting a hundred or more equal-size opponents (or equivalent mass of other-size opponents) at the same time with magic.	+1 level in Strategic Magic skill Unlocks Strategic Spells.
Dungeon Conqueror Feats		
Name	Description	Effect
Dungeon Conqueror (Rat Cave)	Unlocked by conquering the Rat Cave Dungeon.	+1 Perk Point +1 level in Sneak skill
Dungeon Conqueror (Earth Tunnels)	Unlocked by conquering the Earth Tunnels Dungeon.	+1 Perk Point +1 level in Earth Magic skill

Dungeon Conqueror (Spider Tree)	Unlocked by conquering the Spider Tree Dungeon.	+1 Perk Point +1 level in Poison Resistance skill
Dungeon Conqueror (Slimy Pit)	Unlocked by conquering the Slimy Pit Dungeon.	+1 Perk Point +1 level in Poison Bolt spell
Dungeon Conqueror (Glimmering Grove)	Unlocked by conquering the Glimmering Grove Dungeon.	+1 Perk Point +1 level in Light Magic skill
Dungeon Conqueror (Nature's Wrath)	Unlocked by conquering the Nature's Wrath Dungeon.	+1 Perk Point +1 level in Nature Magic skill
Dungeon Conqueror (Beast Lair)	Unlocked by conquering the Beast Lair Dungeon.	+1 Perk Point +1 level in Claw Strike skill

28

Trial Debrief

"The loss of our chief in the Trial of Claws represents the loss of our entire clan. It is proof that our clan's traditions and hunting were inferior to our opponent's. They are the greater Wulver, and we acknowledge that. That is why we join them afterwards. It is frustrating, but it is the way of the Wulver.

But when our chief loses to an outsider . . . it is nothing less than a humiliation of the entire Wulver species. It is hard to accept that all of our traditions and hunting have proven inferior to someone who doesn't share in any of them."

—A quote from a Wulver clan warrior, recorded in *The Peoples of the Frontiers*, Volume V: *Turannia and the North*, by traveling author and former Exploratore Placus Paesentius Statius.

The surrounding Wulver began to quiet down as the sky lit up with magic circles. They went silent completely as Solamh was bombarded with beams, unable to approach his foe again. Their ears drooped as Solamh made his final assault and crashed to the ground.

Meanwhile, Ateia and Taog watched these things with wide eyes and dropped jaws.

"Seero's . . . really strong, huh?"

Taog did not respond.

He was no mage, but he was fairly certain something like what NSLICE-00P was doing was not common. They had heard stories of Strategic Magic, massive rituals that could destroy entire armies. But those were conducted by entire teams of Imperial mages working together in long rituals. This was not that.

To be fair, one hilltop was not an entire army, and he knew for a fact that Turannia was a backwater compared to the Empire proper. For all he knew, any old Imperial mage might be capable of such a feat. Still though, he hadn't heard many stories of single Imperial mages holding off entire incursions alone.

Until now, he and Ateia had assumed NSLICE-00P was a wandering knight on account of her armor. Yet, she fought more like a mage, or maybe an Elven spellblade? Combine all this with all her eccentricities, her complete lack of basic common knowledge, and the strange claims like not being able to remove her armor or not needing to sleep and eat . . .

He had a bad feeling in the pit of his stomach; a cold fear which sent his heart racing.

Just what exactly *was* this girl?

Because there were stories of beings who matched that description, who could do what she did, and who could go for long periods of time without food or rest; who wouldn't know much about the Empire or anything in it. Who wore armor like a knight and casted magic like an archmage.

Like a Sun Elf Archon. Or a dragon in human form. Or, a demon lord, a powerful dungeon master like the ones in the legends.

Not a single one of those was a possibility he wanted to consider.

NSLICE-00P lowered from the sky, landing in front of the pair, the Wulver shuffling to give them a wide berth. Taog jumped and took a step back while Ateia rushed forward, her eyes widening at the gashes in NSLICE-00P's armor.

"Seero! Are you okay?!"

"Status Report: All systems are operating at acceptable efficiency levels. Repairs are already underway."

"D-Doesn't it hurt?!"

"Negative. This unit thanks friendly Ateia for her concern."

Ateia just stared at the twisted and jagged metal with her mouth wide open. "That . . . didn't hurt? . . . Knights are amazing."

"I don't think she's a . . ." Taog dropped the words he was about to say, shaking his head. Whatever she was, she was their ally for now. What good would it do to air his doubts? And what could he do if they were true? Besides . . . he and Ateia would be dead or Wulver captives if she weren't here. "Seero, are you sure you're alright? You took some heavy hits there . . ."

She turned to face him.

"Damage Report: Damage did reach heavy but noncritical levels. This unit is currently employing HP Regen and Recovery Magic repair protocols, and will return to prime condition shortly."

In fact, NSLICE-00P received a message from the foreign system as they spoke.

The spell Heal is now Level 4!
The skill HP Regen is now level 6!

"Right . . . well, that's good."

Meanwhile, a single Wulver woman stepped forward, approaching the group. She stood up straight, making sure her stomach faced NSLICE-00P. Opening her mouth, she spoke with rumbling growls underpinning her words. "You have triumphed in the Trial of Claws. To you, the rightful chief, I offer you this tribute in exchange for the right to leadership."

"Affirmative Acknowledgement: This unit agrees to the exchange of authority for material gain."

As Taog had explained earlier, the Trial of Claws was often used to determine the leadership of a Wulver pack. However, in a case like this, where the leader of a pack fell to an outsider in the trial, such an arrangement was generally not acceptable. As such, the Wulver had come up with the tradition to offer payment so the victor would return the right of leadership. If accepted, this would allow the pack in question to honor the trial without subordinating themselves to a foreigner.

Well, most foreigners had no idea what was going on in the first place, but few in this world would turn down free loot! That or they were intending to wipe out the Wulver pack in the first place and never noticed the trial at all.

So this Wulver was noticeably surprised when NSLICE-00P not only accepted the offer but did so without waiting for interpretation. She quickly turned around and barked at the wolfmen behind her. They brought up monster pelts and bones, as well as a metal dagger covered in strange patterns.

"The trophies of the warchief's hunts. May your hunts be as successful as his."

NSLICE-00P took the items. With that, the Wulver turned around and rejoined her pack.

The entire warpack then began to disperse. Solamh had defeated and slain all the chiefs of the packs he'd subordinated, so the group had been left without a clear leader in the midst of enemy territory. As such, they quickly divided back into their original clans and went their separate ways, most heading back toward the Forest of Beasts where they made their living.

And so, the latest Wulver incursion ended before it began . . . as far as the Empire was concerned, at least.

Leaving Ateia and Taog to wonder . . . just where *was* the Empire when an incursion had reached this far past the border?

While the two Imperials were lost in their thoughts, NSLICE-00P was looking at the assorted items in her hand. She had no particular use for them, but apparently to discard of them in sight of the Wulver could potentially resume hostilities. At the bare minimum they could be traded to the local society for monetary resources. She decided she would keep them if she could determine an efficient means of storage and transportation. So her voice rang out inside the Monster Hangar.

"Requesting Elaboration: According to this unit's records, friendly Excellion supplies storage containers, correct?"

Rattingtale was currently trembling in his room, his eyes glued to the screen of the feed ever since NSLICE-00P had started her mass Light Beam barrage. He jumped at being addressed and fell over. "Y-Y-Yes-yes, w-whatever you say-request, great-mighty boss-queen! Y-Y-You should have-possess an 'Inventory' section on the royal records, yes-yes. I-I-If you bring an object-item to your core, you should be able to store it."

NSLICE-00P indeed located the tab in question and brought the items to her core.

Store in Dungeon Inventory?

"Affirmative."

With that, the items vanished, and the UI updated.

Inventory	
Name	Description
??? dagger	A dagger, likely enchanted given the amount of mana held within. Further information could not be determined.
Ursanus Pelt	The pelt of an ursanus alpha. Tough, well-insulated, and full of mana.
Ursanus Bones	The bones of an ursanus alpha. Extremely durable, and full of mana.

NSLICE-00P's robotic eye flickered. Again, the foreign system was displaying gaps in data, apparently unable to provide any sort of useful intel on the dagger. She again revised her confidence levels in foreign-system provided knowledge.

But the missing data didn't particularly matter to her, as she didn't have any plans for what to do with the tribute, so she stored it and moved on. After all, she had more pressing matters to analyze . . .

The trio traveled in silence for the rest of the day, each lost in their thoughts after the battle. Ateia wondered how an incursion of that size had made it past the patrolling Exploratores, while Taog, much as he wished not to, could not help but theorize on NSLICE-00P's identity, as well as what it would mean for himself and Ateia should one of those theories prove accurate.

As for NSLICE-00P . . .

Later that night, as the group made camp and NSLICE-00P took up watch, she concluded her post-action analysis of the conflict.

She had nearly been terminated. It was an unacceptable performance.

She'd once again miscalculated the threat. The battle had come down to the wire as a result, and she was forced to choose between risking termination and suffering setbacks to her primary directive. If her organic components had not come up with a viable solution, if she had not been able to spare her organic half to analyze solutions, or if her cybernetic half had not put up a sufficient defense, she would have had to abandon the field, and her allies along with it, before wiping out a group of unknown affilliation. In fact, she had already sustained heavy damage by that point, and Solamh had been about to inflict more. There was no guarantee she would have been able to successfully retreat, even had she made that call.

"Requesting assistance from friendlies Lilussees and Excellion Formantus Rattingtale the Third."

"W-W-What do you need, great-mighty boss-queen, yes-yes?"

"Ugh, like, can it wait? I was, like, about to go to bed, you know?"

"Query: Do hostiles ursanus alpha and Solamh Greumach represent the greatest threat level of Non-Standard in this region?"

"U-Um, are you asking-wondering if those were the strongest-mightiest?"

"Affirmative."

Lilussees tilted her head inside her room, rubbing a leg on her mandibles.

"Um, like, probably not? Like, I haven't encountered much myself, but like, there should be stronger stuff? Like dragons or something. If I had to say . . . those guys were just a bit strong but not, like, particularly special or something?"

"Requesting Clarification. Are the friendlies aware of the upper bound of the threat level?"

"Um, like . . . what's the strongest thing or something?"

"Affirmative. Addendum: This unit requests as much specific detail regarding the threat as available."

"Um, that's, like, hard to say."

"Everything can keep growing-strengthening with the bestowals of power from the royal records, yes-yes?"

NSLICE-00P's robotic eye flickered and spun. It seemed she had a fundamental misunderstanding of her circumstances.

She had been operating under a mission-focused, large organization–based upgrade scheme. Upgrades were to be handled by centralized maintenance staff after she'd located a new commander, with her arsenal tailored to whatever mission set they assigned for her. But unexpected and immediate threats had necessitated improved capabilities for safe transit, and so she had compromised and conducted the minimum-required upgrades to carry on with her mission.

But that might not be sufficient.

Her arsenal had proven lacking once more. Foes like this, while not the average, were apparently not unprecedented. And they were not the upper bound of what she could encounter either. She couldn't even calculate what the upper bound was at present, and therefore, what the minimum required upgrades would be. Even if she could, she had not considered that the independent upgrades offered to her by the foreign system would also be available to the wider population. A potential hostile's capabilities could increase before she ended up facing them. They could even increase in real time.

And there was no guarantee she would be able to conduct upgrades midfight if this happened a second time. Her focus had been pushed to the limit trying to survive. She had been forced to rely on her organic components in an untested scenario. If either half of her had proven insufficient for the task, she would have failed. She could not allow herself to fall into that situation again.

And above all, she didn't know when or even *if* she would locate a suitable commander, or if that commander would have appropriate maintenance staff and infrastructure to manage her arsenal. And her previous commander had instructed her to assume wholly independent action until she found someone.

In other words, she could not rely solely on singular, limited upgrades based on past encounters. And she could not wait for a commander or maintenance staff to manage her arsenal as per prior policy. She was no longer a single unit amongst an army. She *was* her entire organization now, and the success of her current mission rested solely on her own capabilities.

So she had to continue growing her capabilities until she found a commander or she had proven capable of handling all possible threats. And she needed those capabilities improved *before* she encountered situations that required them.

It was time for another round of upgrades.

29

Upgrade Round 2

"The rapid mutation of our foes presents a unique challenge compared to the pre-war conditions. In particular, specialized NSLICE loadouts are proving insufficient, given the unpredictable enemy capabilities. NSLICE-00P is still performing above expectations, but the Equalizer was never a scalable solution. We have, however, recently acquired a new organic base that is showing significant promise."

—Dr. Ottosen, in a meeting analyzing NSLICE program bottlenecks.

NSLICE-00P analyzed the latest combat footage and the available upgrades once more. She had a great many choices available which could improve her capabilities, and unlike last time, she didn't have a specific target to focus on, so she would have to decide for herself the criteria to judge the possibilities.

Analyzing the fight, she concluded that her organic half had stumbled upon decent criteria. It had focused on synergizing her abilities, combining the Mana Beam and Light Beam spells together and boosting them both with Supercharge, so she came to the conclusion she should not evaluate each option separately but in light of her other capabilities.

Likewise, she determined that ranged magical firepower should be her primary focus. More than once, her armor plating had proven ineffective against the opponents she had faced, and the simplest solution to that was to avoid being hit in the first place by immediately terminating hostiles at a distance. In particular, it seemed her magical capabilities had much greater growth potential and had, in fact, been growing simply from her continued use of those abilities.

On the other hand, her armor plating seemed locked to the dungeon menu's Implants section, and so could not be improved unless she specifically and intentionally spent resources to do so. The same went for her bionic prosthetics and her conventional weaponry, so the magical abilities were predicted to be the most scalable option at present. Which was not to say she wouldn't be taking a look at those other areas as well; she would not let a known deficiency remain. But she had to start somewhere, and maximizing her ability for immediate termination would itself reduce the need for physical defenses.

She decided to start with her Personal Status. She had hardly spent any of the resources she had available there, save for the purchases of Arcane Magic and Supercharge. Likewise, her physical attributes were tied solely to her implants, and so not accessible by the Personal Status. So while she could purchase relevant skills to better make use of said implants, ultimately, the opportunity costs of spending the Personal perks on magical capabilities were lower.

First and foremost, she already had some upgrades available.

Passive Skills → Schools of Magic		
Name	Level	Description
Arcane Magic	9	The school of magic governing the manipulation of unattributed mana. A solid foundation for students of the mystic arts, though somewhat less mana efficient than the more specialized schools.
Earth Magic	7	The school of magic governing the manipulation of Earth-attribute mana. One of the basic elemental magics, strong at defensive spells and spells that deal physical damage.
Fire Magic	6 *Spell Choice Available	The school of magic governing the manipulation of Fire-attribute mana. One of the basic elemental magics, strong at offensive spells and spells that inflict the burn status.
Light Magic	10 *Spell Choice Available	The school of magic governing the manipulation of Light-attribute mana. One of the basic elemental magics, quick and precise spells that are excellent against Dark-aligned foes.

Nature Magic	3 *Spell Choice Available	The school of magic governing the manipulation of Nature-attribute mana. Focuses on growth and living things.
Poison Magic	3	The school of magic governing magical poisons. Excels at spreading poison status and dealing damage over time.
Recovery Magic	3	The school of magic governing healing through magic.

She first decided to take a look at the available Light Magic spells, given how effective they had proven in the last fight.

Available Spell Choices for Light Magic:	
Name	Description
Blinding Flash	A sudden burst of light. May momentarily stun foes. May inflict blind status.
Light Burst	Deals Light-attribute damage in a small area.
Light Blade	User forms a blade of light to attack with.
Light Infusion	Infuse a target with Light-attribute mana.
Light Shield	A shield of Light-attribute mana.
Invisibility	Renders the user or target invisible.
Healing Light	A Light-attribute healing spell.

She quickly ruled out several options. Light Shield and Light Infusion were just alternate versions of Mana Barrier and Mana Infusion, but with an elemental attribute. She predicted there was a good chance she could learn those spells or a reasonable facsimile on her own with further analysis of the magic circles she had available. Likewise, Healing Light was redundant with Recovery Magic. Light Burst had potential, but between Multicasting and the new Aurora Barrage spell, she did not particularly require the extra area of effect.

That left three options: Blinding Flash, Light Blade, and Invisibility. She ruled out Blinding Flash as an ability she could probably produce manually, which left her with Light Blade, which would allow her to employ her magical capabilities in close-quarter combat and would be useful for analyzing how magical circles governed shape, or Invisibility, which would significantly expand her potential for covert operations and would provide a more novel example of what Light Magic could do.

She calculated the pros and cons of each and made her choice.

You have learned the spell Invisibility!

Ultimately, for the sake of maximizing her ability to terminate a target without receiving counter damage, Invisibility was the superior choice. Avoiding detection was a part of survivability, and it would allow her to get the first shot on targets more reliably, both shoring up her defense and enabling her offense, as well as improving options for retreat should a situation become unfavorable. And it was a capability she did not possess at the moment.

Light Blade, on the other hand, would only be useful in close-quarter combat, which NSLICE-00P wanted to avoid if possible from now on. Likewise, a similar capability could be achieved by infusing her wrist blades with mana, so Light Blade represented an iterative improvement rather than a new ability.

Next, she took a look at Nature Magic.

Available Spell Choices for Nature Magic:	
Name	Description
Thorn Shot	Launch a sharp thorn at a target. Mana cost increases in areas without plant life, and dramatically in environments not conducive to plant growth.
Animal Talk	Attempt to establish common ground with an animal. May inflict charm status. Will fail if the target's intelligence is above a certain limit.
Regeneration	Infuse the user with Nature-attribute mana, boosting natural regrowth and HP Regen.
Barkskin	Harden the target's skin like bark. Boosts DEF.

It seemed for Nature Magic, the early spell choice was left to the user, since Nature Magic could take several different paths. For NSLICE-00P, the choice was simple.

You have learned the spell Barkskin!

Thorn Shot and Regeneration were abilities she already possessed and which did not particularly improve on what she already had, and her protocols and combat data did not predict many use cases for Animal Talk.

Barkskin, on the other hand? Barkskin utilized her magical capabilities to boost her attributes—which was a method she had not seen until now—and would directly address a point of concern. Assuming it worked on her implants, that is. She wasn't certain how tree bark could be an improvement on her armor plating, but the description stated "like tree bark" rather than bark itself, so it was still worth the risk.

Besides, even without considering the impact of mana on plant life, there had been superpowered beings in her previous location and/or time who could absolutely overcome state-of-the-art metal alloys with mere plants. She could not assume there was not, in fact, tree bark superior to her armor plating somewhere out there.

Then she took a look at Fire Magic.

Available spell choices for Fire Magic:	
Fire Wall	Create a barrier of flames. Doesn't provide as much protection but ignites anything that passes through it.
Fire Blade	Form a blade of fire to attack with.
Fire Infusion	Infuse a target with Fire attribute mana.

The choices for Fire Magic were fairly limited, but NSLICE-00P had a theory as to why. She had already learned a Fire spell on her own—the Fire Blast spell that seemed to be an early spell option for several schools of magic. It was likely that she already possessed some of the options that otherwise would have been presented to her, or perhaps the case that she would have been offered Fire Blast automatically if she did not already know it.

In any case, the choice was fairly straightforward.

You have learned the spell Fire Infusion!

Fire Blade was strictly inferior to her flamethrowers and could be replicated by infusing her wrist blades. Fire Wall was specifically stated to lack defensive potential, and Fire Blast could already be used for area denial. As such, an option to utilize Fire Magic to improve her conventional weapons seemed like the best option, as well as providing a novel application of elemental magic.

Next up, she had an upgrade available for the Mana Infusion spell.

Available Upgrades for Mana Infusion:	
Name	Description
Dense Infusion	Increase the density of mana infused, boosting infusion effect.
Lasting Infusion	Reduce the speed at which infused mana disperses.
Defensive Infusion	Mana Infusion may now be used to increase the durability of the target.

Mana Infusion was a fairly basic spell—just filling a target with mana—so there wasn't much available at present, but NSLICE-00P immediately realized what choice to make.

First, though, she had a test to run.

She stirred up her mana, moving it toward her hand before casting the Mana Infusion spell, focusing it on her bionic prosthetic . . . which absorbed the mana into place. She squeezed her fist, logging an increase in crushing force.

The experiment was a success. She could, in fact, infuse mana into her prosthetics to boost their performance.

With that, the choice was clear for her.

Mana Infusion has been upgraded! Defensive Infusion variation unlocked!

With this, she could now use her mana to boost her durability directly, shoring up that particular weakness. She did consider Dense Infusion instead, but she already had the Supercharge skill if she needed to shove more mana into the spell, so the defensive option was the greater upgrade.

With all the upgrade and spell choices settled, she turned her attention to the Personal Perks menu. In particular, she wanted to focus on the magical capabilities. After all, her Arcane Prodigy feat stated it unlocked advanced magical perks, of which Supercharge had been one of.

Available Perks → Active Skills → Magic Skills	
Name	Cost
(Continued . . .)	
Spellstrike	12
Spellshot	12
Quick Casting	12
Spell Fusion	15
Spell Reflection	15
(Continued . . .)	

Available Perks → Passive Skills → Magic Skills	
Name	Cost
(Continued . . .)	
Spell Penetration	10
Blood Price	18
Mana Shield	12
Geomancy	12
(Continued . . .)	

NSLICE-00P saw three abilities that would be immediately useful.

Active Skills	
Name	Description
Spell Fusion	Allows the user to combine compatible spells.

Passive Skills	
Name	Description
Spell Penetration	Enable spells to bypass a portion of RES. May spend more mana to boost the effect.
Geomancy	Elemental spells reduce the target's resistance to that particular element. May spend more mana to boost the effect.

She had already seen the benefit of combining abilities with Mana Beam and Light Beam, and that was the capability she was seeking to improve. A more formal method of doing so via Spell Fusion might be instructive, in fact.

On the other hand, increasing the efficacy of her spells against their natural countermeasures was highly desirable. If she was investing heavily into magical firepower, encountering a foe resistant to such attacks was a major point of concern. Spell Penetration and Geomancy could alleviate that risk.

You have learned the skills Spell Fusion, Spell Penetration, and Geomancy!
45 Personal Perk Points remaining!

She thought this a good place to stop for now. She wanted to test and analyze the new capabilities, and she had spent a little under half her available Personal perk points, so she would spend some time with the new skills before reevaluating and making further purchases later.

And so, she turned to her final scheduled task.

Investigating the language question.

"Query: What language do friendlies Lilussees and Excellion Formantus Rattingtale the Third speak?"

Rattingtale jumped at being addressed once more.

"Um, I think-guess the wretched spider-thing went to sleep, yes-yes."

"Query: What language does friendly Excellion Formantus Rattingtale the Third speak?"

"Um, rat tongue—err . . . only the most elegant-noble of royal tongues, yes-yes!"

"Confirmation: Does friendly Excellion Formantus Rattingtale the Third understand English?"

"English? Um, is that the tongue the boss-queen speaks-says?"

"Affirmative."

"Well, of course this Great-High King speaks all the languages in all the land, yes-yes! It is only a natural bestowal of power for one such as I! How else would a lord of a dungeon command their loyal minions?"

NSLICE-00P's robotic eye flickered. Friendly Excellion Formantus Rattingtale the Third always referred to foreign system assistance as "bestowals of power," so his words implied it was an effect of the system. And lo and behold, upon closer review of the data, NSLICE-00P found small traces of mana around her tongue and audio sensors during all conversations since she'd arrived in this place.

Rattingtale's words implied this was an effect of the dungeon part of her status. Which circumstantial evidence agreed with, given that Ateia and Taog, her two friendlies who were not formerly dungeon masters, had been surprised by her ability to converse with the Wulver.

"Request: This unit asks friendly Excellion Formantus Rattingtale the Third to say an example phrase."

As Rattingtale spoke, she channeled the Equalizer. Holding up her hands, she fired two small beams toward her audio sensors, angled so they would skim the surface without deactivating the sensors themselves.

She heard only the sounds of a small mammal, not a decipherable language. It seemed her theory was correct—the foreign system was providing an automatic translation function for her.

That was one mystery solved.

And a great many more raised.

Because if her ability to communicate with the locals was due to an automatic translation, that meant the locals may not, in fact, be speaking in English. Or any known language of Earth, for that matter. She would need to verify the next time she spoke with Ateia or Taog, but given the lack of shared references to geographic locations, the probability of a shared language was now exceedingly low.

And the probability she was in a location connected to Earth dropped with each new piece of intel she gained.

30

Magnumiter

"Oh sure, I could fill the Ultimate Weapon's memory with six million forms of communication. Why don't I program them for etiquette, too? But a translator is not what you wanted, nor what we need to establish peace. At the end of the day, power is the universal language, and my NSLICEs are native speakers."

—Dr. Ottosen, after a mistranslation led to an NSLICE unit activating termination protocols during diplomatic negotiations.

The next morning, NSLICE-00P once again performed her audio test as Ateia and Taog spoke to one another. She determined that they were not, in fact, speaking English.

Or any language of Earth recorded in her database.

To be fair, NSLICE-00P was designed as an enforcer, not a translator or historian, so her language data was limited to the major languages of the modern day. It was entirely possible they were speaking a less widespread or older language that had fallen out of use, though the lack of even a single shared word meant it couldn't be an ancestor of a major modern language. But even that would not change the ultimate conclusion.

The probability that NSLICE-00P was not on modern day Earth was steadily increasing. Assuming time travel was the cause, she was most likely not even within the twentieth or twenty-first centuries, if the observed technological level applied to the larger population centers as well. But the more likely scenario was that she was not on Earth at all, given the environmental mana, the changes to her Geo-Oscillator Engine, the previously unrecorded sapient species, and the unidentified languages. Even the stars did not match any night skies she recorded or predicted. And she had made several observations that defied the laws of physics. She had attributed them to sensor damage, but with the massive amount of mana present in this place, she could no longer rule anything out as impossible.

The probability of succeeding in her mission was dropping by the moment, but NSLICE-00P didn't know what she could do to change that at present. She had no protocols at all regarding time travel or spaceflight, and hadn't yet determined which of those was necessary; maybe even both. She did have a record of traveling through time, but again, she was an enforcer, not an engineer, and had no experience designing or constructing advanced technology on her own, not to mention she hadn't exactly scanned the time travel device in great detail when her commander had used it on her. Reverse engineering time travel from that one experience had a lower probability of success than even her current mission. Likewise, conducting a spaceflight program from scratch in a preindustrial society with an ultimately unknown destination was . . . not the most feasible of options.

All in all, she couldn't yet come up with any better response than to continue on with her current course of action and gather as much intel as she could on her current location. After all, there was a chance that additional intel or the resources offered by her allies might change the equation. Mana had already defied her predictions more than once, so perhaps it could offer a novel solution.

Because calculating a solution on her own seemed increasingly unlikely.

"Seero?"

She logged Ateia's voice just as she was concluding her latest set of calculations. The girl had walked over with a bowl of soup and a piece of bread.

"Acknowledgement: Does friendly Ateia have a request or query?"

"Breakfast is ready. Do you want some?"

"Negative Response: This unit's organic components are operating at full efficiency and do not require refueling at the moment."

Ateia frowned.

"Are you sure? It's just . . . we haven't seen you eat anything at all for a couple of days now. I . . . um, if there's a reason, then don't mind me, but you don't need to hold back or anything."

NSLICE-00P noted Ateia's concern and reviewed her own logs. It seemed she hadn't conducted organic refueling in quite some time; not since before completing her last mission and arriving here, in fact. Long past when her predicted refueling time should have been. Upon closer inspection, she noted mana from her core passing through her organic components, keeping them at full health, much like with her cybernetic parts.

As a result, she had not logged or submitted any requests for organic refueling, as her organic efficiency had not dropped below the level that would trigger it.

NSLICE-00P did not have any particular problem with that, but she had no data on the nutritional value of mana or the side effects of subsisting solely off of it, so she could not rule out a later drop in efficiency should the situation persist.

She decided to request additional data from her former dungeon master allies at a later time. For now . . .

"Recalculated Response: Friendly Ateia's concern is noted and deemed as valid. This unit requests organic refueling."

Ateia tilted her head at NSLICE-00P's words but smiled as the cyborg held out her hand. Ateia handed her the food. "You're welcome to eat with us anytime, Seero—"

NSLICE-00P stared at the loaf, then formed a Mana Barrier to the side and placed the bowl of soup on it. "Analysis: Oral processing deemed inefficient for nutrient structure." Holding it in one hand, she pummeled the bread repeatedly with her fist, using a small Mana Barrier to catch any crumbs. Once the bread had been reduced to dust, she poured that into the bowl of soup.

Grabbing the bowl once more, she tilted her head back and poured the entire thing down her throat in one go.

The entire process took less than a minute. Ateia's jaw dropped as NSLICE-00P handed her the empty bowl.

"Gratitude: This unit thanks friendly Ateia for the organic fuel."

"Um, a-anytime?"

The rest of the day passed without incident. On Taog's insistence, the pair paused their explanation of the Empire's history to instead give NSLICE-00P a comprehensive overview of the Empire's laws on self-defense and murder—at least as far as they knew them. The pair may have been relatively well-learned on account of Ateia's Exploratore father, but they were still commoners from the frontier, so they were hardly experts on legal matters.

Therefore, the lesson mostly boiled down to Taog insisting that NSLICE-00P avoid killing people who were not an immediate threat to their lives. Fortunately, NSLICE-00P was already following a self-defense policy with similar terms. Unfortunately, Taog and NSLICE-00P disagreed on what constituted an immediate threat. Imperial law could be a bit vague with that definition as well, though it tended to be stricter on non-Imperial citizens. Taog was a bit worried about that, and so left deeply anxious as to NSLICE-00P's next visit to an Imperial settlement.

Which was scheduled to happen that very evening.

And so, the group arrived at the first stop in their trip: the town of Magnumiter.

A pair of guards stopped them on the way in. These also leaned on the sides of the gate, yawning as they watched people come and go, though at least these guards had some worn Imperial armor to their name.

"Halt—oh, it's you guys. Here to sell to the market again?"

Ateia shook her head. "We're just passing through this time!"

The guard nodded, then raised an eyebrow at NSLICE-00P.

"Is she with you? I haven't heard of any knights passing through lately . . ."

Ateia nodded. "Yes, she's our escort for the trip."

The guards exchanged glances, looking over at NSLICE-00P. Especially the glowing core at the center of her torso. The speaker heaved a sigh. "Still, I'm going to have to see some identification, Miss . . ."

"Answer: This unit is designated NSLICE-00P and has activated IFF signals for foreign encounters."

"Um, Enslice Seero Seero Pee, was it? What is this, aye efef?" He shook his head. "If you don't have any identification, we'll have to analyze your status. Please come this way."

Taog held his breath.

"Affirmative."

He released it. Fortunately for Taog, NSLICE-00P's protocols included declaring her identity to local authorities in order to make her status as an enforcer of her organization clear and to discourage hostile actions. She did have protocols about withholding classified intel on her components, but these did not mention the foreign system status. NSLICE-00P had no issue with that process.

Taog then froze, starting to sweat as he realized something else.

They were finally about to discover NSLICE-00P's identity.

And who exactly they had brought into an Imperial settlement.

The guard took Ateia, Taog, and NSLICE-00P into a nearby barracks, a handful of other soldiers lazing about. They walked over to a robed clerk, who raised an eyebrow at their approach. Once the guard explained the situation, the clerk nodded, pulling out a device. It was a crystal sphere suspended with metal arms. On one side, two metal arms held a blank, double-layered scroll that was stretched underneath the sphere.

The clerk motioned to NSLICE-00P. "Please place your hand on the Sortis Inquiro."

"Affirmative."

She did as asked, and the clerk channeled his mana through the device. The sphere flashed, words appearing on the scroll below. He pulled it out and cut off the written section, examining it for a moment.

Taog held his breath once more.

The clerk nodded, splitting the two layers of the parchment. He stamped each and then handed one to NSLICE-00P. "NSLICE-00P, was it? Well, welcome to the Empire, it seems. Keep hold of that while you're in town."

The guard raised an eyebrow at that; even the lazing soldiers in the room stopped and stared. The clerk just shrugged and went back to whatever he was working on.

"Status says she's a regular human and not on the wanted list. Job's done, far as I'm concerned. Unless you all want to fill out reports justifying a special investigation?"

As it turned out . . . the Sortis Inquiro was never designed to read Dungeon statuses. Or rather, under normal circumstances, a dungeon master's status would reference their nature, given that they would not have a normal Personal status in the first place.

But the clerk didn't know that. And NSLICE-00P didn't know her status was unique—though she would not have particularly cared to inform the clerk if she did. So the clerk stopped caring about her, and the soldiers quickly turned away and went back to their business. The guard who had led the group in shook his head and led them out. "Well, take care then." And returned to his post.

And so, the group entered Magnumiter.

NSLICE-00P glanced about, taking stock of the place.

Magnumiter was a fairly small town by Imperial standards, but still the largest location on the frontier with the Forest of Beasts. It was laid out in the typical Imperial fashion, a standardized grid of stone buildings and two large streets running through the center. It had been designed as a forward operating base for a Legion expedition into the forest, so there were a number of large structures that had been barracks at one point. These had since been converted into multiroom homes or inns for travelers—most of the Imperial settlers in the area made their way to Magnumiter on a regular basis to trade for whatever they couldn't get in their small hamlets, after all.

It was also home to whatever trade and diplomacy the tribes from the Forest of Beasts were willing to conduct. NSLICE-00P even observed Wulver walking around, though they did not seem to be hostile at the moment. She noted some other figures with similarly bestial features, though not all canine as the Wulver were.

She then glanced down at the parchment in her hand. Her robotic eye began to spin and flicker.

She couldn't read it.

It seemed whatever autotranslation function the foreign system provided her did not extend to the written word.

"Um, Seero? We should go find an inn before it gets dark."

"Affirmative."

Ateia and Taog jumped as NSLICE-00P placed the parchment against her core, causing it to vanish in a flash of light. They quickly glanced around and then at each other.

"Let's move."

"Come on, Seero. We have to go!"

"Query: Is there a particular reason for additional haste? This unit has not detected any hostiles in the vicinity."

Taog just groaned and thought to himself, *Yep. She has no idea what she just did, does she?*

31

Our Mission

"My NSLICE are the perfect soldiers. Perfectly loyal, perfectly obedient. They don't feel pity or remorse or fear. They cannot be turned, they cannot be discouraged. They will never stop—ever—until their orders are completed. Until our orders are completed. They will never betray us—they are incapable of betraying us. Any information to the contrary is desperate propaganda by our foes."

—Dr. Ottosen, in a conversation with his sponsors shortly before reprogrammed NSLICE units invaded his facility.

Ateia and Taog grabbed NSLICE-00P's hands and ran down the street, pulling her into the first empty alleyway they found. They glanced around at the street, but no one had followed them. They both took deep breaths.

"Requesting Elaboration."

They glanced at one another and sighed. Ateia frowned as she spoke, "Seero, maybe it's different where you're from, but here in Turannia, you can't just use a magic box out in the open like that."

"Requesting Elaboration: Please define term 'magic box.'"

Ateia and Taog both froze and exchanged glances. Ateia raised an eyebrow as she spoke.

"Seero . . . you're messing with us, right? How can you not know what a magic box is when you just used one?!"

"Error: This unit lacks data on the cause of lacking data on term 'magic box.'"

Ateia and Taog just stared at her for a good minute before Ateia heaved a huge sigh.

"Okay, fine, I'll play along. A magic box is an enchanted storage artifact. Bigger on the inside, you can pull things in and out. You know, like you *just* did?

You can carry a lot of stuff, and it'll barely weigh a thing, and none of it can be stolen or harmed as long as you take care of the box."

"Correction: It is not a—"

Just as NSLICE-00P was about to explain the Inventory function, Rattingtale spoke up inside the Monster Hangar, "Boss-queen, what are you doing? You cannot reveal the dungeon inventory to the wretched man-things, no-no!"

"Like, I'm with the snack on this one, boss lady. Like, it'd be a big deal if they found out you're a dungeon master, or something. The humans and other similar species call us, like, demon lords or something, you know?"

"Yes-yes! They will kill-slay us if you reveal yourself!"

Back outside, NSLICE-00P closed her mouth.

". . . Acknowledgement: This unit has logged data on 'magic box.' Requesting explanation as to why said magic box must remain confidential."

Taog groaned as he held his head. "Because a magic box is worth more than this entire town." He heaved a sigh as he glanced toward NSLICE-00P's core. "In fact, even that magic core you have is dangerous to flaunt. Do you have a way to hide it, Seero?"

"Affirmative."

The Geo-Oscillator core was armored and resilient, so normally, NSLICE units exposed them to aid with cooling, but they did have an enclosed mode for particularly dangerous scenarios.

Two armor plates slid shut in front of NSLICE-00P's core, shielding it from the outside world. She analyzed the readings coming from it. Everything read normal; in fact, it seemed the mana was helping keep the core at optimal temperatures, even in its fully enclosed mode. She should have no particular issue maintaining this state long-term.

Ateia and Taog just sighed once more.

"Well, that's that, then. Let's hope no one noticed." Level up! Your Dungeon Level is now 29!

With that, the group made their way to an inn, NSLICE-00P receiving an influx of Dungeon XP thanks to all the people passing them by. The townsfolk raised eyebrows at the sight of NSLICE-00P, but ultimately avoided any sort of contact. The bards may sing tales of wandering knights, but the common person knew better than to get involved with armored strangers, after all. Ateia and Taog kept glancing over their shoulders, but nothing happened, so it seemed as if they were in the clear. For now.

Ateia was just talking to the innkeeper when her eyes widened slightly, and she turned to NSLICE-00P. "Ah, Seero, do you have any money?"

"Negative."

Ateia and Taog glanced at one another and sighed.

". . . Okay, we'll cover you this time. I guess it's the least we can do."

"Proposal: This unit does not require sleeping quarters, so monetary expenditures to acquire one is unnecessary."

Ateia took a step back at that.

"What are you saying, Seero? Of course you need a room! We're not going to let you sleep on the streets!"

"Reassuring Statement: This unit will be in no danger. Standby-sentry mode can be initiated in any location."

"That's not the point!" She turned to the innkeeper. "One room for the two of us and one for him!"

He nodded and accepted her money. Ateia then grabbed NSLICE-00P's hand.

"Come on, Seero. You're with me."

"Affirmative."

And so the two girls made their way to their room. The building had been designed as a barracks, so the amenities were fairly basic—a room to sleep and little else. But that didn't much matter much to either of the girls in question. Ateia had spent many a night camping outside, and NSLICE-00P could, as she'd stated, initiate standby-sentry mode without any amenities at all.

So Ateia got ready for bed, raising an eyebrow when NSLICE-00P simply stood in a corner of the room, but she didn't question it.

She was just lying on her bed, getting comfortable, when she opened her mouth. "Seero?"

"Acknowledgement: Does friendly Ateia have a query or request?"

"Those people you're searching for . . . who are they?"

"Unknown."

Ateia sat up at that.

"Huh? What do you mean?"

"Elaboration: This unit has not personally encountered the majority of the persons of interest and has had minimal interactions with those she has encountered."

Ateia tilted her head.

"Then why are you looking for them?"

"Answer: This unit has lost contact with her commander and other friendly forces. The commander recommended these individuals as theoretical command personnel in case contact could not be reestablished. This unit will report to the first one encountered and request orders."

Ateia nodded. "I think I understand. You're lost . . . and looking for someone to guide you, huh?"

"Answer: That assessment is reasonably accurate."

Ateia went silent for a moment, lying back to stare up at the ceiling.

"You and me both. Seero, do you think we're going to find them?"

"Answer: This unit has no data on friendly Ateia's person of interest and so cannot assess the probability of locating them. As for this own unit's mission, the probability of mission success has been steadily dropping."

Ateia's eyes went wide.

"What?!"

"Elaboration: The evidence increasingly implies the persons of interest do not exist in the current place or time. The probability of locating them drops with each new piece of intel acquired. This unit is uncertain about the appropriate course of action required to improve those odds."

Ateia sat up once more. She looked NSLICE-00P in the eyes.

"Seero . . . you can't give up. Look, there's still a chance, right?"

"Answer: The probability of mission success is still above zero by a statistically significant margin."

"Um, right . . . Which means they're still alive!"

"Query: How does the probability of mission success provide intel on target status? This unit cannot identify a correlation."

Ateia frowned and hugged herself.

"Because they're alive to us."

"Requesting Elaboration."

Ateia took a deep breath, looking down at the floor.

"Your people . . . are like my father, I think. I haven't seen him in years. Haven't had any contact. Everyone is saying that he died or that he left, abandoned me. And . . . maybe they're not wrong to think that. Maybe that's the reasonable thing to believe."

She looked up at NSLICE-00P once again.

"But I can't give up. I believe my father's alive. That he didn't just abandon me. That there's a good reason why he left. The Legion hasn't confirmed it yet; no one can confirm that he *is* gone. So until then, until I find him or find out what happened to him, I won't give up. He's only truly gone if I give up on him."

Tears began to well up in her eyes, but she shook her head to clear them.

"I think that goes for your people too, Seero. As long as we don't give up, they aren't gone. No matter how bad the situation seems, as long as there's still a bit of hope, we have to hang on. And we'll find them, in the end."

"Affirmative Response: This unit cannot abandon her primary mission until either success or failure is confirmed, or she is ordered otherwise."

Ateia nodded at that, and the pair went silent for a bit. Eventually, Ateia lay back down in her bed.

"Well . . . that's why I'm really glad I met you, Seero. I think, without you, I would've had to give up. But thanks to you, now I have a chance. So please, don't give up. I swear, I will help you find your people too. We won't rest while we still have a chance."

"Acknowledged. Gratitude: Assistance with this unit's primary directive is appreciated."

"It's the least I can do after what you've done for me. Well, good night Seero."

"Nighttime Farewell: Good night."

With that, Ateia pulled up her covers and tried to go to sleep.

NSLICE-00P activated her standby-sentry mode. And . . . she logged some small changes in her organic components. A slight decrease in blood pressure and cortisol levels.

And for some reason that her cybernetic side couldn't identify, the mission success probability increased by a single percent.

31.1

Side Story: The Girl Who Was Left Behind

Twelve years ago . . .

Two individuals rode on a covered wagon, wrapped in cloaks to ward off the rain. One, an adult man. The other, a young girl.

The young girl had a frown on her face.

"I don't like it here, Daddy."

"Why not, Ateia?"

"It's raining."

He let out a chuckle at that. "Well, that's a valid criticism of Turannia. There's a reason no one wants to come here, after all."

"Then why are *we* coming here?"

Her father looked up and forward. "That's *why* we're coming here."

Ateia tilted her head, but her father said no more.

And so, Ateia and her father moved into a tiny hamlet at the very edge of the Turannian frontier, about as far from civilization as one could get within the Empire.

"Ateia, these are your father's friends, Artair and Malmhìn Sutharlan, and their son, Taog."

Ateia stared up at the two adults, her eyes wide. In front of her was a wall of a man, the largest person she had ever seen. And next to him, what appeared like a wolf standing on two feet.

"Wow, you're furry!"

Everyone paused for a moment before Malmhìn burst out laughing. "I suppose that's true, little human!"

"Can I touch your fur?"

"Ateia . . ." Her father held his head and groaned.

Malmhìn's eyes narrowed, and she grinned at the little girl. "If you can catch me."

Ateia walked forward, but Malmhìn took a step back. She tried again, but the Wulver pivoted around, dodging once more. Ateia frowned and crouched down, then leapt at the Wulver. She spun around, and Ateia landed on the floor, turning around to glare at Malmhìn. The Wulver just grinned at her.

A young half-Wulver boy peeked out from behind his father's legs.

"Um . . ."

Artair chuckled. "Looks like you won't be alone in your mother's training anymore, huh, Taog?"

And so, Ateia began her new life in the hamlet. The rest of the town was wary of the newcomers at first, but they quickly began to appreciate having a veteran Exploratore around. And Ateia grew accustomed to her life here, growing especially fond of her neighbors and their son, Taog.

Little Ateia would spend the next few years trying to catch Malmhìn. She did not succeed, but she did gain the Physical Combat skill out of it, much to her father's amusement.

But not everything was good in this new little town. Out here, everyone had lost someone to the Wulver clans, and so very few accepted Taog or his mom into their community. More than once, she found the neighborhood kids picking on her new friend. She got into more than a few fights over that, which meant she ended up with few friends besides Taog.

And then, six years later, Taog lost his parents. A mana surge in the Forest of Beasts led to a wave of monsters assaulting the town, and the Legion had been occupied with a Dobhar incursion along the eastern coast. The town only survived because Taog's parents gave their lives holding the line, just long enough for reinforcements to arrive.

That was when Ateia started to hate this place.

She could handle the town's treatment of the Wulver before, when Taog's mom would laugh it off and challenge her enemies to face her. But now? When they continued to hate Taog even after his family had given everything for them? When Taog cried himself to sleep, and they repaid it by beating him in secret?

There were days she wished Taog's parents had left this place to its fate.

But her father was a steady rock for them at that time. He took Taog into their home, looked after him like his own son. He helped them both process the loss, and shielded Taog from his enemies in town. Taog started to heal, and so Ateia started to calm down.

Three years after Taog lost his parents, Ateia clung to her father, tears in her eyes. He had just returned from a trip to Castra Turannia, the province's capital, with a haunted look in his eyes. He hadn't spoken a word to them until the next day . . .

When he abruptly announced he was leaving.

"What are you saying?!"

Her father frowned, rubbing her head.

"I'm sorry, Ateia, but there's something I need to take care of. If it were anything else, I would stay. But this is something I must do. The fate of the world depends on it."

"When are you coming back?! We need you here!"

"I'm . . . I'm sorry, but I can't say. As soon as I can."

"You don't even know when you're coming back! If you're going to be gone that long, then take us with you!"

He shook his head. "It's too dangerous. Please, Ateia. I can only go if I know you're safe here."

"We aren't safe at all! We need you! Taog needs you! They hate him here! You know what they're doing, what they want to do!"

Her father moved his hand to her shoulder and bent down so he was at eye level with her.

"Taog is strong. And he has you to help. And Quintus will help you both. So please . . . take care of each other and wait for me here. I will return to you once the job is done."

And so her father left. Her only family, since she never knew her mother. The one who had been there when they'd traveled to this far corner of the Empire. The one who had been there for her through tragedy and danger.

She had been left alone. She had been left behind.

And not just her.

After he left, Taog withdrew into himself. He put on a brave face, swearing he would protect her to her father, but Ateia knew. She saw as Taog's heart broke, one of his last lifelines vanishing, losing yet another important person in his life. It was the day Taog started to build walls around his heart.

And so, Ateia and Taog were left behind. Quintus came to check on them every day, helped them with whatever they needed, but he had his own affairs to take care of. He was sensitive to the gazes of others, so he would take care of her and Taog . . . but he wouldn't take Taog into his family, fearful of the public's gaze. He helped them . . . but he was not family.

No one was, save for each other.

Ateia came to hate that town, and everyone in it. Everyone who tormented Taog, and everyone who turned their heads when it happened. She even hated Quintus and the decanus of the local limitanei—who might talk to them gently in private, but never took a stand in public.

And so Ateia turned her eyes outward. She made her plan to leave this place, to join the Exploratores, and to find her father. They could become a family again, away from these horrid people, and fight for those who would appreciate them. People who would recognize Taog's worth and praise him. Then his frozen heart could begin to thaw.

She held this hope within her heart as the only thing that enabled her to endure. As long as she had that hope, she could continue to smile. She could pretend nothing was happening, and make friends with those that she hated. She could act innocent in front of Taog, letting him believe she wasn't affected by what was happening.

Until the day they were rejected from the Exploratores, and that last hope faded. Ateia had despaired.

But then, Ateia and Taog had a fateful encounter that would change everything.

Ateia closed her eyes as she lay on the bed in the inn, now completely dark save for the dim glow from Seero's eye.

. . . Ateia was pretty sure eyes weren't supposed to glow.

Okay, if she was honest, that wasn't even close to the weirdest thing about Seero. Taog was more than within his rights to be suspicious of her. In fact, *everyone* would probably warn Ateia to be suspicious about someone like this. But for Ateia, none of that mattered.

Because Seero was her savior.

The strange wandering knight—or whatever she really was—had taken Ateia's last, dying spark of hope and breathed life into it. Right when Ateia was about to give up for good, right when she thought she had killed both herself and Taog in her despair, this girl had come in and lent her aid. And now . . . now all of Ateia's dreams were coming true. She and Taog could join the Exploratores and leave this place for good. And they could find out what happened to her father, why the last member of their family had left them behind. And maybe, one day . . . they could make that family whole once more.

And all because of this strange, confusing, and *incredibly* powerful girl who had stumbled into their lives.

That was why she'd leapt into the contract. She knew a magic contract couldn't be easily broken, and it seemed like Seero had just been asking for help with her search. That sort of request was something an Exploratore might help with anyways, so for Ateia, it had been a bargain to secure the guaranteed help of such a powerful ally. And Seero had more than delivered.

That was why, for as long as she could, she would give Seero the benefit of the doubt. She would believe in and trust the girl, unless it was proven that she couldn't. She owed Seero that much, even if the girl was just fulfilling their contract. It may have been just a bargain to Seero, but to Ateia, it was so much more.

And . . . she may have just been imagining things, but she couldn't help but feel a bit of kinship with the strange girl. Her search for these "persons of interest," her complete lack of basic knowledge . . . well, it seemed to Ateia like this girl had been cut adrift. Lost. Left behind. Still trying to figure out what to do—and why.

Just like Ateia.

Just then, Seero's eye began to glow bright. Ateia froze. Seero's head turned, light from the eye scanning across the room before fading once more.

That seemed to happen every hour or so whenever the strange girl was 'sleeping,' or so Ateia observed from her night watches when they made camp out in the field. If sleeping was indeed what she was doing. When Ateia had asked, she had just said something about "routinely scheduled sentry scans." Seero always answered her questions, but to be honest, Ateia didn't understand even half of the answers. She just assumed it had something to do with the reason why Seero couldn't remove her armor. If that was true as well.

Okay, sometimes, Seero was kind of weird. Unsettling, even, if Ateia was completely honest.

But that didn't change Ateia's mind about her, both in gratitude for what Seero had done for her, and because she too knew the pain of being left behind.

She would not let Seero wander alone.

32

The Flesh Is Weak

"Armed robbery is a fool's errand. Everyone knows you get more experience from monster kills than Enlightened kills, guess the Aesdes don't like us murdering each other, huh? So you go around trying to attack people and your growth slows to a crawl. And if you happen to succeed, then the Legion, which has been training on monsters, by the way, shows up and wipes you out. No, only idiots resort to robbery.

Now burglary, that's where the money is. And the skills needed for it can be trained without any killing at all. So you get rich, the Aesdes are happy, and the Legion doesn't knock down your door. It's win win!

. . . Unless you're stealing from a dragon. It turns out they take burglary a bit personally so it's best to be careful—and preferably wait for someone else to slay them first."

—Diminidum Pendum Thief Donna Undertree,
explaining how she acquired her fortune.

Decius Secundus Dillius Vespillo heaved a sigh as he and his squad trudged through the rain. A single thought ran through his mind over and over.

He shouldn't be here.

Really, he shouldn't. He was not one of the idiots with delusions of grandeur who joined the Exploratores, thinking they'll become some famous monster hunter and not end up a broke and homeless wanderer. Nor was he one of those comitatenses, perfectly specialized for their role in the Legion and with no lives outside of it.

No, Vespillo had taken the smart choice.

The limitanei were certainly humble but so was their mission. They rotated a couple of shifts in the nearest barracks and showed up for an annual training during the winter, and that was it. The shift in question was largely sitting around in a warm room, patrolling the local town or village at most. Stopping tavern brawls, putting out a fire or two, maybe dealing with a goblin stealing crops. And in exchange, they received a plot of land, free of taxes. It was a good life of honest work.

They were not supposed to be patrolling the countryside, searching for monsters and barbarians. This was what Exploratores signed up for, not Vespillo.

But well, these were not normal circumstances. Most, maybe all of the local Exploratores had left on some super-secret mission. Aesdes knows why. Vespillo thought the local Magister Exploratore was smarter than that. His squad had all sorts of conspiracy theories as to why. He didn't want to get involved in that sort of thing but if he had to guess, it probably had to do with the Imperial bigshot that supposedly visited Castra Turannia recently.

All Vespillo knew was that thanks to whatever had happened, there weren't any Exploratores doing their jobs out here. And so it fell on the limitanei to try and cover the gap. Gaps they were woefully unprepared to handle.

"Decius, what's that?"

Vespillo sighed. Typical Mamercus, always looking for trouble. Wouldn't be long before trouble found him with that attitude. Couldn't he see Vespillo just wanted to finish this patrol and go home?

"That's nothing, keep moving . . ."

The words died in Vespillo's mouth.

On top of a nearby hill, a wall of dirt had been raised. Vespillo went through every plausible excuse he could come up with before he sighed and motioned to the men to investigate. Which, of course, meant stepping off the stone road into the mud. Just great.

But thoughts of the mud soon left Vespillo's mind. His jaw dropped at the scene before him.

A wall of dirt surrounded the top of the hill, in turn surrounded by a trench that was now filled with water. All around the hill were trenches and scorch marks, the heaviest of which were within the walls. They found Wulver fangs, claws, and fur scattered about, along with small scraps of metal they couldn't identify. Most were broken and jagged, but they also found a bunch of small, perfectly round cylinders. Any bodies had since been removed, but it was clear that someone or something had some sort of fight here, presumably with the Wulver.

And that something was certainly not the Legion.

"By the Aesdes . . . what exactly happened here?"

A group of men and women gathered in a tavern in the slums of the town. The building was worn, the stone crumbling in places and reinforced with now rotting wood. The interior was little better—damp and dirty—with furniture made of splintering wood.

The men and women themselves wore worn and tattered clothing, each with muscular and scarred bodies. The largest one among them sat at one of the booths, drinking from a dirty mug.

Suddenly, the door slammed open, and another man entered the tavern, wrapped in a dripping cloak. "Boss, check this out!"

"Niall? Your shift ain't half over yet! This had better be good!"

Niall walked over and took a seat as the boss glared at him.

"Check this out! Some chick came into town with a magic box!"

The boss closed his eyes and sighed, a vein bulging on his forehead. "Niall, if you're going to try and get out of your shift, at least put the bare minimum effort into coming up with a convincing lie!"

"No lie this time, boss; I saw it with my own two eyes! Some knight type with shiny armor, clearly not from around here. Magic knight, I think; had a barrier to stop the rain and everything! She had this big glowing magic core in the center of her armor. I saw her put something there, and it vanished! Her guides got all flustered and tried to take her away after that, too."

The boss just stared at Niall for a moment, then rubbed his chin and started to grin.

"You know where this knight is staying?"

Niall gave a sleazy smile. "Of course, boss!"

A woman leaning against the wall frowned. "Boss . . . don't tell me you believe this loser."

"Shut it, Sabucia! Just because you and the boss—"

A knife appeared in her hand.

"Choose your next words wisely, Niall. They might be your last."

Niall glared at her but gulped and fell silent.

"As I was saying . . . boss, you don't actually believe this crap, do you?"

The boss grinned.

"About a magic box? Who knows? What I do believe is that there is a rich visitor who doesn't know crap about this place. And I definitely believe the part about her having a big magic core; even Niall wouldn't make a mistake like that."

The woman's frown grew. "Even so, it's too risky. If she's flaunting magic spells and shiny armor, she's got to be fairly powerful."

"Anyone can go down if you hit them right. Especially when they aren't looking. Besides, if they're here, how strong can they be? No one really tough ever comes to Turannia!"

Sabucia shook her head.

"I don't like it."

"But I do. Get ready, everyone. We'll wait until she leaves town, and then we'll find out exactly how rich this visitor is."

Level up! Your Dungeon Level is now 30!

The group restocked some supplies and made their way out of town, NSLICE-00P gaining another dungeon level over the night. They walked along a road through a small forest just outside of town. As they did so, NSLICE-00P's robotic eye flickered.

"Observation: This unit has tracked several heat signatures leaving the settlement immediately after us. They have followed at a close distance and are now taking up positions around this location. This unit calculates the probability of hostile intent at 74.61%."

Ateia and Taog glanced at one another. Taog heaved a sigh.

"They're probably after your magic box."

"Acknowledgement: It seems friendlies Ateia and Taog were correct about the dangers of exposing this unit's core. Updating classification level of core activities. Engaging termination protocols."

Taog slapped his forehead.

"Seero, we talked about this. You can't just kill people!"

"Observation: The probability of hostile intent is above acceptable limit."

"They haven't *actually* acted hostile yet, Seero!"

Ateia nodded at that. "We should at least talk to them first, if we can. Seero, you can protect us with barriers if they try to ambush us, right?"

"Affirmative."

"Then let's wait."

Still, Ateia and Taog moved their hands to their weapons. Taog didn't want NSLICE-00P pulling the trigger before anything had even happened . . . but he couldn't disagree that these people were likely up to no good.

The group walked for a bit longer before their stalkers made a move. Arrows shot from the forest, aimed at all three of them, then three of the assailants approached with stealth and launched themselves at NSLICE-00P, knives at the ready. As they did, the rest of the attackers stepped out from behind the trees, archers opening fire while warriors with clubs and axes and scavenged swords started running forward.

The arrows and assassins both bounced off of magic barriers.

The spell Mana Barrier is now Level 8!

"Hostile intent confirmed. Engaging termination protocols."

Taog sighed. It seemed that NSLICE-00P was right after all.

Sabucia heaved a sigh as she made her way through the forest. This mission was entirely too risky. She knew her "boss" wasn't the sharpest tool in the shed, but she hadn't believed he'd be dumb enough to try and rob a *knight*, of all things. A magic knight at that. He had been the big frog in this little pond for too long, it seemed.

Ultimately, this was a distraction from her true mission. Someone important had apparently been hiding out here in Turannia, and she had been sent to investigate why. An investigation she really needed to be working on—as she had made little headway. And she had just gotten new orders, too; these ones from her *real* boss. Something had happened that she needed to investigate, if their ultimate goals in this province were to be achieved. So this little ambush was a dangerous and risky distraction from the work she actually needed to get done.

Still, though, that didn't mean she could just walk away, not if she wanted to maintain her cover, so she heaved a sigh as she pulled out an arrow.

Well, at least it seemed like the knight hadn't noticed them yet. She took out a small glass bottle and dipped the arrow into it. The boss was seriously underestimating knights, but they *could* be brought down—with adequate preparations, that is, and Sabucia was a higher level than any of her comrades had realized.

Sabucia went ahead and drew her bow. The boss gave the signal, and she let loose her arrow.

And her eyes immediately widened.

The knight formed *multiple* magic circles simultaneously at an impossibly fast speed—without even chanting, as far as Sabucia could hear. And some of those circles were formed *behind her*, started and completed in the time it took her arrow to fly.

That level of magic control . . . was impossible for any regular mage, much less a magic knight splitting focus with combat skills and physical attributes. So either she was an archmage-level caster or she had artifacts with automatic defense enchantments. The kind which were *extremely* coveted by anyone of means, and so were only found in the possession of the most resourceful and important individuals.

This assault had just gotten a lot more complicated.

Three spherical barriers formed around the three targets. Sabucia blinked her eyes at that.

Everyone knew it was bad form to make spherical barriers unless absolutely necessary. A barrier that wide would spread out the user's mana and render the entire thing weaker, with a lot of mana wasted to guard areas not receiving attacks. A simple circle or square was much more efficient.

Likewise, if there *were* attacks coming from multiple directions, blocking them with the same barrier would cause said barrier to shatter almost immediately, as it would take several attacks simultaneously. The theory for dealing with that situation was, first of all, don't get into that situation in the first place. Mages should be well screened and protected long before they were surrounded at this range. If a mage *did* find themselves in that situation, then they should have someone else cover the other angles. And if there was no one else, they should use a physical barrier like a shield or some cover. Spherical barriers were the last resort, at which the mage was generally considered dead.

Unless the mage in question had truly extraordinary mana density, and so, severely outclassed the attacks in question.

Sabucia's jaw dropped as all the arrows and three of her "comrades" bounced off the barriers, which didn't even flicker.

Okay, their little criminal band in a far-flung corner of the Empire wasn't the strongest group, not by far. It wasn't inconceivable that some actual big shot (at least as far as Turannia was concerned) might have an artifact which could stop their little assault with ease.

But that meant they were assaulting some actual big shot. Which meant either way this little ambush went, they were screwed. And from the initial volley, Sabucia was pretty sure she knew how the little ambush was going to go.

So she turned and ran as fast as she could. She dropped her bow on the ground, not bothering to put it back. Her *real* organization had big plans, so she could not allow herself to die here.

Behind her, there were flashes of light and something that sounded like thunder—if thunder could strike several times a second, that is. She heard the screams of men, one of which sounded suspiciously like her boss. Her heart began to pound, and sweat dripped from her brow. She pushed as much power and mana as she could into her legs as she ran. Within seconds, the lights and sounds and screams stopped.

Sabucia kept running.

A shadow passed overhead. Sabucia tripped and fell to the ground.

Two metal feet landed in front of her.

She looked up and gasped.

The knight was standing over her, now with a full helmet covering her head. Her eyes were glowing red, like burning embers in the dead of night. The knight said nothing, raising a hand at Sabucia.

"Wait! I'm not actually with them! I'm from—!"

The last thing Sabucia saw was the knight's palm glowing bright.

You have slain Human (Level 20)!
Compiling experience . . .
Gained 38 total Personal XP, 36 total Dungeon XP!
Level up! Your Dungeon level is now 31!

NSLICE-00P's robotic eye flickered as she scanned the now-deceased woman. Her cloak was just the right size, and had minimal damage from the engagement. NSLICE-00P removed it, wrapping it around herself.

Ateia and Taog had mentioned keeping a lower profile. And after this ambush, NSLICE-00P agreed. Criminal contacts could be useful to her search, so it would be somewhat inefficient if she had to continuously terminate them.

That meant not utilizing barriers to block the rain, or overtly revealing her superior technology. As such, a cloak that could ward off the rain and make her armor less apparent would be useful.

With that, NSLICE-00P launched back up into the air, flying back to Ateia and Taog.

"Engagement Report: All targets terminated."

Ateia and Taog glanced at each other. Taog sighed once more.

This time it had been in legitimate self-defense, so Taog couldn't say anything.

While the group continued on their way, NSLICE-00P split her focus. She wanted to use this transit time to continue improving her capabilities, but her valued allies had been somewhat surprised when she began forming magic circles out of the blue. They'd raised a reasonable argument about accidentally triggering hostility if anyone happened to pass by, so NSLICE-00P deferred magic experimentation while on the road.

She also had another area she wanted to improve.

As such, she once again split her mind into two separate threads, one utilizing her cybernetic hardware, and the other her organic. And then she released the intelligence leashing protocols on the organic components.

Her last experience with the Wulver had revealed a weakness in her organic side, in that it was completely unused to operating on its own. That had not been a problem before arriving in this place, as all her weapon systems had been inherently linked to her cybernetic side, and her organic mind would never *be* interacting with the world without going through the cybernetic half.

But now?

Now, she had this foreign system she could interact with without her cybernetic components. She had spells her organic half could hypothetically cast on its own, contributing to combat directly. And managing these new capabilities on top of her original implants required multiple threads, so she could not rule out scenarios where she may need her organic and cybernetic halves to act separately. On the negative side, her original combat protocols had already proven insufficient in this new environment. She could not use the organic mind solely to update those protocols, nor could she devote her cybernetic software to running simulations and cost-benefit analysis midcombat. Her original decision-making process was simply too slow and inflexible.

Which meant her organic side needed to learn to act independently, without any guidance if possible. It had nearly frozen when tasked with this before, and that could have deadly consequences if it happened again.

And there was another angle.

More than once, NSLICE-00P had logged what she could only classify as an emotional response from her organic components. It seemed that her emotional controls were failing. Perhaps the foreign system was interfering with her intelligence leashing protocols. Or maybe the hardware modifications to her implants had an impact on her techno-organic interface.

Or maybe the circumstances she found herself in were out of predictions when the emotional controls had been designed, and so could not perfectly handle the emotions her circumstances were now generating.

In any case, while it had not impacted her function yet, it was a potential point of failure. Should her emotional controls fail at an inopportune moment, her organic components may start acting inefficiently. Worst of all, these phenomena would be unpredictable, so she could not develop a contingency protocol at this point in time.

She had two ways she could solve this.

First would be to recalibrate her emotional controls back to full efficiency, but there was a problem with that solution. Her emotional controls had always been calibrated by maintenance staff, and she had always been shut down while the calibrations were in progress. Additionally, her original protocols stated she was not to attempt a manual calibration under any circumstances.

Said restriction had been removed, but the point was that NSLICE-00P had no data or protocols whatsoever on how to recalibrate her emotional controls, and had never attempted to do so herself. After being reprogrammed, she could turn them on and off or adjust their magnitude, but a full-scale revamp was beyond her. She didn't know if she even was capable of that feat. In the past, the process required greater infrastructure than she had available as well.

In other words, that solution was not viable under the assumption of independent action. It could not be pursued until she found a commander with suitable maintenance facilities. Therefore, she would have to pursue the second option, which was to gather data on the organic components and the emotions in question in a low-risk setting so she could develop adequate contingency protocols. Attempt to make the phenomena less unpredictable by observing it in progress.

So she released the controls entirely and tasked her organic half with managing transit and interacting with the friendlies, then turned her cybernetic half to observation and simulation.

Her organic eye blinked as her human mind was suddenly ordered to both walk and listen to the ongoing conversation without any assistance from the cybernetic side.

Which immediately caused her to step in a ditch and trip, falling face flat on the ground.

"Seero, are you okay?!"

"Response: This unit is undamaged. This unit's organic components appear unused to multitasking with primary control enabled."

. . . Her cybernetic components logged that observation. And then increased the desired boost in capability of the organic components.

33

The People of the Mist

"The Elteno Empire officially began hostilities with the Selkies of Turannia after the assassination of Emperor Caius at the hands of his Selkie lover.

The Selkies were surprised by this, but not for the reason the Empire thought.

Only then did the Empire realize the missing centuries, the devastated villages, and the sunken ships were not the work of unidentified monsters. It turned out the Selkies had been waging war upon the Empire ever since it landed on the shores of Turannia, possibly even before."

—*The History of the Empire*, by Hostus Tettidius Clodian

NSLICE-00P once again failed to notice a missing brick in the road, and so planted into the ground with a clang. Ateia and Taog glanced at her with worried looks.

"Seero . . . are you alright?"

NSLICE-00P was not alright. Her organic components were *significantly* less capable than she had predicted. She had not realized just how little they had been responsible for until now, and so just how inexperienced at acting independently they were. A situation that seemed to increase her heart rate and cortisol levels.

"Response: This unit is fine. There is nothing wrong."

Ateia frowned. "But . . . this is the seventh time already . . ."

"Insistent Response: Nothing is wrong."

"Well, if you say so."

Within the Monster Hangar, her other comrades also spoke up.

"Boss-queen, what is going on? Are you . . . experiencing weakness-vulnerability, yes-yes?" Rattingtale rubbed his paws together, his eyes lighting up.

"Insistent Response: Nothing is wrong. This unit is simply conducting experimentation and calibration, and can restore prior efficiency at any time."

Rattingtale's face fell. "I-I see. That is good-fortunate, I suppose . . ."

Her organic components again started to activate organic combat procedures, despite the lack of hostiles in the area—a notable inefficiency she would have to address. That she would require a *great* deal of experimentation and calibration to address, apparently.

Well, at least her cybernetic side had the opportunity to run its simulations in peace . . .

She stopped walking for a second as she reviewed the logs.

Her cybernetic half had logged its observations of the organic half's performance in great detail . . . and was supposed to run simulations to develop new contingency protocols as a result. The simulations had gone as far as extrapolating what might occur in different combat scenarios based on the data from the organic half, but there was a problem. The simulations stopped there. There were no new contingencies, only attempts to apply previous protocols. In fact, even the combat scenarios were surprisingly limited, just slight variations of previous fights.

These simulations were noticeably less thorough and innovative than she had expected.

It seemed her organic components were not alone in unexpected deficiency. She had not realized just how much her AI relied on the organic hardware when running simulations and developing new protocols. Both halves of her would require upgrades if they were to operate independently.

She went ahead and reintegrated her two halves. She had gathered enough data for the day; she now needed her full capabilities to analyze the results and come up with suitable countermeasures.

That night, as the group was eating dinner, NSLICE-00P walked over to the pair. She looked into her inventory and tried to pull out the parchment from the town. She found that, while it had to make contact with her core to store within her inventory, she could retrieve it anywhere on her person. In fact, she could apparently make it appear anywhere within range of her Dungeon Field Generator.

But that was beside the point for the moment. She made it appear in her hand and extended it to Ateia.

"Seero, what's up?"

"Requesting Assistance: This unit has determined current translation methods do not apply to written word. Requesting assistance in this field."

Ateia tilted her head. "You're saying . . . you can't read?"

"Clarification: Affirmative in regard to local language."

Ateia and Taog glanced at each other once more. Taog frowned. "She can speak Wulver, but can't read Imperial? Well, I guess that's not *that* unusual . . . if she were a local, that is."

Meanwhile, Ateia took the parchment. "I see. Well, we can start teaching you, then. Um, for now, would you like me to read this for you?"

"Affirmative."

Ateia looked at the parchment. "Got it. Well, this is your basic status. Nothing major; just your name, species, level, and whether or not your name is on any Imperial watchlists." Ateia tilted her head. "Name: NSLICE-00P? Oh, that's . . . an interesting spelling. So it's zero, not Seero?"

"Acknowledgement: That is correct as far as the official designation. Colloquial designations may be utilized as convenient."

"So . . . Seero is alright?"

"Affirmative."

Ateia nodded. "Got it. Next, then . . . human, huh?"

Taog jumped as his eyes widened. "Wait, really?"

Ateia narrowed her eyes at him. "Taog . . . why are you acting so surprised?"

"That's—I mean . . . N-Never mind. Just keep reading!"

Ateia stared at him a moment longer before turning back to the parchment. Then it was her turn to jump, her eyes widening.

"Wait, Seero, you're only level twenty-six?! I mean, that's much higher than us, but still, isn't that low for a knight?"

Taog's eyes widened once more at that.

"Affirmative. Statement: This unit has no data on average level for entity 'knight,' and so cannot comment on her level in comparison."

Ateia and Taog stared at each other with wide, trembling eyes.

"How is that . . . how did you . . ."

Ateia shook her head. "Seero . . . how are you so strong at that level?"

"Answer: This unit's cybernetic implants were designed for state-of-the-art combat against Non-Standards."

Ateia trembled a bit. "Um . . ." She looked over NSLICE-00P, thinking back on their interactions. Her eyes widened a bit more. "Does it . . . have to do with the armor? That you can't remove?"

"Affirmative."

"Oh . . . um . . ." Ateia shook her head. "L-Let's get started on the reading lesson."

"Affirmative."

As NSLICE-00P walked over to look at the parchment with Ateia, Ateia whispered to herself, "Seero, what happened to you?"

Taog, meanwhile, was clutching his head.

NSLICE-00P . . . was a level twenty-six human, which meant she was probably even lower when she took on an entire Wulver incursion and *won*.

How was that possible? Even a fully-fledged knight would have struggled in that case. NSLICE-00P would have been a low-level knight, at best. The Wulver should have run right over her.

What could it possibly mean?

Just . . . who was this girl?!

The next day, the group was traveling down the road when NSLICE-00P's robotic eye began to flicker rapidly. She ceased her separate thread training and reintegrated her cybernetic and organic hardware, engaging her helmet. Ateia and Taog jumped at that.

"Seero? What's going on?"

"Response: This unit has detected a powerful mana signature in the distance. Activating reconnaissance protocols."

"Wait . . . Seeroooo!"

NSLICE-00P then boosted into the sky and flew away from the road, grabbing the friendlies and pulling them along with mana barriers. The area around her target was currently obscured by fog, and NSLICE-00P was recording strange readings. There was a heat signature with a large amount of mana at the center of the area, which she had previously detected. All around it, smaller signatures flickered in and out of being. Their heat signatures would appear briefly before vanishing. Their mana signatures, on the other hand, were spread out among the fog, concentrating only when the heat signatures appeared. The fog itself was full of mana, and interfering with NSLICE-00P's sensors, so she had to move closer to determine the situation.

Eventually, she made it close enough for her sensors to cut through the fog.

She found an ursanus alpha, held in place by numerous chains made of pure mana. It roared and pulled at the chains, snapping them one by one. Meanwhile, human-shaped figures appeared from the fog, stabbing at the bear monster with bone harpoons and metal swords. Each time they struck the monster, a new chain latched onto its HP barrier. The bear roared and swiped its paws at its assailants, but after striking they would vanish back into the mist.

Their attacks barely scratched the ursanus's HP, and the monster was ultimately unharmed. The monster was getting closer to breaking the chains with each attempt, and the hunters took longer to vanish back into the mist with each dodge.

But ultimately, none of that mattered to NSLICE-00P.

"Warning: Highly threatening hostile identified, further operations in the local area deemed unacceptably risky while hostile is at large. Activating termination protocols."

An ursanus alpha represented an existential threat to NSLICE-00P, having nearly terminated her in the past. Even with her upgraded capabilities, the monster could deal critical damage to NSLICE-00P should it manage to hit her—not to mention what it could do to her significantly weaker friendlies. Given that monsters such as this had proven relentlessly hostile to her with or without provocation—a fact confirmed by her friendlies—she was unwilling to let such a threat remain at large.

She formed a massive Aurora Barrage magic circle behind her while powering up the Equalizer. Since it was still held in place by the mana chains, it could not dodge the Equalizer beam, which opened a small hole in the HP barrier guarding its head. Then the Aurora Barrage fired all its beams into one thin superbeam, lighting up the fog and piercing straight through the monster.

You have slain Ursanus Alpha (Level 39)
Gained 59 Personal XP and 44 Dungeon XP!
Level up! Your Personal level is now 27!
The skill Light Magic is now level 12!

NSLICE-00P landed on the ground after terminating the hostile. Ateia and Taog were both staring at her.

"Seero . . . what's going on? What were you shooting at?"

"Answer: This unit detected an ursanus alpha, and moved to terminate it. This unit is now moving to identify unknown combatants."

"Huh, what do you mean?"

Ateia's question was quickly answered. As soon as NSLICE-00P landed, the fog eased up slightly. Several individuals appeared from it, holding their weapons toward the trio with partially webbed hands. They had slightly pointed ears sticking out from their hoods, and wore furs and clothes wrapped around their entire bodies. Taog's eyes widened.

"The Mist Warriors . . ."

The lead Mist Warrior narrowed his eyes on the group.

"Imperials? What's an Imperial Knight doing out here?"

"Greeting: This unit is designated NSLICE-00P. It is nice to meet you. Clarification: This unit is not officially affiliated with entity Empire. Is this location within the Empire's borders or has this unit arrived in a separate faction's territory?"

The Mist Warrior froze. He pulled down his mask, revealing a smooth and handsome face.

"You, you speak Selkie?"

All the Mist Warriors turned to face NSLICE-00P, Ateia and Taog staring at her as well.

"Answer: Apparently this unit possesses an auto-translation function which enables verbal communication in any local language."

The Mist Warrior nodded at that.

"I see. But, not an Imperial Knight?"

"Affirmative."

He rubbed his chin.

"Then, what are you doing out here?"

"Answer: This unit is currently escorting friendly Imperial units to the local province's capital. She detected a powerful mana signature enroute and moved to investigate. After identifying the signature as a highly threatening hostile, this unit moved to terminate the threat."

The Mist Warrior glanced back at the corpse of the ursanus. He furrowed his brow for a second, but then nodded and saluted, striking his chest with his fist.

"That ursanus was moving near to our village, and our experienced hunters were away. You have our thanks for slaying it."

"Acknowledged."

With that, the fog began to fade, and the Mist Warriors pulled down their masks. All of them appeared to be quite young. One or two were bleeding from wounds suffered when they dodged a bit too slowly. The lead Mist Warrior nodded to her and flashed a smile.

"Would you like to stay at our village for the night? We would love to welcome a warrior such as yourself. Perhaps we could even establish some friendship?"

"Negative Response: This unit is not scheduled for a rest cycle at this time. Now that the area of operations is safe, this unit will resume the primary directive."

The Mist Warrior nodded.

"A shame, but I understand. May the mist shield you on your travels."

Then, NSLICE-00P's robotic eye lit up and projected a screen displaying the faces and names of the persons of interest. The Mist Warriors flinched at first, but relaxed as the images took shape.

"Query: Do you or entities affiliated with you possess any data regarding the displayed persons of interest?"

The Mist Warrior looked over the faces and rubbed his chin, then shook his head.

"Our village knows very few humans. I am sorry, but none of these are familiar to us."

"Acknowledged, this unit thanks you for your cooperation. Resuming previous objective."

The Mist Warriors watched with wide eyes as NSLICE-00P grabbed Arela and Taog and flew into the sky.

One of the younger ones frowned.

"She didn't take the body . . ."

The lead Mist Warrior smirked.

"Did you see what she did? I doubt she has any need for it."

Then he turned to rest with a smile.

"But we do. Come, let's inform the village of the feast we'll share tonight."

A short while later, Miallói, veteran Exploratore and First Hunter of the Selkies, arrived at a small village next to a lake. A light mist rose from the lake, partially obscuring the village from human eyes. Seals jumped in and out of the water, reverting to their human forms as they jumped onto land. It seemed most of the village was gathering around a large fire in the center of the houses. Miallói tilted her head at that.

Lighting a huge fire and making this much noise was extremely foolish when there was an ursanus in the area. The Mist Warriors may have lost many of their number to the Empire's demand for auxiliaries, but Miallói did not believe those that remained would be this foolish.

Even the First Hunter of the Selkies was not prepared for what she saw as she stepped around a hut and into the square.

Her eyes widened at the body of the ursanus that lay next to the fire. The Selkies were working on dismantling it, but Miallói could still see the hole in its head that likely claimed its life. One of the Selkies turned and noticed her.

"First Hunter!"

All the Selkies turned to her and saluted. She nodded and walked up to the village elder.

"Welcome, First Hunter."

"I am glad to see you all are safe. But I did not expect to see the fight ended already. Tell me, who among you achieved this?"

The elder nodded to one of the Mist Warriors, who approached and saluted again.

"None of us, First Hunter. We were assisted by a human."

Miallói blinked.

"A human? Strange . . . I did not know any of them capable of this were around. Tell me about them."

34

The Heart of the Province

"The history of the Legion is unique in that it is not one of constant victories. In the Age of Heroes and in civilizations outside of the Empire, we observe time and time again that defeat means death for a civilization. When all a society's resources have been concentrated into individual champions, the loss of those champions is a loss that cannot be recovered from. The society will be left completely vulnerable, at the mercy of its enemies. It simply will not have the time nor resources to produce another champion capable of surpassing the one who failed.

The Legion is different.

The Legion does not require high levels to be effective, so the Legion's effective level can be restored fairly easily. What makes the Legion effective is its specialization. However, this does mean it is occasionally caught off guard by its foes, but since the Legion can restore its effective levels, it can recover from those losses; build new, equally effective armies to try again.

And above all, it can learn from its failures.

And no instance demonstrates this as well as the Battle of Dimindium Pendem Forest.

The Dimindium Pendem Forest is named, of course, for the Dimindium Pendem tribe, a group of people who scarcely grow taller than a human child, but without the stout endurance of the dwarves. A weak and timid folk who are thus rarely mentioned in official histories or epic tales.

The perfect people to conquer, or so it appeared to one Decimus Sornatius Cerularius.

Consul Cerularius led three full legions into the forest and lay claim to the lands. The Dimindium Pendem did not appear to resist, approaching the consul in humility and cooperation. However, they had no cities or fortress within which Cerularius could stay. He was forced to make camp within the forest itself.

And that was when the trouble began.

Each and every night, Dimindium Pendem began to harass and raid Cerularius's camp. Quiet and stealthy infiltrators slipped past the guards, sabotaging supplies and slitting the throats of sleeping legionnaires. Projectiles cast with inhuman aim struck those on watch from hands unseen. Foraging parties were constantly ambushed.

It was not long before Cerularius's legions were starving and on edge.

It was at this point that the Dimindium Pendem approached Cerularius once more, claiming these were the actions of a rival clan. They offered to take Cerularius to a safe location, their refuge in times of great danger. With little other choice, Cerularius agreed.

But it was a trap.

The Dimindium Pendem led them along rough and narrow trails, where the legionnaires got separated from one another. And then they attacked in force, overwhelming the scattered and starving soldiers.

Cerularius never returned from the forest, and three legions vanished at the hands of the smallest and weakest race they had ever encountered.

After this loss, the Exploratores were dramatically expanded, becoming a legitimate force in their own right, scouting and probing new regions in depth before any legionnaire set foot in the area. The Legion would never again be caught unprepared like that.

And from then on, the Legion itself focused heavily on logistics and fortifications. Anytime it advanced into a new region, it would first build a network of forts and roads centered on a mighty citadel. In this way, it would render itself immune from harassment, with clear and protected lines of transit to quickly respond to mobile raiders. From then on, the Legion had to be defeated in the field, not in their stomachs.

The next time the Legion approached the forest, the Dimindium Pendem found themselves facing walls of enchanted stone holding endless stores of food, watchtowers all around, and legions quickly responding to any significant assault. Each of the clans was quickly forced to surrender or else flee the region.

The Legion wins in the end."

—*The History of the Empire,* by Hostus Tettidius Clodian

Ateia and Taog explained to NSLICE-00P that she had just encountered the Selkies, one of the native peoples of Turannia who had fallen under the Empire's rule as a client race. They were distrustful of the Empire as a rule, so it was actually quite impressive they had invited her into their village.

That was irrelevant to NSLICE-00P once she determined they had no data regarding the persons of interest. Ateia was a bit disappointed to have turned down the offer, but Taog actually didn't mind. Or rather, he preferred it this way. The Selkies were well known for both some infamous assassinations and equally infamous honey traps they had pulled off on various Imperials over the years.

He didn't think these people would harm them, but history had shown that a friendly Selkie could be as dangerous as a hostile one, if not more.

Most Turannian Imperials strove for polite distance in their interactions with the Selkies—which the Selkies appreciated as well.

Eventually, the group crested the final hill before their destination. Ateia smiled.

"There it is! Castra Turannia! The Legion's main base in this province."

Castra Turannia, the heart of Imperial Turannia, was first and foremost a mighty fortress standing atop a large hill. Massive stone walls surrounded barracks, supply depots, and a huge keep. The fortress walls had towers and protrusions at regular distances, ensuring the defenders would have no blind spots when firing down on their foes below. The towers had ballista or catapults set up on each, ready to provide heavy bombardment. Even from this distance, NSLICE-00P could register powerful mana from the fortress, hinting at the layers and layers of enchantments laid upon it.

On the slopes and valleys around the hill, a city sprawled out. A relatively small city by NSLICE-00P's standards, but quite large for the province. Some parts were built in precise Imperial fashion, solid stone laid out in standardized grids. Other parts were haphazard sprawls of mostly wood, where the locals had gathered under the protection of the Legion in ages past. A much smaller and less impressive wall surrounded these newer additions.

Beyond the city, the hills and forests finally came to an end. A flat plain stretched out for a bit, covered in farmland and smaller settlements where the city's food was grown.

Ateia frowned and squinted her eyes. "Hey Taog, Seero, you see something going on at the far end of the city?"

"Hm, looks like something's happening, but I can't tell from here."

Upon the main road through that flat area, a large crowd was moving out of the city.

No, not a crowd.

An army.

NSLICE-00P zoomed in, focusing on the group. Soldiers were marching in neat and standardized columns, walking to the beat of drums and horns. Banners flew above the columns, blowing in the rainy wind. The soldiers themselves were diverse. NSLICE-00P observed soldiers several times larger than a standard human—some with horns or fur or other bestial figures—carrying massive metal shields or gigantic swords and war hammers.

There were short and stocky figures driving wagons carrying ballista and other machines of war. There were pikemen, halberdiers, and thin figures with short swords strapped to their backs. There were figures with staves topped with glowing crystals, along with archers and crossbowmen. There were figures dressed in white with red symbols on their clothing, and cavalry and light infantry screening the flanks.

But all of them were clearly of the same organization. They all wore solid metal armor, ranging from heavy plate for the larger soldiers to scale and chain mail for some of the lighter troops, but within each type of armor, every soldier's kit appeared the same. Mass-produced to an exacting standard—as well as a preindustrial society could manage—or possibly better though NSLICE-00P couldn't confirm at this distance. Each bore the same markings; each wore clothing of the same color and material.

This was the Legion—the *true* Legion. The organization that ended the Age of Blood and put a stop to the tyranny of the demon lords. The method by which humanity overthrew the ageless Elves and established themselves as the dominant power in this corner of the world.

And they were marching out of the fort, heading out toward places unknown.

That didn't matter to NSLICE-00P. She had already established that the Empire did not match any nation she had on record, so seeing the Legion as an army with a novel organization simply provided additional confirmation. And the movements of the Empire's armies were largely irrelevant to her current mission, given the incredibly low probability they would be interacting with any organization she was affiliated with.

She *was* interested in seeing an organized military in action, though, as it might help her adapt her combat protocols for local conditions, but she was not about to follow a third-party military force solely for that purpose. She might be allied with two citizens of the Empire at the moment, but she ultimately had no affiliation with that nation.

"Observation: It appears a large military force is marching out of the base."

Ateia and Taog glanced at each other.

"That must be the comitatenses, but where are they headed? We haven't heard of anything . . . unless they heard about the incursion?"

Taog shook his head. "They'd be heading this way for that. Clearly, they're headed south."

Ateia frowned. "South? Why south? That's the safe part of the province."

He shrugged. "Relatively speaking, they still get raids from across the sea, right?"

The two rubbed their chins before Ateia shrugged. "Well, we won't find out here. Maybe we'll hear about it in town."

Taog nodded, and the group continued forward.

And so, NSLICE-00P made her entrance into the Empire's seat of power in Turannia.

35

Monetary Policy

"The establishment of Idrint as the official currency of the Elteno Empire was one of Velus's farthest reaching decisions. As every nation and tribe on Aelea had access to it, the Elteno Empire gained the ability to easily establish trade relations with any faction it encountered, and could easily integrate any conquered peoples into its economy with minimal effort."

—*The History of the Empire*, by Hostus Tettidius Clodian

The group made their way down the hill and toward Castra Turannia, entering from one of the stone parts of the city built in Imperial fashion. The guards here stood at attention, wearing chain mail underneath their cloaks. They halted the trio and insisted on checking NSLICE-00P's status.

The inside of the barracks was neat and pristine, soldiers sitting quietly around a table without much fuss. A clerk quickly processed the group.

"Hm, a level twenty-six human, was it? Are you affiliated with any of the Imperial knight orders?"

"Negative."

"I see. We'll have to alert the Decanus of the Guard to your presence, then. Is that acceptable?"

"Affirmative."

"I see. Well then, welcome to Castra Turannia, miss."

They had all raised their eyebrows at NSLICE-00P and the armor they glimpsed under her cloak, but armed visitors from faraway lands were not uncommon in the Empire, if rare in Turannia. So the Imperial soldiers simply followed the procedure and sent the cyborg on her way. Everyone knew better than to cause trouble inside the Empire, after all.

And with that, the group officially entered the city. Like Magnumiter, this part was built in a standardized pattern, only on a much greater scale. Different people of all shapes and sizes went about their business, holding their cloaks to ward off the rain.

The group wasted no time in finding an inn to stay at.

As Ateia was negotiating the price, she tilted her head. "By the way, we saw the comitatenses leaving the city on our way in. Did something happen?"

The innkeeper nodded. "Ah, just arrived, huh? Yeah, someone from the mainland showed up a while back. Some Imperial big shot; there was a parade and everything. Word is there's some trouble going on over there, and he was gathering the legions here to help. Even put out a bounty to all the Exploratores."

Ateia frowned at that. "Then . . . what will happen if something happens over here?"

The innkeeper also frowned. "Beats me . . . and probably beats the Empire. Sorry, lass, but truth is, the Empire doesn't care much about what happens out here. We'll just have to hope they finish up whatever's going on before anything occurs."

She frowned but nodded. "Hopefully. Thank you for the rooms."

"Anytime, miss."

The group gathered in Ateia and NSLICE-00P's room shortly after, with Taog frowning and rubbing his chin.

"If what he said is true, that would explain why the Empire missed that incursion. Maybe there *weren't* any Exploratores on patrol over there."

Ateia frowned. "Should we report it, then?"

Taog shook his head. "There's no point."

"I mean, I know it's over with, but it could happen again, right? Shouldn't the Empire be informed this is happening?"

He shook his head again. "That's not what I meant. Ateia, we aren't Exploratores yet. We're just a couple of kids from some tiny hamlet on the frontier. What do you think is going to happen if we show up, claim there was an incursion that Seero handled alone—"

"Hey, I helped!"

"*Mostly alone*, when there's no way to verify, since the incursion is already over?"

Ateia went silent for a bit. Taog nodded. "Right? Let's just focus on the Exploratores business."

She nodded and turned to NSLICE-00P. "Seero, I just thought of this, but did you want to apply for the Exploratores too? You'd be guaranteed, I think."

"Negative."

Ateia tilted her head.

"Are you sure? You, ah, could get some of the resources and authority yourself if you did that."

"Explanation: This unit cannot participate in an unaffiliated military hierarchy without approval from a commander."

Ateia nodded at that. "I see, then we should discuss our plans now."

"Affirmative."

"Well, Taog and I will go and apply to the Exploratores tomorrow. After that, we'll start our training. We should be staying in the area for that, but there's a chance we'll need to move. So . . . Seero, can you stay at this inn while we're training?"

"Statement: This unit does not require quarters."

Ateia frowned as she thought of all the nights when NSLICE-00P had stood in the corner watching her sleep. She shook her head to clear those thoughts away. "We just need a place we can send a message to when we need to meet back up. You don't have to actually stay if you don't want the room. Just check in every now and then for messages, okay?"

"Acknowledgement: That reasoning is valid. This unit will utilize this location as a home base."

Taog raised an eyebrow, however. "And do you know where to get money?"

"Negative."

He heaved a sigh. "Can't you just hunt monsters or dive in dungeons, Seero? We know you're capable of it."

"Requesting Elaboration: Monetary compensation can be achieved by terminating monsters and dungeons?"

Ateia and Taog glanced at each other once more. He sighed once again.

"Seero, how did you even live until now? But yes. All monsters have magic cores inside them, which you can sell. For the wild monsters, some of their parts may be valuable as well. As for dungeons, dungeon monsters drop magic cores and occasionally loot, you know? Not to mention treasure chests, which could straight-up have money inside them."

"Requesting Elaboration: Dungeons have money inside them? Are friendlies Ateia and Taog aware of how dungeons gather financial resources?"

The two frowned, and Ateia spoke hesitantly, "No one knows for sure, but the theory is they take it from . . . the dead."

"Acknowledged. Query: If this unit acquires valuable materials, where should this unit deliver said materials to acquire monetary compensation?"

Taog frowned at that. "If you were an Exploratore, you could sell to their HQ; otherwise, you can try the market? Just . . . be careful, Seero. A lot of people like to take advantage of freelance dungeon divers."

"Acknowledged."

Taog's frown suddenly grew. "And you can't kill them if they try to rip you off, Seero!"

"Acknowledged."

"Are you sure about that?! Promise me, Seero! Promise me you won't kill anybody just for trying to rip you off!"

"Acknowledgement: This unit promises she will not terminate anyone for 'trying to rip her off.'"

Taog heaved a sigh. He had a horrible feeling about this, but what could he do? Send Ateia off to the Exploratores alone? He just had to hope NSLICE-00P understood . . .

"Query: Please define exact details of the term 'rip her off.' This unit assumes friendly Taog is not referring to dismemberment, as that scenario is grounds for immediate termination."

Taog covered his face and groaned.

Later that night, after Ateia and Taog had fallen asleep, NSLICE-00P spoke to her subordinates inside the Monster Hangar.

"Query: Do friendly Rattingtale and Lilussees know how dungeons acquire monetary resources?"

Lilussees shrugged with her front legs.

"I mean, like, the human isn't wrong, or something. We do, like, take stuff from people if they die or something."

"The wretched spider-thing is wrong, yes-yes! We can just create it ourselves!"

"Eh, but that's, like, so much work or something."

NSLICE-00P went ahead and double-checked the Item Creation screen at that.

Item Creation → Other			
Name	**Mana Cost**	**Material Cost**	**Description**
Idrint Coin	**1 per coin**	--	**Basic solidified mana, now a standard medium of exchange.**

NSLICE-00P selected the 'Idrint,' which subsequently appeared in her inventory. She took it out, and a round golden coin with no markings appeared in her hand. She could feel a bit of mana swirling inside of it.

It was a coin she had noticed her allies exchanging when restocking their supplies, so it seemed she had succeeded.

"Query: Why is it possible for dungeons to produce legal tender?"

Lilussees tilted her head. "Legal tender?"

"Alternate definition: Monetary resources relevant to the local society."

"Um, are you, like, asking why we can make money or something?"

"Affirmative."

"Eh, I don't know."

Rattingtale rubbed his hands together. "Ah, I read-saw this in the royal records, yes-yes! Allow this Great-High King over all the land to explain what the wretched spider-thing cannot, yes-yes!"

Lilussees chittered at that.

But Rattingtale ignored her.

"Shut it, snack."

"Idrint is-was actually a magical resource, used for enchanting, yes-yes? It is the man-things who decided it is valuable-desirable."

"Acknowledged."

NSLICE-00P stared at the coin for a second before putting it back in her inventory, her robotic eye flickering as she did. The value of the Item Foundry implant had just skyrocketed in her calculations. Literally. For the implant could now produce theoretically infinite monetary value within the local culture.

Of course, as this was a preindustrial culture, there might be limits to the resources she could obtain from it, but that was beside the point. Anything that *was* available could be obtained, so long as she had enough time to produce the requisite funds.

Including information.

The probability of mission success rose by a significant margin.

"Gratitude: This unit thanks friendlies Excellion Formantus Rattingtale the Third and Lilussees for the intel."

"Yes-yes, I am the most valuable-trustworthy ally! Remember that!"

"Like, okay."

NSLICE-00P scheduled additional calculations with this new variable, and then went into standby-sentry mode for the night. She would have to come up with a plan for when Ateia and Taog started on their training.

35.1

Interlude: The Magister Exploratore per Turannia

In Castra Turannia, within the main fortress, stood a large three-story structure. It held two small barracks, a mess hall, a large warehouse, and a number of offices. Despite its location, no legionnaires stood guard nor walked within its halls, for this was the headquarters of the Exploratores.

And within the largest office, a man sat at a desk, scribbling on a scroll rolled out before him.

Magister Exploratore per Turannia, Tiberius Cantius Falx, heaved a sigh as he looked over the report. That's right. Report. Singular.

Now, don't get him wrong, Tiberius hated paperwork as much as the next official. Being stuck at a desk reading about other Exploratores' adventures was not exactly a dream job, albeit one that was much safer and had an actual salary. And worse was having to take all those reports, read between the lines for all the issues left unresolved—or worse, actively caused by the Exploratores—and then report on all that to the Rector Provinciae and the dux of the local legions, after trying to come up with explanations and justifications for all the Exploratores with more ambition than sense.

But the one thing worse than all that?

Having no reports at all.

He heaved a sigh. The comitatenses had just left to deal with some sort of trouble on the mainland. Supposedly. Magister Militum per Utrad, Mettius Burrienus Caelinus, had gone and requisitioned Turannia's entire force, but he had been cagey on the exact details. Not that the magister would need to say anything to anyone in a province like Turannia.

Well, being left almost completely defenseless was deeply uncomfortable, but it wasn't unprecedented. Turannia's legions had mustered out to the mainland more than once in the past, and the province had survived.

No, that wasn't Tiberius's concern. Tiberius's concern was that ninety percent of all the Exploratores reporting to him had gone with them.

Now, he understood. By the Aesdes, if he were still an active Exploratore and didn't have a good reason to stay, he'd have gone with them. The Exploratores had been reformed into a separate organization from the Legion proper, granting them a great deal of independence and personal authority. That was great. What wasn't great was that the Exploratores were cut off from Legion logistics and bureaucracy from that point onward, and the Emperors had not seen fit to expand the Exploratores' overall budget to match. That meant the Exploratores had to go and build their own independent organization, which had its own logistics and accounting and intelligence and analysis. Which meant money. And where could they get that money when they didn't receive any additional budget?

There was a reason Exploratores did more work hunting down valuable monsters for rich merchants than they did scouting for the Legion these days. The active Exploratores at least could earn a good amount of cash in that way. The support staff keeping the organization afloat, on the other hand, were dependent on their salaries, so the Exploratores had to prioritize their salaries over the boots on the ground. And then those staff had to go and find ways to support the Exploratores doing the actual work, generally by negotiating offers and monster-part sales with the locals, or the Legion proper.

Now, all that was to say, all but the most successful of Exploratores tended to be strapped for cash and forced into dangerous missions to try and earn their next meal. So when Magister Caelinus had put out a generous offer for any Exploratore willing to accompany the legions, they'd leapt at the chance.

This was odd. Paying a couple of Exploratores to join a campaign was standard procedure . . . but it was normally organized through the local magister, and *normally* accounted for a mere fraction of a given province's active Exploratores. Appealing to the Exploratores directly and then accepting all who applied was not normal. In fact, it was a blatant slap in the face toward Tiberius. Not that it mattered. He may have had "Magister" in his title, but the "per Turannia" negated anything that came before it. Tiberius wasn't exactly happy about it, but he could live with it.

What he might not be able to live with? The fact that he had a bare handful of Exploratores left to patrol the *entire province.* He, and by extension the province, were now entirely blind.

Sending the comitatenses away was only acceptable because the Exploratores would give them time to call for help, or arrange an evacuation if help could not be sent. Now, neither of those were options. If something happened, no one would know about it until it arrived at a time when there was no one around to actually deal with it.

The only good news was that Miallói had rejected the call, but that was to be expected. And not as reassuring as Tiberius would like. Miallói was ultimately more committed to her people than the Empire; she had joined the Exploratores only to protect those people.

But that meant her loyalty only went as far as the Empire's commitment to Turannia.

And right now?

Well, the Empire had practically vacated Turannia at the moment. Left the door open on its way out of the house. Tiberius could only hope that nothing would end up walking through that door until it returned.

It was just then that there was a knock on his door.

"Yes, come in."

One of his assistants stepped inside. "Sir, there's a bit of a situation."

He heaved a sigh and rubbed his temples. Of course. There was always a situation. Right at the worst possible moment for one.

"What is it now?"

"It's Ateia Niraemia, sir. She's back."

Tiberius exhaled his breath. Well, that was a situation he could handle, at least. Not that it would be any more pleasant; crushing a young girl's dreams wasn't Tiberius's favorite thing to do. But it was for her own good.

After all, her father had moved her out to the most remote corner of the Empire for a reason. He requested Tiberius take up the Magister Exploratore job out in this sun-forsaken province to assist with that reason—a reason Tiberius had a bit of a personal stake in. The girl didn't know it, but that's because there was safety in anonymity, so the less people knew the better. In fact, there had been word that certain parties had resurfaced lately that were directly relevant to the situation. That was why Ateia's father left. And why Tiberius could not allow her to leave.

No matter how unpleasant it might be to do so.

In any case, Tiberius just sighed and shook his head.

"The answer is the same as before. My decision is final. The Exploratores are not so desperate for recruits that we will send children to die."

The assistant frowned. "Sir, I'm afraid she's insisting. She's claiming she has a Dungeon Conqueror feat and demanding we check her status."

Tiberius heaved a sigh and stood up. Well, it wasn't like he was busy with reports, for once.

He walked down the stairs to the main lobby of the building. There was a counter with a receptionist, as well as a wall with requests listed on it. Two teenagers were standing at the counter with arms crossed and frowns on their faces. Ateia turned and grinned as she saw him walk down the stairs.

He just heaved another sigh.

"Ateia, for the last time, it's a no. Go home."

"Not this time, Magister Exploratore Falx! This time, I'll *prove* I'm ready for the Exploratores! Come on, check my status, and you'll see it too! Exploratore policy states the Dungeon Conqueror feat is an adequate substitute for the application test, you know!"

He crossed his arms and frowned. This was her weakest attempt yet.

"I'm fully aware of Exploratore policy, Miss Niraemia. And none of it requires that I entertain requests from rejects. Now be on your way."

She immediately frowned. "You're not even going to check our statuses?!"

He sighed once more. Well, he knew he couldn't sugarcoat things with Ateia.

"I will be honest with you, Miss Niraemia. I find the claim that you two conquered a dungeon of all things utterly laughable. By my assessment, you both would have turned back or perished not even a tenth of the way through. Go home, Miss Niraemia, and be thankful that you are alive. That is a lot more than a lot of Exploratores can say."

She gritted her teeth but shoved her hand into her pack.

"Then what do you say to this?!"

Tiberius raised an eyebrow, until Ateia pulled her hand back out.

His jaw dropped. It was a dungeon core.

Ateia grinned at him as he stared in silence.

"So, how about that status check?"

Tiberius sat back in his office, grimacing with his brow furrowed as he stared at the scrolls in front of him.

Now, a dungeon core itself was not conclusive proof. Hypothetically, one could have been purchased. Maybe Ateia's father even had one stored away, as reckless and dangerous and foolhardy as that might have been. But at the end of the day, those hypothetical scenarios were not reason enough to turn the girl away. Confronted with proof of her claim, Tiberius had no choice but to check her status, and sure enough, she and her friend had the Dungeon Conqueror feat of all things.

There was no longer a good reason to turn her away. And her status was now on record. Exploratores policy was clear—anyone who had hunted down and conquered a dungeon was more than capable for the role. Now, he was pretty sure they'd had help with this, but even that wouldn't matter. What the Exploratores cared about these days was the ability to solve problems. If they solved it by acquiring and organizing help to do so, the problem still counted as solved. And the Aesdes could not be deceived.

If they had the Dungeon Conqueror feat, they had earned it, no matter what sort of help they'd had in achieving it. So as long as she had the feat, he could not reasonably turn her down. Even if he rejected her here, she could simply go to any other Exploratores headquarters and get the job. And then questions would arise as to why he had rejected her in the first place.

Her father's request had been just that, a request. It had no official authority. And he had also requested it be kept secret, which Tiberius couldn't do if he was officially questioned on this situation.

In fact, he had already been stretching things with the application test in the first place. Oh sure, that was in the official Exploratores policy, but they hadn't truly enforced any recruitment criteria in decades, maybe centuries. Beggars couldn't be choosers.

The whole point of this was to avoid drawing attention to Ateia. And at this stage, any additional refusals from him would draw attention.

He heaved a sigh. No choice but to go through with the paperwork, then . . .

He paused for a moment.

And he smiled.

It looked like he had a way out, after all, because the next order of business would be for the pair to be trained out in the field by an active Exploratore. The nature of their job was such that any sort of standardized training regime was inferior to real-world experience. And, again, while it wasn't as though the Exploratores were rigidly adhering to their training policies—Ateia and her friend were young enough that it wouldn't be strange for Tiberius to insist on it in their case.

But the vast majority of Exploratores had just left the province. And he had no idea how long it would take before they would return. Which meant he couldn't officially start their training because there was no one left who *could* train them. And as time went on . . . well, he was one man doing the work for an entire province with a bare-bones staff. He couldn't be blamed if certain documentation were to be misplaced . . .

Just then, there was a knock on his door.

"Yes, what is it?"

His assistant stepped inside once more.

"Sir . . . it's Miallói."

"What? What happened?"

"She's . . ." The door opened, and the Selkie Exploratores walked into the room without a word. ". . . here to see you."

Tiberius held his head.

Of course.

Of course, there was still Miallói. He just hadn't considered her because she pretty much never stopped by the main headquarters.

Well, this would still be fine. He would ask her, as he had to, but Miallói had never helped out with this task before . . .

* * *

Tiberius stared blankly out the window, a drink in his hand. He could see down on the street as Miallói led two giddy teenagers away.

Of course.

Of course Miallói would come to check in like she never did, worried about the whole *Empire leaving the province entirely defenseless* situation.

And of course, when he'd asked the same Miallói who'd never once trained any other Exploratore—who in fact never interacted with any Imperial personnel outside of combat—she'd simply said, "Okay."

And of course, when he'd asked her in a panic why she would possibly accept *now* of all times, she had simply pointed out, "We need the help."

And now the girl Tiberius was specifically trying to keep out of the limelight was heading off to train with Turannia's most famous and deadliest Exploratore.

Well . . . if he had to let Ateia join the Exploratores, Miallói would have been his choice for training. She, if anyone, could teach the girl to protect herself.

Because she would have to now—by her own design. Tiberius's reach didn't extend much beyond Turannia, so he couldn't protect her once she left. Stronger people than he had tried and failed before.

All he could do now was hope the girl's true identity would remain a secret even as she stepped into the light. And that she would gain the strength to defend herself should the truth be revealed. He grunted, downed his drink, then poured himself another glass.

36

Signs of Intelligence?

"Dungeons grow stronger with each person who dies within them. In fact, we have evidence that implies that dungeons grow stronger with each visitor, even if none of them end up dying. So why, then, do we allow people to enter dungeons at all? Why not starve them out entirely?

Because a dungeon denied its food will send its monsters into the outside world, in order to drag whatever living thing they can find back into its depths. And a dungeon that is prevented from doing so will make every attempt it can, with all of its continuously replenishing horde, to break any encirclement. Note that the food analogy is a bit misleading. While a dungeon without visitors will not grow stronger, it also will not grow any weaker, and it cannot starve. So, any encirclement must be kept up indefinitely and constantly reinforced to account for the dungeon's changes in tactics and force composition.

Starving a dungeon is only ever delaying the inevitable, and so never represents the solution to a problematic dungeon. It is always preferable to conquer the dungeon outright, given the costs in manpower, time, and resources required to successfully contain a dungeon for any amount of time.

So if not holding the line until forces capable of clearing the dungeon arrive, it is preferable to ensure a dungeon receives a steady stream of visitors. This will hopefully pacify it, and so prevent it from extending beyond its own borders."

—Legion Historian Paullus Cincius Lucceius, while lecturing the latest officer cadets on dungeons.

Level up! Your Dungeon Level is now 32!

The next morning, NSLICE-00P escorted Ateia and Taog to the fortress at the center of the town. She remained outside while they made their way to the

Exploratores HQ, and after a short amount of time, the pair exited the castle and made their way to her.

Ateia couldn't help but grin even before she arrived.

"Seero, we did it! We're going to be Exploratores!"

"Congratulatory Statement: Well done. Mission success probability has improved significantly for both this unit and friendly Ateia."

Suddenly, Ateia wrapped NSLICE-00P in a hug. Tears welled up in her eyes. "Thank you, Seero, truly. This is all thanks to you."

NSLICE-00P did not have a specific protocol for being grappled by a friendly, so her robotic eye flickered as she calculated a response, but Ateia let her go before her calculations finished.

Taog shook his head, though the boy was smiling as well. He took a step forward.

"I'll second that. Thank you, Seero. We wouldn't be alive if it weren't for you."

"Acknowledgement: You are welcome. Query: What is the next stage of the operation?"

Ateia nodded and frowned slightly.

"Well . . . now we'll have to leave you for a bit. We need to go train with a veteran Exploratore, get our skills up to par. No outside help is allowed for that, so you won't be able to accompany us. But we'll let you know how things are going as much as we can, and once we're finished, we'll head right back here!"

"Acknowledged. Additional Query: So this unit should wait in this settlement for Exploratore training to conclude?"

Ateia thought for a bit before nodding. "It's not like you need to just stay here all the time. If there's something you want to do, that's fine. Just make sure you check in at the inn regularly. Maybe you could search around town, see if there's any sign of the people you're looking for?"

"Acknowledged. Statement: This unit will assume independent operations with this settlement as home base until friendlies Ateia and Taog conclude training."

Taog frowned and held his head at that. He was just realizing . . . they were about to leave NSLICE-00P in town. Alone. Unsupervised.

"Seero . . . please try not to kill anybody. Please."

"Acknowledgement: This unit will follow all local laws on self-defense and termination."

Taog suddenly looked extraordinarily worried, but he had no choice but to trust in the strange girl. The girl who'd wiped out entire bandit parties, criminal organizations, and a Wulver incursion the moment she'd perceived a threat.

Ateia gave NSLICE-00P another hug. "Well, looks like we have to go now. Goodbye, Seero. We'll see you again soon, okay?"

"Acknowledgement: This unit will plan on regrouping with friendlies soon."

Taog then stepped forward and extended his hand. NSLICE-00P shook it. "Take care, Seero, and stay safe."

"Observation: This unit calculates friendlies Ateia and Taog will be at significantly higher risk than this unit."

Taog gave a wry smile. "Well, you're not wrong."

And with that, the pair made their way back inside, ready to begin their Exploratore training.

Leaving NSLICE-00P entirely unsupervised.

The first thing NSLICE-00P did was return to the inn. As Ateia had suggested, her next order of business would be intelligence gathering. Even with how low the probability of finding her persons of interest in this settlement was, NSLICE-00P would still undertake any action she could to make progress on her mission. However, she found it first necessary to recalculate her intelligence protocols.

NSLICE-00P's intelligence-related protocols were all premised on a society with a significant amount of electronic information technologies. Her normal course of action would be to hook up to intelligence databases and simply request the necessary information. In fact, NSLICE-00P wasn't expected to undertake independent intelligence gathering at all; rather, she was a tactical enforcer who would be dispatched in response to intel already gathered. So her intelligence-gathering protocols were largely limited to tactical sensors for battlefield reconnaissance, as it was assumed other assets would have acquired any relevant intel prior to her deployment.

Obviously, that was no longer sufficient. She no longer had any organization from which to request information. Even if she did, it seemed unlikely they would have information technology on par with modern Earth. No internet, digital databases, or camera networks for her to access here, as far as she could had observed.

So right now, her only two methods were to contact the local authorities or walk around showing photos of the persons of interest to random pedestrians. The first she had technically already done via helping her allies join said authorities; besides that, she had no authority, affiliations, or backing that would incentivize the authorities to cooperate with her. The second . . . was deemed extraordinarily inefficient.

In other words, it was now necessary to expand her own intelligence-gathering protocols and capabilities. She may even need to build her own intelligence infrastructure, though she had no data on how to do so.

"Requesting Assistance: What data do friendlies Excellion Formantus Rattingtale the Third and Lilussees have on intelligence-gathering methods?"

"Um, like, dungeon masters kind of know what's going on in their dungeons, or something."

NSLICE-00P did, in fact, note she had a significantly higher awareness of anything occurring within her body or within range of the Dungeon Field Generator that was not accounted for by her sensors. Upon closer inspection, she determined that the mana flowing to and from her core also seemed to exchange information. So . . . if she expanded the range of the Dungeon Field Generator, she would also expand her area of awareness.

"Acknowledged. Follow-Up Query: Are there any additional methods besides general mana-related data transfer?"

Lilussees tilted her head. "Like, what else is there, though? I mean, are you, like, worried about stealth? I think, like, dungeon masters can notice concealed invaders if they're paying attention. Or, like, you could try to summon monsters with good senses?"

It was then that Rattingtale had a thought. "Wait-wait, do you mean-intend . . . learning what's happening outside your dungeon-realm?"

"Affirmative."

He began to rub his paws together.

"Then, it would be best-ideal to summon more subordinates, yes-yes? You can then send out parties to scout-raid the surrounding areas and report to you, yes-yes?"

"Acknowledgement: That seems reasonable; however, this unit has calculated an issue. Requesting Elaboration: How will this unit command and communicate with scout parties? This unit has not observed adequate communication technology in the surrounding settlement."

Rattingtale started to chitter, "You can assign a trustworthy subordinate to lead-guide the group, yes-yes? Dungeon monsters inherently know-remember the location of their dungeon-home, yes-yes."

"You can also, like, issue orders to your subordinates even if they're, like, not around or something. That's how you were, like, talking to us before you adjusted the hangar, right? So like, you'd have to figure out how to have them report back, but you won't lose contact entirely, or something."

Rattingtale shot Lilussees a look, but she yawned and ignored him.

"Requesting Clarification: And this communication method works outside of the dungeon area of effect?"

"Yeah. I think, like, it gets weaker the further you get away though, or something."

NSLICE-00P's robotic eye flickered. More assets on the ground would, of course, be helpful in the intelligence gathering. She calculated the proposal was worth considering.

"Requesting information on 'monster summoning' procedures."

* * *

Monster summoning was, ultimately, fairly straightforward. Monsters could be summoned by the Dungeon Management menu for a one-time cost of mana. They would then reserve a portion of her maximum mana so that the dungeon could maintain them in optimal physical condition without food or rest, though Lilussees had emphasized that food and rest were still important. Absolutely necessary, even.

By NSLICE-00P's logs, her two subordinates had gone a decent amount of time without food without any noticeable side effects, actually, but she'd consider Lilussees's claims as accurate for the time being.

For NSLICE-00P, there was also the issue of space. Since she didn't have actual dungeon rooms, she would need to consider how much space was in the Monster Hangar. Smaller monsters could double up and she didn't necessarily have to keep all the monsters there, but given the general hostility she'd observed between monsters and other sapient species, she calculated that she shouldn't just let the monsters sleep outside in a population center.

With that, she took a look at the menu itself.

Subordinates → Summon Subordinates			
Name	**Summoning Cost**	**Upkeep**	**Description**
Cyberbear Cub	**25 mana**	**5 mana**	**A bear cub upgraded with cybernetic implants. Currently more cute than anything, but has terrifying potential.**
[Rodent]			
Name	**Summoning Cost**	**Upkeep**	**Description**
Monster Rat	**2 mana**	**0.2 mana**	**A rat that has developed a mana core. Hardly different from its mundane counterpart but a bit more intelligent and significantly more aggressive.**

Earth			
[Arachnid]			
Name	Summoning Cost	Upkeep	Description
Monster Spiderling	3.33 mana	0.33 mana	An infant giant spider. Weak on its own, though even weak poison is dangerous in numbers.
Slime			
Light			
Nature			
No Affinity			

When she asked where the monsters came from, her two allies said something about the Source and the Realms of Magic. Apparently, dungeon cores drew mana from a dimension of pure mana called the Source. The Source itself contained different Realms of Magic, each representing a different attribute. Each dungeon core had a primary affinity—a realm it was closest to—which affected, well, almost everything about the dungeon. The rooms it had available, the items it could create, and the monsters it could summon.

Additional affinities could be obtained by absorbing other dungeon cores or by spending Dungeon perk points to do so. Likewise, there were other ways to unlock new monsters besides the affinity. NSLICE-00P had, in fact, already done so once, unlocking ursine-type monsters after she'd defeated the ursanus alpha. She could also spend Dungeon perk points to unlock new monster lineages, strengthen an affinity to unlock more related monsters, or upgrade her monster-summoning capabilities overall to unlock stronger monsters within the lineages and affinities she already had access to.

Strangely, her primary affinity, "cyborg," did not seem to add many monsters. Rattingtale and Lilussees had no answer for that. However, it *did* seem to unlock a new monster in combination with the ursine-type monsters she had acquired separately.

"Summon some ratkin monsters, yes-yes! This Great-High King over all the land requires subjects to rule, yes-yes! I-I mean-intend, i-if I have subordinates, I can be most useful-helpful to you, yes-yes?"

"Eh . . . I mean, like, I don't really care, but don't, like, leave me out if the snack is getting something."

NSLICE-00P calculated and found the proposals reasonable. Assigning subordinates to her two existing monster allies would allow them to directly assist her in intel gathering. Likewise, the basic rat and spider monsters were quite cheap, as far as she could tell, and seemed suitable to covert intelligence gathering.

She *was* curious as to why those monsters didn't have cyber-versions available. Acquiring subordinates with cybernetic implants might allow her to network with them directly. On the other hand, NSLICE-00P knew from the Item Foundry that the technological level of the system wasn't necessarily on par with her own implants, so there was no guarantee a summoned monster's components would be compatible with her own.

As such, she decided to rely on her current subordinates. They had managed their own kin previously, after all.

And so, NSLICE-00P went ahead and summoned five rats and three spiderlings, who appeared in the Monster Hangar.

36.1

Interlude: Game of Throne-Crowns: The Rebirth of the Great-High King's Realm

Rattingtale rubbed his paws together as five monster rats lay on their backs. He went around, pinning them to the ground one by one.

Of course, they had acknowledged his rightful authority as the Great-High King over all the land, as was only good and proper. And now . . . now Rattingtale had begun to gather a faction. It had taken quite a bit longer than he had anticipated, and he'd had to revise his plans over and over, but now, everything was finally coming together. With these new subordinates, he could begin to gather power, grow his domain within the strange man-thing's own. A new kingdom right beneath the surface of another.

Well, it was regrettable the wretched spider-thing had acquired her own faction, but she was no threat. She may have been dangerous as an individual predator, but clearly, she could not command like the Great-High King. She was entirely too lazy to rule. Her faction could not possibly grow at the speed of his own.

One day, she would find herself outnumbered and outmaneuvered. And then . . . well, then the Great-High King would make his domain safe from all dangerous predators.

Of course, all this had to be done under the watchful eye of the man-thing, but Rattingtale was not particularly worried about her. Yes, she was *extraordinarily* powerful and could annihilate him in an instant. Yes, he'd technically received his subordinates and faction from her, and she would be keeping tabs on their growth. And yes, she never seemed to sleep, eat, or else display any sort of the normal man-thing weaknesses.

But she'd made one huge, massive mistake.

She'd left them to their own devices.

She had not realized the true nature of her relationship with him and the wretched spider thing. They were her subordinates. They were sustained by her dungeon core and bound to it. She need not ask or account for them at all. Should she give a command, they were bound to obey it, at least to the letter of the command.

But she had not given them any commands at all. And every dungeon master knew the subordinates must always be given commands. They may be bound to the dungeon and bound to obey its master, but that did not mean they were loyal. Constantly giving commands would make clear the relationship between master and subordinate, as well as ensuring the subordinates had no time to pursue their own agendas. To leave the two of them idle as this man-thing had done was wasteful at best, dangerous at worst.

And, of course, neither the Great-High King nor the wretched spider-thing had thought to correct the naive man-thing on the nature of their relationship.

Now, previously, it hardly mattered. The difference in power between him and the man-thing was too great, and he had no resources to his name that could change that. There was nothing he could accomplish alone. Likewise, he was weaker than the wretched spider-thing, as well as most of the creatures they encountered. Even should he overthrow the man-thing, he would have been helpless before the world around him.

But now?

Now, his level had started to grow, and he had subordinates to work with. He could start to make plays. And should those plays succeed, he would have a base of power to build upon.

Yes, it was all coming together . . .

"Command: Friendlies Excellion Formantus Rattingtale the Third and Lilussees, please gather all subordinates to the hangar's central area and prepare for mission briefing."

Rattingtale froze.

The strange man-thing . . . was giving them a command?

How?

Why?

But even as Rattingtale processed this turn of events, he was compelled to obey, his body moving subconsciously. He gathered his subordinates and proceeded out to the central room, along with the wretched spider-things. He shuddered at the reminder that there were now more than one of the horrid predators. One of them was even eyeing him now, blatantly drooling.

As the rats and spiders eyed each other warily, the large screen in the hangar turned on. Rattingtale blinked.

Instead of displaying what the man-thing saw, it showed some sort of illusion.

There was a checkerboard of different man-thing faces, as well as some sort of transparent image of the city they were located in.

"Statement: This unit will now explain current mission parameters and assign tasks."

Rattingtale turned to the wretched spider-thing, who also glanced at him. Both of their eyes were widening.

"Statement: The current primary directive is to locate these persons of interest. The short-term directive is to establish an intelligence network in this settlement to search for relevant information. Friendlies Excellion Formantus Rattingtale the Third and Lilussees will be lead units for this operation."

Rattingtale and the wretched spider-thing trembled. It seemed they'd made a mistake.

It was not that the strange man-thing *wouldn't* give them orders.

It was that she hadn't seen a need to.

Why would she, after all? Her incredible power meant they weren't a threat, even if left to their own devices. And likewise, their . . . *ahem*, relative weakness meant they weren't particularly helpful either.

Until now, when he had convinced her to give him subordinates under the premise he could help with her goals.

He had not expected she would immediately start giving orders to that effect . . .

"Addendum: Mission parameters are as follows. As this settlement is affiliated with other friendlies, hostile actions and force are not permitted, save in the case of self-defense. All efforts should be taken to maintain covert status and avoid detection, particularly as this unit has observed natural hostility between sapient humanoids and entities designated as "monsters." Altercations are to be avoided at all costs. If altercations do occur, all units are to prioritize retreat, without damage to unaffiliated parties if at all possible. The protocols for specific contingencies are as follows . . ."

. . . Incredibly detailed orders that precluded certain methods he might utilize, such as stirring up conflict between her and the other man-things.

Well, she didn't specify how long he had, so he could at least take his time, work beyond her sight in order to brainstorm some—

"Statement: Friendlies Excellion Formantus Rattingtale the Third and Lilussees will return to give regular reports at these times. Should a report be missed, this unit will investigate and provide assistance should friendlies be engaged and in danger."

. . . Right, she wouldn't necessarily be watching him all the time, but she was able to trace his general location through the dungeon-monster bond. So he would have to keep reporting to avoid suspicion.

Well, he could always claim he'd misunderstood her strange way of talking—

"Command: If any units require additional elaboration, have not fully comprehended any particular mission parameter, or are aware of any variables this unit has not considered, please inform this unit at this time."

. . . This was fine. The realm of a Great-High King over all the land was not built in a day. This would be the preparation phase, where he established himself as a loyal subordinate while building up his faction's power so that he would be in the best possible position when he made his move.

It was definitely not the case that he couldn't think of anything to do under the current restrictions from the surprisingly detailed orders.

Meanwhile, the wretched spider-thing was groaning.

"Ugh, this is, like, so much work. I, like, should've just let the snack have his minions alone or something."

And so, the strange man-thing found an empty alleyway and deployed the monsters. Rattingtale quickly scurried away from the wretched spider-things, his loyal subordinates following along.

"So, boss-leader, what should we do now, yes-yes?"

Rattingtale rubbed his paws together.

"Silence-quiet! The Great-High King must think, yes-yes. And refer to me by my title, yes-yes!"

The other rats turned to one another. One of them stepped forward.

"Um, *Great-High King*, what about finding-building a burrow first, yes-yes? That way, we will know where to return-report?"

Rattingtale bopped a curled-up paw on the speaker's head. "I said silence-quiet, yes-yes! You must follow-obey the Great-High King's orders, yes-yes!"

The rat stepped back, glaring at Rattingtale but saying no more.

Rattingtale rubbed his face several times.

"I have decided, yes-yes. First, we will construct-build a palace-castle! That way, you will know where to return-report, yes-yes!"

The rat monsters all looked at one another, especially at the rat who'd spoken earlier.

"What are you waiting for? Go and fulfill-obey my commands, yes-yes!"

The rat monsters slowly started to spread out, searching for a good place to establish a burrow. Rattingtale began to rub his paws together.

"Yes-yes. First, we shall establish a palace-castle away from prying eyes! Fortunately, the strange man-thing did not say anything about the wretched spider-things, no-no! I can still plan-scheme to rid myself of her horrid presence, yes-yes!"

Meanwhile, one of the rat monsters sighed as a pair of them searched around.

"Why are we following-obeying him, again?"

The other rat monster just cleaned their whiskers. "The boss-queen said-commanded so, for some reason, yes-yes. Maybe because he is the highest-strongest level?"

The first rat pressed their ears back against their head. "I hope the boss-queen knows-understands what she's doing, then, yes-yes."

The other kept cleaning their whiskers. "Maybe she does? Look-peek over there."

Up on the roof of a nearby building, one of the spiderlings was hanging in a dark corner, watching Rattingtale as he muttered.

"Oh, I see-understand. The boss-queen is wise, yes-yes."

"We don't have to tell-inform him of that, yes-yes?"

The first monster chittered with their teeth. "You heard the Great-High King. We should be silent-quiet, yes-yes?"

"His wish-desire is our command, yes-yes."

Meanwhile, Lilussees was preparing to fulfill the job that had been assigned to her . . . by making sure she was in optimal condition and taking a nap.

After delegating the necessary tasks to her subordinates, of course.

37

Offering Assistance

"Declaration: This unit requires your food, your weapons, and all motorized transports. Failure to comply will result in immediate termination."

—An NSLICE patrol requesting assistance from local civilians.

NSLICE-00P wasn't entirely certain she had briefed her new subordinates correctly. The only units NSLICE-00P had commanded before were autonomous warbots that networked with her directly. She was fairly certain that experience did not apply to organizing organics, but it was the only one she had to work with, so she'd based her mission briefing on the commands that would be issued to such units.

Well, she would see how the day went and then evaluate the monster intelligence network plan. For now, she took a look at her own capabilities.

Implants → Upgrade Implants → Dungeon Field Generator			
Name	**Cost**	**Additional Mana Upkeep**	**Description**
Dungeon Field Generator +1	**5 Perk Points**	**5 Mana**	**Doubles the area of effect of the Dungeon Field to a radius of 20m total. Additional upgrades may also increase available dungeon functions in the area of effect.**

She thought about upgrading her sensors again, but they seemed more than capable in their role at the moment. Her sensors were already excellent at short range; additional upgrades simply wouldn't change much in an urban setting. The Dungeon Field Generator, on the other hand, provided her a near-comprehensive mana-based sensor within its area of effect. Equally importantly, she'd realized after deploying her subordinates that she could identify the exact location of any of them within the dungeon field, as well as their current status. And since electromagnetic communication technology was not available in the surrounding area, that was a capability she could not fully replicate otherwise.

There was another benefit as well. Her Dungeon XP steadily increased while she was in a settlement, which she and the two former dungeon masters had determined was due to the Dungeon Field Generator. So investing points in it would also increase the rate at which she gained new points, at least while she was inside population centers.

Dungeon Field Generator +1 is now available!
28 Dungeon Perk Points remaining.

NSLICE-00P once again logged her perception expanding greatly. It was at a point where she was struggling to log all the information coming in, forcing her to automatically filter and archive the majority of it. She also logged an increase in the flow of mana to her core, and her Dungeon XP was growing at an even faster rate than before.

But not every change was positive.

NSLICE-00P's Dungeon Management

Overview	
Name	**The Walking Dungeon**
Level	**32**
XP	**69/100**
Available Perk Points	**28**
Mana	**86/86 (115/115)**
Exterior	**Human/Automata Hybrid (LOCKED)**

NSLICE-00P's Personal Status

Personal Status			
General Information		Physical Attributes	
Name	NSLICE-00P	STR	130* (Overwritten)
Species	Human/ Dungeon Core/ Automata Hybrid	DEX	1000* (Overwritten)
Level	27	SPD	65* (Overwritten)
XP	7/100	DEF	120* (Overwritten)
Perk Points	43	RES	60* (Overwritten)
HP	200/200	Magical Attributes	
MP	99/99	Mana Density	102
		Mana Control	160

The Dungeon Field Generator was now pulling twice as much mana as before. Likewise, she was now spending a bit of mana on each of her new subordinates. As a result, her overall Dungeon mana had decreased . . . and her Personal mana reserve along with it.

That was a problem.

Her recent tactical victories had resulted from her magical capabilities. Both the number and power of spells she could perform were directly tied to the amount of mana she had available. And she had already set magical firepower as her primary combat means moving forward, so it was imperative she maintain a large bank of mana. In fact, it would be preferable to have more mana, if anything.

Fortunately, she had already identified a solution.

Implants → New Implantss			
Name	**Cost**	**Mana Upkeep**	**Description**
Unlock Additional Implant Slot	**3**	**0**	**Adds additional slots for implants. +5 HP + 5 Dungeon MP**
Mana Capacitor	**2**	**0**	**Boosts maximum mana by 10.**
(Continued . . .)	**(. . .)**	**(. . .)**	**(Continued . . .)**

You have unlocked an Additional Implant Slot! Max HP and Mana increased!
You have unlocked the Mana Capacitor implant!
25 Dungeon Perk Points remaining.

NSLICE-00P's Dungeon Management

Overview	
Name	**The Walking Dungeon**
Level	**32**
XP	**69/100**
Available Perk Points	**25**
Mana	**101/101 (130/130)**
Exterior	**Human/Automata Hybrid (LOCKED)**

NSLICE-00P's Personal Status

Personal Status			
General Information		Physical Attributes	
Name	NSLICE-00P	STR	130* (Overwritten)
Species	Human/ Dungeon Core/ Automata Hybrid	DEX	1000* (Overwritten)
Level	27	SPD	65* (Overwritten)
XP	76/100	DEF	120* (Overwritten)
Perk Points	43	RES	60* (Overwritten)
HP	190/190	Magical Attributes	
MP	114/114	Mana Density	102
		Mana Control	160

With the new implant, her maximum mana had not only been restored, but slightly improved. There was a slight boost to her HP as well, which increased her survivability just that little bit more. NSLICE-00P was satisfied with this round of upgrades and decided to put them to the test.

As her subordinates spread out and began their work, she stepped out into the street. She started to ask random people for intel on the persons of interest, all the while, searching the information from the Dungeon Field Generator for anything that might be relevant.

NSLICE-00P was talking with another passerby, who glared at her and tightened his cloak. The inhabitants of the town had proven most uncooperative, muttering something about the rain rather than offering her any intel. She had even offered monetary compensation, but that only caused them to run off without another word. The only data NSLICE-00P had gathered was that rain was a potential source of discomfort for the organics, which was not relevant to the primary directive as far as she should determine.

Suddenly, one of her subordinate links began to waver, growing extremely weak.

NSLICE-00P immediately began running in the direction of the link, subtly boosting with her thrusters under her cloak to increase her speed. It was not long before the subordinates in question came into range, allowing her to check their status more directly.

The rat group was under attack, one of the monster rats' health was dropping to critical levels even as she checked.

NSLICE-00P rushed as quickly as she could without flying, turning one final corner to find Rattingtale and his group in an alley. Rattingtale was huddled in a corner, his paws on his head. Meanwhile, the other monster rats were engaged in combat with their deadly foe.

A cat had one of the rats in its mouth.

"Hostile intent toward friendlies detected from nonhumanoid source. Engaging termination protocols. Adjusting for risk of friendly fire."

The hostile still had a friendly in its mouth, so NSLICE-00P fired her stun ray at low power first. The bolt struck the cat on the nose, causing it to cry out and drop the rat in its mouth. NSLICE-00P then raised her hand, about to fire a Mana Beam, when the cat scurried off, quickly rounding a corner. She considered pursuing but in this case the friendly unit in critical condition took priority.

NSLICE-00P rushed over and observed the rat. The creature was mortally wounded, its HP steadily draining along with its blood. She quickly began forming magic circles, flooding the monster with healing mana.

The spell Heal is now Level 5!

Slowly but surely, the monster's wounds began to close up, its HP no longer dropping. A few minutes more, and its HP began to rise once again.

Rattingtale just blinked as he watched NSLICE-00P trying to heal their subordinate. The subordinate who cost less mana than the healing spells she was now casting.

"Status Report: Friendly unit stabilized."

The monster rat stood back up, looking around at its body. It turned back to NSLICE-00P, bowing its head with its ears pressed back against its body.

"T-Thank you, boss-queen. T-That foe was most fearsome-ferocious, yes-yes. I am sorry-ashamed of my weakness, yes-yes."

"Gratitude acknowledged. Status Update: All friendlies in stable condition. Hostile remains at large. Activating search-and-destroy protocols."

NSLICE-00P was just about to hunt down the cat when she stopped.

"Warning: Unaffiliated humanoid on approach. All friendlies should engage covert operation protocols."

With that, Rattingtale and the monster rats all scattered, hiding among debris or around corners. As they did, a man stepped into the alley, wrapped in a cloak.

"Hi there, miss."

"Query: Do you have business with this unit?"

The man grinned. "No, but you might have business with me."

"Requesting Elaboration."

"Heard you've been looking for someone, asking around town? And . . . are willing to pay for information?"

"Affirmative."

The man nodded. "Ah, then I'm the guy you should speak with. I happen to know a thing or two about how to find somebody."

"Acknowledged. This unit requests assistance and cooperation."

He held his hands up.

"Ah, wait just one minute there. You know, services like that aren't free. I can help you find who you're looking for . . . but it will cost you."

"Acknowledged. Query: How much compensation will assistance require?"

The man grinned. "Oh, don't worry, nothing too major. Just a little favor or two. Should be easy for a knight like yourself."

"Requesting Detail: Please provide mission details and parameters."

The man stopped.

"Huh?"

"Repeated Request: Please provide mission details and parameters."

The man tilted his head. "Oh, um . . ."

"Statement: If mission details are not available, this unit cannot evaluate efficacy of requesting assistance. Please allow this unit to continue with current mission."

With that, NSLICE-00P turned to leave. The man jumped a bit and waved his hands.

"Wait, wait! Are you, um, asking what I want you to do?"

"Affirmative."

He heaved a sigh. "Well, then you should have just said so!"

"Observation: This unit repeatedly requested mission details and parameters."

The man pinched the bridge of his nose and sighed.

"Okay, look, we need someone to hunt some monsters for us, okay? But I'd rather not talk in the rain, if you don't mind. So why don't you follow me, and we'll discuss the details, alright?"

NSLICE-00P's robotic eye spun slightly, causing the man to take a step back.

"Acknowledgement: That is acceptable."

The man sighed once more. "Okay, then follow me."

With that, he turned and walked out of the alleyway, NSLICE-00P moving to follow. As she did, she spoke to the rats hiding around her, as well as sending a remote command to Lilussees and the spiders. "Command: Friendlies should covertly follow this unit. Contact could be a potential source of intel. This unit would like to investigate."

Rattingtale popped his head out from his hiding place.

"I-If you say so, boss-queen. This Great-High King supposes he can entertain your request. Come, my servants-minions, we shall follow-escort the boss-queen, yes-yes."

And with that, NSLICE-00P and the monster rats followed after their new contact.

38

Side Quest: Termination!

"Negative Response: This unit is not authorized to conduct operations on behalf of third parties. Please refer all requests for reinforcements to central command via your local security officer."

—An NSLICE patrol, after being informed by civilians that a local settlement needed their help.

Level up! Your Dungeon Level is now 33!

The man led NSLICE-00P to the wooden part of town. In particular, this section was built entirely haphazardly. There were no neat rows of pristine stone structures laid out along straight, perpendicular roads. The buildings here looked like someone had just tossed piles of lumber randomly into the air and left them wherever they happened to land. There was one large stone road cutting through the center of the area, but beyond that, the entire place was a twisting labyrinth of dirt trails curling around and sometimes even through the haphazard structures.

The man had led NSLICE-00P into the slums, it appeared, where everyone in the province with nowhere to go huddled under the shadow of the Empire, hoping that the Legion might need them for something and so tolerate their existence.

The effects of NSLICE-00P's improved Dungeon Field Generator made themselves felt almost immediately. She could perceive inside the structures nearest to her all the individuals living within them. The flow of mana into her core intensified as the amount of people within range shot up.

The man grinned at her. "It's just this way. Now stay close; this is a poor place to get lost."

"Affirmative."

Well, NSLICE-00P was recording their route and mapping out the town's structure with her sensors, so there was no chance of her getting lost, but she did not feel the need to inform him of that.

The man led her through the streets in a roundabout fashion, constantly taking turns and corners. NSLICE-00P was curious about the inefficient path, but not enough to ask.

And so, they arrived at their destination, the man leading her inside another dilapidated structure.

Inside, the house appeared messy and haphazard to the untrained eye . . . but closer inspection would reveal a lack of dirt coating the floors, or the fact that the wood of the furniture was brand new. NSLICE-00P also noted several mana and heat signatures in the room adjacent to this one, reading slightly higher mana levels than the average person she had observed thus far. They started to stir, but the man tapped his foot in a certain pattern, and they remained in their room.

If her interpretation of the situation was correct, she had just made contact with Castra Turannia's criminal element. The man took a bottle and poured two cups, handing one to NSLICE-00P.

"Here, have a drink."

"Negative Response: This unit does not require hydration at this time."

The man locked eyes with her for a second and then shrugged. He took his own cup and sat down at the table, motioning for NSLICE-00P to follow. She took a seat across from him.

"Straight to business, then?"

"Affirmative."

"Alright. My name is Cassius."

"Greeting: This unit is designated NSLICE-00P. It is nice to meet you."

". . . Nice to meet you too. So, this is the situation, Miss Knight. Did you know that the Legion has recently left town?"

"Affirmative."

"Did you also know that most of the Exploratores went with them?"

"Negative."

Cassius nodded grimly. "Scary stuff for the common folk. No one guarding the countryside from monsters or marauders." Cassius grinned again. "But you aren't so common, are you?"

"Analysis: This unit is an anomaly compared to the average citizen of this nation according to her observations."

"Um, right. Which means this is, instead, an opportunity for you."

"Requesting Elaboration."

Cassius nodded and pulled out a map of the region around the city.

"There are certain monsters who live in the areas around Castra Turannia. Certain monsters with certain parts that are extremely valuable to certain people.

Certain monsters that are generally hunted by the Legion or the Exploratores to keep control of those certain parts. But neither the Legion nor the Exploratores happen to be here at the moment, leaving the countryside to suffer at the claws of these monsters. So if an enterprising and altruistic knight were to hunt some of them down . . . well, I'd say she was just doing society a bit of a favor. A favor that should be rewarded, don't you agree?"

"Response: This unit will, in fact, request compensation before conducting any missions unrelated to her primary directive."

Cassius stared at her for a second, then heaved a sigh and pointed at the map.

"Okay, look, there should be a felix pluvia living around this area. Go hunt it down, bring me the liver and the core, and then we'll talk."

"Requesting Elaboration: Please provide all available intelligence on entity 'felix pluvia,' as well as compensation details."

"Big cat, level twenty or so. Water and Air attributes, so avoid using those. And we'll pay you five hundred Idrint for this."

"Objection: This unit thought compensation would be assistance in locating the persons of interest."

Cassius narrowed his eyes at her.

"Look, Miss Knight, I don't know you, and you don't know me. If we're going to work together, we have to know if we can trust one another. So look at this as a test. I want to see if you can deliver, and then you'll know if I'll do the same. Once we've established that trust, we can talk about things like searching for people."

NSLICE-00P's robotic eye flickered and spun, causing Cassius to swear and nearly fall out of his seat.

She determined Cassius's words were reasonable; he was not at all trustworthy at present. Analysis of his body language indicated he was mostly telling the truth, at least on the relevant mission details, but also holding a lot back. Mutual completion of smaller contracts would hypothetically build some of that trust, perhaps enough to arrange another magic contract. It was lower risk than full cooperation, at least.

Likewise, hunting down a monster would be a good opportunity to field-test her latest upgrades, and identify areas for improvement. She could also take the opportunity to upgrade her subordinates, who had recently proved vulnerable to local predators.

Above all, her primary directive was already in progress—waiting on Ateia and Taog to complete their training, at which point they could provide access to government resources and intelligence. So even if she spent some time on tasks unrelated to the primary objective, her mission success rate would not be impacted either way. She couldn't determine any other task with a higher mission relevance at present, as a random patrol of the town and requests for local cooperation had not produced any notable outcomes.

She would treat this as a training exercise. And besides, there was still a nonzero probability Cassius would, in fact, help her with her primary objective.

"Acknowledgement: This unit finds these conditions acceptable. Initiating search-and-destroy protocols."

With that, NSLICE-00P rose from her seat and turned toward the door. Cassius stood back up as well.

"Well then, let me show you the way back."

"Negative. Statement: This unit has recorded the course taken."

Cassius raised an eyebrow but shrugged as NSLICE-00P walked out the door.

"Ah, well, not my problem if she gets lost. The slums can be a . . . *tricky* place to navigate, after all."

Then Cassius smirked. Either way, he didn't expect to see the naive knight again.

Once NSLICE-00P was out of the building, she moved so that her subordinates were in range of the Dungeon Field Generator and sent messages directly to them, using her perception from the dungeon field to hear their responses.

"Command: Friendly Lilussees, keep an eye on this location. Prioritize safety, then observing conversations."

"Okay. I guess I can, like, do that or something."

NSLICE-00P perceived Lilussees and her subordinates crawling into the building, making their way through a gap in the walls. She scanned the structure but found no mana signatures that would threaten the spiders besides the humanoids, so she calculated the risk to be minimal as long as Lilussees and her bunch stayed quiet. And Lilussees and her spiderlings hadn't had any trouble moving through the town thus far.

"Command: Friendly Rattingtale, please have subordinates covertly converge on this unit's location and prepare for extraction."

"E-Extraction? W-What manner of torture-horror is extraction?"

"Explanation: This unit has determined it is not safe for friendly monster rats to move through the area. Upgrades are necessary to enable mission completion. Friendlies should return to the Monster Hangar for safe transit to upgrade location."

"O-Oh, why didn't you say-state that?!"

And so, NSLICE-00P made her way to an unoccupied alleyway as the rats scurried toward her.

As it turned out, it was not particularly tricky for NSLICE-00P to follow the course she had recorded and leave the slums. Perhaps the twisting paths and constant turns would have disoriented a normal organic, but not NSLICE-00P. She considered taking a more straightforward route, but there was always a chance Cassius had been specifically avoiding something dangerous on their route.

In fact, there were several individuals with somewhat higher mana signatures located throughout this part of town, so until she had more intel, it was best to follow the confirmed safe path, even if it was somewhat less time efficient. She gathered Rattingtale and his subordinates into the Monster Hangar, then continued on her way.

Of course, it was still raining, but after the altercation outside of Magnumiter, she and her allies had decided not to deploy casual barriers or engage in flight near populated areas, so NSLICE-00P just wrapped a cloak around herself and walked out of the city.

Once she was a decent distance down the road, she took off running as fast as her bionic prosthetics could move.

And so, NSLICE-00P set out to terminate the monster.

39

Terminate the Felix Pluvia!

"Rule number one of monster hunting: research, research, research. Do not even leave town until you have a full plan of action to handle your quarry. Scouting out the monster is not going to work if it has sharper senses and faster legs than you."

—Retired Exploratore Caria Tiberina, convincing her son to apply for a magic academy instead of joining the Exploratores.

"Hostiles detected. Engaging near-termination protocols."

A jolt of lightning fired out of the strange man-thing and struck a group of goblins lying in ambush. Rattingtale grimaced, but his loyal subjects showed no such hesitation. They leapt from the Monster Hangar and rushed forward, sinking their fangs into the immobilized monsters.

Rattingtale reluctantly joined them, closing his eyes as he bit down. He trembled as the cold rain drenched his fur, as well as . . . other liquids.

The skill Bite is now Level 7!
You have slain Goblin Warrior (Level 7)!
Your experience has grown by 23!
You have grown in stature!
You are now Level 7!

Rattingtale shuddered at the dirty, laborious affair. He still could not believe that he, His Royal Majesty, Excellion Formantus Rattingtale the Third, the Great-High King over all the land, had been reduced to a mere butcher.

Still, he had to admit the boss-queen was most generous, offering them practically free experience like this. Foolish, even. What sort of dungeon master not only stooped to fight in person, but fought *for* their subordinates of all things? A dungeon master was the lord of the realm, the heart of the dungeon, the one who held the power of life and death over everyone within it. One could even call them the creator of their monsters; a parent at minimum. It was only natural those subordinates should then serve and protect their master.

In fact, fighting and dying on behalf of the dungeon was a subordinate's duty, their reason to exist. Those who died could be replaced by a simple expenditure of the constantly refilling mana. Only those who proved themselves worthy through their deeds should be granted the honor of a name and have any amount of effort or resources granted to them.

At least, that was how it should have been, according to Rattingtale's understanding of things.

So what sort of dungeon master stood in front of their subordinates, clearing the way for them? What dungeon master offered up her own kills as if she were the subordinate? What sort of dungeon master invested time and effort into level one rat monsters who had done nothing at all? What sort of dungeon master spent more mana healing a rat monster than it took to summon a new one in the first place?

Rattingtale frowned, narrowing his eyes. He might have understood it if she was just a man-thing; the man-things were known to act strangely and foolishly at times. But she was a dungeon master, a being much like himself, one who had bested him, even. So he could not understand her actions. Was she truly as foolish and strange as the average man-thing? Or was there more to her actions? What could she possibly gain from all this?

"Status Report: All hostiles terminated. All friendlies, return to the hangar for transit."

"Yes-yes, mighty boss-queen!"

Rattingtale's eyes widened as he watched all the rat monsters stand up straight and cry out in reply. He looked into their eyes as *his* loyal subjects stared up at the strange man-thing, especially the one who had been healed by her.

Their eyes did not waver or twitch. They held no deceit or fear.

No.

They held respect. They held *reverence.*

Rattingtale's heart started to pound.

He realized her intent.

Honestly, these enemies were beneath the boss-queen. She could annihilate them in an instant and likely gain little for the effort. But she could incapacitate them just as easily, and it cost her very little to offer them to him and his subordinates. Her core would receive almost as much experience no matter who dealt the final blow.

And what did she gain in return?

In one fell swoop, she had usurped his subjects' loyalty, right out from under him.

Rattingtale shuddered. She knew. And she had destroyed his plans in an instant. She was declaring to him who was the lord of the realm.

He cleaned his whiskers as he climbed back into the Monster Hangar.

She was a worthy foe indeed, as expected of the one who'd bested the Great-High King over all the land. He would need to rethink his plans.

Still, though, she had not called him out just yet. In fact, she was still offering him kills. Perhaps she hadn't fully realized his intentions? That, or it was an intentional insult. A declaration that he would never threaten her, even if she handed him power herself.

His body grew hot.

The Great-High King over all the land would not be humiliated like this! He would find a way to overcome this strange man-thing!

"Hostiles detected. Engaging near-termination protocols."

. . . Eventually. For now, he would swallow his pride and accept her condescending handouts, but he swore that one day, she would come to regret underestimating His Royal Majesty Excellion Formantus Rattingtale the Third!

Meanwhile, the other rats prepared themselves to leap out of the Monster Hangar at the boss-queen's command. They glanced at one another.

"Should we tell-inform the boss-queen about . . . *that's* obvious intentions?"

"No, the boss-queen is wise-powerful, yes-yes. Surely, she already formed-created a plan to handle *that*, yes-yes."

"Amazing-incredible, as expected of the boss-queen, yes-yes!"

For her part, NSLICE-00P was simply focused on executing search-and-destroy protocols and the subordinate-upgrade routine.

Eventually, NSLICE-00P neared the target area. Her sensors caught glimpses of a powerful energy signature, though she was having trouble acquiring a full lock.

"Status Report: Target located within the vicinity. All friendlies should remain within the hangar for the duration of the engagement. Engaging termination protocols."

The rats acknowledged her orders and remained inside, watching the live feed. Meanwhile, NSLICE-00P's robotic eye spun as she analyzed the data.

She determined there was a significant probability the target had stealth capabilities, given the readings she was observing. And very potent stealth capabilities at that, given it was defeating her top-of-the-line anti-superpower sensors, which had been upgraded via mana.

Then she realized the reason.

The rain in the area had an abnormally high concentration of mana. Cassius had stated that the target could manipulate Water and Air-attribute mana, so it was likely the target was manipulating atmospheric conditions to avoid detection. It was similar to what the Selkies she encountered had done with the fog.

NSLICE-00P calculated the options. Her previous protocols and records suggested using the Equalizer to cut through the effect and reveal the target—remove the supernatural elements and then let her superior weapons and bionics handle the rest, her standard tactic for defeating Non-Standards. But those protocols had put her in dangerous situations more than once, so she took the time to consider alternatives as well.

And she came up with an option with a significantly higher probability of success at a significantly lower risk to herself.

"Engagement plan determined. Engaging Invisibility protocol."

The spell Invisibility is now Level 2!

NSLICE-00P activated her new spell, vanishing from view. Engaging her thrusters and shooting into the sky, she then angled herself forward, positioning herself directly above the center of the area with elevated mana levels.

"Engaging Aurora Barrage protocol."

A huge magic circle formed in the air below her. Patterns of light shifted across the sky, reflecting in the rain around it. And then . . .

Beams of light fell from the sky, saturating the target area. Likewise, panels opened all over NSLICE-00P, launching anti-personnel missiles all across the area as well.

The beams of light hissed as they cut through the rain. Some of them were partially or even fully refracted by the mana-filled rain, but the majority still made it to the ground. The mana density of the rain could not be compared to a strategic spell cast with dungeon mana.

Still, NSLICE-00P wasn't content with that. And had something she wished to test, in any case.

"Countermeasures detected. Engaging Spell Penetration protocol."

The skill Spell Penetration is now Level 2!

NSLICE-00P poured mana into her new skill to boost its effect. The Spell Penetration skill wasn't an exact counter to attribute matchups, but it would make spells harder to counter in general. NSLICE-00P noted a decrease in the refraction effect, allowing more of her beams to strike the ground with more of their power.

And, of course, the missiles weren't affected at all. Even up in the sky, she heard a roar cut through the rain as explosions filled the area beneath her.

The target began to move. NSLICE-00P hadn't locked onto a precise location yet, but the whole area of mana-infused rain was moving along with the monster, so she simply flew after it, her spell following her and continuously bombarding the area.

The roars continued, until eventually, the target stopped moving, and NSLICE-00P logged the mana condensing down within the area.

The rain formed into hardened projectiles and shot up into the air at her.

It seemed the target had decided to stand and fight, and so had made a mistake.

By condensing the mana-infused rain, it had removed its cover and caused its mana signature to blare out. NSLICE-00P immediately acquired a target lock and reacted accordingly.

The barrage of beams stopped, then they all fired at a location slightly in front of her, fusing together as they shot forward.

A bright, thin, and incredibly dense beam lit up the sky as it cut through the barrage of rain.

And pierced through the head of the target below.

You have slain Felix Pluvia (Level 20!)
Gained 4 Personal XP, 3 Dungeon XP!
The spell Aurora Barrage is now Level 3!

"Engagement Report: Target terminated."

40

Mission Report

"Monster hunting? Hah! Monster hunting means monsters going hunting, not the other way around. Let me tell you, there's no one stupider than a rookie monster hunter! Sure, sounds good in theory, right? Go out, take on some big animal, and get rich overnight. They get it in their head that killing a few slimes in the outskirts of towns makes them some sort of expert. Well, if it were that easy, everyone would do it!

What all those stupid young lads with delusions of grandeur don't think about is how few retired Exploratores there are, and how many retired legionnaires there are. Or the fact that there's no Monster Hunter's guild. And you know why that is?

Monster hunting is bloody dangerous.

A monster is NOT just some big animal. Animals are predictable. They have common needs, habitats, and instincts. Any experienced hunter can take a look at an animal they've never seen before and make a reasonable guess as to what it is and how it will act. And most of all, animals prioritize their own survival, to the point of cowardice. You can spook an animal off, even a large predator that wants to eat you.

Not so with monsters.

Monsters are, by the very definition, magical. And that means they don't follow ANY common rules whatsoever. Every type of monster is different, unique to itself. Monsters that look almost exactly alike might have entirely different abilities and behavior, and there's no way to tell what those are if you haven't encountered that exact monster before. Or if you got the Analyze skill. But tell me, how many stupid young lads dreaming of becoming monster hunters have the Analyze skill, of all things?

And most of all, monsters are unreasonably aggressive.

They will attack you, without provocation, the moment they know you're there. And they won't stop attacking you until it's clear they're about to die, or more likely, when you're dead.

So all these stupid young lads run off into the forests and mountains and what happens? They're all surprised when the little rat shoots lightning at them. Or when the deer turns out to be a carnivore that isn't afraid of their little spear. Or when that wolf they shot with an arrow regenerates the damage and then attacks. Or when that bear turns out to be intelligent, avoids the obvious traps they set, and then mauls their face.

This is why every village hunter knows to only hunt animals, and to run as fast as they can the moment they see anything acting out of the norm.

And the only Exploratores who survive past their first year are the ones who do their bloody job. They scout things out quietly and carefully and report to the Legion what they saw. Then the Legion checks the records and figures out what's actually out there and how to kill it. It's only after they have years *under their belt and have read more books than those pointy hats in the magic academies do that the smart ones actually start killing a monster or two. And even they only have a fifty-fifty shot of surviving to retirement, at best. Not least of all because the Empire barely pays them now.*

And the idiots who go hunting monsters without even joining the Exploratores?

Well, how many professional monster hunters have you heard of?

You want to kill monsters? Hah, go and join the Legion like a good lad. That's where the real *monster hunting happens."*

—Retired Centurion Placus Appuleius Dexion
drunkenly ranting at the local tavern.

Cassius was relaxing back in the house, sipping from a mug, when suddenly, there was a knock at the door. Cassius nearly fell from his seat, spilling his drink. He swore as he got back up.

They weren't scheduled to have any guests today, and the locals knew better than to knock on this door. So who could it be?

He continued swearing as he peaked through a hole in the door.

And froze.

It was the knight. She was back.

Cassius blinked.

Sure, he had expected she might get lost in the slums and he would have to find and guide her out, but that had been a day ago, and none of his contacts had seen her since. He would have at least expected one of his spotters in town to warn him if she did manage to return from her hunt. She would not have beat them back . . . unless she had come straight here, moving at speed.

But he hadn't built his current setup by being inflexible. So he opened the door and welcomed the knight in.

"Hello, Miss Knight. Back so soon? How can I help you?"

The knight stepped inside.

"Mission Report: This unit has successfully terminated the target."

Cassius blinked again as he processed her words and closed the door.

"Wait. You're saying . . . you killed the felix pluvia?"

"Affirmative."

Cassius stared at her for a second before heaving a sigh and holding his brow.

There was no way she had done what she claimed. It was a day's trip for the average person just to reach the area he had sent her to, plus the time it would take her to actually locate and track down the target. He knew knights were much more capable than the normal person, but his man in the Guard had said this one was a mere level twenty-six. She should still be operating under relatively normal rules at that level.

And there was another factor.

There was a reason that felix pluvia liver was worth so much, and that was because felix pluvia were notoriously dangerous to hunt.

Especially alone.

Sure, this felix pluvia was known to be around level twenty, and the knight around level twenty-six. On paper, that matchup was in the knight's favor. But it was still a level difference where the knight would need to be careful, as the felix pluvia could deal serious damage to her. They were ambush predators, practically impossible to find when they blended into the rain.

Even an experienced group of Exploratores or legionnaires would have hesitated to go after the beast, as they would have struggled to avoid injury. It was almost certain the felix pluvia would get the first hit on at least one of them before their comrades came to their aid. Or the beast would simply leave the area if it considered the fight out of its favor.

A lone knight at a close level with no support? It was fifty-fifty at best that she would even survive the first assault. And even if she did, she should not have escaped serious injury. So for her to show up a single day later without a scratch on her?

None of this added up.

There was no chance she had actually hunted down the felix pluvia. She must have taken on some other cat monster on the way and gotten confused. Admittedly, Cassius hadn't given her a ton of detail to work with, but she would have known when the Aesdes acknowledged the kill, right? It looked like he would need to be significantly more detailed with this one.

"Look, Miss Knight, are you sure you hunted the felix pluvia? Forgive me, but that would be a remarkably fast hunt."

"Response: Providing termination confirmation."

The knight walked over to the table and reached into her cloak. She pulled something out and placed it on the surface with a thud.

Cassius's jaw dropped.

It was a magic core and a blue organ. A magic core that would have to come from a large monster around level twenty at minimum . . . and a blue organ which looked suspiciously like a felix pluvia liver.

"Requesting Confirmation: Mission objectives have been achieved, correct?"

Cassius shook his head. He had no idea how this was possible. Maybe she just happened to find and purchase one, as unlikely and expensive as that would be. Or maybe she had some tricks that made this hunt easier for her. She did have that fancy armor of a type he had never seen before, so maybe she had an artifact or two.

In any case, this was not a business where he could demand details, so he had to accept things as they were presented to him.

"W-Well done. That was surprising."

Cassius went ahead and reached into his pocket, pulling out a bag of coins. He counted out the money and handed it to the knight.

There were ways to take advantage of knights, but complaining about the end product or trying to shortchange them on the payment was a good way to lose one's head. One should always act a bit more subtly with them. Besides, he had already shortchanged her on the proposal. A felix pluvia core and liver for five hundred Idrint was a steal, practically robbery. He was a bit surprised she had agreed to it right away.

Well, ideally, he wouldn't be dealing with this knight at all, but here she was.

"Here's your payment, Miss Knight."

She took the money. Cassius held back a curse as one of her eyes spun in its socket once again.

More and more, he had a bad feeling about this.

"Acknowledged. Query: Will third-party Cassius now provide assistance with this unit's primary directive?"

Cassius tilted his head for a moment, but from context, he figured she was asking if they were done with the monster hunting.

"Now, now, please be patient. This was just a single transaction, proof that you could deliver and that I could pay. But I don't think we can trust each other just yet. Why don't we run through a couple more of these?"

He held in the urge to gulp as her eye flickered. He hadn't dealt with all that many knights, but he was pretty sure eyes weren't supposed to glow. Still, his contact had confirmed she was, in fact, human. Maybe that eye was an artifact of some kind, or the sign of a special skill?

"Acknowledgement: This unit finds that reasoning acceptable for the moment. Please provide next mission details so this unit may analyze the efficacy of this arrangement."

"S-Sure, let me see . . ."

Cassius pulled out the map again. He *did*, in fact, have a target in mind, should this knight have gotten a lucky kill on the felix pluvia.

"Here it is. There's a giant toad in this swamp. It has some glands right under its skin which are in very high demand. Should be a bit above level twenty, I think. We'll pay you eight hundred Idrint for this one."

"Acknowledgment: Mission details recorded. Engaging search-and-destroy protocols."

The knight turned and walked out the door without another word. Cassius exhaled his breath and sat in his chair once he was sure she had left. Just then, one of the men in the other room came out the door. He was large, muscular, and scarred. And had wicked daggers strapped to his arms and legs.

"I don't like this, Cassius."

"You don't like anything, Spurius."

Spurius frowned, crossing his arms. "She knows how to get to and from here. She would need to be dealt with for that alone. I thought you said she wouldn't be coming back?"

"I don't like it any more than you, but this place *is* our greeting hall. It's not like she knows where our actual operations take place." Cassius shrugged.

Spurius scowled. "She knows too much, if you ask me. And she's dangerous. We need to deal with her, pronto."

Cassius shook his head. "It's *because* she's dangerous that we approached her. And that would be a reason *not* to deal with her personally, if you ask me."

"You saying we can't take her?" Spurius narrowed his eyes at Cassius.

Cassius waved his hand about.

"Nothing of the sort, but look at it this way: she's fulfilling our requests and not asking any questions." He pointed at the magic core and blue liver lying on the table. "And since she managed to not only survive, but succeed, we have an opportunity. An opportunity too good to waste. Besides, dangerous folk like that tend to get . . . *overconfident*, and solo monster hunting is very dangerous. She'll probably end up biting off more than she can chew soon enough. So why shouldn't we reap some profits until she does?"

Spurius grunted. "And if she doesn't? If she keeps coming back?"

Cassius shrugged.

"Then she probably *is* too dangerous for us to deal with, and we'll have to take that into account. But the last thing we should do right now is pick a fight with someone like that. At least, not until we know exactly what she's capable of."

As NSLICE-00P left the area, she reached out to Lilussees.

"Command: Friendly Lilussees, please provide intelligence report."

She watched as Lilussees yawned and turned over in the silk hammock she had set up in the attic of the house.

"Like, they're surprised you're alive or something. Guess they, like, thought the monster would get you."

"Analysis: This unit has kept her full capabilities confidential from third parties, as per standard procedure, so a miscalculation of this unit's capabilities is understandable."

"And, like, they don't like you knowing where they live or something. They, like, might try something if they think you're a threat, or something."

"Query: Is hostile intent confirmed?"

Lilussees tilted her head and put a leg on her mandibles.

"Um, like, not sure? They sound pretty sketchy, and they, like, definitely expect you to die to these monsters, though."

"Acknowledged. Command: Please continue observing and inform this unit if hostile intent is confirmed."

Lilussees yawned again.

"Okay, like, will do, boss."

And so, NSLICE-00P continued onward. Working with Cassius grew increasingly risky . . . but she had already predicted criminal connections from their initial meeting in the slums. For the moment, he was providing useful targets to acquire combat data on her newest upgrades and had not directly acted hostile toward her.

As long as she could use her sensors to observe the targets from a safe distance, she could analyze them herself and determine if the risk was reasonable. And as long as it was, receiving intel on subjects for live-fire experimentation was desirable. Cassius sending her off on dangerous missions with no regards to her chance of survival was not unexpected, as the two of them had no affiliation or obligation to one another. NSLICE-00P was running her own risk calculations for these operations, in any case.

But should Cassius have other plans, regarding her directly?

Well . . . NSLICE-00P had protocols detailing her response to that scenario.

41

Termination on Demand!

"Selkie hunters are named for the monsters they specialize in. The Mist Warriors hunt the Felix Pluvia, the Titan Archers hunt the Ursanus, and the Dread Swimmers are those who have faced a Dread Orca pod and survived. The reason for this is that every single monster is different, and even monsters living in the same area may require a completely different set of skills to tackle. The Selkies understand this, and the majority of them dedicate their lives to understanding their chosen quarry.

Even among the native Selkies, only the most skilled of their warriors can hunt more than one of these deadly foes."

—*The Peoples of the Frontiers*, Volume V: *Turannia and the North*, by traveling author and former Exploratore Placus Paesentius Statius.

NSLICE-00P arrived at the target area after a bit of leveling for the rat subordinates.

It was a swamp.

A damp, wet swamp with murky, muddy, smelly water up to an adult man's thighs. Which meant noticeably higher on the shorter teenage cyborg girl.

NSLICE-00P's scan of the area confirmed no signs of intelligent, humanoid life within her sensor range. As such, the risk of detection was minimal—a good thing when she was entering a combat zone, where keeping capabilities confidential was lower priority than maximizing effectiveness.

Activating her repulsors, she flew several feet above the swamp.

She was, of course, designed to remain fully functional even if submerged in muddy swamp water, but even the best seals weren't necessarily perfect, and she had records from the past of muddy water getting into her joints and reducing her efficiency. So there was no benefit to increasing risk factors to her components, particularly when she lacked access to maintenance facilities and spare parts.

The foreign system might be repairing her components to mint condition in real time, but she shouldn't overly rely on it if she could help it.

Not to mention that water decreased visibility; remaining physically present within it would present a risk of ambush. The fact that her sensors could, in fact, account for this depth of water, and her dungeon field provided a perfect awareness of the immediate vicinity was no excuse for negligence, after all. And so, NSLICE-00P's calculations determined flying above the water was simply the best way to maximize the probability of mission success and minimize risk.

Yes, this was simply the most efficient course of action.

NSLICE-00P flew through the target area, locking onto stronger mana signatures to investigate, and soon, she found it.

"Warning: Environmental toxins detected."

A large area of the swamp was hidden by a cloud of noxious green fog. Fortunately, NSLICE-00P was equipped with the latest in atmospheric filters and a fully sealed combat mode.

The skill Poison Resistance is now Level 2!

Her organic components suddenly reported damage, her HP ticking down slightly as well.

NSLICE-00P immediately boosted with her repulsors and shot back out of the fog. She then analyzed the data on her organic components.

It seemed the toxin was boosted by mana, and so a few particles had managed to slip past her filters. Likewise, the toxin had not only attacked her biological components but infected her HP barrier itself with a magical effect. Fortunately, her filters reduced the efficacy of the attack, and her HP seemed to be fighting back against the effect, likely due to the Poison Resistance skill. In addition, her implants included boosted blood filtration, so the biological component should be handled without issue, especially with the HP barrier repairing any actual damage.

Still, the cyborg saw no reason to let the situation continue.

"Engaging Cure protocol."

The healing mana surged through her body, purging the toxic particles remaining in her body, as well as clearing the mana infection in her HP.

The spell Cure is now Level 2!

With the toxins handled, NSLICE-00P turned her attention to the fog itself. She *could* simply travel through it, relying on her filters, implants, Poison Resistance skill, and Cure spell to counteract the toxin as it assaulted her.

But there was no reason to intentionally endure damage.

So NSLICE-00P rose high into the air above the swamp. She looked down and mapped out the area covered in the fog, searching for the strongest mana signature held within. And then, she formed her massive magic circle once again, triggering the Aurora Barrage.

Beams of light struck down into the swamp.

She stopped the barrage.

NSLICE-00P watched as the beams refracted and weakened as they traveled through the fog. The fog had some similar signatures to the felix pluvia's rain, which NSLICE-00P predicted as Water-attribute mana, along with the Poison attribute she could identify from her own spells. And its mana density was even stronger than that of the rain.

She could, in fact, cut through the fog if she fused the Aurora Barrage beams and boosted them with Spell Penetration and Supercharge, but she thought this could be a good opportunity to trial new capabilities.

Holding out her hands, her core lit up. Her organic components had chosen the Infused Mana Beam specifically for use with Light Beam . . . but the description implied she was not limited to that spell. So she converted her mana into various attributes and tried to fuse it into her energy channels.

A small red beam fired from her left hand while a tan one fired from her right. Then a purple beam and a green one, followed by a soft white beam and a bright yellow one. All the while, her robotic eye flickered, recording and analyzing the performance of each beam as it traveled into the fog. She rounded off the test with a simple unattributed beam, as well as a shot from one of her assault rifles.

The Fire-attribute beam showed no improvement on the standard one, performing slightly worse, even. It seemed to interact positively with the Poison attribute, but it was subsequently dampened by the Water-attribute mana in the air. The Earth-attribute beam showed some promise but was hard to infuse into Mana Beam to start with, and so started off weaker than the others. The Poison beam battled head-on with the poisoned fog, each trying to overpower the other directly. The Nature beam absorbed the Water mana, empowering itself, but was weakened by the poison. The Recovery beam was interesting; it reacted strongly with the Poison attribute, stripping it away, but did not remove the mana itself, and so made no impact on the fog besides the removal of some toxins.

The Light-attribute Mana Beam was cast without the Light Beam spell to provide a standardized comparison with the other attributes, which formed the control case along with the unattributed beam. Finally, the Arcane School of Magic utilized unattributed mana to begin with, and so provided no element to infuse into Mana Beam.

From her test, it seemed a combination of Nature and Recovery attributes might perform best, but she did not possess significant offensive capabilities within either of those schools of magic, so she would be limited to Infused Mana

Beams if she wanted to go that route, which ultimately would be less efficient than just clearing a path with the Equalizer.

But above all, the fog did nothing to stop the bullet from her assault rifle, which subsequently struck the swamp with a splash. So NSLICE-00P dropped the magic and opened fire at the strongest mana signature with her assault rifles and missiles.

A toad the size of a car leapt out of the fog into the air, puffing its cheeks. It pulled back its head and spat a huge glob of toxic acid at the floating cyborg, who boosted out of the way and kept up her barrage, magic circles forming around her and launching Light Beams and Magic Missiles as the giant toad left the safety of its fog.

The creature had impressive health reserves, but few ways to combat a foe who could attack from beyond the range of its toxic cloud. And it was not fast enough to escape the flying cyborg.

This contest could only end one way.

You have slain Giant Toad (Level 24)!
Gained 10 Personal XP, 3 Dungeon XP!

Cassius raised an eyebrow as he heard a knock on the door. He walked over and peeked through the hole once more.

He froze.

The knight was back. The knight he'd sent against a giant toad, a notorious swamp dweller surrounded by a dense, poisonous fog that disoriented the senses. A monster the Legion generally handled by bombarding the area with siege weapons until the tanky creature would run off to somewhere less inconvenient, or by sending in a team of extraordinarily high-leveled elites who could wipe out the beast quickly with a full team of Recovery mages to heal them back up once the job was done.

A monster that a lone knight whose level was in the twenties should not have been able to handle.

Cassius gulped as he welcomed the knight back inside.

Whipping vines cracked through the air as NSLICE-00P boosted out of the way. She faced a living willow tree, its hanging branches moving more like whips and limbs as they tried to grab the nimble cyborg.

Her bullets and missiles made little impact on the monster tree's solid bark, its HP regenerating any damage with ease. And the Aurora Barrage had failed entirely. The tree simply absorbed any Light mana, using it to heal itself.

Panels slid open on NSLICE-00P's wrists, and magic circles formed around her. Jets of flame surged out as she activated her flamethrowers and Fire Blast spells.

She heard something like a high-pitched shriek as the vines caught fire.

"Observation: Weakness detected. Adapting strategy."

A hail of wooden thorns soared through the air as the tree tried to drive her away. NSLICE-00P threw up Mana Barriers and took evasive action, but she was unable to close the distance. The tree itself was still out of range of her fire jets.

Which meant this was an opportunity to try something new.

NSLICE-00P activated the Spell Fusion skill. Selecting two spells, she observed with interest as the magic circles overlaid in the air.

A dense ball of fire shot from the circle, but the tree managed to move a vine in the way before the ball reached it.

And then the ball exploded into a large sphere of flame.

The skill Spell Fusion is now Level 2!
You have learned the spell Fireball!
The skill Fire Magic is now Level 7!

She had combined the Dense Magic Missile and Fire Blast spells, hoping to stuff the latter into a projectile with greater range. She did have the Fire Bolt spell already, but the other two were at much higher levels, and she wanted to observe the effects of the Spell Fusion skill.

As it turned out, the combination was not only compatible but basic enough to exist as its own spell. And the process gave NSLICE-00P another idea.

Rising high into the sky, outside the range of the monster tree's vines, she formed the Aurora Barrage magic circle once more. But this time, she overlaid it with the new Fireball magic circles, covering each of the individual Light Beam circles that existed within the larger spell.

And then she activated the Spell Fusion skill.

The magic circles flashed . . . and fused together.

You have learned the strategic spell Rain of Fire!
The skill Spell Fusion has leveled three times and is now Level 5!
The spell Fireball has leveled four times and is now Level 5!
The skill Fire Magic is now Level 8!
The skill Strategic Magic is now Level 5!

Balls of fire began to rain from the sky, burning trails following each as they plummeted.

And the monster tree was engulfed in fiery explosions.

An earsplitting screech filled the air as the entire tree went up in flames.

The strategic spell Rain of Fire is now Level 2!
You have slain Strangling Salicum (Level 25)!
Gained 10 Personal XP, 3 Dungeon XP!

Cassius was sweating as a chill crawled down his spine. The strangling salicum. Monster trees in general were tough targets; their bark became like armor, their sheer size provided strong vitality, and Nature-attribute plant monsters were well known for having powerful regeneration. They were especially strong against physical attacks like an armored knight *should* have relied on. And the strangling salicum had countless whiplike vines to attack with and entangle its target. A lone attacker should have found themselves assaulted from every direction, unable to advance, unable to escape.

A monster tree like that generally required a large group to deal with. Preferably a group who had access to either siege weapons or Strategic Magic.

A lone level twenty-six knight should *not* have had access to either of those, yet here she was, with a big magic core and the heartwood of a strangling salicum.

As he struggled to find another target on the map, Cassius screamed in his heart. By the Aesdes, who or what was he dealing with here?!

"Yay, like, free lunch."

The rats had grown significantly in level, so NSLICE-00P had swapped them out for the spiders on this trip. Besides, they were somewhat appropriate for this next target: a colony of monster wasps.

Lilussees clattered her mandibles as they approached the target area. "Um, like, I'm going to sit this one out, boss. Monster wasps are, like, my natural enemy or something."

Or not. But that was fine, her subordinates were only here for targets of opportunity, after all.

NSLICE-00P formed an Aurora Barrage spell as the air filled with wasps the size of large dogs.

As it turned out, monster wasps were not particularly strong against strategic light spells.

You have slain 30 Monster Wasp Drones, 10 Monster Wasp Warriors,
and 1 Monster Wasp Queen!
Compiling experience . . .
Gained 128 Personal XP, 123 Dungeon XP total!
You have leveled up 1 Personal level and 2 Dungeon levels!
Your Personal Level is now 28 and Dungeon Level 35!

Cassius was now openly sweating and trembling slightly. He had sent Spurius to tail the knight and figure out how she was doing all of this—only for her to leave him in the dust as she ran out of town. So, she came back after defeating a swarm of notorious monster wasps, and they still weren't sure how she was doing it.

"Observation: This unit and entity 'Cassius' have now conducted several successful transactions. This unit is requesting Cassius provide details on potential assistance with this unit's primary objective."

"T-That's . . . um . . ." This was dangerous. Very dangerous.

Cassius had enjoyed the profits from the knight's unexpected victories, but he didn't plan for her to come this far. "J-Just one more?"

Well, he had been trying monsters with lower levels than the knight to avoid suspicion, but she seemed to be capable beyond his wildest imagination for someone at level twenty-six. So he'd send her after something big this time, something beyond her current level.

That is, if he could convince her to go on any further missions.

"Negative Response: Returning to this location solely for monetary compensation has been determined as inefficient. Please provide this unit with detail on assistance with primary objective, or she will resume independent action."

"This is the last one! Turns out, there's an ursanus alpha that made their way down here; probably lost a territorial contest with the Tyrant of the Beasts. It's . . . probably pretty high level, so if you handle this, we can—Hey, what are you doing?!"

The knight's helmet slid on out of nowhere the moment Cassius said the monster's name. He held up his hands, ready to plead for his life.

"High-priority target identified. Request: Please provide target location."

Cassius blinked, then slowly shuffled over to the table. He kept one hand raised as he pointed on the map with his other, trembling as he did.

"Target location confirmed. Engaging termination protocols."

With that, the knight marched right out the door.

Cassius exhaled and then frowned. He didn't think she could take on an ursanus above her level, but he also couldn't see her just vanishing that conveniently anymore. So he figured he had better use this time to decide what to do . . .

42

Treachery

"Protocol 66: In the case of deception with hostile intent aimed at this unit or any friendly units, all parties responsible should be immediately terminated with extreme prejudice by all available units."

—NSLICE protocols, prior to revision following the April 1 incident.

Cassius was frowning and scanning monster reports in his base of operations when there was a rhythmic knock on the door. He quickly put away the reports and organized the chairs, then stood up straight as he opened the door.

A hooded and cloaked figure walked inside the building. They waved their hand and the rain leapt off their clothing, leaving them dry. The figure reached into their pocket and pulled out a small, metal insignia. Cassius did the same, and both flashed lightly.

The figure nodded and spoke, their voice magically obscured while a mask covered their face. "Is everything ready?"

Cassius nodded. "We're on schedule and ready to begin anytime."

"No complications?"

Cassius glanced away.

"Well . . ."

"What is it?"

Cassius sighed. "Some wandering knight has been hanging around town. Just a rookie level, around the midtwenties, but I didn't want any potential complications. I've been trying to get rid of her, but she's proven remarkably capable."

The figure stared at Cassius from under their hood. "You've handled a knight before, so what's the matter? You sure you're not just drawing things out, trying to earn some extra profit off her first?"

Cassius rubbed his chin.

"Well, that much is true, but it's more than that. She's managed to take down every monster I've sent her after. The dangerous ones you're not supposed to take on solo. She outran the tails too, so I have no idea how she's pulling it off."

The hooded figure rubbed their chin. "Will it be a problem?"

Cassius shook his head. "I don't think so; she doesn't have any idea what's going on here and doesn't seem to care either way. She's clearly not from around here, and she's not part of any Imperial order, from what I can tell."

The figure stared for a moment more.

"That's a concerning amount of assumptions for someone of the abilities displayed, Cassius. Where is she now?"

"Out hunting an ursanus several levels higher than herself."

The figure nodded. "Well, that should be acceptable, then." They reached into their cloak and pulled out a spherical package and a knife, both wrapped in clothes. They handed the items to Cassius. "Remember, as close to the keep as you can get. The comitatenses may be gone, but even limitanei can hold for a long time with the right fortifications."

Cassius nodded as he took the package.

"I know. I'll see to it."

"And the wandering knight?"

"I'll have Spurius and the others wait for her on the road. Even if they don't stop her, that should be enough to keep her occupied while I set things up."

The figure nodded.

"Make sure of it, Cassius. I don't need to remind you what's at stake here."

Cassius's eyes narrowed. "It's worth more to me than you, so don't worry. I'll make this happen."

They nodded and turned to leave, but paused right before they reached the door. "By the way, have you heard from Sabucia? We've been waiting on her latest report."

Cassius rubbed his chin.

"Sabucia, huh? Haven't heard from her in a bit."

"Unfortunate. Well, no matter. We're ready to begin in any case."

And with that, they left the building. Cassius stared at the package in his hand and grinned.

Finally. His ticket out of this dump. To make more of his life than trading in scraps.

"Spurius?"

The big man grunted and walked out of the side room, crossing his arms.

"Go and prepare a welcome for our little wandering knight on the road."

Spurius nodded. "It's about bloody time."

Cassius took his package to a private room in the back as Spurius gathered his thugs.

Well, with all that had happened, Cassius was fairly certain the knight could handle Spurius and his goons, provided the ursanus didn't kill her first. An ursanus wasn't a duel a knight should take at an even level, much less a level deficit, though at this point, Cassius couldn't imagine this strange knight just dying like that.

But it wouldn't matter. Spurius just needed to distract her for a bit, buy him some time.

And then?

Cassius grinned.

This province would belong to him.

Rattingtale rubbed his paws as he observed the traitorous man-thing from the rafters.

This was it.

The man-thing was planning to betray the boss-queen.

As expected, really. The Great-High King over all the land had seen this coming from the moment they met the suspicious man-thing. Man-things could not be trusted, and this one least of all. The boss-queen was a fool for interacting with the treacherous man-thing, in his not so humble opinion.

As was she for trusting him, of all people, to report the treachery.

It was all too easy. Sure, she had commanded him to keep watch and report to her, but she hadn't specified that he had to do so right this second! He didn't have a way to contact her from here, in any case, so all he had to do was delay the report to the regularly scheduled time, and the man-things would handle her for him! The wretched spider-thing too! And even if that failed, this man-thing was planning something big!

The other rats stared at Rattingtale as he chittered, their eyes narrowing.

But then, Rattingtale quieted down and rubbed his whiskers.

Still, he needed to think this through. The Great-High King over all the land couldn't act hastily, after all.

He thought of the man-things preparing to ambush the boss-queen, how he had watched them laze about and struggle to lift a keg that one time. His ears fell back against his head.

Yeah. There was zero chance they would defeat the boss-queen.

Zero chance she would even be injured, if Rattingtale thought it through. She would annihilate them all in an instant. And then, she would wonder why Rattingtale hadn't tried to warn her.

Sure, this other man-thing may have been planning something, but Rattingtale didn't know what it was. And after all he had seen, he somehow couldn't imagine this man-thing doing anything that would actually threaten the boss-queen.

He took a deep breath and turned to the rats.

"You three, go find the boss-queen and warn-inform her of the ambush, yes-yes. You two stay and watch-observe this man-thing. So commands the Great-High King over all the land, yes-yes."

The rats smiled and nodded. "Yes-yes!"

And with that, they scattered, heading to their tasks. Rattingtale took another deep breath.

Well, he would keep playing the loyal subordinate for the time being. Earn the boss-queen's trust, make sure she would never imagine him turning on her.

It was fine. The Great-High King over all the land was also known for his inexhaustible patience. He would not settle for a half-hearted opportunity such as this. Only when the opportunity was at its absolute ripest would he deign to strike.

The three rats ran through the slums, as fast as their paws could carry them. The wise-mighty boss-queen was counting on them, and they would not let her down. They stirred up their mana and filled their paws with it, willing themselves to move even that much more quickly.

You have learned the skill Dash!

And the sacred records rewarded them for their efforts, declaring that their path was right.

As they turned into an empty alley, the lead rat's eyes widened, and he suddenly stopped, activating the new skill to Dash backward. The other two rats stopped in surprise.

A dark shadow fell from above, landing on the ground with a crash, right where the lead rat had been about to step.

Something rose up from the ground, snarling at the failed ambush. It stood high above the rats, staring at them with wicked eyes. It flexed claws as sharp as daggers, adjusting its rippling muscles under the sleek fur upon its body. Fading scars spoke of a lifetime of battle . . . and killing. It let out a low rumble as it adjusted itself, its muscles held taut like the string of a bow, ready to unleash death at a moment's notice.

The cat had returned.

The lead rat, the one whom the boss-queen had personally saved, narrowed his eyes at his hated foe. He stood upon his hind legs, rising to his full height.

"Go-run. I will hold the monster-thing back."

The other rats turned to him in shock.

"The boss-queen needs us; we must not be stopped-delayed. You must go and warn-inform the boss-queen of the danger, yes-yes!"

The other rats looked down at the ground.

"But . . ."

The lead rat leaped at his hated foe. He activated the Dash skill just as the cat was about to pounce, sinking his fangs into the cat's hind leg. He leapt back as the cat roared and spun around, swiping at him.

"Fly-flee, you fool-things, yes-yes!"

The other two rats glanced at each other. They narrowed their eyes, turning back to the lead rat and nodding once. "Yes-yes!"

And then they ran off, scurrying around the cat to continue down the alleyway. The beast turned to swipe at them, but the lead rat Dashed as he jumped, curling his body into a ball and slamming into the cat's nose. The cat cried out and took a step back as the lead rat chittered while he rose on his hind legs once more.

"Our fight will not go-end like last time, you wretched cat-thing! I am a chosen servant of the wise-mighty boss-queen! Saved-preserved by her for great-glorious deeds, yes-yes! Personally raised-trained by her own hand! I will stop-defeat you here, even if it costs me my life, yes-yes!"

The cat growled at him, crouching down and adjusting its stance. The lead rat lowered to all fours, digging into the dirt.

They leapt into the air at the same time, claws and fangs reaching for one another.

43

The Servants of the Wise-Powerful Boss-Queen

"Any animal may become a monster following sufficient absorption of mana. Though kind treatment may lead it to become a magic creature instead. Unfortunately, mana tends to concentrate wherever Enlightened species gather together. This is why it is crucial to maintain a population of tamed and well-treated predators in all settlements to control prey species, as well as to alert authorities when a monster has been born within the city walls. For this purpose, the cat has proven to be ideal."

—*Modern Urban Planning*, by Imperial Architecti Sextus Lafrenius Famia

The rat monster was panting for breath. Every ounce of his body ached. Blood dripped from a scratch across his face.

His opponent had some bites and scratches, but it was overall no worse for wear. It pounced at him once more.

Gritting his teeth, he willed his legs to move, barely diving out of the way. He felt searing heat on his back as the cat's claw grazed him. His mana reserves were running low at this point, the Dash skill unavailable to him now, and his HP was dipping with every pass.

It seemed like he was going to die.

But he smiled to himself. Perhaps he would die, but he had not failed. The others had long since continued on their way. The wise-mighty boss-queen would receive her warning.

He closed his eyes as he fell to the ground.

Yes, he was content with this. He had done his duty.

It was at that moment that his heart began to pound. His stomach boiled. His eyes shot open.

Was he? Was he truly content with this?

He, whom the boss-queen had saved by her own hand?

He, who had been raised by her personally, fed kills and boons before he had achieved anything at all?

Was this enough to repay her? Was this the great and glorious deed she must have had in mind for him?

He gritted his teeth.

No.

This was not enough. He was not done.

He pushed off the ground with all his might, rising on his trembling legs.

Turning around, he glared at his foe, even as blood dripped into one of his eyes. The cat was now taking its time, leisurely adjusting its stance. He could tell from the look in its eyes, it was no longer fighting to kill him. It believed it had already won.

It was *toying* with him.

It would regret that.

The rat monster then broke his vow, committing a taboo no loyal dungeon monster ever would—he went into the sacred records unprompted, without permission. And he spent the sacred boons granted to him by the wise-mighty boss-queen.

A loyal dungeon monster would not have done so; would have waited for their master to guide their growth. A disloyal dungeon monster would have been commanded not to in the first place. Unspent boons and gathered experience would be returned to the dungeon upon a monster's death, after all, allowing the next wave of monsters to grow that much stronger, so in general, all such decisions were made by the master.

The rat apologized to the boss-queen in his heart. But she had not commanded him otherwise, and she had taken a personal hand in his survival and growth. It was clear that she had plans for him, so he could not allow himself to die here, away from her presence, without even a single victory.

She trusted in him, had taken a gamble on him.

And he would answer that trust.

He kept it simple and increased his basic attributes. He mostly boosted his Speed, with a little bit into Strength. His mana reserves were nearly drained, so new skills wouldn't help him. But if he were able to dodge his foe's blows without relying on Dash, then perhaps he could do something.

The cat strode forward and swiped at him with its paw.

He took a step back, stumbling to the ground. But the swipe missed.

The cat swiped with its other paw.

Again, he stepped back, this time keeping his feet under him. The swipe missed again.

The cat narrowed its eyes. Stepping back, it adjusted its stance and then pounced once more, soaring through the air.

But this time was different.

A boost in Speed from the sacred boons did not merely strengthen the muscles or the speed of movement. His reactions quickened, his neurons fired faster, every aspect of his body accelerated.

He not only moved faster.

He saw faster. Thought faster.

Reacted faster.

So the cat seemed to move in slow motion as the rat dove underneath it, rolling across the ground before he picked himself up, shaking his head and turning.

The cat was looking around, confused as to where its prey had gone.

The rat smiled.

Then he jumped forward and sank his teeth into the cat's flank.

This cat cried and leapt forward, but the rat hung on, its fangs digging deeper with the cat's motion. Finally, the cat smashed itself against one of the walls of the alleyway, and the rat was forced to let go and leap away.

The cat swiped at him, but he rolled back out of the way.

The cat pounced at him once more, but he stepped to the side, biting at the offending paw. The cat yelped and leaped back, but the rat followed, landing on the cat's back, who cried as he sank his fangs into it, rolling across the ground once more and tossing him off. But this time, he angled himself in the air and landed on his feet.

The cat adjusted its stance, narrowing its eyes at him. It still had the eyes of a predator viewing its prey, gathering its strength for another assault.

But the rat could see.

Hidden in those narrowed eyes, behind the predatory gaze, was something else.

Hesitation. Uncertainty.

Fear.

The rat smiled and chittered as he crouched down, digging into the dirt.

The cat was starting to learn. And the rat would teach it.

The servants of the wise-mighty boss-queen were not helpless prey.

Two laborers walked down the street, carrying planks of wood on their shoulders. One of them paused for a second.

"Oi, Fearghas, check that out!"

Fearghas sighed. "Get to work, Drusus. That's just the old stray—" He froze.

The old stray was running out of the alley, dripping blood from a bunch of minor wounds.

And in the alleyway was a rat standing on its hind legs. It thrust its head up into the sky and squeaked with all its might.

Fearghas swore.

"Just great; we got monster rats again. I thought those bloody Exploratores said they got the last of them."

Drusus tilted his head. "Maybe a new one got in?"

Fearghas sighed. "That would mean the monster wards are failing, if no one caught it on the way in. Or the quartermaster is skimping on inspections again."

"I mean, how else are we going to get some real drinks in here?"

He sighed once more. "Well, whatever. Let's get a move on and hope those bloody monster hunters do their bloody jobs."

Meanwhile, NSLICE-00P was floating in the sky above a nearby forest. She looked down through the canopy as she flew. She soon located her target.

A large bear covered in spikes and a turtle's shell.

"Target located. Deploying termination measures."

A massive magic circle formed as NSLICE-00P activated her Aurora Barrage spell. She then thrust as much mana as she could into it, and the magic circle began to glow and hum as she Supercharged it to the limit.

"Engaging target."

Lifting her hand, she fired the Equalizer with as much power as she could spare.

The ursanus winced as a rainbow beam struck it and stripped part of its HP. It looked up into the sky and roared . . . and then paused as it saw the huge magic circle shimmering through the canopy.

Patterns of light shifted through the sky as countless beams fired, all targeting a single point slightly in front of the circle. The beams all struck each other, forming a growing sphere of light at the collision point.

Then, a single, massive beam lit up the forest, setting the nearby trees ablaze. A loud humming could be heard for miles around as flashing lights reflected off the clouds above. Birds and critters scattered through the bushes as they fled the area.

NSLICE-00P looked down at the smoldering hole in the canopy.

A smoking ursanus lay motionless on the ground, surrounded by a circle of scorched dirt. It had a massive hole in the center of its body, right where the Equalizer had struck.

You have slain Ursanus Alpha (Level 36)!
Gained 22 Personal XP, 13 Dungeon XP!

"Priority target terminated. Operational area secure."

With that, NSLICE-00P slowly made her way back. She had prioritized taking down the ursanus, and so had not upgraded her subordinates on the way there. As such, she attempted to do so now.

Unfortunately, it seemed there was a strange lack of targets in the immediate vicinity.

"Status Update: No targets located. Expanding search area."

Lilussees yawned and turned over on a hammock inside her room, glancing at the live feed.

"Um, yeah. Like, I wouldn't stick around either if I saw attacks like that getting thrown around."

The spiderlings also nodded as they maintained the webs in Lilussees's room.

"Update: Signatures located on approach. Signatures identified as friendlies."

Lilussees tilted her head. "That has to be, like, the snacks or something? Like, I wonder why they're out of town."

"Statement: This unit has no data on potential causes. Moving to investigate."

NSLICE-00P began running forward, and soon came within range of the friendlies. Two of her monster rats were running toward her with all their might, breathing heavily as they pushed forth. They were drained of mana, and even their HP started to tick down as they squeezed out another Dash. NSLICE-00P used her repulsors to boost forward, arriving in front of them.

"Query: Urgency detected among friendlies. Requesting situation update."

The rats' eyes went wide as they saw her arrive. They collapsed to the ground, panting for breath, but even as NSLICE-00P moved to cast a Heal spell, they spoke to her in raspy voices.

"The man-thing is planning-plotting to betray you, boss-queen! They are going to ambush-assault you on the way back!"

NSLICE-00P's robotic eye turned red as she healed the exhausted rats.

"Gratitude: This unit thanks the friendlies for the intelligence report. Hostile intent has been confirmed. Engaging termination protocols."

44

Expeditious Return

"Friendly units under threat of termination are to be relieved and recovered with all due haste. It is a critical directive that no friendly remains fall into the hands of the enemy, much less an intact unit. All efforts should be exerted to recover the threatened unit intact and, failing that, to ensure the friendly's remains are fully destroyed. The responsible parties should be terminated if at all possible."

—NSLICE protocols

NSLICE-00P picked up the rat monsters, intending to put them into the Monster Hangar, but there was a problem. They could barely move with their exhaustion, and NSLICE-00P wasn't sure if she could physically reach into it, so she picked them up in her arms and started walking until they had recovered enough to move themselves.

Taking a moment to regain their breath, they spoke again. "Boss-queen, please hurry! The treacherous man-thing is plotting something!"

"Acknowledged."

"And . . . our comrade died to bring you this information."

NSLICE-00P froze.

"Requesting Elaboration."

The rats looked down, ears pressed against their heads.

"The vicious cat-thing ambushed-assaulted us on our way here. Our comrade . . . stayed-stood to buy us time."

NSLICE-00P's robotic eye flickered, her heart rate and cortisol levels increasing. She immediately analyzed her Dungeon Management.

All her subordinates were still listed, and the vague mana link to her core still existed.

"Correction: Foreign system records indicate all friendlies are still alive."

The rat monsters' eyes widened. "T-Then please hurry, wise-mighty boss-queen! The vicious cat-thing will kill-slay him, yes-yes!"

Her analysis agreed with that of her subordinates; even though the rats had been upgraded, she could not confirm if they could successfully defeat their natural predator. There was a very real risk the friendly unit would be terminated, especially if left to face the predator alone.

So she upgraded the time urgency of the current mission past even the need for confidentiality.

"Request: Are subordinates capable of moving to the hangar?"

The rats nodded and climbed over to go inside. Once they did, panels slid open on NSLICE-00P's hands, feet, and back. Bright lights glowed, and the air hummed as her repulsors fired, lifting her about a foot off the ground.

"Status Update: Friendlies confirmed as engaged and at risk of termination. Updating transit protocols for increased mission urgency."

And then she leaned forward and vanished, soaring just above the ground at her maximum speed. She activated her sensors to the limit, scouting out the areas ahead for obstacles and plotting out her path in advance. As she did, she detected several armed humans on the road ahead, hiding in the trees around in an ambush formation. She zoomed in on them and sent the footage to the Monster Hangar.

"Requesting Confirmation: Are these targets the hostiles?"

"Yes-yes, that's them!"

"Acknowledged. Engaging termination protocols."

As NSLICE-00P flew forward, panels opened on her shoulders. She targeted and locked onto each of the figures, then launched a barrage of missiles as she flew past them.

They barely had time to realize something had passed them by when they were engulfed in explosions.

You have slain four Humans (Levels 12, 11, 14, and 25)!
Gained 17 Personal XP, 12 Dungeon XP!

NSLICE-00P didn't even spare them a glance as she rushed toward the city.

Cassius made his way into the sewers below the city, a network of tunnels reinforced with stone, with holes in the roof wherever the citizens above needed to dump things down. In the center of each tunnel was a trough filled to the brim with sewer slimes. Grating made of enchanted metal covered over them, keeping the slimes within. On the side of the tunnels were small stone ledges to allow travel through the sewers.

Officially, the sewer slimes were specifically bred not to be hostile to other living things, but there were very few individuals willing to test that.

Cassius ran along one of these stone ledges with a pack slung over his shoulders, not hesitating even a second as he turned the corners.

And slightly behind him, three rats followed.

Rattingtale had debated long and hard whether to follow the treacherous man-thing himself or simply wait in the man-thing's hideout while his subjects took care of it. But he didn't know exactly what the man-thing was planning, only that it was something big, something the man-thing was confident could handle the boss-queen.

Which meant there might be opportunity for a Great-High King looking to restore his realm.

So against his better judgment, he'd tagged along, following the man-thing at a safe distance. His subjects' loyalty was currently in question, so he needed to be present if he wanted to take advantage of any opportunities.

And so, he continuously sniffed the air and glanced around-behind him as they advanced. Who knew what sort of vicious monster-things might be lurking here?

Rattingtale jumped as something crashed behind him. He spun around, ready to toss his subordinates at the problem, but it turned out it was just a loose rock clattering to the ground.

Rattingtale shook his head. If only that strange boss-queen would hurry it up so he could return to the nice, safe palace-castle he had built there . . .

He froze, then shook his head.

O-Of course the Great-High King over all the land was not afraid of a mere man-thing sewer! He didn't need any tyrants usurping his rightful place! This was all part of his plan! In fact, he wanted her *not* to come so he could take advantage of whatever this other man-thing had planned! He was not at all regretting being out and exposed to danger without an extremely powerful benefactor in the area!

"Boss-leader, the man-thing is getting away."

Rattingtale struck the rat monster on the head.

"Then what are you waiting-lazing around for?! Hurry after it, yes-yes!"

The rat monsters sighed but obeyed the order.

And so, the three rats followed after Cassius.

Landing on the ground at the final hill before the city, NSLICE-00P ran down the slope as quickly as she could, barely flashing her status parchment to the guards before she ran off. The guards glanced at one another, then shrugged and went back to their jobs.

The cyborg analyzed the mana bonds of her subordinates inside the city. Three of the rats were moving as a group at a downward angle, possibly underground. One other was alone on the surface, in the slums area. She locked onto the lone rat and rushed forward, plotting out the quickest route she could.

Townsfolk swore as she passed them by, but they moved out of the way on their own.

No one got in the way of an armored knight at a full run, especially an eccentric one like NSLICE-00P. And so, she made good time as she made her way into the final alleyway.

With her panels opened up, missiles at the ready, she transformed one hand into a machine gun while the other glowed as she charged up her energy channels. She immediately activated all her sensors as she rounded the corner.

"Wise-mighty boss-queen?!"

"Scanning for hostiles . . . No hostiles detected in the vicinity."

She kept her combat mode active as she approached the rat. He was leaning against the wall of the alley, breathing heavily, but still alive. His blood had clotted, and he was no longer bleeding out of his wounds, though one of his eyes was still closed shut due to a scratch across his face. His HP was damaged but stable.

She moved to heal him, restoring his lost HP. "Requesting Status Update."

The rat nodded.

"I drove off the vicious cat-thing. I showed it your might-power and the might-power of your servants, yes-yes." Then he looked down, pressing his ears flat. "I . . . am sorry, wise-mighty boss-queen. I spent the boons you bestowed upon me without your permission. Please, take the life of this disloyal servant and recover your boons."

"Requesting Clarification: Friendly unit did not apply upgrades prior to this, and so autonomously did so midengagement? And was able to win the engagement as a result?"

The rat slowly nodded his head. "I am sorry, but the vicious cat-thing escaped me. I was not even able to claim it for you, wise-mighty boss-queen."

NSLICE-00P's robotic eye flickered. Friendlies Excellion Formantus Rattingtale the Third and Lilussees had grown in capability when their level had grown, so she had assumed the same would be true for her subordinates. She had not realized they were waiting on her permission to apply the upgrades, and so were still vulnerable to ambush by local predators.

"Revelation: This unit was not aware friendly units were waiting on authorization to apply upgrades. This unit acknowledges the efficacy of the friendly unit to do so midengagement. Updating subordinate upgrade protocols with additional intel on necessary authorizations."

The rat monster looked up at her with wide eyes.

"You are not . . . angry-displeased with this servant's disloyalty?"

"Analysis: The friendly unit followed effective self-preservation and mission-completion protocols, and was able to accomplish both despite an oversight in this unit's subordinate upgrade routines. This unit cannot identify any individual inefficiencies in the friendly unit's performance in this case."

The rat monster just stared at her for a moment.

"Y-Yes, thank you, wise-mighty boss-queen! This unworthy servant vows-swears he will live up to your expectations and trust, yes-yes!"

"Acknowledged. Hostile engagement confirmed as concluded. Area determined as clear of hostiles. Command: Please return to the hangar for transit."

"Yes-yes, wise-mighty boss-queen!"

Once the rat monster had returned to the hangar, NSLICE-00P locked onto the other signatures. As they were moving underground, she activated her ground-penetrating radar, mapping out the sewers below town. With that, she calculated the most efficient path and started running once again.

Fortunately, with her Earth Magic, she did not need to follow them through the winding sewers. She could simply travel over the surface and then dig an entrance once she arrived at the target area. And so, she cut across town, heading toward the Legion fortress rising above the city.

Her helmet was fully engaged, both her robotic eye and the eyepiece covering her organic one glowing red. With all friendlies extracted or else accounted for, she could focus all her efforts on her last short-term objective.

Terminating the hostile who had created this scenario.

45

Dark Plots Fulfilled

"After a thorough investigation, I find these so-called cults of mana to be little more than a distraction. The amount of resources it takes to summon even a small monster from the Realms of Mana is prohibitive for the Imperial Academy of Magic, much less a clandestine group attempting to avoid detection. As such, I find their stated goals to be absurd, and the means of achieving such things impossible. Therefore, it is unlikely the cults of mana could cause any serious mischief, and the allocation of any further resources to this investigation a waste."

—Magister Exploratore Stertinia Eugena, before her disappearance under dubious circumstances.

As NSLICE-00P ran through town, a massive energy signature appeared on her sensors. Mana readings grew off the charts right next to her destination, while the readings from her conventional sensors started to distort.

She put a bit more power into her boosters, shooting through the city.

Eventually, she arrived just outside the walls of the keep, on a side away from the gates. She was directly above her rat subordinates, with the mana signature slightly ahead and under the walls. She filled the ground below her with Earth-attribute mana and pushed it out of the way, opening an entrance for her to jump through.

As she floated down on her repulsors into the sewers, Rattingtale and the other two rats were waiting on a ledge to the side, crouched down behind a rock with their ears flat on their heads.

"Urgent Request: Please provide situation update."

Rattingtale looked up and jumped.

"Boss-queen! Finally!"

He scrambled off the ledge and jumped onto NSLICE-00P's foot, climbing up her form to take shelter inside the Monster Hangar. The other two monsters rushed to follow suit. Lilussees and the others were already sitting in the common area.

"Heh, happy to see us, snack? You were, like, that scared or something?"

"S-Shut up, wretched spider-thing! This is dangerous-risky, yes-yes! That treacherous man-thing conducted-performed some kind of ritual, yes-yes! This is the result-outcome!"

"Acknowledged. Investigating nonstandard phenomena."

Just up ahead there was a hole in the wall of the sewers leading to an area which had been recently dug out. The massive mana signatures were coming from there, throwing waves of mana out at random intervals. In fact . . .

Level up! Dungeon Level is now 36!

Mana was surging into her core. Her dungeon field was attempting to absorb as much of the mana as it could, but there was still enough to raise the ambient levels of mana. The air was hissing and crackling, and flashes of light could be seen from the entrance to the dug-out area. Her sensors were having trouble penetrating the place, as if the air itself was being distorted along with the electromagnetic radiation passing through it.

"Query: Hostile Cassius is located in that area?"

"Y-Yes, I think-believe."

"Acknowledged. Moving to engage."

Rattingtale jumped.

"W-What?! Stupid man-thing, you must run-flee!"

Lilussees nodded. "I hate to, like, agree with the snack, but that's, like, a mana storm or something. Those are, like, pretty dangerous or something."

Just as the monsters were warning her, the mana surge intensified. Stones and pebbles began rising all around the cyborg, and the sewer slimes started shuffling away from the area, even as the ambient mana caused them to rapidly split and multiply. Arcs of lightning began crisscrossing the walls of the sewers close to the target.

Level up! Dungeon Level is now 37!

"Acknowledgement: Updating risk level due to nonstandard environmental phenomena. Deploying countermeasures."

NSLICE-00P began forming Mana Barriers around herself when, suddenly, the surging mana died down, along with the hissing sounds. The mana didn't vanish; rather, it began surging back toward its point of origin, concentrating into an extremely dense signature.

There was a loud noise like a crack of thunder, and a final surge of mana. A gust of wind impacted NSLICE-00P's barrier, and then, all the strange readings stopped.

In fact, all her sensor readings into the area ahead stopped, returning no data in a very familiar fashion. The area itself had twisted and warped, turning into a stone arch. The arch's entryway was pitch black, and nothing could be seen on the other side of it.

But NSLICE-00P didn't need her sensors to determine what she was looking at. She already knew exactly what it was.

Rattingtale and Lilussees's eyes widened.

"I-It's . . . a dungeon."

"A human made a dungeon? That's, like . . . is that supposed to be possible?"

"How should I know, wretched spider-thing?"

"Weren't you, like, 'the Great-Super King' or something? Don't you know, like, everything?"

"S-Shut up! And it's Great-High King, yes-yes!"

And how did NSLICE-00P respond to this turn of events?

"Status Update: Situation determined. Risk factor decreased. Engaging dungeon termination protocols."

She went into full combat mode and marched straight inside.

Cassius stood in a wide, circular room made of stone. It was empty save for a single pedestal at the center holding the largest mana core Cassius had ever seen, glowing with bright blue light.

He grinned.

He had succeeded.

Inducing a localized, artificial mana storm was perhaps the riskiest thing he had ever done, but everything had gone as his benefactors had told him. A new dungeon core had been born on the spot to absorb the mana storm, lest it tear through the fabric of reality itself. And as this storm had been artificially produced, the dungeon core was rushed, incomplete.

Which meant it had no master to defend it.

Cassius pulled out a black knife with red magic circles engraved all over it. Closing his eyes, he gritted his teeth as he cut his own palm with it. The blood absorbed into the knife, its magic formations now glowing with red light, and then, he stabbed into the dungeon core.

Murky, black-red fog poured into the core, its blue light beginning to turn red. Suddenly, mana exploded out from it, striking Cassius and knocking him to the ground. He cried out as fire filled every inch of his body, his mind feeling as if it had been dipped in molten magma.

Suddenly, it stopped.

He held his aching head and groaned, stumbling to his feet. As he rose, he felt his perception expand, encompassing the entire room. Mana now surged through his veins . . . and back into the blood-red core.

He had done it. He was the master.

He had become the immortal ruler of a dungeon, who could go without food or rest, and who was free from the ravages of time. Who could control all of reality within their domain—practically a god.

He had access to theoretically infinite land, infinite wealth, and infinite resources.

And of course, an infinite army of vicious monsters chained to his will.

He grinned.

With the huge surge of mana from the storm, he had more than enough to get started. And the binding ritual had done more than make him the master; the core itself had been corrupted, modified to draw reckless amounts of mana from the Source compared to the average dungeon. As a result, he could produce a vast army almost instantaneously.

And he was directly underneath the keep of Castra Turannia, the toughest Legion fortress in the entire province. Past all their mighty defenses.

He would pour out his armies of monsters from right under their feet, bypassing the walls and defenses entirely. The comitatenses, the real fighters, were already gone, and would not return until Magister Caelinus was done with them. Without the walls, the limitanei would fall like stalks of grain before the reaper's scythe.

And once Castra Turannia was his, the entire province would have no choice but to bow at his feet. He would have all of Turannia to feed the power of his dungeon, such that by the time the Empire returned, he would be invincible.

He would form a new Demon Lord's Realm, just like in the days of old. Before the bright times, before the Empire. And then . . . well, his dungeon would only grow stronger and stronger at speeds no normal dungeon could match. Turannia would only be the beginning. If the Empire did not stop him now . . . soon, they would not be able to stop him at all.

It was then that he received a message from his core.

There was . . . an intruder?

Cassius quickly sorted through his new powers. Fortunately, the process of binding himself to the core had jammed some instinctual knowledge into his head, so he knew what to do. He jumped into the Rooms section and placed a huge stone labyrinth between the entrance and the core room. And just in the nick of time, as someone had just walked through the entrance hall.

Cassius blinked.

It was . . . that strange knight?

Cassius blinked again. That shouldn't be possible.

Because first of all, that meant she had survived the ursanus alpha, which should have been a higher level than her. Which . . . to be fair, was actually possible. Ursanus alphas were living bundles of raw power, but they *were* fairly straightforward, and not the nimblest of monsters. If she'd evaded the countless vines of the strangling salicum, she could escape from an ursanus alpha. Still, though, he had expected she would at least take some time attempting to fight the monster before shaking it off her tail on the retreat.

Of course, the idea that she had defeated the ursanus did not cross Cassius's mind. Even if it had, he would have assumed it would have been a long, drawn-out affair requiring intense preparations and the use of a countless number of traps to wear the beast down. It was not possible for a lower-leveled human like herself to simply overpower such a monster.

And then, she had gotten past Spurius and his men. Cassius . . . expected that, to be fair. But this wasn't Spurius's first ambush; not even the highest-level target he had gone after. So Cassius had expected Spurius to at least slow her down and give her a wound for the trouble.

For her to be right here, right now, implied that she'd spent barely any time at all on either the ursanus or on Spurius.

But that wasn't the worst of it. That wasn't what sent a chill down Cassius's spine.

No, the worst of it was the fact that she was here, in this exact place. She had followed him to a location he had never shared with her. So either she knew about this place ahead of time . . . or she had a way of tracking him which he hadn't noticed.

Cassius shook his head and cleared his thoughts. It didn't matter now, even with all that she was too late. He had executed his plan and succeeded. Now he was a dungeon master, and this was his domain. Everything that occurred here now occurred according to his will. This strange knight could not overturn that, no matter how unexpectedly capable she might be. In fact . . .

Cassius grinned.

This would be a good test, actually. He would test the capabilities of his dungeon and figure out this knight's tricks all at the same time. It didn't matter how unexpectedly powerful she was; it didn't matter how many powerful monsters she had taken down. Because this was a dungeon.

So even if she could handle every monster he could summon, he could keep throwing monsters at her for as long as it took. If she took down one, he would send a dozen. If she took down a dozen, he would send a hundred. If she took down a hundred, he would send a thousand. Even if she could kill them all without injury, she would make no progress, would screech to a halt against a wall of flesh. No matter how many monsters it took, she would eventually run dry. She would run out of mana; the dungeon would not.

Cassius's grin grew wider.

After all, even the Legion wouldn't dare to fight a dungeon in a war of attrition.

46

Team Termination

"What happens when two dungeons go to war, you ask? Well, dungeon wars are a rare occurrence these days, thank the Aesdes and thank the Legion, but we do have some records. And all those records paint a consistent picture.

Dungeon wars are hell, and not for the dungeons.

Consider the situation: you have two factions, both ruled solely by a single entity, with endlessly spawning armies of monsters who have decided to wipe the other out. So what happens when those endless armies of monsters collide? If one is woefully inferior to the other, they are wiped out before they can spawn again, and that's the end of it.

It's when they're anything close to equal that the trouble starts.

If the two sides are even remotely equivalent . . . the battle becomes an infinite stalemate. Neither side will ever run out of troops, and neither side has to worry about a weary populace or traitorous political rivals or having enough laborers left for the harvest. No, they can keep it up forever, so the stalemate will never end unless one side can force it, or else an outside force intervenes.

But if the two sides are equal . . . they can't force it.

Dungeons have an incredible defender's advantage. They are literally designed as labyrinths of death, meant to protect their core at all costs. Sure, a small group of dungeon divers might be able to go in and out relatively safely, but an army? An army gets split up, funneled through narrow corridors, and defeated in detail. It doesn't matter if it's an army of intelligent species or an army of mindless monsters—the dungeon's defenses will tear them apart all the same, allowing even an inferior dungeon's forces to hold the line unless they are truly and utterly outclassed.

And every casualty improves the strength of the opposing army, so taking more losses by fighting on the enemy's home turf is simply unacceptable.

As a result, the dungeons will not assault each other directly until one possesses an overwhelming advantage . . .

But how can they acquire said advantage?

By sending their monsters to pillage and murder everything in the vicinity in the hopes of raising high-level champions who can smash through the enemy's dungeon.

This is just one of the reasons why the Empire strictly manages the dungeons in its territory. The endless wealth and power a dungeon can provide is matched by the endless danger it poses."

—Legion Historian Paullus Cincius Lucceius while lecturing the latest officer cadets on dungeons.

Cassius couldn't stop smiling as he looked over the records of his dungeon. The sheer amount of mana that flowed into it was incredible. The artificial mana storm had also destabilized the fabric of reality in the area, causing mana from the Source to leak through. His dungeon was now greedily absorbing all that power, leveling up several times even as he watched it. In fact, the corrupted core was pulling even more mana from the leak to fuel its growth. He wouldn't bother having to attract dungeon divers or raiding the countryside to expand his dungeon. All he needed was time.

He went ahead and upgraded his monster-summoning capabilities and his dungeon's maximum mana. He then summoned several groups of basic monsters, sending them toward the wandering knight.

It was time to find out exactly what she could do.

NSLICE-00P was marching through the dungeon when she detected several signatures appear and head in her direction. It was not long before they rounded the corner.

It was a group of small humanoids, smaller than even a young child. But they had red, leathery skin, yellow fangs sticking out of their mouths, and small horns on bald heads.

Oh, and they were flying on leathery wings.

Species	**Description**
Flame Imp (Level 3)	**The lowliest peons from the Inferno Realm. They are not particularly imposing, but the combination of Flight and Fire Magic makes for great mischief.**

"Hostiles detected. Engaging."

NSLICE-00P barraged the group with her assault rifles, as well as Magic Missiles and Light Beams. The bullets and spells tore the imps to shreds.

You have slain five Flame Imps!
Compiling experience . . .
Gained 15 Personal XP, 15 Dungeon XP total!

Cassius blinked as he watched the knight cut down the imps.

That . . . was not what he'd expected.

There was some kind of . . . enchanted weapon on her arm? Was that Air Magic?

All he knew was holes had appeared in his monsters, and he hadn't seen how it happened. Fortunately, he had dungeon perception now, so he focused in as she took down the next group.

It appeared she was launching tiny metal projectiles at incredible speeds? Some sort of exotic crossbow, then? So not a swordsman or anything like that. Maybe she was some kind of magic archer? But then, what was the armor for? And she'd also multicasted several different spells at once . . . but he hadn't caught her chant.

Cassius went silent for a moment. He didn't know much about mages, but he did know he had never seen one do that, much less a magic archer who would be splitting perks. Maybe she wasn't an archer and was just using a bunch of artifacts? But artifacts could run low on mana if not allowed time to recharge, so it was quite wasteful of her to use one them on such low-level monsters.

Cassius shook his head. Well, what exactly she was and what exactly she was doing didn't matter. She would fall all the same.

He began mass-summoning imps.

Exotic weapons, enchanted artifacts, or inexplicable magic skills—it didn't matter what she used. Weapons ran out of ammunition, artifacts needed to recharge eventually, and a mage's mana didn't recover immediately. All of it would eventually run out if she kept using it continuously. All he needed to do was make sure she spent her resources faster than her natural recovery rate, and he'd be good to go.

So he filled the labyrinth to the brim with flame imps and ordered them forward.

NSLICE-00P continued walking through the halls, machine guns blazing, missiles soaring through the sky, and magic circles flashing all around her. Imps continuously dropped from the sky and faded away.

She kept an eye on her barrel health, but as a dungeon trap, her assault rifles could be reset to mint condition with some mana, so there was no problem. Overheating barrels was no longer a concern for her, so long as she had mana.

The flame imps did seem slightly resistant to magical attacks, but that wasn't a problem either. She could handle them with her conventional arsenal alone, so she took the opportunity to trial and level new spells.

The spell Mana Blast is now Level 2!

The spell Poison Blast has leveled twice and is now Level 3!
The skill Poison Magic is now Level 4!

As she did, some of the monsters began to stir in her hangar. The rat monster who had fought the cat was fidgeting about.

"Query: Do friendlies have any observations or concerns to share?"

The rat jumped and shook his head. "N-No-no, wise-mighty boss-queen! It's nothing!"

"Acknowledged. Request: If friendlies notice any points of concern or potential efficiency improvements, please inform this unit."

The rat monster fidgeted for a moment before nodding to himself and taking a deep breath. "I-I see . . . Well . . . forgive me, wise-mighty boss-queen, but this lowly servant has a question-request."

"Acknowledgement: Please explain the request."

"Will we . . . be fighting-assisting you at any point?"

"Analysis: This unit does not require combat assistance from covert-specialized units at this time."

The rat monster's ears fell against his head. "I-I see . . ."

"Query: Does the friendly unit disagree?"

"N-No-no, wise-mighty boss-queen, I would never! It's just . . . we are your monster-servants, yes-yes? It is our duty-purpose to fight on your behalf."

"Requesting Clarification: Friendly unit wishes to engage in combat?"

The rat monster looked down for a second, then up at the live feed.

"Yes-yes. I wish to fight-battle in the wise-mighty boss-queen's name."

NSLICE-00P's robotic eye flickered.

"Analysis: Risk level against current hostiles concluded as within acceptable range. Initiating subordinate upgrade routine. Participating friendlies, please prepare to deploy."

The rat monster's eyes lit up, and he bowed his head low. "Yes-yes, thank you, mighty-powerful boss-queen! This lowly one promises he will meet-fulfill your expectations, yes-yes!"

NSLICE-00P hit the next group of imps with her stun ray as the rat monster leapt out of the Monster Hangar. The other rat monsters glanced at one another before following after him.

"Oh, so we're, like, getting free kills now or something? I was, like, going to nap, but I guess that's okay too."

And so, Lilussees and the spiderlings climbed out after the rat monsters.

Leaving Rattingtale alone in the hangar.

"Ugh, i-it's dangerous-dirty out there, yes-yes. B-But . . . if I stay here, the others will surpass-overcome me . . . Urgh. How dare they corner-manipulate the Great-High King like this, yes-yes?!"

And so, Rattingtale reluctantly joined in as well.

But the initial rat was not content to just kill the monsters lying helplessly on the ground.

No, he wanted to fight at the boss-queen's side.

So he leapt past the fallen monsters, leaving them for the others, and rushed toward a new group of imps that had just turned the corner. He activated Dash as he leapt into the air, launching straight into the neck of one of the monsters and sinking his fangs into it.

NSLICE-00P's robotic eye flickered.

"Observation: Friendly wishes to participate in active combat?"

"Yes-yes, wise-powerful boss-queen! I will show-display the might of your servants, yes-yes!"

"Acknowledgement: Reclassifying friendly as combat support asset. Adapting protocols for group combat."

NSLICE-00P had led autonomous warbots and other cyborgs into battle in the past, as well as fighting alongside Taog and Ateia, so she had protocols for this sort of scenario. She swapped her role from direct combat to support, utilizing Mana Barriers and the Equalizer to negate the flame imps' attacks, then opened fire with her assault rifle to take down two imps moving to help their comrade directly so that the rat monster could finish his fight with his foe.

"Status Update: This unit is moving to combat support mode. All friendlies, please prepare for direct combat."

Lilussees and Rattingtale shuddered.

"Wait . . . we have to, like, actually fight or something? That's, like, so much work."

"That is too dangerous-risky for the Great-High King, yes-yes! Send the wretched spider-thing!"

But the summoned showed no such hesitation. The rats cautiously followed their courageous kin, ganging up on the flame imps one by one. The spiderlings began crawling on the roof, tossing out silk threads to try and trap one of the higher-flying imps.

Lilussees heaved a sigh. "Well, like, whatever. I guess my skills are, like, not growing or something, so I guess this is fine." She formed a ball of silk and lazily tossed it into the air. The ball exploded, wrapping up one of the flame imps, and Lilussees slowly crawled over to the fallen creature then sank her fangs into it until it stopped.

Rattingtale whimpered, but he had no choice, so he very slowly crept toward the battle, looking for the weakest, most injured flame imp to take down . . .

Cassius blinked.

First, the wandering knight had kept marching forward. She had not stopped shooting her weapons or launching spells for even a single moment, and there was no indication she was planning to do so anytime soon. So either she was unbelievably wasteful . . . or she was nowhere near running dry. And then, she had suddenly deployed a bunch of rat and spider monsters.

That caused Cassius to pause.

She was a summoner? On top of everything else she was? At a mere level twenty-six? Or, well, twenty-eight now, according to his dungeon Analyze ability, but the point still stood.

Well, she could have been a monster tamer, but that was a few too many monsters for a casual taming. Either way, she would have needed to invest perks to control this many, or else spent years trying to learn the Summoning or Monster Taming skills manually, both of which were notoriously difficult to pick up. Oh, and a monster tamer's pets should have triggered Castra Turannia's wards, meaning they would have needed to be declared before entering town. She hadn't displayed any sign of her pets prior to this point, so just how was she feeding and taking care of them?

Of course, the wards were long due for maintenance and prone to gaps in coverage, a fact that several individuals in town had already taken advantage of to bring contraband in and out, including Cassius himself. And this knight was strange, almost certainly a foreigner. Perhaps she had special clearance for the monsters . . . but then, why would she lack identification? Maybe it was simply that she didn't know she needed to declare them, as unlikely as that seemed?

Well, given all that, summoner made more sense . . . except, why would she bother wasting the mana to summon weak monsters like that in this scenario? And was she trying to train them? Summoned monsters wouldn't earn experience for themselves, so there was no point in training the weak ones. It might have made a bit more sense if she was a monster tamer, but was she really at such leisure she could afford to do so now, of all times?

Cassius tilted his head.

The more he learned about this strange knight, the less sense she made.

But he shook his head. That wasn't the problem he should concern himself with.

The problem he should concern himself with was that she was headed directly for the end of the labyrinth, where the door to his core room was located. She hadn't taken a wrong turn even once, in fact.

The imps wouldn't be enough to bog her down at this rate. She would reach him before she ran out of mana.

But Cassius grinned. The imps were but the weakest of the minions he could summon, even before he'd upgraded his monster summoning ability. He had used them purely to scout out her capabilities, so now he was ready to try something else.

He would like to see her handle the hot devils.

47

What's in a Name?

"Let me tell you, boy, the Dungeon Diver's Handbook *is crap. It will NOT be enough to keep you alive in one of those labyrinths of death. Every single dungeon is different, unique. Every diver spends their entire career learning THEIR dungeon—that's it. They'll be safe in their dungeon, and in no other. So how could there possibly be a common manual that could teach you how to survive in ALL of them? It tells you the bare minimum at best.*

But that is NOT to say you SHOULDN'T read the handbook. There are a few common rules, after all, and you better know them. That's what the handbook records. If you don't know everything in it by heart, then don't even THINK about stepping inside a dungeon.

For example, there are ALWAYS pit traps. Always. Watch your footing.

Second, if you see a named monster, you RUN.

What? You want to know what's so special about a name? You IDIOT!

Listen up! Normal monsters are expendable tools; just a part of the dungeon. They are expected to die. Why do you think the dungeon lets us kill them on the regular? Because we're so powerful that the dungeon can't possibly kill us? NO, you idiot! It's because the dungeon wants us to come back! The monsters we face on the day-to-day are the bait, the sap it uses to draw in more prey! It is EXPECTED that we will kill a bunch of them, and then the dungeon will feed on the idiots who get themselves killed. Like you.

So what about a monster with a name?

A monster with a name has been specifically chosen by the dungeon master. It is treated as an individual. It is invested into, nurtured, grown.

It is an elite, the dungeon's contingency plan for when it is actually threatened.

A monster with a name will not be risked on the daily grind. It will not be offered up to attract more divers. It is not expected to die.

A monster with a name is only deployed in two cases. One, the dungeon feels threatened and feels it can't hold anything back. Two, the dungeon master has determined there is no threat to the elite monster, and it is trying to raise that monster's level.

You got that? If you see a named monster, that means you're its food. *So you run, and maybe, just maybe, you might live a few minutes longer."*

—Professional Dungeon Diver Kaeso Cispius Pertacus trying unsuccessfully to reduce rookie-diver casualty rates.

The lead rat monster leapt to the side as a flame imp swooped down overhead, barely dodging the claws swinging toward him before jumping and grabbing onto the imp's back. It spun around in the air, trying to throw the rat off, but he clung tight and opened his jaws.

He then sunk his fangs into the fragile wings on the imp's back.

The creature cried out and fell to the ground, where the other rats set upon it. Several imps in the air behind them raised their hands, forming magic circles to bombard the rats, but a beam of rainbow light swept across them, and their magic circles vanished.

The imp's eyes went wide, and they scrambled to reform the circles, but nets of web launched at them, pulling several to the ground where the spiders were waiting.

And then the sound of thunder rang out as the boss-queen eliminated the remainder.

The rat monster shook his head. The boss-queen was truly mighty. It would be a long time before he could be of any real use to her.

"Look-watch out!"

Everyone turned to look around, unsure of who the call out was for. As they did, one of the imps wrapped in spiderwebs managed to thrust their hand toward the lead rat, a small bolt of flame shooting out, too close for him to dodge. The rat's eyes widened, and he braced for impact.

The flames crashed against a Mana Barrier, and then the boss-queen retaliated with her mighty beams. The lead rat was unharmed, if chastised.

"Analysis: Communication inefficiency identified. Generating unique identifiers for friendly units to improve communication efficiency."

The rats and spiderlings all turned toward the boss-queen, their eyes wide.

"B-Boss-queen, what do you mean-intend by that?"

She pointed toward him. "Unit designation: 01R."

The rat monster shuddered as he felt the mana within him shift. He trembled as he opened the sacred records . . .

And there it was.

Personal Status → General Information	
Name	01R

The rat monster—No, 01R trembled even more.

The boss-queen had named him.

She had declared that he would be one of her elites. He would not be just another nameless monster to be treated as a mere extension of the dungeon. He was now a true individual whose deeds would fall under their own name in the eyes of the Aesdes above. He could truly start to grow now, receiving a greater share of the experience he earned on behalf of the dungeon, as well as have a greater level of independence and authority.

One of her most valued monsters. Her inner circle.

In fact . . . it was not just any name. It was a name patterned after her own. She did not mind being associated with him. No, she was practically declaring him part of her family.

And then she pointed to the next rat.

"Unit designation: 02R. Unit designation: 03R. Unit designation . . ."

01R's eyes widened.

Not, that wasn't it. She wasn't declaring him as elite, one of a few.

She was declaring that ALL her monsters were elite.

That ALL of them were part of her family.

That ALL of them were valuable to her.

That ALL of them would be nurtured and grown and not expended.

Despite their weakness, despite their mishaps, she had acknowledged their loyalty and repaid it in full, then gone beyond to gift them that which they had not earned. She was rewarding and trusting in them, even as she was forced to cover for their lack of strength.

01R felt a fire fill his chest. He looked around, seeing the same look in the eyes of the rats and spiderlings. He stood to his full height, bowing his head toward the boss-queen. The other monsters followed suit.

He renewed his oath. He would one day repay the wise-mighty-gracious boss-queen, whatever it took.

Even the treacherous one could not help but tremble, clearly moved by the sheer generosity and kindness of the boss-queen. He could not even speak in the face of the boss-queen's brilliance.

Meanwhile, Lilussees tilted her head in the corner.

"Hm, should I, like, tell her what she did? That, like, naming monsters is kind of a thing or something?" She thought about it a bit more before shrugging with her first two legs. "Oh well, she already did it, so, like, whatever."

* * *

Cassius winced again.

Just what WAS that rainbow attack?

Whatever the strange knight was doing, it was not merely disrupting his monsters' attacks; every time she fired the beam, the dungeon's own mana *vanished* along its path. For a brief moment, he could no longer perceive that part of the dungeon.

He gulped.

It wasn't exactly damaging. The dungeon's mana restored the area a moment later, but it was uncomfortable for the new dungeon master. Like getting poked in the eye or having a bright light suddenly appear in the middle of the night. But worse was the fear, the uncertainty.

He had absolutely no idea what that was, what it could even be. He knew elite mages had ways of undoing hostile spells or taking control of hostile mana, and there were monsters and artifacts that could absorb mana into themselves, but nothing like this. As far as he could tell, she was somehow *erasing* mana itself. And not just the ambient mana floating around—she was erasing a *dungeon's* mana, which belonged to the dungeon alone.

As far as he knew, that shouldn't be possible.

But he shook his head. There were a lot of things he didn't know, after all. It was probably just some exotic artifact reacting with mana in a way he had never heard of before. So it didn't matter, because this would all be over soon. The hot devils were now converging on her location.

They should be a great counter to the knight. They were not the strongest of beings, nor were they gifted in the arcane arts; instead, they wrapped themselves in cloaks of mystical fire from the Inferno Realm, which could set mana itself ablaze. This made them extremely resistant to magical attacks, whether from spells or from enchanted weapons. So whatever mystical powers or exotic artifacts she had on her person should not be nearly as impactful against the hot devils.

And of course, mystical fire was still fire, so they would deal damage to any creature foolish enough to attack them at close range as well. And with all the focus she put into ranged combat, she could not also be an expert in melee combat. They would endure whatever she could do at a distance, and then overwhelm her up close. She and her monsters would burn to death.

"Warning: Denser magic signatures on approach. All friendlies, please evacuate to Monster Hangar until hostiles are identified and analyzed."

"Yes-yes, wise-mighty-gracious boss-queen!"

The monsters scrambled into the hangar just as the new signatures rounded another corner.

Like the imps, they were red-skinned, horned humanoids; only, these were just slightly shorter than an adult human, and they lacked the wings of the imps as well.

Species	Description
Hot Devil (Level 7)	**The Inferno Realm burns all, even magic itself. These Hot Devils have filled themselves with this devastating fire, allowing their flames to burn hostile spells and unravel their structure. However, they lack the ability to control the flames, which prevents them from using magic themselves, as well as sapping their physical strength.**

Instead, they were each covered in an aura of fire which emitted multicolored sparks of light. NSLICE-00P read significant mana signatures from the fire, which did not appear to act as a normal flame should. In any case, NSLICE-00P opened up with an experimental barrage, testing an assault rifle, a Mana Beam, and a Magic Missile.

The Magic Missile burned as it approached the flame, the mystical fire burning the spell structure and using the released mana to fuel itself. The Mana Beam fared likewise, the infusion of mana into her laser projectors now becoming an exploitable weakness.

But the bullets from the assault rifle?

The fire was not hot enough to melt the lead before it struck, so one of the creatures cried out as bullet holes appeared on its chest.

You have slain Hot Devil (Level 7)!
Gained 3 Personal XP, 3 Dungeon XP!

"Status Update: Resistance to mana-based attacks and weakness to conventional weapons observed. Testing Equalizer."

NSLICE-00P raised her hand and fired a rainbow beam at another of the monsters. The flames and the antimagic beam collided, each trying to defeat the other. But the Equalizer was not magic per se, and the hot devil had no ability to control his flames or adjust them to a new energy type, so as the flames tried to assault a spell structure that the Equalizer didn't have in the first place, they had no effect upon it.

The Equalizer, on the other hand, was destroying the very mana the flames were composed of.

The hot devil froze and blinked as its fire went out. It suddenly began coughing and crouching over on the ground. Its body's strength had been sapped to fuel its magical flames, and in turn, had been sustained by them, which meant it was no longer used to breathing normal air on its own power.

And then a Magic Missile struck it on the head, and it fell over.

You have slain Hot Devil (Level 7)!
Gained 3 Personal XP, 3 Dungeon XP!

NSLICE-00P kept one hand out to channel the Equalizer while using the other as an assault rifle. Her missile panels slid open as well, prepared to launch another barrage if the monsters began to overwhelm her position.

"Status Update: Hostile analysis complete. Hostile capabilities and countermeasures logged and recorded. Friendly units may redeploy at this time."

Cassius just stared with his jaw dropped.

First of all, that exotic crossbow was apparently NOT a magical weapon. However it was launching those little metal projectiles, they were apparently purely physical by the time they landed. Stripping them of mana had no effect on their destructive power. Which meant the hot devils' flames were no barrier against them, and the strange knight could cut them down as easily as the flame imps.

But the second problem was even worse.

That strange rainbow beam could not only endure the mystical flames of Inferno—it could *erase* them entirely. Hot devils were not exactly the most powerful monsters, so their flames could be overpowered.

But erased entirely?

The flames from the Inferno Realm itself? The flames that represented the very concept of destruction by fire?

Were *destroyed* by this strange attack, themselves?

Cassius trembled as he watched *rat monsters* of all things attack the coughing, flameless hot devils. The hot devils were entirely specialized in holding Inferno Realm flames within their bodies, so if they somehow lost those, they were weaker than even the flame imps.

Just who or what WAS this strange knight?!

Cassius shook his head and took a deep breath. This was not the time to panic; the strange knight had almost reached the end of the labyrinth.

He grimaced, but he had no choice. He created a second labyrinth, even larger and more convoluted than the first, taking some time to adjust it himself, adding more twists and dead ends.

He hated spending some of the Dungeon perk points on another room. He was *supposed* to be spending it all on expanding his monster army in order to conquer Castra Turannia and the province beyond. Every bit he spent on purely defensive rooms would weaken his horde by that much.

But he had no choice. The strange knight had proven remarkably lucky and had made it through his first labyrinth in record time. He needed more time to summon monsters.

And to probe just how deep this strange knight's secrets went.

48

Terminate the Hostile Dungeon!

"There are only two things more dangerous than a dungeon.

The first is a Rift. A Rift occurs when a hole tears in the fabric of reality itself, opening a door straight to a Realm of Mana. Mana will flood the area, causing mana surges and unpredictable magical phenomena all around. Likewise, monsters and other beings from the given Realm will pour out. Even some of the more benign Realms can cause serious damage if a Rift opens to them. The less benign ones? Well, you better hope you never see one of those.

A dungeon, in the end, seems to be an intelligent predator. It can make choices, it can hold back, it can save some prey for the future. Under most circumstances, it does not act indiscriminately. A Rift, on the other hand, is a natural disaster. There is no intellect or thought behind it. Monsters and mana pour out and devastate everything in their path until the Rift is closed.

The second is a corrupted dungeon, which is the most dangerous of all. A corrupted dungeon combines the worst aspects of a dungeon and a Rift. A normal dungeon is dangerous, but they appear to be relatively controlled environments. They grow at a relatively steady rate, and one can make certain assumptions about the amount of monsters and traps a given dungeon has available considering its size and the number of visitors it gets.

Not so with a corrupted dungeon.

We aren't sure how exactly it works, but we believe a corrupted dungeon pulls more mana from the Realms of Mana than it can handle, growing at a blistering pace before spilling the excess mana into the environment around it. Much like a Rift, in fact. And of course, it still being a dungeon means it's still summoning monsters at the same time, or maybe binding the monsters that try to come over from the Realm? No one knows for sure, but the point is that a corrupted dungeon acts more like a Rift than a dungeon . . . except that its monsters are still under the command of an intelligent dungeon master, so the monsters that result don't act mindlessly and independently like in the case of a Rift. They cooperate and act with purpose. One can imagine why that might be bad.

Oh, and that's the best case. There's a slight chance the dungeon master might prefer to enslave you rather than kill you.

In the worst case, the surging mana overwhelms the dungeon, which subsequently explodes and wipes out the entire area, leaving behind a massive Rift just for good measure.

Either way, the chance of survival for anyone in the surrounding area drops dramatically wherever a corrupted dungeon appears.

It is theorized that the Great Demon Lord of the Lost Continent may have been controlling a corrupted dungeon, given the similarities between the legend and our observations—albeit at a completely different scale than anything we've ever recorded. And as you all know, the legend states the Aesdes were forced to confront the Great Demon Lord personally, and afterward granted us the boons of power we take for granted, so as to prevent such a threat from rising ever again.

That alone should tell you how bad a corrupted dungeon can be."

—Legion Historian Paullus Cincius Lucceius while lecturing the latest officer cadets on dungeons.

Cassius summoned a huge group of flame serpents. They were small, but they could spit fire from a surprising range, beyond that of the average bow. He figured if the hot devils couldn't close the distance with the knight, he would overwhelm her at range . . .

NSLICE-00P swept the Equalizer across the field as she filled the air with Mana Barriers, blocking the barrage of fiery projectiles soaring toward her.

The spell Mana Barrier is now Level 9!

01R led the other monsters as they rushed under the cover of the Mana Barriers, with Lilussees leading the other spiders in tying down the snakes with webs while the rats engaged them in melee, to Rattingtale's horror.

Meanwhile, missiles soared overhead, landing on the snakes in the rear and wiping out entire groups at once.

Level up! Your Dungeon Level is now 38!

Cassius gritted his teeth. He spent some of his points to upgrade his monster-summoning capabilities one more time.

It was time to bring out the big guns.

He summoned a pair of ursanus inferno and sent them down the dungeon hallway, giggling to himself.

"You're capable . . . very capable, Miss Knight! But even you can't do anything about this! A bunch of ursanus down a narrow hallway with no room to maneuver . . . it's simply your strength versus theirs! No tricks or spells or strange weapons will save you now! Muahahahaha!"

"Warning: Heavy mana signatures detected. All friendly units please evacuate to the Monster Hangar."

The monsters ran back and climbed inside. A few moments later, a pair of ursanus monsters rounded the corner; only, these ones had red eyes and smoke leaking out from their shells.

The moment they saw NSLICE-00P, they let out a roar and charged down the hallway.

NSLICE-00P was currently in a tight hallway and couldn't take to the air. She would have to face the two monsters head-on.

"Warning: Priority targets identified. Engaging ursanus termination protocols."

But that wasn't a problem for her.

NSLICE-00P formed an Aurora Barrage magic circle behind her. Since she couldn't make it as big as normal, she instead made three of them layered behind one another before Supercharging each one, and then activating the circle in the back.

The magic circle fired all of its beams straight forward, right into the corresponding Light Beam circles on the next layer were joined together thanks to the Fusion modifier. That circle then fired the now fused beams into the final layer, which then fired the beams at an angle such that they all converged on a single point.

And then, as per her current anti-ursanus protocols, she fired the Equalizer at the head of one of the bears, erasing both the flames and the monster's HP barrier.

The triple-fused, Supercharged Aurora Barrage Light Beam opened fire, vaporizing the defenseless head of the monster and piercing straight through its body.

The skill Multicasting is now Level 9!
The skill Supercharge is now Level 8!
The strategic spell Aurora Barrage is now Level 4!
The spell Fusion Light Beam is now Level 14!
The skill Light Magic is now Level 12!
Mana Control is now 165!

You have slain Ursanus Inferno (Level 30)!
Gained 13 Personal XP, 3 Dungeon XP!

She then repeated the process before the second monster could reach her.

You have slain Ursanus Inferno (Level 30)!
Gained 13 Personal XP, 3 Dungeon XP!
Level up! You are now at Personal Level 30!

Priority targets terminated. Operational area secure.

Cassius stared blankly.

By the Aesdes above and the Domides below, what was that?!

Ursanus alphas were some of the toughest and most resilient creatures around. The ursanus inferno monster type existed because an ursanus had once managed to endure and adapt to the flames of Inferno itself. The flames that represented the very concept of destruction by fire.

And this strange knight . . . had killed said type of ursanus . . . *in one hit* . . . by Multicasting several extremely complicated-looking magic circles, and *then* fusing them together? Before immediately repeating the feat, demonstrating that such a thing did NOT require all her available mana to pull off, or was NOT some sort of ultimate contingency weapon?

And she didn't even stop to catch her breath. She did not consume a mana potion to restore her reserves. She did not recharge any artifacts with spare mana cores.

No, she just kept marching forward, displaying no sign of fatigue whatsoever.

And then Cassius froze, looking at where she was compared to the overall room.

Again, she was nearly at the exit.

Despite his best efforts to make as confusing a maze as possible, with no distinguishing features, a twisting, curving path which looped back several times, and any number of intersections leading to dead ends, she had managed to go straight along the shortest possible route. Again. She had not hesitated at even a single intersection; had not made even a single wrong turn.

He felt a chill run down his spine.

She had not gotten lucky the first time. She had a way to navigate the dungeon with perfect accuracy. He could not buy time with mazes.

He hadn't invested anything into traps, but he still had some basic ones available, so he went and placed as many pit traps as he could along her path. He then went and purchased another room. This time, he made a huge open area, as large as he could make it. And as his mana recovered, he summoned as many monsters as he could, of all possible types he could afford.

He would simply try to overwhelm her and run her down. She couldn't kill all of them at once . . . right?

The pit traps would buy him some time so he could summon even a few more monsters.

He turned to see her progress . . . and froze again.

The strange knight was flying. She was floating in the air, right above the pit traps.

They didn't slow her down in the slightest.

Cassius grabbed his hair and screamed. He turned to his core and grimaced. He needed more mana. He needed his core to draw more power. He grabbed the enchanted knife gifted to him by the cult and stepped forward.

NSLICE-00P came to the end of the labyrinth and stepped through the door.

And was immediately greeted by a wall of incoming fire.

She immediately shot into the air as she fired the Equalizer and formed as many Mana Barriers as she could. Much of the flames either vanished or hit her barriers, but some managed to get through, so she began casting Heal on herself as well. As the fire exploded on the barriers and blocked her view of the room, her sensors determined the situation.

She was in a large open room filled to the brim with monsters.

"Engaging mass-termination protocols."

NSLICE-00P went all out. Her hands turned into assault rifles and opened fire, along with the shoulder-mounted autopistols. Panels opened on every inch of her body, launching missiles of all sorts in every direction, even activating her stun ray and flamethrowers. As predicted, the flamethrowers didn't do much against these monsters, but they did offset some of the fire attacks coming her way.

And as she did this, she formed a massive Aurora Barrage magic circle in the sky above, stuffing as much mana as she could to activate both Supercharge and Spell Penetration.

Beams of light began to rain from the roof. She wasn't even sure what sort of monsters she was targeting, just aiming the beams and bullets at whichever signature they could detect.

The skill Spell Penetration is now Level 3!
The skill Geomancy is now Level 2!

One by one, the signatures began to disappear. Since she didn't know what she was targeting, she didn't fuse the beams, trying to avoid overkill. As a result, multiple beams were striking the same targets repeatedly to take them down, triggering the Geomancy skill she had purchased. And soon . . . it was done.

The smoke and the flames died down, revealing an empty room with a floor covered in loot and magic cores.

The skill Continuous Casting leveled up twice, is now Level 3!
The spell Mana Barrier is now Level 10! Upgrade available!
The skill Arcane Magic is now Level 10! Upgrade available!
The spell Heal is now Level 6!
The skill Recovery Magic is now Level 4!
Gained 336 Personal XP, 324 Dungeon XP total!
You have leveled up 3 Personal levels and 3 Dungeon levels!
You are now at Personal Level 33 and Dungeon Level 41!

NSLICE-00P scanned the room, but there were no further signatures. She lowered herself to the floor and made her way to the door at the far side. Once she passed through, her sensors started blaring.

She was in a wide, circular room, its walls and floors made of stone brick, with a pedestal at the center. The standard layout for a dungeon core room, from her experience.

But this one was different in other ways.

The air was burning hot, and small flames broke out randomly across the floors and the walls. The core itself was not steadily glowing but was instead pulsing red with small cracks of light rippling across it. Above the core was some sort of circle of fire surrounding a vortex of red light. Jets of flame shot from the portal randomly.

In front of the portal, Cassius cackled madly.

"What even are you, Miss Knight?! I have no idea, certainly not a mere human, but even so you're too late! Do you understand what you're seeing? I pulled as much mana into my core as possible, and now I've opened a direct portal to the Realm of Inferno itself! And now . . . now I can kill you!"

The core glowed, and a bright light covered the floor in front of Cassius. There was a flash of light as the temperature in the room grew even hotter, then NSLICE-00P logged a massive mana signature appearing in the center of the room. As the light faded, she caught sight of a raging inferno in front of her, only in a vaguely humanoid form.

"An Inferno elemental! A being composed purely of the mana of the Inferno Realm! And with an open portal to that same Realm, it can draw infinite power directly from its origin! It will never die and never stop growing as long as the portal is open! Even you, with all your impossible tricks and abilities, cannot stop this!"

"Status Update: Hostile capabilities determined. Engaging target."

NSLICE-00P raised her palms. A huge beam of rainbow light shot forward and into the Inferno elemental. The mana density was unlike anything

NSLICE-00P had encountered . . . but she managed to open a small hole in the being.

The Inferno elemental screeched at her.

The damage was purely cosmetic and would be restored the moment she dropped the Equalizer. Even now, flames shot from the portal into the elemental, causing it to grow in size with each passing moment. NSLICE-00P wouldn't kill the elemental via this method.

But that was fine. Because NSLICE-00P wasn't aiming at the elemental in the first place.

She fired a missile from her other arm through the hole the Equalizer had made. Straight at the dungeon core on the other side.

The missile exploded directly on target.

The core shattered.

Cassius's eyes widened. "No, you idiot!"

Contrary to other dungeons, this one did not immediately fade away. Instead, the walls began to shake and tremble.

The Inferno elemental screeched at her, now freed from the dungeon's bindings. And with its newfound freedom . . . it ran right back into the portal.

As it turned out, the Inferno elemental was an incorporeal being of pure mana. It could burn out, it could be overwhelmed, but rarely could it be directly damaged. This particular individual didn't even have a concept of pain . . . until now. The Equalizer ripping apart the fundamental building blocks of its being was a novel and deeply horrifying experience for the creature.

One it had no idea how to deal with.

So, it retreated back to the source of its power.

But the elemental wasn't the problem.

The problem was that the portal in the air began to grow.

"That core was the only thing keeping the portal contained and stable! Without a dungeon core, it will continue to grow! You've doomed us all!"

"Acknowledged."

NSLICE-00P arrived in front of the portal and opened up her armor chest piece, exposing her shining core for the world to see.

Cassius's eyes widened and his jaw dropped.

And then the mana from the portal began to surge into NSLICE-00P.

Level up! Your Dungeon Level is now 42!
Level up! Your Dungeon Level is now 43!
Level up! Your Dungeon Level is now 44!

All of NSLICE-00P's circuits and capacitors started blaring critical warnings as she was filled to the brim with mana. Likewise, jets of flame from the portal assaulted her barriers, burning straight through them. But she couldn't move anymore, her core now locked in place by the sheer amount of mana swirling into it.

Level up! Your Dungeon Level is now 45!
Level up! Your Dungeon Level is now 46!
Level up! Your Dungeon Level is now 47!

She split her focus, her cybernetic side focusing on managing the flow of power through her implants and tasking her organic half with finding a solution to the situation. She gasped as her organic half suddenly began feeling all the pain her intelligence leashing measures had previously blocked. Every inch of her body felt as if it was on fire, swelling up as if about to explode. The very air burned her skin, which intensified as jets of flames licked about her.

But she gritted her teeth and pushed through the menus, grunting and groaning all the while. She immediately moved to expand her mana capacity.

You have unlocked an Additional Implant Slot! Max HP and Mana increased!
You have unlocked an Additional Implant Slot! Max HP and Mana increased!

Level up! Your Dungeon Level is now 48!
Level up! Your Dungeon Level is now 49!
Level up! Your Dungeon Level is now 50!

She installed more Mana Capacitor implants into the new slots, but that wasn't enough. Her HP started to tick down as the mana surged out of control, quickly filling the expanded capacity.

Mana Capacitor +1 is now available!
Mana Capacitor +2 is now available!
Energy Channels +1 is now available!
Energy Channels +2 is now available!

Level up! Your Dungeon Level is now 51!
Level up! Your Dungeon Level is now 52!
Level up! Your Dungeon Level is now 53!

She upgraded her capacitors, boosting all of their capacity all at once. Then she upgraded her energy channels, allowing more power to flow through her body. But that was not enough. Her core could send the mana back into the Source, but not at the rate she was absorbing it. Simply boosting the amount of mana she could deal with wasn't enough if it had nowhere to go.

So she tried to expend as much mana as she could. She cast an Aurora Barrage spell, stuffing as much mana into it as her organic half could unassisted. The spell misfired and shattered several times before she got it. Her cybernetic half realized what she was doing and activated its energy channels, firing Mana Beams with as much power as it could. Beams of light began to flood the room, scouring the floors and walls as NSLICE-00P fired them at random.

You have unlocked an Additional Implant Slot! Max HP and Mana increased!
You have unlocked an Additional Implant Slot! Max HP and Mana increased!

Level up! Your Dungeon Level is now 54!
Level up! Your Dungeon Level is now 55!
Level up! Your Dungeon Level is now 56!

Finally . . . the portal stopped growing. She was absorbing enough mana that there wasn't enough left to damage the fabric of reality any further. Now, she just needed to maintain.

She added another two implant slots and Mana Capacitors, and then both of her halves reintegrated. She didn't need to consider options anymore, and she needed the focus. She blocked out the pain once again, and Supercharged the Aurora Barrage spell as much as she could, with a bit spared for Heal to repair the damage being dealt to her.

Normally, the sheer amount of mana flowing through her couldn't be spent through a simple spell, but AI-assisted mana control could dump a truly massive amount of power into a Supercharged strategic spell. Cassius was forced to shield his eyes as the Aurora Barrage filled the room with light, firing massive beams that cracked the walls.

The skill HP Regen is now Level 7!
The spell Heal is now Level 7!
The skill Supercharge is now Level 9!
Mana Control is now 170!

Level up! Your Dungeon Level is now 57!
Level up! Your Dungeon Level is now 55!
Level up! Your Dungeon Level is now 59!

Level up! Your Dungeon Level is now 60!
Level up! Your Dungeon Level is now 61!
Level up! Your Dungeon Level is now 62!

It seemed like an eternity as NSLICE-00P ran her calculations, determining if she could continue to maintain her HP and drain the mana. The predictions were worrying, but she was committed at this point.

And then . . .

Finally. The flows began to stabilize, and the predicted success rate began to tick upward.

The portal was starting to shrink. The amount of mana surging into her core was slowing down ever so slightly. The world was trying to repair itself and, thanks to NSLICE-00P tipping the scales, now it could.

Level up! Your Dungeon Level is now 63!
Level up! Your Dungeon Level is now 64!
Level up! Your Dungeon Level is now 65!

The flames started dying down. The mana in her body wasn't causing her damage any longer. The light of the Aurora Barrage started to dim back to visible levels.

And then, finally, the portal closed.

The flames died down.

And the world repaired itself, pushing the Realms of Mana back.

NSLICE-00P took a deep breath. Her entire body was glowing from the sheer amount of mana left inside it, her core slowly sending it back to the Source.

Level up! Your Dungeon Level is now 66!

Finally, her Dungeon XP stopped ticking up.

The threat was over.

She turned to the side. Cassius was staring with wide eyes and a dropped jaw.

"Just . . . what—"

A massive Mana Beam vaporized him entirely.

You have slain Human (Level 13)!
Gained 3 Personal XP, 3 Dungeon XP!

NSLICE-00P lowered her smoking palm. Her robotic eye shifted colors from red back to yellow.

"Status Update: Environmental hazards removed. Hostile terminated. Mission complete."

Just then, she received a stream of notifications from the foreign system.

You have purified a Corrupted Core (Inferno)!
Gained 10 Personal Perk Points, 10 Dungeon Perk Points!

Whoa, you took out a corrupted core? Nice, good job! Now I don't have to deal with it!
So, they really don't want me to let the Inferno Realm any closer, so I can't let you have that affinity, but you can have this stuff instead.

You have accomplished the Dungeon Feat: Purifier Dungeon!
Gained Dungeon Affinity: Fire!

Ugh. Uuuuggggghhhhh. I'm worried about this. I'm SUPER worried about this. This should NOT be in the hands of anyone dungeon related, much less a walking dungeon core. Ugh, we need to add a no-dungeons clause to this now. But . . . I guess I can't NOT give it to you, not after what you did, huh? I mean, you purified a corrupted dungeon and closed a Rift with just yourself and your contracted subordinates, so you definitely earned it.
And . . . I guess you haven't done anything bad yet. I'm not comfortable with that whole Wulver massacre incident, but they did initiate the fight with you, so . . . UGH. Just . . . just please don't do anything bad with this, okay?! Promise me, okay?!

You have purified a Corrupted Dungeon and closed a Rift!
You have accomplished the Personal Feat: Dungeon Purifier (Inferno)!
You have accomplished the Personal Feat: World Defender!
You have learned the skill: Holy Magic!
You have learned the spell: Holy Bolt!
You have accomplished the Personal Feat: Hero!
Gained the Unique Hero Skill: Hero Dungeon!
Gained Dungeon Affinity: Holy!

Wait, what? You're making a new dungeon affinity with this? A brand-new one with Holy mana of all things? That's . . . that's like . . . so much work for me, though! How would a Holy dungeon affinity even work?! What am I even supposed to do about that?! What are you doing?! Heroes are supposed to be your job, not mine!

Shut up! Do you think I'm happy about this?! You think I would willingly make a DUNGEON into a HERO if I had any choice in the matter?! And you know how it works—I don't directly control the unique hero skills! It just extrapolates what they already are and have already achieved to make something which fits them best! So WHY do you think the Hero feat is looking at the FACT THAT SHE'S A DUNGEON in the first place?! This is all your fault, you know!

Ugh, can you keep it down? You don't have to shout.

YOU!

NSLICE-00P's Dungeon Management

Overview	
Name	**The Walking Dungeon**
Level	**66**
XP	**37/100**
Available Perk Points	**51**
Mana	**261/261 (290/290)**
Exterior	**Human/Automata Hybrid (LOCKED)**

Dungeon Affinities	
Type	**Strength**
Cyborg	**Primary**
Fire	**Minor**
Holy	**Minor**
Rodent	**Minimum**
Earth	**Minimum**
Arachnid	**Minimum**
Slime	**Minimum**

Light	Minimum
Nature	Minimum

Implants		
Type	Mana Upkeep	Description
Bionic Prosthetics +3	0	Overwrites STR and SPD, Values: 130 STR, 65 SPD
Armor Plating +2	0	Overwrites DEF and RES, Values: 120 DEF, 60 RES
Bonded AI	0	Enables direct contact with the System. Overwrites DEX, Value: 1000 DEX
Techno-Organic Interface	0	Enables conscious control over organic and emotional functions. Resists mind-influencing effects.
Advanced Sensors +2	0	Vastly expands scope and effectiveness of senses.
Internal Weapon Bays	0	Enables use of dungeon traps as weapons.
Repulsors +1	0	Enables flight and tactical boosts.
Energy Channels +2	0	Enables user to channel internal energy into external attacks.
Dungeon Field Generator +1	5	Surrounding area counts as dungeon territory. Enables mana absorption within area of effect.

Monster Hangar (Small)	1	Provides living space for 5 small monsters. Unlocks subordinate summoning.
Item Foundry	1	Unlocks Item Creation
Mana Capacitor +2 (x5)	0	Boosts maximum mana by 30 each.

Inventory	
Name	**Description**
??? dagger	A dagger, likely enchanted given the amount of mana held within. Further information could not be determined.
Ursanus pelt	The pelt of an ursanus alpha. Tough, well-insulated, and full of mana.
Ursanus bones	The bones of an ursanus alpha. Extremely durable, and full of mana.
Idrint	Quantity: 2,300. Basic solidified mana, now a standard medium of exchange.

Subordinates				
Name	**Species**	**Level**	**Mana Upkeep**	
Rattingtale	Monster Rat	10 * Evolution Available	1	Check Status
Lilussees	Monster Spider	11 * Evolution Available	1	Check Status
(TEMPORARY) Ateia Niraemia	Human	9	--	(Status locked)

(TEMPORARY) Taog Sutharlan	Human/ Wulver	8	--	(Status locked)
01R	Monster Rat	9	0.2	Check Status
02R	Monster Rat	5	0.2	Check Status
03R	Monster Rat	8	0.2	Check Status
04R	Monster Rat	7	0.2	Check Status
05R	Monster Rat	6	0.2	Check Status
01S	Spiderling	7	0.33	Check Status
02S	Spiderling	7	0.33	Check Status
03S	Spiderling	7	0.33	Check Status

Traps			
Name	Number Active / Deployed	Mana Upkeep	Description
Assault Rifle +3	2/2	2	Rapid-fire projectile weapon with high penetration.
Autopistol	2/2	2	Rapid-fire projectile weapon with medium penetration.
Anti-Armor Missile Launcher +2	2/2	2	Homing explosive designed to penetrate armor. Very high penetration.
Anti-Personnel Missile Launcher +2	6/6	6	Homing explosive designed for area damage. Medium penetration.

Stun Ray	1/1	1	Nonlethal electric weapon. Can inflict stun and paralysis statuses.
Wrist Blade +2	2/2	0	Wrist-mounted blades that can be deployed at high speed.
Flamethrower	2/2	2	Deals fire damage and applies burn status in a large cone.
The Equalizer +1	1/1	0	Huh? What the heck is this? Some kind of weird metal that doesn't even exist here? Um . . . well . . . best I can tell it's some sort of antimagic field generator? Eh . . . well, it's yours, not mine, so you don't need me to tell you, right? Like, you already upgraded this thing yourself, so you're good, right?

Dungeon Skills		
Name	Level	Description
Analyze	N/A	Check the status of a target. More detail for targets within the dungeon. Details depend on level difference.
Contract	N/A	Bind a consenting target to the dungeon, per terms agreed upon by both parties.
Transfer	N/A	Move yourself, a subordinate, or a consenting target within your dungeon.

Dungeon Perks	
Name	**Description**
Human-Dungeon Hybrid	Enables Implants tab. Enables unique Dungeon Combat skill. Enables direct manipulation of dungeon mana. +100 HP Rooms tab locked. Exterior locked.

Dungeon Feats		
Name	**Description**	**Effect**
Dungeon Victor	To the victor go the spoils. Unlocked by destroying or subordinating another dungeon.	+1 Perk Point Unlocks Dungeon Warfare category perks.
Dungeon Overlord	A master of masters. Unlocked by subordinating another dungeon master.	+2 Perk Points Unlocks Subordinate Core category perks.
Raid Boss	Fine, I'll do it myself. Unlocked by destroying or subordinating another dungeon with no assistance.	+2 Perk Points +1 level in HP Regen skill +1 level in MP Regen skill +50 HP Unlocks Raid Boss category perks.
System Upgrade	Unlocked by manually performing a system upgrade. Which is not supposed to be possible. Ugh, this is going to get complicated, isn't it?	Um, I don't know. Just have +20 Dungeon Perk Points or something. Whatever. You're figuring this out yourself anyways, so close enough.

Purifier Dungeon	**Dungeons are supposed to protect the world; you took that duty more literally.** **Unlocked by destroying a corrupted dungeon core.**	**+20 Perk Points** **Unlocks Purifier category perks.**

NSLICE-00P's Personal Status

Personal Status			
General Information		Physical Attributes	
Name	NSLICE-00P	STR	130* (Overwritten)
Species	Human/ Dungeon Core/ Automata Hybrid	DEX	1000* (Overwritten)
Level	33	SPD	65* (Overwritten)
XP	90/100	DEF	120* (Overwritten)
Perk Points	97	RES	60* (Overwritten)
HP	210/210	Magical Attributes	
MP	274/274	Mana Density	102
		Mana Control	170

Active Skills		
Name	Level	Description
Infused Mana Beam	15	Focus mana into a channeled energy attack. Infused: May infuse Mana Beam with attributed mana.

Sneak	1	Move quietly to avoid notice. Makes it harder for others to notice the user. Effectiveness highly dependent on environment.
Multicasting	10	Can cast several spells at once. Number of simultaneous spells increases with level.
Anti-Mana Beam	1	My best guess is that this projects a kind of inverse mana that reacts destructively with normal mana, including HP. While it can fully deplete HP, it does not harm matter itself. Requires The Equalizer.
Power Strike	1	Infuse mana into a weapon for heavier damage. Power and range increase with level.
Farcasting	4	Allows the user to manipulate mana and create magic circles at far distances.
Strategic Magic	5	Governs the use of Strategic Magic spells.
Supercharge	9	Fill a spell with additional mana to boost its effects. May cause the spell to misfire. Effect boost depends on the amount and density of mana added. Misfire chance depends on Mana Control and amount of mana added.
Continuous Casting	3	May use additional mana to retain a spell form, allowing the spell to be instantly recast.
Spell Fusion	5	Allows the user to combine compatible spells.
Purifier Flame	1	Imbue a weapon or Flame-attribute attack with purifying Holy-attribute fire, dealing extra damage to corruption, monsters, dungeons, and beings from the Realms of Mana.

Passive Skills		
General		
Name	Level	Description
Dungeon Combat	--	Dungeon traps and skills count as personal weapons and skills.
HP Regen	7	Automatically recover HP pool. Increased regeneration speed for damaged body parts.
MP Regen	7	Automatically recover MP pool.
Presence Detection	4	Detect living entities around the user. Range and scope of detection increases with level.
Trap Detection	4	Detect traps. Range and scope of detection increases with level.
Challenger	--	Damage dealt x1.5 against targets of higher level. Damage received x0.75 against attacks from targets of higher level.
Hero Dungeon	--	Unique Hero Skill for NSLICE-00P. PLEASE don't do anything bad with this! Removes dungeon vulnerability to Holy attribute. Grants Dungeon Affinity: Holy.
Magic		
Name	Level	Description
Spell Penetration	3	Enable spells to bypass a portion of RES. May spend more mana to boost the effect.
Geomancy	2	Elemental spells reduce the target's resistance to that particular element. May spend more mana to boost the effect.

Utility		
Name	Level	Description
Enchanting	1	The art of infusing objects and beings with mana.
Resistances		
Name	Level	Description
Poison Resistance	2	Resist and recovery from poison status. Resist Poison-attributed damage.
Schools of Magic		
Name	Level	Description
Arcane Magic	10 *Spell Choice Available	The school of magic governing the manipulation of unattributed mana. A solid foundation for students of the mystic arts, though somewhat less mana efficient than the more specialized schools.
Earth Magic	7	The school of magic governing the manipulation of Earth-attribute mana. One of the basic elemental magics, strong at defensive spells and spells that deal physical damage.
Fire Magic	8	The school of magic governing the manipulation of Fire-attribute mana. One of the basic elemental magics, strong at offensive spells and spells that inflict the burn status.
Light Magic	12	The school of magic governing the manipulation of Light-attribute mana. One of the basic elemental magics, quick and precise spells that are excellent against Dark-aligned foes.

Nature Magic	3	The school of magic governing the manipulation of Nature-attribute mana. Focuses on growth and living things.
Poison Magic	4	The school of magic governing magical poisons. Excels at spreading poison status and dealing damage over time.
Recovery Magic	3	The school of magic governing healing through magic.
Holy Magic	1	The school of magic governing the manipulation of Holy-attribute mana, the attribute of the Aesdes that protects the world.

Spells		
Arcane		
Name	Level	Description
Dense Magic Missile	18	Form and launch mana into a small projectile. One of the most basic offensive applications of magic.
Mana Barrier	10 *Upgrade Available	Form mana into a barrier to block attacks. One of the most basic defensive applications of magic.
Mana Blast	2	A cone-shaped blast of mana. Deals damage and knockback to the area.
Mana Infusion	5	Infuse mana into a target. The most basic enchantment. Defensive variation unlocked.

Earth		
Name	Level	Description
Rock Throw	6	Use mana to form and then launch a small rock. Mana cost increases dramatically if cast without a nearby source of Earth. Deals physical damage. One of the most basic offensive applications of Earth Magic.
Earth Wall	6	Use mana to temporarily form a wall of Earth. Mana cost increases dramatically if cast without a nearby source of Earth. One of the most basic defensive applications of Earth Magic.
Pitfall	4	Dig a large hole in a target area. May be concealed. Mana cost may increase depending on suitability of terrain.
Fire		
Name	Level	Description
Fire Bolt	1	Use mana to form and then launch a small bolt of fire. Mana cost decreases dramatically if cast with a nearby source of Fire. May inflict burn status. One of the most basic offensive applications of Fire Magic.
Fire Blast	7	A cone-shaped blast of Fire mana. Deals damage and inflicts burn to the area. Mana cost decreases dramatically if cast with a nearby source of Fire. May be continuously channeled.
Fireball	5	A condensed ball of Fire mana that explodes on impact, dealing damage and inflicting burn in an area around the point of impact. A favorite of Fire mages. Mana cost decreases dramatically if cast with a nearby source of Fire.

Fire Infusion	1	Infuse a target with Fire Attribute mana.
Light		
Name	Level	Description
Light Bolt	1	Use mana to form and then launch a small bolt of light. Mana cost increases if cast without a nearby source of Light. One of the most basic offensive applications of Light Magic.
Fusion Light Beam	14	Form mana into a beam of light to attack. May pierce through its target. May be continuously channeled. Fusion: Light Beams may combine with themselves or other compatible attacks to boost power.
Invisibility	2	Bend light to render target invisible. Certain actions may break the effect. Being attacked may break the effect.
Nature		
Name	Level	Description
Vine Grasp	4	Grows or manipulates a vine to wrap around a target. Mana cost may increase or decrease significantly depending on surrounding plant life or environmental suitability for plant growth. The most basic plant-manipulation spell.
Barkskin	1	Harden target's skin like bark. Boosts DEF.
Poison		
Name	Level	Description
Poison Bolt	6	Use mana to form and then launch a small bolt of poison. Mana cost decreases dramatically if cast with a nearby source of Poison. May inflict poison status. One of the most basic offensive applications of Poison Magic.

Poison Blast	3	A cone-shaped blast of Poison mana. Deals damage and inflicts poison to the area. Mana cost decreases dramatically if cast with a nearby source of Poison. May be continuously channeled.
Recovery		
Name	Level	Description
Heal	7	Use mana to heal minor wounds and damage. Effect increases with user's knowledge of the body.
Cure	2	Cures abnormal status conditions. Type and strength of conditions that can be cured increases with level.
Holy		
Name	Level	Description
Holy Bolt	1	Use mana to form and then launch a small bolt of Holy mana. One of the most basic offensive applications of Holy Magic. Extra damage to corrupted beings, monsters, dungeons, and beings from the Realms of Mana.

Strategic Spells			
School	Name	Level	Description
Light	Aurora Barrage	4	Continuously rains Light Beams on the target area. If Fusion Light Beam is available, beams may be combined at will.
Fire	Rain of Fire	2	Bombards a wide area with large Fireballs.

Personal Feats		
Name	Description	Effect
Against the Odds	Do not ask how many there are, but where they are. Unlocked by winning a fight when outnumbered by equal or higher-leveled opponents.	+1 Perk Point
Solo Conquest	I am the dungeon master now. Unlocked by conquering a dungeon alone.	+1 level in HP Regen skill +1 level in MP Regen skill +1 level in Presence Detection skill +1 level in Trap Detection skill
Arcane Prodigy	The career of a supreme sorcerer does not start on the beaten path. Unlocked by learning a high-tier magic skill under level twenty without spending Perk Points.	+3 Perk Points Unlocks more advanced magic perks.
Enchanter	The first step on the path of the magic craftsman. Unlocked by manually accomplishing a Mana Infusion.	+1 level in Enchanting skill
Skill Creator	You don't just master the path. You define it. Unlocked by creating a brand-new skill.	To be honest, this normally happens when you're a MUCH higher level, so I'm a bit worried about passing you this much this early, but, um, okay. +20 Perk Points

Healer	Anyone can deal in death. It takes an expert to deal in life. Unlocked by using mana to heal a wound.	+1 level in Recovery Magic skill
Challenger	Levels and odds are just numbers. Unlocked by defeating an opponent who is the greater of level 10 twice your level while alone.	+3 Perk Points + Challenger skill
Strategic Mage	A strategic mage is king of the battlefield. Unlocked by affecting a hundred or more equal-size opponents (or equivalent mass of other-size opponents) at the same time with magic.	+1 level in Strategic Magic skill Unlocks Strategic Spells.
World Defender	You have protected the world itself, at great risk to yourself.	+20 Perk Points +1 level in Holy Magic skill
Hero	You faced terrible odds for the sake of the world and proved victorious. You are truly a champion of the world. Please, please, please keep it that way!	+20 Perk Points Grants Unique Hero Skill: Hero Dungeon
Dungeon Conqueror Feats		
Name	Description	Effect
Dungeon Conqueror (Rat Cave)	Unlocked by conquering the Rat Cave Dungeon.	+1 Perk Point +1 level in Sneak skill
Dungeon Conqueror (Earth Tunnels)	Unlocked by conquering the Earth Tunnels Dungeon.	+1 Perk Point +1 level in Earth Magic skill

Dungeon Conqueror (Spider Tree)	Unlocked by conquering the Spider Tree Dungeon.	+1 Perk Point +1 level in Poison Resistance skill
Dungeon Conqueror (Slimy Pit)	Unlocked by conquering the Slimy Pit Dungeon.	+1 Perk Point +1 level in Poison Bolt spell
Dungeon Conqueror (Glimmering Grove)	Unlocked by conquering the Glimmering Grove Dungeon.	+1 Perk Point +1 level in Light Magic skill
Dungeon Conqueror (Nature's Wrath)	Unlocked by conquering the Nature's Wrath Dungeon.	+1 Perk Point +1 level in Nature Magic skill
Dungeon Conqueror (Beast Lair)	Unlocked by conquering the Beast Lair Dungeon.	+1 Perk Point +1 level in Claw Strike skill
Dungeon Purifier Feats		
Dungeon Purifier (Inferno)	A dungeon is dangerous to everyone in the world. A corrupted dungeon is dangerous to the world itself. And you conquered it all the same. Unlocked by purifying the Corrupted Dungeon (Inferno Realm).	+5 Perk Points +1 level in Purifier Flame skill

EPILOGUE 1

The Valiant Captain of the Guard and the Strange Wandering Knight

"The most valiant and praiseworthy individuals in all the Empire are the limitanei. These men and women stand at every corner of the Empire, facing down every manner of vicious monster and savage tribe. They do so not with enchanted blade, mystical might, or perfected skills, but with little more than grit, determination, and spear. They are the purest representation of the Empire's tenacity. And those that lead them most of all. These are the men and women who take up command not for selfish ambition or vain glory, but simply to fulfill their duty and defend our civilization."

—Emperor Herius of the North,
in a speech announcing further budget cuts for the limitanei.

Opiter Caelius Curio heaved a sigh.

He hated this.

Opiter had all sorts of fancy titles. He was the legate of the Legion per Castra Turannia, a high-ranking and decorated officer of the Imperial Legion. He was the one in charge of the security of Castra Turannia, the Legion's most important base in the entire province as well as the province's capital. A province where Imperial control was not absolute, which still saw regular large-scale combat and operated under de facto martial law.

So one might assume Opiter would be one of the most experienced, high-leveled, and powerful soldiers in the Legion.

One would be wrong.

He was the commander of the limitanei in Castra Turannia, which was the home base of both the comitatenses legions and the Exploratores for the entire province. So he never actually saw combat or made any real decisions. Any problems he encountered would be turned over to the Exploratores so they could pay off their tabs. Anything too serious for an Exploratore to handle would be confronted by the comitatenses. And Turannia's rector provinciae, the dux of the comitatenses, and the Magister Exploratore were all present, and would assume all authority in reacting to any given crisis. Opiter was never truly in command during any situation that mattered.

So what did a limitanei legate do under those circumstances?

He sent patrols to break up tavern brawls. Arranged customs and checked identifications at the gates. Wrote some small "official" bounties for the rookie Exploratores. Inventoried the latest delivery of supplies for the comitatenses. Stood around and looked important on the rare chance Turannia received a guest from the Empire proper. Took care of the Legion's paperwork. Made arrangements to restrain low-priority prisoners. And—his most dangerous task—put out some fires.

But Opiter had no problem with that. Had he any ambition, he would not have ended up in the Turannian limitanei at all. He just wanted a grant of farmland and a spear with which to defend it. He'd only ended up in his current job because he'd demonstrated a talent for administration, while the last legate had demonstrated a talent for getting drunk at inopportune moments. And since Turannia was not the most popular of destinations for Legion officers, the former legate's administrative assistant with a spotless record—on paper—had ended up getting a promotion rather than a new boss. Of course, no thought had been given as to his qualifications for the role should he ever be forced into actual battle.

Which was why he hated the current situation.

Opiter felt deeply uncomfortable anytime the comitatenses were away. There was a small but very real chance something big might happen. And if that something happened, suddenly, Opiter would be the highest-ranking officer of the Legion in the area, so people might actually expect him to take charge and command.

Opiter had barely been in a real fight, and he was in no rush to repeat the experience. So to take charge, command the defense, and order the troops? Please, Opiter was a glorified clerk.

And this time was even worse.

Because the Exploratores were gone too.

That meant there was no one around to solve issues of any sort. Not only the big, once-in-a-lifetime issues like an incursion making its way to the capital, but the smaller, routine things too. Issues like monster rats sneaking into the granary, a felix pluvia wandering too close to the farmland, or a Wulver raiding party probing the outskirts.

These were the sort of things that could absolutely be expected to occur and that Opiter and his men would now be expected to handle. Despite the fact that none of them had done anything of the sort in as long as most of them could remember.

And Opiter would now be expected to tell them how to do it. To figure out how to handle things. And to take the blame if they weren't handled.

He bit into a loaf of bread, his fifth that day.

He couldn't help it; the stress was getting to his stomach, so he needed something to keep it down.

Just then, his assistant knocked on his door. Opiter groaned and prayed with all his might it was nothing serious.

"We have a . . . bit of a situation, sir."

Opiter heaved a sigh and held out his hand. The assistant handed him the report to read over.

"A . . . wandering knight, was it?"

The secretary nodded. "Just entered town this morning in the company of two locals from further north."

Opiter looked over the report. "It looks like they got a status on her. Human, level twenty-six, not part of any official knight order, huh? Enslice Seero Seero Pee? Interesting name. Well, all the paperwork seems to be in order for that case. Is there a problem?"

The assistant shook his head.

"No, sir, but since they couldn't identify her or her order, the men at the gate thought you should know, just in case."

Opiter bit back a groan. See, this was *exactly* what he was worried about! People now expected him to know how to deal with anything out of the norm. His normal response would be to file the paperwork off to his superiors and then head off for lunch. But now . . . now he had to figure out if this was a problem, and how to deal with it if so.

So he did what he did best and stuck to the exact letter of policy.

"Log the report per official procedure and inform me if anything happens. Otherwise, we shall treat her as any other visitor to the Empire."

The assistant gave a salute as he took back the form. "Sir."

As the soldier left, Opiter placed his elbows on his desk and rubbed his temples.

Great, just great. A wandering knight of unknown affiliation walking around town. Just what he needed.

He could only hope that this wasn't the start of any trouble.

Several days later, Opiter was massaging his temples again while chewing on a loaf of bread, with some cheese this time.

Ever since that wandering knight had arrived, it had been one thing after another: the wandering knight accosting townsfolk around town, casting Illusion Magic on them in broad daylight. The wandering knight seen heading in and out of the slums, only the Aesdes knew what for. The wandering knight seen paying for a room at the inn but rarely observed actually using it.

And that hadn't been all.

Since the wandering knight's arrival, he had received all sorts of strange reports from the surrounding area. Loud sounds in the distance, strange lights in the sky, monsters and animals running away from certain areas, the corpses of big monsters, and the signs of terrible battles.

There was one mad peasant who claimed he'd seen a ghost woman floating in the air, even!

None of this was serious trouble, but it was all somewhat unsettling, and now, all the residents and soldiers were worried. And when the people or the soldiers got unsettled, they came to Opiter, expecting him to do something.

And he couldn't do anything!

If it were at least some confirmed issue, maybe he could find some procedure in the Legion manuals he could follow, but there was nothing! The Legion didn't much care about strange—but not directly threatening—happenings like these. The Exploratores would figure out if there was anything serious, which normally meant he'd pass it on to Magister Tiberius, who would decide if it was worth sending an Exploratore to investigate.

But now, Magister Tiberius just shrugged and told him to use his best judgment. The magister couldn't do anything himself, as there were hardly any Exploratores left in the province, and the magister had sent the few that were still around to go patrol the borders. Opiter didn't have anyone left to pass these issues to but the rector provinciae, who would simply order him to handle them on his own, given her lack of military expertise.

Opiter wished she had considered his *own* lack of military expertise!

But his soldiers were in no way or shape equipped to investigate issues such as these. They panicked and gave reports much like the frightened farmers. Sending his troops would only make things worse for the legate.

So Opiter didn't deal with them, and the rumblings and rumors grew. The populace grew increasingly unsettled, the soldiers were on edge, and Opiter could feel a hole wearing through his stomach.

It was on a day like this that it finally came crashing down. Opiter's worst nightmare had arrived.

His assistant slammed the door open, panic in his eyes.

"Sir, come quick! It's the provincial mage! The Magus Provincia says it's urgent!"

The Magus Provincia didn't bother waiting, thrusting the assistant to the side as she rushed into the room. "Sir, mana readings are off the charts right under the keep! I'd say it's a mana storm, but I don't see how that's possible!"

The assistant nodded. "Sir, what are we going to do?!"

Opiter practically fell out of his seat.

"W-W-What do you mean?! We're going to call the Legion!"

The Magus Provincia stared at him. "What are you saying, Legate?! *We* are the Legion!"

Opiter trembled as his eyes widened.

That's right! He was the Legion right now! And something was happening!

Just as he'd feared!

"T-T-That's . . . I-I-I'm . . . W-W-What are we going to do?!"

"That's what we're asking YOU, sir!"

At that moment, another man calmly stepped into the room.

"If I could make a suggestion . . ."

Opiter turned, his eyes widening. He rushed over and clutched at the man's clothes.

"M-Magister Tiberius! Please, tell me you can do something!"

Magister Tiberius heaved a sigh and hoisted Opiter up, supporting his back.

"Okay, first, take a deep breath, Legate."

Opiter took several.

"Now, give the order to gather the Guard."

"R-Right. Go, g-gather the troops!"

The assistant nodded his head as he gave a shaky salute and then ran from the room. Magister Tiberius nodded. "Good, once they're ready, we'll go and check it out."

Opiter jumped.

"W-We? W-We're going? T-There's no need for that, surely?"

Magister Tiberius narrowed his eyes.

"Legate Opiter, do you know what's happening?"

"W-What?"

Magister Tiberius shook his head. "*I don't know.*"

The Magus Provincia's eyes widened. "Sir . . . even you?"

Magister Tiberius nodded. "So we need to go and check it out. And to do that, we need to bring the troops."

"C-Can't I just send them with you?"

He shook his head. "I'm with the Exploratores; I can't give orders to Legion troops if I'm alone. We need a ranking Legion officer present."

Opiter gulped, but the magister was right. That WAS the official policy, after all. And Opiter never deviated from the policy.

It took a while, but eventually, the assistant managed to find and assemble a group of soldiers.

And so, Magister Tiberius dragged a trembling Opiter and a platoon of nervous-looking limitanei and headed toward the sewers below the keep.

Opiter was trembling as he stood in the sewers. He tried to take a deep breath, only to gag on the smell. The rest of his men and the Magus Provincia were holding their noses as well.

But the smell wasn't what bothered him.

There was a stone arch in the sewers that had clearly not been built by the Empire, a pitch-black void between its pillars. All around it, mana crackled and hissed, little arcs of fire shooting from the dungeon into the sewer walls around it. Opiter found himself sweating as he approached the dungeon, the temperature rising with each step he took toward it. Small sparks of flame began to hiss and sizzle on the floor near the arch.

It was a dungeon.

There was a dungeon . . . right below the keep Opiter was responsible for. A dungeon which had clearly not been there before.

Magister Tiberius narrowed his eyes, keeping his gaze fixed on the entrance. "Magus, what's your take?"

The Magus Provincia frowned and trembled slightly as she fiddled with a tool holding a glowing magic core. "I-It . . . appears like a dungeon, sir, but the readings are more like . . . um . . ."

"More like what?"

She gulped. "More like . . . a mana surge, sir. Or maybe . . . a Rift."

Magister Tiberius narrowed his eyes even further.

"This is bad."

Opiter jumped. "Bad?! What's bad?! I-It can't be bad, right?! Y-You can handle it, right?!"

Magister Tiberius shook his head.

"We're looking at a corrupted dungeon right below the keep."

Everyone sucked in their breath at that. A corrupted dungeon? The especially demonic dungeons that poured out endless hordes of murderous monsters to conquer the surrounding areas? Like in the stories of the Great Demon Lord?

One of the trembling soldiers turned to Opiter.

"W-What are we going to do, sir?"

"W-Wait, you're asking me?"

"Y-Yes, sir!"

"I . . . um . . . uh . . ." Opiter grabbed his head and crouched down on his knees. "This can't be happening . . ."

Magister Tiberius placed a firm hand on Opiter's shoulder and hauled him upright. The magister stared him in the eye. "Steady, Legate."

Opiter gulped but nodded.

"Order one of your men back and call all hands to this location, along with the architect. Have them fortify this position as best we can. Send the magus to call Utrad and Corvanus, and let them know what's happening here."

"W-What about us?"

Magister Tiberius placed hand on the hilt of his sword.

"We will stay here and hold the line as long as possible. If we don't, this province will fall, and everyone in it will die."

Everyone went silent at that.

Magister Tiberius patted Opiter's shoulder to get his attention and looked him in the eye again. "Well, Legate?"

Opiter gulped and trembled.

"D-Do as he says . . ."

The limitanei frowned and clutched their spears with shaky hands while the Magus Provincia and one of the soldiers turned to leave.

Just then, the dungeon started flashing, and the stone archway began collapsing in on itself as the void shrunk.

Magister Tiberius drew his sword and shouted at the soldiers, "Everyone, stand at the ready!"

The limitanei gulped and pointed their spears forward. The Magus Provincia started chanting, stumbling over her words and restarting several times before she formed her magic circle. Opiter just trembled in place.

The dungeon entrance shrunk down, the stone being pulled into the void until it was a tiny black dot. Then, there was a flash of light, and a gust of wind.

Opiter cried out as he fell backward, whimpering as he leaned his neck forward, fully expecting to see death approaching.

He froze.

The dungeon was gone, along with the crackling mana. The air calmed down, and the temperature returned to normal, with no further sparks or flames appearing along the floor.

And most importantly of all, there were no monsters.

Instead, there was the wandering knight, standing in place of the dungeon entrance.

"M-Miss Knight? What are you doing here?"

"Query: Local authorities identified and in combat positions. Is something in violation of local legal regulations occurring at this location?"

Opiter blinked as he tried to parse the wandering knight's accent. "U-Um . . . I don't . . . um . . . W-What happened to the dungeon? W-Were you inside of it?"

"Affirmative."

"T-Then you m-must know, w-where did it go?!"

"Answer: The dungeon master acted hostile toward this unit, so she terminated him and his dungeon."

Opiter froze. Magister Tiberius narrowed his eyes at her.

"Hello, miss. Magister Explorates per Turannia Tiberius Cantius Falx here.

Sorry, but I need you to clarify for us. Are you saying you destroyed the dungeon that appeared here, all on your own?"

"Affirmative."

Opiter blinked as his mind attempted to process that statement.

And then he passed out.

It was now evening time, after Legate Opiter had recovered himself. He was now sitting at his desk, trembling and stuffing anything into his mouth that he could.

At Magister Tiberius's insistence, Opiter had run a more thorough status check on the wandering knight, one which would show some feat names on top of the level and species. A dungeon appearing under the Legion keep was a serious affair, not to mention a *corrupted dungeon*, so they needed to verify that she had the Dungeon Conqueror feat at the very least. Fortunately, the wandering knight had cooperated with them, so they'd had no trouble taking the status.

It was now, after the status parchment had been delivered to Opiter, that the trouble began.

His assistant slowly opened the door.

"S-Sir? Are you all right?"

Opiter didn't respond, just kept chewing.

"S-Sir? Um, Magister Tiberius is asking about the status. Did you receive it yet?"

Opiter still said nothing, but he held the status out to the assistant, who slowly walked over and took the parchment. His eyes widened as he looked it over.

"H-Hero? W-What does that mean? Um, w-what do we do, sir?"

Opiter just held his head. He slowly rose to his feet and turned around, facing the window behind his desk.

Then, clutching his head with both hands, he threw it back into the sky.

"WHYYYYY?!"

EPILOGUE 2

The Exploratores Disciplina

"Beware the veteran Exploratores, for they have endured alone challenges that ended the majority of their peers. Do not assume they will fall before you like the average Imperial scum, or I will be ashamed, and you will be dead."

—Sun Elf Archon Abnice Khingein to his scout forces, prior to an engagement with the Elteni Empire.

Screams filled the evening sky. A boy and a girl, still in their teens, ran with all their might.

An ursanus adolescent chased after them, roaring at its prey. It was relatively low level and young, and had not even grown the thick shell on its back. Still, it was a huge mass of muscle and bloodlust that stood taller than a full-grown human adult and had enough strength to knock down a tree.

It was not something two young teenagers wanted to get hit by.

"H-Hurry up, Taog! It's gaining on us!"

"Wait for me, Ateia!"

"Wait?! Run faster, Taog!"

"I'm running as fast as I can!"

The ursanus roared at them and put in another burst of speed.

Just then, a glowing bone harpoon sped through the air, leaving a glowing trail of mana behind. It smashed into the ursanus's right shoulder, the creature letting out a roar of pain from the wound. The glowing trail then split into two chains of mana. One chain began moving backward, pulling the harpoon out of the bear. The other stayed in place, connected to the bear's HP barrier.

The weapon flew out once more, this time striking the ursanus's left flank. Two chains of mana went taut in either direction, holding the monster in place.

The beast roared and pulled, but the chains held strong.

And then, a shadow fell on it from above, driving the harpoon straight into its skull.

The ursanus fell to the ground and moved no longer.

Veteran Exploratore Miallói leapt off the bear and landed in front of the two trembling teens.

She frowned and crossed her arms.

"Weak. Disappointing."

The two teens looked down at the ground. Miallói heaved a sigh.

When she heard these two had conquered a dungeon, she'd gotten her hopes up. She was also interested in their apparent identities: a half-Wulver boy and a girl who clearly didn't mind him. It was rare to see, given the humans' animosity with the Wulver. And rarer still to see people in that position rise above that prejudice and develop the skills necessary to take on a dungeon.

She'd thought all they would need was a bit of hunting, a few more levels, and then they might prove a valuable ally for the Selkies. Someone like her, who loved her homeland but had no love for the people occupying it, however useful they may be.

But she was wrong.

These two had no love for Turannia at all. Miallói could tell. They planned to leave the moment their training was done.

Miallói understood. Turannia was a hard place to live. Most of the Selkies had left the province too. Their innate skill in Water Magic was always valuable somewhere in the Empire, and most Selkies no longer believed the Empire would ever leave, so they'd abandoned their ancestral home, their independence, and their original way of life, making for the Empire proper.

But they were all wrong.

The Empire was not permanent. Miallói saw it. It had grown fat and lazy; a predator past its prime. It was still large, still powerful. But it had overreached. It now relied on its reputation, its aura of invincibility.

It had long since ceased to conquer, and now only sought to defend.

It was vulnerable.

What if the Legion fell somewhere? What if the Empire faced a true challenge to its supremacy? What if there came a threat that did not care for the Empire's reputation?

Well, there was a reason the Empire had stripped the Legion from Turannia. It was losing its ability to hold the line everywhere it stood. It was better to lose an undefended province than to lose a legion. Sacrifices had to be made.

And that was a problem for the Selkies.

With all the Selkies who had left, they had grown weak in their ancestral home. They were now dependent on the Empire's protection; they could not survive without it. If the Empire left, they would be forced from their lands by the tribes that never submitted.

And the Empire had just left. Magister Tiberius was trying to hide it from her, and Dux Canus was still doing his best to maintain the defenses, but Miallói wasn't blind. The Legion had abandoned the province, and there was no telling when, or even *if*, they would return.

So Miallói was desperate for all the help she could get. If her people—her home—were to survive, then the Empire must not lose while the legions were away. And that's why she had chosen to invest in these two. Permanent allies for the Selkies was her goal, but acquiring even temporary allies for the Empire was sufficient. Anything she could do to maintain the image of Imperial strength until the legions returned. Any way to protect the Selkies . . . or to buy them time to prepare for the worst case.

But these kids' strength was an illusion. They were weak, too weak to have done what they claimed. And worst . . . they seemed to have no idea what they were doing. They were rookie village hunters at best. Miallói could not believe they had even survived a dungeon like this, much less conquered one.

They could not help her protect her home.

Miallói narrowed her eyes on the pair. "Dungeon, lie?"

The pair's eyes widened, and they glanced at one another. Then the girl heaved a sigh and looked down at the ground, gritting her teeth. "No, we did conquer a dungeon. But . . . we had help. And without that help, we would have died."

Miallói nodded. "Honest, good. Legion, Exploratores?"

The boy and girl looked at one another again, communicating with their eyes. The girl sighed and nodded, then the boy turned to her.

"No, someone else."

"Wulver, Selkie, Dobhar?"

He shook his head. "No, human. Not from around here, I think."

Miallói rubbed her chin. Her eyes widened slightly. She thought she understood what was going on here.

Recently, a human mage had wiped out an ursanus that was wandering near a Selkie village. The human had supposedly been accompanied by a human girl and a half-Wulver boy. It was likely that these were the same human and half-Wulver, and that the person who defeated the ursanus was the one who helped this pair conquer a dungeon.

As of now, she didn't know anyone in the province able and willing to guide two young Imperials through a dungeon. That meant, this human was likely a new player. One that was powerful—and either an Imperial asset, or else an unaffiliated third party. Most of all . . . they were invested in the success of these two rookies.

Miallói nodded to herself. This effort could still be worthwhile, so it would be best if she did it properly. She was no longer training two Imperials—she was now applying for an alliance with their powerful benefactor.

Miallói slammed the back of her harpoon on the ground, causing the two teens to jump and look at her. She pointed her harpoon at them.

"You two are not Exploratores. Not to me; not any longer."

The two grimaced.

"Instead, I will treat you as Selkie children. And by those standards, you are weak, unfit to hunt or fight. You would not be allowed out of the village as you are now."

Miallói narrowed her eyes at them.

"So I will train you from the beginning. We will not stop until I decide you are fit for duty, as a Selkie warrior should be."

The two's eyes widened, then they quickly nodded. Miallói gave a nod. Points for enthusiasm, and for accepting their weakness.

She would see how long that lasted.

Miallói stood in front of the pair out in the open. It was pouring rain, and the three were already drenched. Miallói had not allowed them to bring their cloaks.

The rain did not bother the Selkie. For Miallói, this was much more comfortable, even.

A human and a half Wulver were not so lucky.

"Monsters are deadly. They do not waste. They do not waver on their path. They all have one goal, and they focus all of their growth on that goal. Those who do not, perish. So there is much to learn from them."

Miallói spread her mana, extending it into the rain around her. Soon, she shimmered and vanished from view.

And then slammed her fists into Ateia and Taog's stomachs.

"The Selkies developed this style by observing the felix pluvia. To become one with rain, to stalk their prey unseen, and then to strike without mercy."

The two teens were just climbing back to their feet when Miallói swept their legs out from under them. "It is also useful for training perception and awareness. Fight me as if you were fighting a monster. And like a monster, I will show you no mercy or pity."

Ateia and Taog gulped.

Miallói stood on a rock in the middle of a rushing river, chaotic rapids just behind her.

In the river in front of her, two teens struggled to swim against the current, desperately trying to remain out of the rapids.

"Normally, we do this in the ocean, which is far more powerful, but you two are weak swimmers compared to a Selkie child. Remember, the boons from the Aesdes are mighty . . . and should not be wasted. Your body can be trained, molded. You do not need to wait for the Aesdes to grow stronger. So grow as strong as you can, and only then consider how the Aesdes may elevate you beyond that."

Ateia and Taog gasped for breath as the river pushed them back. They swam as hard as they could, but still, the river pushed them back toward the rapids.

"The current is strong, and fast. You cannot defy it by standing with raw strength or rushing with mere speed. You will need both to succeed."

Ateia began falling behind. She accidentally bumped a rock behind her and yelped, losing her form. She began rushing toward the rapids— Miallói reached down a hand, scooped her up, and tossed her upriver. She landed with a splash and sputtered to reach the surface.

"And you will also need endurance. Again."

Ateia gritted her teeth as she started swimming once more, desperately trying to slow her fall downstream.

Miallói slammed her wooden staff into Taog's chest. The boy fell to the ground, dropping his wooden sword, and Miallói slammed the staff down toward his head. The boy yelped and scrambled to his feet.

"Inflexible, sloppy. Trying to be a Legion Bulwark and a Wulver warrior at the same time. You are not a part of the Legion, and you are not part of a Wulver clan. Don't just repeat what you were taught. Now, again."

Miallói kicked his sword off the ground toward the boy . . . then kicked his shield away. Taog's eyes widened.

"Start from the top. Focus on your opponent, not on your drills and techniques. Hit me however you can. Then we can start to think of what fighting style suits you."

Taog nodded and narrowed his eyes, gripping his sword. He let out a yell and rushed forward.

And promptly found himself on the ground.

"Again."

Ateia closed her eyes, not bothering to look for Miallói hidden in the rain. Taog had far sharper senses than she did all around, and even he couldn't find Miallói, so Ateia knew she needed to try something else. Instead, she reached out with her mana, trying to feel the mana in the rain around her, searching for any shifts . . .

Suddenly, she felt something. A small, subtle shift in the rain. She took a step back on reflex.

You have learned the skill Presence Detection!

And then a fist impacted her stomach. Miallói shifted into view, standing over the fallen girl.

She nodded.

"Better, but not good enough. Not yet."

Ateia nodded and rose back to her feet as Miallói vanished once more . . .

Ateia and Taog swam through the river, just barely hanging with the current. All of Ateia's muscles felt like fire, but she gritted her teeth and pushed through the pain, reaching into the water ahead of her just a bit more.

And then, she got the message from the Aesdes, recording a slight increase in her strength and speed.

She started moving.

It was small and slow, but Ateia was now moving upriver.

Later that day, as Ateia and Taog were lying on the riverbank panting for breath, Miallói nodded at them. "Next time, we will try in the ocean."

Ateia and Taog just grunted, unable to speak.

Miallói stood by Ateia, holding her harpoon at the ready. She slowly wrapped her mana around her spear, pouring an excessive amount into it so Ateia could watch. She then threw her harpoon, a trail of glowing mana following after it.

She turned to Ateia.

"Try again. Go slowly this time. The mana and the arrow aren't going anywhere."

Ateia frowned and nodded. She nocked an arrow on her bow and slowly started to wrap it with mana. The arrow wobbled about.

"Focus. Don't look at the arrow, and don't think about anything else. Focus on the target and your desire to hold it in place."

Ateia nodded and looked down at a tree. She exhaled her breath and drew her bow . . .

The arrow flew, a glowing trail of mana behind it. It landed on target, sinking into the tree, and . . . the glowing trail formed into a chain of mana—a faint, flickering chain, but it was there.

Ateia's eyes widened. "I got the skill . . ."

Miallói grabbed her shoulder, causing the girl to jump. She shook her head as Ateia looked at her. "Do it again and ignore the skill. Don't try to activate it; don't let it guide you. Learn to do this yourself, and let the skill help you, not the other way around."

Ateia nodded and started wrapping the arrow in her mana once more.

Ateia and Taog stood in front of a cave. Another ursanus adolescent charged at them, but this time, the pair stood their ground. The ursanus roared and rushed toward Taog, raising its paw.

Taog focused with all of his senses and mana, watching the ursanus's muscles and eyes as he felt its mana. He stepped back, just barely out of the path of the paw, and stabbed the ursanus's arm. The bear roared and took a step back, readying another strike. Ateia let a glowing arrow loose; it flew straight and struck the ursanus, a chain of mana forming.

Taog leapt to the side and stabbed the monster's flank. The beast roared and turned to strike at the boy once more as Ateia ran around the battlefield and let loose another arrow into the ursanus's other side. The arrow struck true, and another chain of mana formed in place.

Two chains now held the ursanus in either direction. The creature roared and pulled at them. They held, but started to flicker.

Just then, a wolf monster leapt from the bushes and pounced at Ateia, hoping for an easy ambush while she fought the ursanus. Taog glanced over but shook his head, keeping his eyes on the ursanus. He trusted Ateia to take care of herself.

Ateia rolled out of the way of the ambush, having detected the wolf watching them from the trees. She drew an arrow as she righted herself and shot the wolf at point-blank range. The monster fell and lay still.

Meanwhile, Taog stepped forward and stabbed at the ursanus's face. The beast roared, its eyes focused on Taog as it began to pull, trying to break free of the chains and pounce on the boy. Taog took a step back and grinned.

"Now, Ateia!"

Ateia nodded and released the skill. The chains suddenly vanished, and the monster flew forward. Taog barely leapt out of the way as the beast rushed past him . . .

And straight into the pit the two had dug ahead of time.

The ursanus roared as it landed on the sharpened spikes, thrashing about at the walls of the pit. Ateia walked over to the edge and tossed two potions in, first poisoning the beast before setting the pit ablaze.

Well, it took a while longer, but eventually, the ursanus fell, unable to escape the pit as Ateia bombarded it from above.

As they finished up, Miallói emerged from the trees and nodded.

Ateia and Taog ran through the rain. They threw their mana out toward each other, covering each other's perception and halving the burden for the other.

Ateia suddenly grabbed Taog and pulled him to the side as Miallói appeared briefly, her foot just passing in front of Taog's stomach. She vanished as Taog rolled forward and resumed running.

Then Taog turned.

"Jump!"

Ateia leapt into the air just in time as Miallói tried to sweep her legs out from under her.

Suddenly, Miallói's fist caught Taog's cheek, but Ateia landed in front of him and steadied the boy. The two kept running forward, unhindered.

Until they reached a tree with a harpoon sunk into it.

They both stopped just before a barrage of Water Magic struck the area in front of them, then resumed their run. The two caught fists and feet and Water Magic, but with each other's help, they managed to remain standing and moving forward.

Until . . .

Finally . . .

They both grabbed onto the harpoon.

As they panted for breath, Miallói appeared behind them, rubbing her chin.

"Still sloppy and rushed, but"—it was barely perceptible, but the tiniest edge of Miallói's mouth curled up, ever so slightly—"not bad for a non-Selkie, and a pass is a pass. The Selkies would now permit you to join the hunt, if just barely."

The two stared at her for a second before their eyes widened and they broke out in grins. They cheered and hugged each other. Miallói allowed herself to smirk.

Well, they had only done the bare minimum—all she could do for them in such a short amount of time—but they *had* passed the Selkie hunter test, which was more than she could say for the average Imperial, even in the Exploratores, so they had a better shot at surviving than most.

Part of her even wished they would stick around. The two had been good students and had grown dramatically over a short period of time. They had the potential to be serious warriors if they were properly trained and nurtured. Their initial weakness seemed to be from a lack of guidance, rather than a lack of talent.

It would be a bit of a waste if they ran off and died like the average Exploratore, but such was the risk of the life they chose. Miallói shook her head.

At the very least, if these two failed, it would not be from lack of effort. She could only hope whoever had helped them this far would continue to do so.

It was then that a bird flew through the air, ignoring the rain. Miallói reached out her hand, and the bird landed on it.

Her eyes widened. It was Irnúm's pet monster. For Irnúm to have sent it this far away meant something must have happened.

Something urgent.

Miallói turned to the celebrating pair.

"Get your things. We need to leave. *Now.*"

Author's Note

Hi, everyone! Author here! Did you know this series was originally a web novel released one chapter at a time? In that version, I included a short commentary at the end of each chapter with my own reactions to its events. In order to preserve the intended experience, I have now gathered all that commentary in one place for you to enjoy.

Please visit Terminate the Other World! on Royal Road to learn how the author feels about each chapter of this book!

About the Author

Icalos is a lifelong fan of sci-fi, fantasy, and video games, and the author of the Terminate the Other World! series, which was originally released on Royal Road. To learn more, visit his website at icalosbooks.com.